A WAR OF WIZARDS

BOOK V OF THE BLACKWOOD SAGA

Layton Green

To John Strout and Rusty Dalferes,
for this journey and all the others

ISBN: 978-1-7338188-6-5

Published by Cloaked Traveler Press.
Cover design by Sammy Yuen
Interior by JW Manus

Books by Layton Green

THE BLACKWOOD SAGA

Book I: *The Brothers Three*

Book II: *The Spirit Mage*

Book III: *The Last Cleric*

Book IV: *Return of the Paladin*

Book V: *A War of Wizards*

THE DOMINIC GREY SERIES

The Summoner

The Egyptian

The Diabolist

The Shadow Cartel

The Resurrector

The Reaper's Game (Novella)

THE GENESIS TRILOGY

Genesis

Revelation (forthcoming 2021)

Ascension (forthcoming 2022)

OTHER WORKS

Written in Blood

A Shattered Lens

The Metaxy Project

The Letterbox

THE TALE SO FAR . . .

The Brothers Three

The Blackwood brothers have very different outlooks on life: Will is a dreamer and fantasy addict stuck in a dead-end job; middle brother Caleb is a charming, happy-go-lucky bartender; and the eldest, Val, is a driven corporate attorney. One night in their hometown of New Orleans, after receiving a strange inheritance from their father—a pair of bracers, a staff, and a sword with a silver hilt—the Blackwood brothers are attacked by a wizard named Zedock who raises a manticore from a bag of bones and stops bullets with a glance.

Disbelieving, fearing for their lives, the brothers accept a key from a mysterious old man named Salomon and are transported to an alternate Earth ruled by wizards, where magic is real and monsters prowl the land. To survive in this deadly new world, the brothers hire a band of mercenaries, led by an alluring but deadly adventuress named Mala, to recover a trio of magical items from an abandoned sorcerer's keep. The brothers manage to recover the items, take a portal back to New Orleans, and confront Zedock in a cemetery. Will and Caleb follow the necromancer through a portal and manage to defeat him, but end up trapped on Urfe.

The Spirit Mage

Desperate to save his brothers, Val enlists the Myrddinus Society to help him return to Urfe. After landing in the dangerous underbelly of New Victoria, he concludes the only way to find Will and Caleb is to enroll in the Abbey—the school for wizards—and somehow gain access to a gateway called the Pool of Souls.

As Val struggles to survive, his brothers undergo an even deadlier trial. Reeling from the loss of Mala, who is adrift in the mysterious Place Between Worlds, Will and Caleb and Yasmina are captured by slavers and taken to the mines beneath Fellengard Mountain.

Trapped in a land of dreams and nightmares, afraid of losing their home world forever, the brothers manage to survive, but are forced apart yet again. After Val is thrown into a wizard prison for trying to use the Pool of Souls, Will and Caleb escape the Darklands, only to find themselves besieged by wizards in a city called Freetown, home of the Revolution.

The Last Cleric

The Blackwood brothers have become entangled in events that threaten to upend the Realm. Sentenced to die in wizard prison, Val wins his freedom by undertaking a quest to an alternate dimension—but taints his soul in the process.

Reunited with an old lover, Caleb braves the dangers of the Barrier Coast to warn his ancestors of the coming invasion by the Congregation. He survives the journey, but at a cost so high it will change him forever.

And in a distant unexplored jungle, Will finds his warrior spirit as he and Mala lead a party of adventurers in search of the Coffer of Devla, a fabled artifact thought to reside in the lost pyramid of a sorcerer king. Used to annihilate the enemies of its possessor, the Coffer might be the only hope for the struggling Revolution. While the expedition is a success, prophecy holds that the Coffer can only be used by a cleric of Devla—and yet it mysteriously opens for Caleb during an attack by the Congregation.

Return of the Paladin

Distraught by the slaughter of his loved ones, Caleb embarks on a mission of revenge against Lord Alistair and the Congregation, traveling along the Barrier Coast with the Brewer to seek the Tower of Elarion. The tower is a forgotten outpost said to exist outside of time and space—and which Caleb believes might hold the key to unlocking his inexplicable new powers.

With Caleb gone and Mala fleeing a deadly assassin from her past, a half-human and half-vampire dhampyr named Nagiro, Will agrees to lead a band of adventurers to recover the stolen Coffer of Devla. The last-ditch attempt to save the Revolution takes Will, Yasmina, Mateo, and Dalen through a portal to Praha, the most dangerous city on Urfe: a place seething with thieves, monsters, and weird magic from another age.

In New Victoria, unbeknownst to his brothers, Val is taken under the wing of Lord Alistair and ordered to perform a very important task: find the Coffer of Devla and secure it for the Congregation. Val's mission leads him from the dangerous sewers beneath the city to the underwater kingdom of the Kethropi and, finally, to a Cretan isle where Val reunites with Will and Mala. Together, they manage to wrest the Coffer away from a powerful sorcerer, and Val opens a portal to Lord Alistair, expecting him to send Will home to Earth in exchange for the Coffer. But Lord Alistair has deceived them, and instead sends Will to a dungeon in an unknown location.

After surviving the trials of the Tower of Elarion, Caleb joins the Revolution, along with the Brewer and Allira and one of the Blackwood brothers' oldest friends, Lance Wesson, who has mysteriously returned to Urfe. The Prophet continues to believe that Caleb is the last true cleric of the age: the Templar foretold in the *Canticles of Urfe*, the one who will break the will of the world.

As the brothers' lives on Urfe spiral further and further out of control, their individual journeys become a fulcrum for the fate of the Realm—and a forge that threatens to consume them.

Dramatis Personae

EARTH

Will Blackwood: The youngest brother; apprentice builder; wielder of the legendary sword Zariduke

Caleb Blackwood: The middle brother; bartender; thought by the followers of Devla to be the Templar, a warrior who prophecy has foretold will lead their people to freedom

Val Blackwood: The oldest brother; attorney; spirit mage and member of the Congregation

Yasmina: Zoology PhD Student; wilder of the Realm

The Brewer: Former rock star from New Jersey; bard

Lance: Former police officer and Marine; Will's best friend in New Orleans

URFE

Lord Alistair: Chief Thaumaturge of the Congregation; arch spirit mage

Mala: Adventuress; master thief and swordswoman; daughter of Clan Kalev

Allira: Healer from a land beyond the oceans

Marguerite: Former member of New Victoria Rogue's Guild; Caleb's deceased wife

Luca: Roma child adopted by Caleb and Marguerite; deceased

Dalen: Young illusionist from Macedonia

Mateo: Roma warrior and cousin to the Blackwood brothers

Tamás: Leader of the Revolution

Adaira: Cuerpomancer and daughter of Lord Alistair

Dida: Bibliomancer from the Kingdom of Great Zimbabwe

Synne: Majitsu loyal to Val Blackwood

Kjeld Anarsson: Head Don of the Order of Majitsu

Yasir Ookar: First General of the Protectorate Army

Alaina Whitehall: Governess of the Protectorate

Braden Shankstone: Highest Ranking Cuerpomancer of the Congregation

Kalyn Tern: Highest Ranking Aeromancer of the Congregation

Rucker: One-armed adventurer

Professor Groft: Dean of Spiritmancy at the Abbey

The Prophet: Leader of the followers of Devla

Branyn: Geomancer; follower of the Prophet

Elaina: Geomancer; follower of the Prophet

Salomon Elder: Spirit mage

Core Disciplines of the Congregation

Pyromancy (fire)

Aquamancy (water)

Aeromancy (air)

Geomancy (earth and stone)

Sylvamancy (the natural world)

Cuerpomancy (the human body)

Alchemancy (transformation)

Spiritmancy (spirit and astral travel)

Other Disciplines

Electromancy (lightning and related phenomena)

Necromancy (scrying and the dead)

Menagery (adaptation, breeding, and fusing of species)

Illusomancy (illusion and light)

Artisamancy (magical artistry)

Entomancy (insects)

Cyanomancy (sound)

Relicmancy (creation of magical items)

Bibliomancy (runes, wards, and lore)

Phrenomancy (exploring the inner mind)

NEW VICTORIA, URFE

-1-

As dusk fell on New Victoria, the soaring spires atop the wizard compounds began to wink on across the city, a forest of multihued celestial lances illuminating the capital of the Protectorate. Lord Alistair observed the breathtaking vista through a window in his observatory atop the tallest tower in the city, gazing proudly down on his fiefdom.

Briefly, the Chief Thaumaturge pondered what kept him tethered to his home world, when the entire multiverse was his to explore. Yes, he had power here, an entire continent under his thumb. But he could have that anywhere. No other being of the terrestrial planes—at least of which he was aware—could match the power of an elder spirit mage.

True, he found Urfe the most beautiful planet he had ever seen, its magic the richest and most complex. But there were plenty of worlds that came close, and an untold number left to explore.

He loved his daughter above all else, but he could take her with him.

In the end, he knew he was loyal to Urfe simply because it was his home. He was not a shiftless wanderer like the wretched gypsy clans. On the contrary, he longed to *improve* the land of his birth. The Realm was but one of many kingdoms on Urfe, with plenty of territory left to conquer, much of it firmly in the grasp of ignorant pagans. His dream was to transform Urfe into a beacon of progress and enlightenment that would shine throughout the multiverse.

With himself, of course, as the emperor supreme.

Yet before he expanded the borders of the Realm, starting with the Mayan Kingdom, he had a final thorn to extract from his side. At that very moment, the Prophet and the middle Blackwood brother were leading a ragtag army of

Devla scum and gypsies through the Ninth Protectorate, hoping to march to New Victoria and force a confrontation with the Congregation.

What was causing Caleb Blackwood to act so rashly? Was it simple revenge for his deceased spouse and the boy, Luca, who Caleb had known for less than a month?

Lord Alistair reflected on the death of his own wife. *Yes, if there had been someone to blame instead of the ravages of disease, then I, too, would have waged a war.*

Yet according to his sources, this behavior was entirely out of character for the middle Blackwood brother. Lord Alistair suspected Caleb's rage would burn itself out long before he left the Ninth Protectorate. Most likely, he would come to his senses after finding solace in the arms of a barmaid in some far-flung village.

No matter. Freetown was destroyed, Zariduke secure in Inverlock Keep, and the Coffer of Devla under the protection of his own powerful wards deep beneath the Sanctum. Even if the rebels *were* in possession of the sword and the Coffer, they would not have lasted a day, or even an hour, against the combined might of the Congregation and the Protectorate army. And without those artifacts, their cause was less than hopeless: it was a farce of epic proportions. Lord Alistair might as well send a regiment of drunken, halfwit tuskers to deal with them.

And yet, while he doubted the gypsies would even make it through the perils of the Ninth, he continued to let them march for a very important reason: the prophecy a phrenomancer had delivered long ago, right after Lord Alistair had taken power as Chief Thaumaturge.

> *When the sword born of spirit returns to Urfe, war is imminent, and one born of Roma blood will destroy you.*

War had come to Urfe, of that there was no doubt. Lord Alistair himself had ushered it in. Yet the second part of the prophecy . . .

Let the gypsies march, he thought, *and draw every single one of their miserable kin to their cause. I'll gather them together and destroy them all in one battle.*

Beneath the window, he absorbed the dreamscape of wizard compounds, the pyramid of the Sanctum, and the red-gold pillars of the Hall of Wizards. In the distance, the vast sprawl of the city merged into the horizon. After drinking in the view a final time, Lord Alistair spun on his heel and strode away from the window. An amber glow orb kindled in the center of the room, revealing support columns mind-painted by an artisamancer with artistic renditions of the astral plane. Star charts covered the walls beneath a domed and tinted glass ceiling.

To his left, a cloaked being drifted away from the wall. Streaks of silver light pulsated across a face that resembled a congealed shadow, and the silhouette of its features were molded in bas-relief from the darkness, offering a faint remembrance of the man it once had been.

The sole remaining Spirit Liege grasped an obsidian helm in one of its gloved hands, an offering for its master. Lord Alistair had ensorcelled a cloak and pair of gloves for his creation, so that it could interact with the world without destroying it.

A glance at the line of Spirit Helms on the wall told him the missing helm belonged to Inverlock Keep, his ancestral stronghold across the Great Ocean. After dismissing the Liege, Lord Alistair placed the Spirit Helm on his head, his vision blurring before it revealed the throne room in his cloud fortress. He was now seeing through the eyes of Fesoj Gelmene, a wizard banished from the Realm for the unlawful practice of menagery. Lord Alistair found Fesoj loyal and highly useful, while Fesoj relished the opportunity to continue his illicit craft in secret.

"Milord," the menagerist whispered through the Spirit Helm. "The phrenomancer has gazed with the Blackwood boy."

After Alrick, the best phrenomancer in the Realm, had tried to betray him, Lord Alistair no longer trusted anyone to gaze into his own mind. Since he had long suspected that his fate was tied to the sword and that infernal Blackwood family, he had ordered a gazer to travel to Inverlock Keep and probe the youngest Blackwood brother instead.

Lord Alistair tensed. "Go on."

"The probability of one of the Blackwood brothers fulfilling the prophecy is almost nil."

Alistair exhaled a breath of relief. This was the first gazing session since he had seized the sword and the Coffer. Unlike oracles, who claimed to commune with divine forces and which Lord Alistair considered charlatans, phrenomancers traveled the pathways of the mind to search for possible outcomes, branches of probabilities that were in a constant state of flux, skeins of fate that depended on how events unfolded in the conscious world. Skilled phrenomancers were incredibly good at evaluating future possibilities.

The so-called "Prophecy of the Sword" had always been one potential outcome among many. The first phrenomancer who had glimpsed it had claimed the percentage of fulfillment was roughly thirty per cent. A terrifying prospect. Since that day, Lord Alistair had worked ceaselessly to lower the odds and combat the hated prophecy. It seemed his efforts had finally borne fruit.

"Almost nil, you say?"

"Nearly every pathway led to your victory and the death of all three brothers."

"And those pathways that did not?"

"So unstable they could not be traveled."

"I see. All else is well? The youngest Blackwood is secure?"

"His prison will be his grave."

Lord Alistair clasped his hands behind his back and paced the room, relief pouring through him. He would sleep much better knowing the prophecy was all but extinguished. "I expect to have the remaining brother in chains before the week is out. Once that occurs, we'll have no reason to keep any of them alive.

The menagerist's voice assumed a note of eagerness. "Milord, would you consider granting me permission to utilize the brothers' newly deceased corpses for experimentation? The fusion of interworld specimens raises intriguing possibilities that I might not have another chance to explore. I would have to employ the services of a necromancer, of course."

Lord Alistair swallowed his revulsion at the request. Fesoj was a necessary evil, and it was best to feed his unwholesome nature a morsel of nourishment from time to time. "I don't see why not."

-2-

As he was dreaming, Will Blackwood knew that someone was in the back of his mind, like a squirrel poking around in an attic, and that this was exceedingly strange. Though aware he was experiencing a lucid dream, he couldn't seem to make himself wake up. He tried shouting at his uninvited cerebral visitor to vacate the premises, but no one responded, and Will was incredibly frustrated that he couldn't *see* anyone, even inside the dream. It felt as if an invisible doctor was performing brain surgery while he slept.

The location of the dream changed. Will yelled as he leaped off his horse, rattled his sword, and dashed across the stage of Medieval Nights, the joust-themed dinner theatre in New Orleans where he used to work nights and weekends. He was stoked about using his new warrior skills to impress his peers, especially the raven-haired bartender with the killer smile who had never given him the time of day.

Things were different now. Will had thick stubble and blond hair down to his shoulders, the sort of physique found on the covers of men's magazines, and he knew he could defeat the entire staff of Medieval Nights in a sword fight all by himself without breaking a sweat.

At first the papier-mâché red dragon lurched awkwardly back and forth, controlled, as Will knew, by a puppeteer inside the belly of the beast. But then the monster started to grow. As the crowd roared in appreciation, Will slowed as he approached, gawking as the dragon doubled in size and raised its long neck in a sinuous movement far too controlled for any puppet. He realized the beast was not made of papier-mâché, but covered in scabrous red scales as supple as leather and so hard they could repel edged weapons. When the dragon opened its mouth to unleash a geyser of flame, Will could feel the residual heat from the magical fire, and saw a forked tongue and rows of teeth as long and sharp as daggers.

Ohmygod. This dragon is real.

Is the dream real, too?

Will looked down and realized he was not holding Zariduke, but a plastic sword that would snap in half as soon as it connected with the dragon's thick scales. As he backed away, the cheers from the crowd turned mocking, and then to the sort of bloodthirsty cries one would expect in a Roman amphitheater.

They wanted to see the dragon win.

They wanted to see Will burn.

The dragon stomped forward, swung its head around, and prepared to unleash another cone of fire. Will knew he had no defense. He was going to die. He wasn't Will from the Blackwood Forest, champion of the Roma clans, wielder of Zariduke and a paladin's shield, the fearsome slayer of wizards.

He was Will Blackwood from New Orleans, apprentice builder and fantasy geek, proud owner of a clunky Honda Civic and a dead-end life and a history of panic attacks that left him on the floor at the slightest hint of danger.

Orange-red flames poured out of the dragon's maw and enveloped him. Will screamed as the fire seared his flesh and lungs, the hottest fire he had ever experienced, hotter than anything he could ever imagine, the fire of Hell itself—

With a start, he woke from the dream, groggy and trembling, sweat pouring off his skin despite the cold stone floor beneath him and the frigid temperature inside the cell. It took him a moment to realize he was no longer dreaming. It had all felt so *real*, especially the part when someone had been inside his mind.

Had that really happened? And had it somehow exacerbated the dream with the dragon?

He had heard of people called phrenomancers who could enter people's heads and read their thoughts. Had his captors probed him for information while he slept? He shuddered at the prospect. He might prefer torture over someone rummaging inside his head, messing with his thoughts and memories.

He checked himself for burns and other wounds. Though intact, he was stiff from spending the night on a dungeon floor. Someone had taken Zariduke and his buckler shield while he slept. No surprise there. They had taken everything, in fact, except the clothes on his back and his armband which allowed him to understand all manner of languages. A useful tool, though it bothered him that he couldn't take it off. He still wasn't sure if it was a blessing or a curse.

The cell was ten feet by ten feet with no windows and a set of iron bars serving as the front wall. The floor, walls, and ceiling were made of solid stone. So was the hallway outside, and the empty cell across from him. The dungeon looked as if it had stood for a thousand years and would stand for a thousand more. Soon after he arrived, Will had run his experienced contractor hands over the walls and iron bars and knew he wasn't breaking out. The place was as solid as a mountain.

Thirst clawed at Will's throat. Hunger pangs had set in. He estimated a day had passed since Lord Alistair had sent him hurtling through the portal to this dungeon. Were they going to let him rot in here?

"Hey! Is anyone out there! I need some food and water!"

No one answered, but an hour or so later he heard footsteps approaching from the hallway outside his cell. The footsteps grew thunderous, echoing off the stone walls, causing him to wonder what sort of being could make such a racket. He scrambled to the back of his cell as a giant leather boot appeared, attached to a hairless thigh as big around as an oak trunk. Above the thigh was the bottom of a white tunic level with the top of the iron bars.

The giant stopped in front of the cell. Will caught a strong whiff of musky body odor. The giant's knees bent, and a hand as big as a trash can lid lowered to shove a blanket, a loaf of bread, and a flagon of water through the bars.

Will didn't dare move within reach of the giant hand. With a grunt, the being straightened and then returned the way it had come, followed by the sound of a door slamming shut.

His knees a little watery from the size of the jailer, Will picked up the bread and sniffed it, took an exploratory sip of water, then made short work of the pitiful little meal.

Though devastated by his banishment to the dungeon, he was equally worried about his brothers. What in the world was Val thinking? How could he place an ounce of trust in Lord Alistair? Not to mention that Val now had far greater control of his powers, and appeared to be a member of the Congregation. What had happened during all those months?

As infuriating as Val's actions had been, Will knew his older brother was only trying to help, and must have had no idea of Lord Alistair's true intentions.

Which meant Val, too, was in mortal danger.

Caleb was even worse off, running off to confront Lord Alistair in battle. A death wish if Will had ever heard one.

Madness, it's all madness.

Will had to get out of this prison and bring his brothers to their senses. He stalked to the bars of his cell and yanked as hard as he could, over and over, before sinking to the floor.

Hopeless.

It also hurt that Mala had disappeared when Lord Alistair showed up, just when the going got rough. He supposed he couldn't blame her—how was she supposed to fight someone like that? But still, no one else had run away or tried to hide. They had stood by his side to the bitter end.

Which probably means they're all dead or in the Fens.

You should have listened to Mala and stopped trying to be a hero.

As time passed, he grew so cold he was forced to wrap himself in the filthy blanket the giant had left. After shaking it out, worried it was infested with bed bugs, he lay on his back near the bars of his cell, wallowing in depression, second-guessing all the choices that had led to this dungeon.

Something fluttered down the hallway to his left. He turned to see a young boy about twelve years old walking towards his cell, dressed in a tailored gray coat, boots, and a high-collared dress shirt. Will stood and gripped the bars, but his plea for help died on his lips as he noticed the deathly pallor of the newcomer's face and hands, realized his footsteps made no sound, and saw that his boots barely seemed to brush the floor when he moved. When the figure stopped right in front of his cell and faced him with a mute expression, Will could see right through him. He realized he was looking at a shade or apparition.

Was this a ghost? Despite all the monsters Will had seen on Urfe, and the magic he had witnessed, the possibility of confronting a being from beyond the grave induced a numinous shiver that creeped him out more than any monster he had faced.

"Um, hey there," Will said.

The spectral figure did not reply, but he was staring at Will with an expression so intense Will knew he was trying to communicate. The boy's high forehead and aristocratic features looked familiar, though Will couldn't put a finger on why.

"What's your name?" Will asked. "Where are you from? Is this your castle?"

Knowing he was babbling, Will shut up and tried to remember the lore he knew on spirits. The popular opinion, both in the fantasy literature and embraced by real-life mediums, was that ghosts usually formed after a traumatic and untimely death. Often they stuck around because they wanted to impart a message, or had a strong unfulfilled desire. Sometimes these lost souls needed to be "led to the light" before they could rest in peace.

Will stepped right to the bars, so close he could see what appeared to be food stains on the collar of the boy's shirt. "Are you trying to tell me something? Did something happen to you?"

He felt a little foolish asking these questions. When the boy didn't respond, the silence of the ancient stone dungeon seemed to deepen. Will became more and more unnerved, acutely aware that he was alone with a ghost with nowhere to run or hide.

What if the boy is malevolent? What if all the lore is wrong and it can reach out and harm me? What if it wants to drag me down—

"Boo!"

At the sound of the voice, which had come not from the apparition but from behind Will in the cell, he jumped about three feet in the air and thought he might have suffered a mild heart attack.

"I wonder," said a sardonic female voice, "what all those adoring barmaids up and down the Barrier Coast would think about seeing the legendary Will Blackwood spooked like a frightened child? It's just a ghost, after all."

Will had to blink a few times to convince himself the woman who had somehow appeared in the cell with him, a dark-haired beauty with dancing violet eyes and a mocking smile, the Roma adventuress with whom he had fallen deeply in love, was real.

"So this is your home world?" she continued. "No wonder you emigrated."

"Mala!"

"My name has not changed, Will the Builder."

"But what—where—how did you get here?"

She fingered an amulet attached to a silver chain around her neck. The striking talisman, called the Decagon of Kirna Tuluth, was made of tiny pieces of amethyst that formed a ten-pointed star. Will remembered she had used the magic of the talisman, which connected two souls across vast distances in some mysterious way, to find him on the isle of Takros.

"I sense the magic of the talisman has dispersed," she said. "I'm afraid that was the last use, which does not bode well for our escape from wherever it is we are. I don't suppose you know?"

"'Fraid not." Suddenly remembering the ghostly figure, Will turned but saw no sign of it. *I wonder what he wanted.* He asked Mala, "What do you think the appearance of a ghost means?"

"That someone has died."

"Yeah. Thanks. You missed your calling as a jester." As she smirked, he felt the familiar shiver of attraction which Mala's proximity always induced. She was dressed in her typical black leather pants, calf-high boots, a lace-up crimson shirt, and colorful jewelry. He was relieved to see that her weighted sash, pouches, and weapons had arrived intact.

"You came back for me," Will said. "I thought you had..."

"Run away?"

"Pretty much."

"But of course I did, foolish boy. Why would I stay and do battle with the Chief Thaumaturge of the Congregation? I prefer to live, and confronting one such as he is a sure way to die. I told you before I don't believe in heroes. If I hadn't acted as I did, I'd be dead and you would rot in this dungeon."

He couldn't deny the truth of that. "Where did you go? What happened to the others?"

"I've no idea. I remained concealed until Alistair sent you through the portal, and then used the decagon to return to New Victoria. I knew Alistair was not being forthright and would never send you home."

After dwelling on the encounter for a moment, he took a step closer and said, "So on the island, after you found me, if you're able to sense the decagon's magic, you knew it had at least one charge left."

"And?"

"And you stayed. You could have warned me about Ferala and left at any time."

She brushed a strand of hair from her eyes. "As I said before. You'd have stood no chance against the dhampyr."

"But you also went inside Takros's stronghold, where Ferala was unlikely to be, and where a world-class illusionist awaited. Do you know what I think?"

"Pray tell, Will the Builder."

He walked right up to her and wrapped her in his arms. "I think you can't bear to see me in danger." Instead of pulling away, he felt her relax in his arms, and he kissed her long and deeply.

When she disengaged, her face was flushed, her voice soft and throaty. "You have quite the annoying habit of attempting to seduce me at inopportune times. In case you've forgotten, we're imprisoned in a dungeon of unknown origin, and if our captors—loyal to Lord Alistair, I presume—find out I'm here, they'll likely kill me on sight. Since I've oft repeated that I prefer to live, I will not be wasting another moment responding to your amorous advances."

He held her by the waist, frustrated by circumstance once again, but also buoyed by the real passion he had felt in their kiss. "Is that a definite no?"

She patted him on the cheek, disengaged, and stepped around him to approach the door to the cell. After running her hands over the iron door plate, she extracted a set of thieves' tools from one of her pouches and reached through the iron bars to work the lock. It took her far longer than usual—Will had never seen a lock survive longer than a minute against Mala—but ten minutes after she started, the door creaked as it swung open, causing him to cringe.

She reached out quickly to hold the door still. "Hurry now," she said, as she tossed him one of her daggers.

Wishing he had his sword, he followed her into the dungeon corridor, where they craned their necks to regard the stone ceiling high overhead. He told her about the giant guardian he had seen.

"About twelve feet tall and hairless?" she said. "Thick legs and wearing boots?"

"That's right."

"It could be a number of races. I'd need to see more."

They crept down the dungeon corridor in the opposite direction from which the giant had arrived. Empty cells lined both sides of the passage, though most contained the skeleton of a past resident.

They reached a dead-end, forcing them to backtrack and continue in the opposite direction. Soon they came to a T-intersection with a closed stone door befitting a giant. The iron pull ring was level with Will's head. Five feet above that, a small window overlooked the hallway.

"Hold still," Mala said, positioning Will under the door and then springing agilely onto his shoulders.

"Be careful," he said.

"If someone was looking through the window, they'd have noticed us already."

She stood on his shoulders without using the door for support. Moments later, she hopped down. "Empty," she said, "though obviously a guard room. I saw keys hanging on the wall."

"Do you think it's the way out?"

"I think it's highly dangerous to proceed in that direction, and I'm not sure we can. I didn't see a visible means of egress, which leads me to suspect there's a trap door in the ceiling, pressurized or weighted in some manner, accessible only to those with superhuman size and strength. I've heard of such doors utilized by the more intelligent of the giant races."

"So this castle belongs to some giant? I don't understand. Why send me here and not prison in New Victoria?"

"Think about it."

He did, and came to the obvious conclusion. "Because Alistair doesn't want anyone else to know I'm here. He wants the sword for himself, and is keeping me alive for some reason."

"Probably as leverage against your brothers."

"Why would he need leverage? He has the Coffer and the sword."

She pursed her lips. "Now that is an excellent question."

Worried there wouldn't be another way out, they headed down the passage to the left of the door, encountering a hallway lined with cells large enough to fit a giant.

Still no signs of life. The passage branched two more times, and each one dead-ended at a stone wall. Their hopes sank lower and lower until they encountered a door at the end of the corridor to the right of the T-junction. An iron bar as thick as Will's waist barred the door from the inside, which they both found strange. Reaching above his head, Will could just barely reach the iron bar, and it took all of his strength to lift it off. His knees buckled as he lowered it, but he managed to keep it from clanging against the floor.

"Well done," Mala said, as he rubbed his forearms from the exertion. After inspecting the door for traps, she lifted her sash off her belt and began to twirl it, gripping her short sword in her other hand as she motioned for Will to open the door.

He could tell by the hinges the door opened outward. Pushing on the handle had no effect, either because the door was stuck or too heavy. He pushed harder, putting his weight behind it. The door burst open and he stumbled forward—right into open air.

In a panic, flailing with both arms as he started to plummet, he felt Mala grab the collar of his leather jerkin and pull him backwards. She wasn't strong enough to stop his descent, but Will managed to clutch the door frame with his fingers and pull himself back to solid ground.

Who puts a dungeon on the top floor, and a door that opens in the middle of the sky?

His heart pumping with adrenaline, he crept to the edge of the ledge and looked out. Above him and to either side he saw the tops of granite ramparts, towers, and other indicia of an enormous castle. Looking down, he saw a mass of thick white cotton he realized with a shock was a bank of clouds. He lowered to the floor, edged out on his elbows, leaned down, and swallowed when he saw that, impossibly, nothing supported the structure from below.

The castle was floating in the sky.

-3-

"Hold steady!" Tamás screamed into the cold night air, "Await the command!"

Above the wild-haired clan leader, beneath the light of a crescent moon, hundreds of mountain trolls raced down the steep mountain slope, spindly limbs flying, their bare and gnarled feet slapping on the stony ground as they grew closer and closer to the contingent of Roma and Devla warriors massed behind Tamás and his companions.

On the clan leader's left was Yasmina, sitting astride her chestnut horse, clutching Elegon's staff in her right hand. Allira was on Tamás's other side, her tattooed skin darker than the night, twirling a deadly boomerang in each hand. Just behind that trio were a hundred archers on horseback, followed by the bulk of the forces, nearly five thousand Roma and newly trained Devla fighters spread out across the slope.

Caleb, sitting astride his hulking gray stallion named Margo, alone at the head of the small army, knew everyone was tensely awaiting his order to attack. Just behind him, Lance and Tamás, both far more experienced in the art of warfare, would tell Caleb when to act. But the troops massed behind them, and especially the Devla, drew their courage from the Templar, the man they considered the representative of their god on Urfe.

Caleb knew the eerily quiet approach of the mountain trolls would strike fear into the heart of his army, as it had once done to him. He watched with a strangely detached air while the rage built inside him, whispering to him that these foul creatures stood between him and the realization of his deepest desire. He could hardly continue on his mission to confront Lord Alistair and avenge his loved ones while these filthy brutes lived to block the way.

Ranging between ten and eleven feet tall, the hairless trolls were clad in shabby loincloths and bear pelts draped over their ashen skin and ropy, almost skeletal frames. But appearances were deceiving. Their knotted limbs were as dense as ironwood, each troll had the strength of two men, and they had a cunning intelligence that made them far more dangerous than their cousins in the hills.

The mountain trolls hefted roughhewn spears and clubs as they approached. Caleb had witnessed their battle prowess firsthand, as well as their cruel natures, when a pair of them had ambushed him and the Brewer on the way to the Tower of Elarion. They would have eaten them for dinner if the Brewer hadn't lulled them to sleep with a magical story.

But that was then, before Caleb had survived the tower's trials, found the diamond-headed mace, and gained an army of followers.

And this was now.

In broad daylight, lower down in the valley or on a wide-open plain, the trolls would not have attacked such a large group. But the terrain limited the mobility of the human army, and the trolls had come on fast, with no time for their opponents to flank them. Plus, fall was receding into winter, food was becoming scarce, and Tamás had warned everyone they might be subject to raids in the Dragon's Teeth as they tried to cross the treacherous peaks.

Grimly remembering his horrific ordeal with the Brewer, Caleb suspected the mountain trolls would look to strike fast and hard, kill the men on horseback, take enough captives for dinner, and lope back to their lairs high in the mountain peaks where no one could reach them.

Except you won't be taking a single human back to your vile cooking pots. Not while I'm in charge.

When the trolls drew close enough that Caleb could see the guards of spiked bone on their shins and forearms, Tamás told him it was time. Caleb stood tall in his stirrups, wrapped in the black cloak with silver stitching he had taken from the Coffer, and which offered protection from the elements. He raised his mace high in the air, roaring at the top of his voice.

"With me! Forward!!"

The resulting cry of support from his followers boiled his blood and gave him a surge of adrenaline. He kicked his heels, urging his steed onward to clash with the mountain troll at the vanguard of the attack. The troll was so tall he stood eye-to-eye with Caleb, even atop his horse. With a sneer at the puny human who dared combat him, the troll launched his spear at Caleb's chest. The missile streaked through the air, almost impossible to avoid from astride a horse, but Caleb didn't bother dodging it. He gave a contemptuous sneer of his own and flicked his wrist at the last minute, causing the spear to shatter when it struck his ensorcelled leather vambrace.

Startled but undeterred, the troll raised its forearm in defense, prepared to use its bark-like skin as a shield as Caleb swung the diamond-headed mace. While it did not take a magic weapon to hurt a mountain troll, their hardened skin could deter blows from most blunt weapons and even edged ones, unless wielded by a powerful warrior.

Caleb guessed the monster's thoughts. That it would not be worried about this lean man with the fine-boned face, far too pretty and smooth-skinned to be a warrior of consequence, swinging a mace with a funny-shaped diamond head.

Yet Caleb's blow blasted right through the outstretched forearm and then the skull of the unfortunate creature, as if the mace had encountered no resistance. Aware of his weapon's capabilities—it crushed most objects, including iron and steel, as easily as a rock smashes through a glass pane—Caleb maintained his balance and shattered another troll skull on the backswing.

A glance over his shoulder told him the ragtag army had surged forward to hold the line. Yasmina and Tamás worked in tandem, Tamás trying to penetrate the trolls' thick hides with expert thrusts of his blade while Yasmina inflicted heavy blows with the owl head of her staff. A troll tried to rush Yasmina from behind, only to scream in agony when a harpy eagle landed on its face and tore out its eyes with knife-like talons. Not far away, using a war hammer and a shield, Lance fought toe to toe against an enormous troll until Allira took the creature down with a boomerang throw to the temple.

Not everyone fared so well. The archers had trouble injuring the trolls unless an arrow pierced an eye or a throat. The trolls took vicious swipes at the legs of the archers' steeds and brought many of them down. All along the front line, mountain trolls could be seen spearing and clubbing people to death, or ripping them apart with their bare hands.

A commanding tenor rose above the chaos of battle. Caleb glanced to his left and saw the Brewer riding through the crowd with his sword raised to the sky, belting out a battle hymn in an unknown language. Though no one could understand the words, the power of his friend's voice gave Caleb's army a surge of strength, and caused the trolls to fall back a step.

When Caleb turned around, he noticed a cone of light illuminating three mages standing atop a rocky outcropping on the left side of the mountain slope. Two Roma women flanked a young man with flowing brown hair, all three of them geomancers who began levitating heavy rocks off the battlefield and launching them into the ranks of the enemy, shattering skulls and pinning mountain trolls to the ground.

The unexpected ferocity of the resistance, along with the appearance of the mages, was too much for the trolls. With howls of rage, they broke off from the battle and raced back up the slope. A few dozen of them scooped up unfortunate fighters on the way out, a last-ditch attempt to carry back meat for dinner.

Urging his steed forward, Caleb managed to run down the nearest troll carrying a prisoner and cut down the creature from behind. Allira freed another by smashing a troll in the head with a boomerang, causing it to stumble and release its captive. Lance bellowed and rushed forward, but Tamás held him back. "Don't follow them up the mountain," the clan leader warned. "They move like goats on the slopes. You too, Caleb. We can't risk it."

With a snarl, Caleb ignored him and spurred his horse forward, barking commands to the mages as he rode. "Follow them! They don't take a single prisoner!"

The mages obeyed, whipping up more rocks and fallen logs to pester the fleeing trolls, causing many of them to release their captives so they could take cover. Caleb tried to catch up with another straggler, but the slope became so steep and rocky his horse was forced to walk. Frustrated, he could only watch as the brown-haired mage named Branyn flew past him. When they locked eyes for a moment, Caleb saw the same determination reflected in the young man's eyes. *No one goes in the cooking pots.*

Branyn flew ahead of the trolls, followed by the two Roma mages, all three of them landing higher up the slope, well ahead of the monsters. One by one, they began to systematically cut down the trolls carrying prisoners, striking them with stones or causing the ground to erupt beneath them and send them tumbling. The trolls finally got the hint and began releasing their captives—but not before a spear launched from below pierced one of the mages through the side.

Still rushing up the hill, followed by Yasmina and Lance and Allira, Caleb helped the fleeing prisoners to safety, and met the two unharmed mages as they flew their wounded companion down the mountain. Caleb remembered the name of the injured geomancer was Lavinia, and he gripped her hand as they passed. "Thank you for your bravery."

"As best I could tell," Branyn said, "we freed all the prisoners."

With a grim nod of thanks, Caleb let them continue down the slope.

Later that night, after the dead were buried and the injured given care and the chaos of the attack had receded, Caleb attended a meeting inside the administrative tent. The mages had set perimeter wards as best they could. Besides the three geomancers, only eleven other mages—all of them junior and bereft of battle experience—had made the journey from Freetown. The Congregation attacks had severely decimated their numbers, and most of the surviving mages had elected to travel to their home villages to search for those in need. Others had simply disappeared. Not everyone had the stomach for a cross-continent march to New Victoria with almost no chance of success.

But sometimes, Caleb knew, those with no hope were forced to make terrible decisions, and cross borders they would never otherwise have crossed.

"How many did we lose?" he asked in a quiet voice as he entered the tent, joining Tamás, the Prophet, Yasmina, and the Brewer on a rug around a portable log stove that poured out heat. Yasmina had arrived the night before, sent through a portal opened by Lord Alistair at her request. She had told Caleb all about the incredible events on the isle of Takros, and begged him not to continue on his mission. Though Caleb was glad Will was safe back home in New Orleans, the loss of Zariduke and the Coffer of Devla were heavy blows, and Val's alliance with Lord Alistair was a troubling turn of events Caleb wasn't sure how to process. Yasmina had also come with a message: that if Caleb turned himself in to the Congregation, he would be sent home to join Will, with no repercussions.

Yasmina had begged him to accept the offer.

Caleb had cursed Lord Alistair and walked off.

A flap at the top of the tent allowed the smoke to vent and the stars to shine. Lance was part of the inner circle, but he was still with the troops, offering advice and encouragement after the battle. Though Allira was tending to Lavinia, the silent healer had made it clear she did not want to take part in decision making. Caleb was surprised none of the elders had been invited to the gathering, and he soon found out why.

"We lost fifty-three people," Tamás said, stoking the fire as everyone settled in. "All things considered, and with respect to our fallen brethren, not a terrible result for a surprise attack by so many mountain trolls."

"The question is how many attacks there will be," the Brewer said, "and by whom? We might run afoul of a larger troll colony, or a roving tribe of tuskers, or something much worse."

"We also face the prospect of winter snows," Yasmina said, laying her staff across her knees as she sat cross-legged between Caleb and Tamás. Having her steady presence by his side helped calm the rage and turmoil in Caleb's soul, if only a fraction. "The snows will arrive in days, not weeks."

No longer did anyone question how the wilder knew things about the weather, flora, and fauna that others did not. Time after time, her observations had proven true.

Tamás slammed a fist into an open palm. "Queen's blood! We'll never make it over the mountains in time."

The strategy, Caleb knew, was to cross the mountains on foot before the snows arrived. If the weather held, this was a much faster way to reach the plains than by taking the entire army far to the south and then east through the Caraxi Pass. Once they reached the other side of the Dragon's Teeth, they planned to purchase wagons and horses from the towns and Roma clans on the plains, with the hope of swelling the army's ranks on the march to New Victoria.

Not that a few thousand additional foot soldiers are going to matter, Caleb thought darkly. *It's the Coffer we need.*

Everyone knew the Coffer was in Lord Alistair's hands. Yasmina had told them what had happened, and Tamás had relayed the news to the camp during an assembly. Silence had reigned until the Prophet stood on a stump and reminded everyone of the prophecy foretold in the Canticles of Urfe, the holiest text of the Devla religion.

Who is this savior?
When will he come?

When shall we be free?
O, Devla!
Not until the prophet shall herald
And the people shall hear
The roar of the last true cleric of the age, the Templar
Your fist, Your scorn, Your righteousness
The one who unseals the Coffer
As he breaks the will of the world.

He did not go so far as to predict victory, or to say *how* they would retrieve the Coffer, but he had told those gathered to stay the course and trust in their god. While some had left the camp after learning the Coffer was in the hands of the Congregation, to Caleb's surprise, the vast majority had chosen to stay.

Were they acting out of faith, or a loss of hope?

Face flushed, Tamás turned to the Prophet. "We should have gone south to the pass, as I suggested."

"Devla will return the Coffer to His people before we reach New Victoria," the Prophet replied, repeating verbatim the words he had spoken atop a tree stump to bolster the spirits in the camp. "He will find a way."

"Acting on faith is one thing," Tamás said carefully in reply, "making foolish and irrational decisions another."

"Following the will of Devla is not a decision," the Prophet said, with maddening serenity, dressed in the same coarse, belted tunic woven from animal hair he always wore. "It is obedience."

Unwilling to cross the spiritual leader, Tamás closed his eyes for a long moment. "Even so, the elders are not faring well. Some of them, perhaps many, won't last a winter in the peaks. Not to mention the children."

The Brewer raised his palms. "Why haven't we seen a death squad? Surely they know we're here."

"We're too large for the death squads to handle," Tamás said, "even if they travel with a mage."

"Then why haven't they sent an airship? Why bother destroying Freetown and not finish the job?"

"Because they want us to come," Caleb said grimly. "We're making their job easy, picking up stragglers on the way and coming right to their door."

"Perhaps," Tamás murmured.

The Brewer nodded. "It makes sense. Once we reach the plains, they can destroy our entire army any time they choose with a single airship, long before we reach the city."

"I don't think they'll commit mass murder in front of witnesses," Yasmina added. "I think they'll provoke a battle, force us to retaliate, then claim a moral victory over the pagans and oath avoiders."

As if he wasn't listening to the conversation, the Prophet turned to Caleb and said, "When we're finished, perhaps you would care to attempt healing the wounded, my lord?"

"I'm not your lord," Caleb growled, "and I told you, I can't heal anyone. You've seen me try."

"Perhaps your first attempt was untimely. Or you might try invoking Devla's blessing," the Prophet gently suggested.

"I didn't say a prayer because I don't *believe* in him."

"I would humbly propose another effort," the Prophet said, undeterred as always by Caleb's lack of faith. "Perhaps Devla will see fit to bestow a blessing."

Caleb believed in the Coffer's power, and in the existence of magic, because he had witnessed both firsthand. What he refused to do was attribute either to some invisible deity. He realized the inner workings of magic existed in an unseen realm. So did science back home.

But there was no rhyme or reason to the world, as far as he could tell.

There was only suffering.

After an uncomfortable silence, in which it was clear Caleb wasn't going to respond, Tamás said, "We need to make a decision. Do we continue across the mountains or turn south?"

Everyone looked to Caleb. He stared down at his hands, unable to bear the thought of retracing their steps, turning south, and losing weeks if not months. He couldn't wait that long for revenge. He simply couldn't. After pushing to his feet, he cast his gaze around the room and said, "I don't expect any of you to come with me, but I start across the mountains in the morning."

"Excellent, my lord," the Prophet murmured. "The Devlan will be at your side."

After a frustrated glance in Yasmina's direction, Tamás sighed and said, "I'll have to discuss it with the elders. I suspect they'll want to continue, against my better judgment."

After a disinterested nod, Caleb swept his cloak around him and stepped into the cold moonlit night.

-4-

The fetid desolation of the Fens disappeared into the eastern horizon. In the distance behind Val, the spires of New Victoria receded as he flew above the murky waters of the swamp. His feet were planted firmly on a Magedisc, a sort of enchanted hoverboard which allowed him to fly without expending magic. Lord Alistair's proclamation of war against the advancing Roma army and their supporters had spurred the deployment of the Magediscs and other combat-ready artifacts.

Behind Val, two aquamancers stood at the prow of a pair of bog boats the Protectorate used to patrol the Fens from time to time. A hybrid of a rowboat and an oversize pontoon, the flat-bottomed vessels had a dozen oars attached to each side, manned by Protectorate soldiers. If needed, the aquamancers could propel the boats on magic-generated waves, but they preferred to save their strength.

Flying at the vanguard of the strike force, Val's eyes swept the watery wasteland of the Fens, cringing at the clusters of unfortunate souls withering away on boards and wooden planks lashed together by reeds. The floating colonies survived by collecting rainwater and scouring the swamp for food. Guards stationed on the periphery of the swamp ensured no one tried to leave. The last port of call for the poor and homeless and oath avoiders banished from the city, the Fens were populated by the diseased and dying, the defeated and the damned.

They were also home to the last remnants of the Black Sash gypsies, the criminal revolutionaries who had almost been eradicated in New Victoria in recent weeks. Tired of their terroristic attacks on upstanding citizens, Lord Alistair had issued an edict to wipe out the organization in New Victoria once and for all.

Val couldn't agree more. He would never forget his first encounter with the Black Sash, when a roving band of their ilk had assaulted Val and Mari in the middle of the Gypsy Quarter. The leader of the gang had killed Mari in cold blood, and Val had almost suffered the same fate. Though Val had taken his revenge on that particular leader, he had never forgotten that awful night, or the Black Sash's attempt to kidnap Adaira, or the ambush in the sewer tunnels beneath the city.

No, Val would shed no tears for these murderers.

"There! South ten degrees!"

As Val bore to the right, he glanced back and saw Yasdril Oofar, the reptilus who had shouted, lowering his spyglass. Yasdril was the nephew of Yasir Oofar, First General of the Protectorate army, a brilliant commander for whom Val had the utmost respect.

Soon a sprawling platform of rotting boards and planks came into view, tenuously supported by long poles driven into the muck. It was the largest settlement they had seen on the Fens, and, according to their intelligence, one of the last remaining outposts of Black Sash resistance. Their cowardly leaders had taken to hiding in plain sight among the downtrodden.

The two bog boats pulled alongside the edges of the floating settlement. A pair of soldiers lowered anchors in the shallow water. Staff in hand, Val worked hard not to gag at the stench of garbage, human waste, and disease-ridden flesh as he cautiously led the way into the settlement. Many of the residents lay prostrate in the hot sun, too hungry or sick to move, their last hope a swift and painless death. In his head, he knew the poor suffered everywhere, at least every place he had ever been, but his heart recoiled at the sight of so much human misery.

The best way to help these people, Val thought, *is not to overthrow the wizards, because there will always be an elite class, but to work harder to raise the standard of the poor, and invest in education and opportunity for all.*

The world doesn't need revolutions. It needs enlightenment and progress.

Val estimated a few hundred people were congregated around the cooking fires, water barrels, and canvas lean-tos in the center of the settlement. Mosquitos and flies swarmed the Protectorate soldiers as they fanned out across the rickety structure, checking each person for weapons, sashes, and Black Sash tattoos. Similar raids were occurring all across the Fens.

"Valjean!"

Val whipped to his right, just in time to summon a Wizard Shield. As the arrow struck the invisible barrier and fell harmlessly to the plank below, men and women wearing black sashes sprang out from under lean-tos all over the settlement. More revolutionaries climbed out of the water and onto the wooden planks, surrounding the invaders. At a glance, Val estimated the Black Sash outnumbered his forces more than two to one.

Yet Val did not spot a single mage among them. Nor did the Black Sash have highly-trained Protectorate soldiers wearing fine chainmail armor, a trio of Congregation wizards, and a very angry majitsu rushing towards the woman who had dared fire an arrow at her wizard charge.

Synne, who had ridden along in the bog boat behind Val, tore through the crowd as the Black Sash fighter rushed to nock another arrow. The dark-haired woman was standing thirty feet away and should have had plenty of time, but she had not accounted for the preternatural speed of Synne, whose feet barely touched the ground as she leaped across the planks, flew into the air, and kicked the woman in the chest with the heels of both feet, caving her sternum and sending her flying into the water. A crocosaur circling the settlement bit her in half before she could scream for help.

Like his uncle, Yasdril was calm and collected as he issued battle orders. The Protectorate soldiers, already gathered in a circle around Val, expanded outward to meet the threat, creating a phalanx of shields and steel. Shouts of dismay and terror arose from the Black Sash fighters as they found themselves pulled into the swamp by the long, suffocating coils of water elementals summoned by the aquamancers.

The permanent residents of the Fens either scurried as far away from the battle as they could, or watched with listless eyes, too sick and depressed to care about their personal safety.

Where Val would once have struggled to summon a basic Wizard Shield, he now maintained it effortlessly, without thinking, as the battle raged around him. The shield of hardened air was child's play compared to the Spirit Armor he could now employ, though he had no use for such a powerful spell against common fighters. Even a Wizard Shield was draining, however, and he could not cast other spells while using it.

But the fighting was almost over before it began. Cowed by the whirling fury of Synne and the well-trained regiment, the remaining Black Sash fighters threw down their arms and begged for mercy.

Val allowed himself a smile of satisfaction as the Protectorate forces rounded up the prisoners and put them in chains. Not a single Protectorate life had been lost. With any luck, the soul of the Black Sash Gypsies would be crushed by nightfall.

After exchanging a word of thanks with Synne, he drifted back to the bog boat on the Magedisc, safely above the squalor and filth beneath him, wishing the world were different but reminding himself of the greater good.

Just after dusk, starving and exhausted from the long day on the Fens, Val watched the city come alive through the open window of his carriage clacking down the worn cobblestones of Magazine Street. It was the same street—at least in name and flora—where his brothers used to live in New Orleans. It always made him think of home, though home had never seemed so far away.

Would he ever return to Earth?

Though he missed certain things back home terribly, Val had never felt this alive. When they arrived on Urfe, his goal of returning home had consumed him. He had thought Will would be the one who accepted the new world. And, after his youngest brother had learned to control his panic attacks, he had indeed embraced life on Urfe.

Caleb, as always, had almost seemed indifferent. With a chuckle, Val suspected that if the brothers had found a small village with a good pub when they had arrived on Urfe, and decided to stay, Caleb might not have blinked.

At least before the events of the last few months.

But now, Val had fallen in love with Adaira, he had come to appreciate the unspoiled beauty of Urfe, and he enjoyed being a wizard. Not just the power and prestige it conferred—though these things were important to him—but for the sense of fulfilment he got from learning and casting spells. Magic was *hard*, harder than anything he had ever attempted. And Val was very good at it. He had always liked to be challenged, and working with the primeval forces of the multiverse was about as challenging as it got. And to be a spirit mage . . . to plumb the essence of reality and summon primal fire and unlock the nature of space and time . . . how could flying on a jet across the Atlantic hold a candle to soaring across worlds, dimensions, universes?

After traversing St. Charles Avenue beneath a canopy of live oaks and

Spanish moss, the carriage left the Garden District and entered the busy commercial area. When they passed the New Victoria Magick Shoppe, Val remembered how excited Will had been when they saw it for the first time. A sharp pang of love for his brothers welled up deep inside Val, causing him to clench his fists at his sides.

Val didn't want to think about how long it might be before he gained enough power to travel worlds and see his youngest brother on Earth again. But at least he was safe. That had always been Val's first priority in life, at least since their father had died.

One more brother to go.

According to Lord Alistair, Caleb was leading a ragtag army of gypsies and Devla worshippers through the Ninth Protectorate in a laughable attempt to . . . what, exactly? Val had his doubts as to the accuracy of the information. He thought someone might be controlling or using Caleb for some unknown reason. But either way, the army had about as much chance of reaching New Victoria, not to mention sticking a thorn in the side of the Congregation, as a Boy Scout troop had of marching across the Alps and defeating Napoleon.

Even if Caleb was just along for the ride, as was usual for him, what the hell was he thinking? Val knew that Caleb's wife and adopted son had perished during a confrontation with the rebels of Freetown. According to the Congregation, the rebels had provoked the attack, but Val knew both sides were to blame. If you send an airship to intimidate someone, you have to expect blowback. Yet why had the rebels started a battle they couldn't win? The news had shocked him—Caleb got married??—and made him sick to his stomach with grief. But this mission of revenge did not at all sound like his freewheeling, peace-loving middle brother. Val hoped with all his heart that Caleb would come to his senses, or he might get killed before Val could intervene.

The carriage stopped outside the Gryphon's Beak, a tavern on the edge of the Guild Quarter. Glow orbs atop slender, curvilinear bronze poles illuminated the busy street. The nip of fall was in the air.

"How now, laddie," Gus called down from atop the carriage. "What time ye be needin' me again?"

Val stepped onto the street, the azantite tip of his staff gleaming beneath a glow orb, the crescent sickle mirroring the moon above. Now that he didn't have to hide his identity, his father's staff never left his side, and he was proud to carry it. When one of the older Congregation mages recognized the staff, it caused them to look at Val with new eyes: sometimes admiring, sometimes uneasy, but always respectful. Though Dane Blackwood's legacy depended on who one asked, everyone agreed he had been one of the most powerful spirit mages of his generation.

"Take the rest of the night off, Gus. Adaira and I will find our way back."

A frown split Gus's bearded face beneath his top hat. "Ye sure about that, laddie? I know yer a powerful wizard and all, but the Black Sash don't discriminate in their targets. After Garbind, no one's safe with that sword around."

Val was amused but also touched that Gus thought Val was safer with him. "I appreciate your concern, old friend. But after today, let's just say the Black Sash no longer concerns us."

"Oh? Is there somethin' I be missin'?"

Val flashed a thin smile. "I expect a public announcement will come soon, but we dealt them a death blow today. Their leaders and sorcerers are dead or imprisoned. As for the sword . . ." Val lowered his voice. "I can't speak about that, but between you and me, that won't be a problem, either."

Gus's bushy eyebrows lifted, and he took a long puff on his wooden pipe. "That's good news. In that case, laddie, I advise you to enjoy your evening with the lovely lass."

"Thanks, Gus."

The driver was still looking at him with an oddly concerned expression. After a moment of hesitation, he said, "Black Sash or not, ye just watch yer back, ye hear?"

"Gus—Is there something I should know?"

The driver clamped down on his pipe. "I'm just a lowly driver, though right proud to be one, and especially proud to be yers. There's a safety in bein' in low places, if you know what I mean, because yer neck ain't stuck out for everyone to see." His shrewd eyes narrowed. "Ye made a rapid rise in the Congregation, laddie. Not everyone might be so pleased by that as I am. I'm not speaking specifics, here. That's far above me station. But I don't need to. There's always people that ain't happy when someone leapfrogs their position in life. Ye understand me, laddie?"

"Perfectly," Val said softly. As always, he was impressed by Gus's street smarts, and his instincts were spot on. Val had indeed caught jealous stares from some of the older mages, especially Braden, now that Lord Alistair had taken Val under his wing and no longer considered the cuerpomancer his heir apparent.

"There's somethin' else," Gus said, looking both ways down the street. "This is just a feelin' . . . but I've got those same jitters in my bones I get when a hurricane is on the way. Even though there's no sign of a storm. If ye know what I'm sayin.'"

Val stepped closer and patted Gus warmly on the knee. "You worry too much, Gus. I appreciate the concern, but after today, the city's never been safer."

"I suppose yer right. I dunno what's come over me." He tipped his hat. "Don't ye worry about the grumblings of a nervous old man. Enjoy yer night with yer friends and lady. Ye deserve it."

"So do you." Val flipped a silver groat onto his driver's lap. "Have a nice meal on me tonight."

Gus's smile revealed a mouth full of crooked, tobacco-stained teeth. "Thank ye, laddie!" he said as he snapped the reins, spurring the horses to action on the cobblestones. "Queen's luck to ye!"

Val grinned to himself as he turned to enter the Gryphon's Beak, though it bothered him that Gus felt so uneasy. He hoped it was nothing to do with his driver's personal life. If so, Val would do everything in his power to help him. Val prized loyalty above all other traits, and he returned that loyalty with his own.

A gush of pleasing aromas greeted him inside the tavern: wood smoke wafting off of the grill inset into the far wall; worn, well-oiled leather from the boisterous crowd of adventurers and mercenaries; the tang of golden ale; and the mouthwatering sizzle of fat dripping off fire-crisped meat.

The rough crowd grudgingly made way as Val strode past the tables dotting the front of the room and skirted the central wraparound bar festooned with pennants, flags, and coats of arms from around the world.

He found Rucker at his familiar table near the hearth in the back corner. Val had never seen anyone else sitting at that table, even when the burly one-armed adventurer wasn't there, because everyone was too afraid Rucker might walk in and find a stranger at *his* table. Val chuckled. He'd be afraid of Rucker too, if he didn't know him so well.

And maybe he was a little bit afraid anyway.

Another familiar face had joined the scarred and grizzled adventurer: a tall, bald young man from the Kingdom of Great Zimbabwe. Dida rose to greet Val, tripping over a table leg and almost falling on his face before Val caught him. The bibliomancer gave a sheepish smile, and the two men exchanged a warm arm clasp.

Val knew better than to offer the same greeting to Rucker, so he nodded and took a seat between the two men. Though Synne did not like to leave Val's side, he needed his space at times, and he also knew that Kjeld Anarsson, the nasty and hot-blooded head of the Order of Majitsu who hated Synne, liked to frequent the tavern. As capable as Synne was, Kjeld was a monster of a man and as gifted in magic as most wizards. The last time they had met, in this very tavern, Kjeld had almost killed her before Adaira intervened.

"I was having a good night drinking alone," Rucker grumbled, "and now there's two of ye?"

"Sorry I'm late," Val said to Dida.

"Ye two jesters planned this?" Rucker said, shaking his head in disgust. "And wizards are always late. Too high and mighty for the rest of us. Where's yer attack dog and the princess?"

"Synne took the night off, and Adaira should be here later. She's eager to see you."

"Bah," Rucker said, waving his hand before taking a swig of foamy red ale to conceal the pleasure in his eyes. His long gray hair was caught in a ponytail beneath a worn battle helm, and his silver axe—Demonbane—hung from a notch in his leather belt.

After making small talk over a round of beer, their conversation turned to Lord Alistair's recent declaration of war. "If I was a younger man," Rucker said, "it'd be good for business. But I'm older and wiser and know a rat when I smell one."

"What do you mean?" Val said carefully.

"Tell me something, boy: why does the most powerful collection of wizards in the Realm need to go to war against an army that isn't even an army?"

"What should he do? Let them march on the city and burn it down?"

"The gypsies were keeping to themselves in the Ninth before Lord Alistair sent the airships."

"The Ninth doesn't belong to them. The airships were sent to scout the

Mayan border and survey coastal territory. The Freetown mages attacked the airships, forcing them to respond."

Rucker guffawed and slapped the table. "What do ye think, Dida? Should we try to sell him farmland in the Fens?"

The bibliomancer looked uncomfortable at the turn the conversation had taken. His forehead wrinkled, and he said, "That's what our embassy was told as well."

"I know there's animosity," Val said. "The presence of the airships provoked the rebels, no doubt. But again, it's not officially their land, and I've seen first-hand what the Black Sash gypsies are capable of."

"Not all gypsies are black sash, just as not all mages cozy up to the Congregation."

Val's eyes narrowed at the slight. "I know the Congregation has its flaws. But the fact remains that the Roma people, *all* Oath avoiders, have a choice. They can take the oaths and pay their taxes like the rest of us. There's no need to revolt."

"Easy for ye to say, since it's not yer way of life yer giving up."

"You forget who my father is. I'm Roma too, Rucker."

"Ye didn't know ye were until ye arrived. It's different."

"Thanks, but I'll speak for myself on my heritage. It's a complicated world. I sympathize with the oath avoiders. I know they're just doing what they think is right. But there are other ways to go about it. Overall the Congregation is a force for good, and progress has to be made. I'd rather live in a modern but imperfect world than one where our kind is slaughtered like pigs by the . . ."

Rucker's face reddened, and he slammed his beer mug on the table, spilling half its contents. "Say it, boy. By the *common born*. Our kind, is it? Ye've risen so high above the rest of us ye can't smell yer own stink."

"Oh, don't be ridiculous. You saw what happened in the alternate dimension. They tried to hang Adaira from a *tree*. If you think that can't happen again, and history can't repeat itself, then you're the one who's naïve." Val's face was tight as he stood to leave. "I'm sorry, Dida. I don't think my presence is welcome anymore."

Dida's intelligent brown eyes slipped downward.

Rucker jabbed a finger as Val gathered his cloak and staff. "Ye've got wool in yer eyes. A man like Lord Alistair will never be satisfied. He'll slaughter your kinsmen, the Mayans, and the whole of Urfe unless someone stops him. He'll say the right words in public, but little by little, he'll take our freedoms away. He'll turn on ye, too, one day. Mark my words."

"I can look out for myself," Val said.

He swept out of the tavern, only to be caught outside the door by Adaira. "Val! What's wrong?"

He took a deep breath to steady himself. "Rucker and I have a difference of opinion on, oh, about everything right now. I had to leave before I said something I'd regret."

Adaira was dressed in calfskin boots and a light blue cloak that matched her eyes. "Did it involve my father?" she guessed, causing Val to nod. He didn't want to get into the details and upset her.

"I know you wanted to see Rucker," Val said. "Why don't you say hello and come to my place later?"

She looped an arm through his. "It's fine. I know where to find him. There's something I need to tell you, and I want us to be alone."

He noticed a strange look on her face, a faint, mysterious, almost ethereal smile that made him curious. "What is it?"

"Not here," she said, peering up at him almost shyly. "Come," she said, levitating off the street, inviting him to fly with her.

Soon after, guided by strings of teardrop-shaped glow orbs, Val strolled arm-in-arm with Adaira down a pebbled path that wound through hedgerows of vivid tropical flowers and groves of palms and banana trees.

The grounds of the Oasis Café, tucked inside the high brick walls of the finest pleasure garden in the city, were just as stunning as he remembered.

Adaira chose a familiar table, candlelit and made of emerald quartz, perched on the edge of a courtyard surrounded by live oaks. Across the courtyard, the spires of the Wizard District backlit the silver arch of the Canal Bridge. The beauty of the setting and the subtle spice of Adaira's perfume—a heady mix of cinnamon and rose—left Val feeling intoxicated even before the granth arrived.

"Our first date," he said as a multicolored waterfall burst out of the fountain in the courtyard. "Down to the very same table."

Adaira removed her cloak, revealing a silver blouse that clung to her lithe figure that drew Val's eyes even more than the first time they had met. Her pale skin shone like moonlight under the glow orbs as she fingered her black pearl choker.

"Our first time here," she said wistfully, "we barely knew each other." She eyed his high-collared dress shirt and black dinner jacket which the maître d had loaned him. "I liked how you didn't conform to the fashions of the day, though unbeknownst to me at the time, you had no clue what they were."

"I still don't," he said wryly.

She laid a hand atop his. "Exactly."

A waiter in white livery dropped off two glasses of house granth and a plate of artfully arranged shellfish appetizers. Except for the narrow view of the courtyard, their table was hidden within the foliage, ensconced in the sublime calm of the garden. Val stared into Adaira's eyes, remembering how beautiful she had looked that first night, amazed at how their relationship had blossomed. He never imagined he would fall so deeply in love.

"And now here we are," she said. "No longer wide-eyed students but mages who have traveled to a new dimension, battled demons, and slain a member of the Alazashin. Lovers and companions, survivors of trials and tribulations."

"Here we are," Val said steadily, meeting her gaze.

Where is she going with this? Has her father pressured her to marry?

Though not averse to the thought of marriage—in fact, it was increasingly on his mind—he would betray nothing until he knew her intentions. Maybe she was about to tell him she had fallen for someone else, or her father no longer thought they should be together.

She leaned forward, the candlelight illuminating the curve of her neck as her flaxen hair brushed her arms. "You told me once that you see the world in layers of gray."

"I suppose I did."

"You said it was hard to express who you are, even to yourself."

"I said all that?"

A small smile creased her lips. "I've often thought about what you said, and wondered what it meant for the two of us."

Val gazed into the shadows at the edges of the courtyard, thinking about his mindset when he had made the comment. "After being with you," he said, facing her once again, "I can say that I know myself better than I ever did before. Who I am. What I want to be. And I . . . I can't think of a higher compliment."

She nodded slowly, still with that faraway expression. "I feel the same. I wouldn't even want someone who understood themselves, or thought they understood me, with perfect clarity. I just need you to love me, as I do you. Do you love me, Val?"

The directness of the question caught him off-guard. He looked her in the eye and said, with all honesty, "I do, Adaira. I truly love you."

"Good," she said softly. "Because I'm pregnant."

-5-

Will stood at the end of the dungeon corridor, staring into the patch of open sky that surrounded his floating prison. "What is this place?"

Beside him, Mala replaced her sash and sword and crossed her arms, gazing outward with a thoughtful expression. "I believe I might know."

"Another world or dimension?"

"No, I believe we're still on Urfe. I remember hearing that Lord Alistair has an ancestral home in the northern reaches of Albion, deep in the Craglands of Argyll. Obviously it's been imbued with powerful magic to keep it fixed among the clouds."

As she peered out, Mala balanced on her tiptoes on the ledge, unconcerned by her precarious position. Will gripped her arm just in case, put his other hand on the door frame, and leaned out to get a better view. He couldn't get over how the bottom of the castle dropped into empty sky beneath him, while the gray stone wall rose a hundred feet or more above their heads, all the way to a set of ramparts bordered by a pair of squat towers.

"Do you see that window—" Mala began, then cut off when they heard a series of faint booms, followed by the appearance of a colossal humanoid atop the ramparts in the distance. A pelt of animal fur draped the shoulders of the gigantic male being, adding a layer of warmth to the leather armor with sky-blue buckles that protected his torso. A mass of shaggy, curly white hair covered his head and face, and a thicket of icicles hung from the bottom of his beard. The giant held an iron club the size of a small tree in one hand. As he leaned over the edge of the parapet to scan the sky around the castle, Mala and Will backed away from the ledge, closed the door as quietly as they could, and crept back down the corridor.

"Do you think he saw us?" Will whispered, his hands trembling from the encounter.

"I don't know. Queen's prayer he didn't."

"What kind of giant was that?"

"No giant, Will the Builder. That was a titan, largest of all the humanoid races. They're extremely rare, quite intelligent, and hermetic. I've never seen one before, and was unsure if they still existed."

The faint booms began again—the titan's footsteps, Will presumed—then faded away. "Existence of terrifying titan guarding the ramparts of Lord Alistair's sky castle—check."

"No lore I've encountered has mentioned titans serving humans," she said. "In fact, it was the other way around. But with Lord Alistair, one never knows. Now, of course, the appearance of your jailer makes sense. That must have been a younger titan, perhaps his son."

"He was big enough to break me in half," Will muttered.

"Make no mistake," Mala said, "challenging a titan is far beyond our capabilities. Perhaps we could manage to overcome the young one—with luck, and *if* you had your sword—but an adult male of that size . . . that is the province of an elder mage, and a powerful one at that."

Will shuddered. "Judging by the size of that thing, I don't doubt you one bit."

Mala twisted a silver bangle around her wrist. "We might have one thing in our favor. If I'm right, and this is Lord Alistair's stronghold, then I would bet a thousand florins there's a nontraditional means of egress."

"Because Lord Alistair isn't going to fly across an ocean from New Victoria every time he gets nostalgic for his childhood home."

"Precisely. He's a spirit mage, but I suspect he won't rely on his magic alone to travel. That can be risky." She flashed a grim smile. "My suspicion is a portal to New Victoria lies somewhere in the castle."

"So if we can find it before we're killed by that demigod up there," he said, "or by some other deadly defense Lord Alistair has in place, then we might have a chance to escape."

"You have a talent for seeing to the heart of the matter, Will the Builder."

Later that night—Will wasn't sure of the exact time, but he guessed well past midnight—he paced his cell after forcing down another ration of murky water and moldy bread, waiting for Mala to come for him, praying nothing had happened since they had split up.

Earlier, Mala had hatched an insane plan to climb straight up the outside wall, through the window they had seen high above them, and into the castle proper.

Will was terrified of the climb, and of being spotted by the titan, and of what they would encounter even if they made it through the window. But he had to admit it was their best chance—maybe their only chance—of escaping the dungeon.

Since the castle wall was so exposed, Mala reasoned they would have a greater chance of avoiding detection if they climbed under the cover of darkness. After they parted, Will had hurried back to his cell to lock himself inside before the jailer made his daily rounds. Mala had spent the day hiding out in an unused portion of the dungeon.

"Fancy an escape from a wizard's keep?"

Will jumped to his feet as she appeared in front of his cell. "About time. I was getting worried."

"I've no idea whether titans are nocturnal, but I haven't heard footsteps on the ramparts in some time."

She picked the lock to the cell again, and the iron door swung open. Will hurried out, hoping he never again saw the wrong side of a set of iron bars. Mala locked the door behind him, and together they raced through the dungeon and returned to the door they had found.

Will heaved off the iron bar and carefully set it down. "We won't be able to replace the bar once we start climbing. Though the jailer will probably notice my absence long before he wanders into this part of the dungeon. I'd say we have a couple of hours at best."

"Less talk," Mala said, easing the door open to expose a blast of cold air. "More action."

Will knew he was stalling. A stiff gust of wind blew his hair into his face, making him even more nervous. What if the wind blew him right off the castle wall? Or what if his fingers froze before they finished? It was far colder outside than in the castle. As high up as they were, the inside temperature must be magically controlled.

He leaned out to study the rough-cut stone blocks that comprised the castle. Each block was about two feet tall and three feet wide, with a millimeter of indentation in the mortar. The smooth face of the wall made him swallow. "You know I can't climb like you. How am I supposed to do this?"

She withdrew a tiny silver canister from one of her pouches. Inside was a white paste she applied to her fingertips. "This spidergel will help, but be warned: it is not a safety net, and will not hold your weight. It is a climbing aid, nothing more."

Will stuck his fingertips into the canister and covered them in the gooey odorless paste. After flexing his fingers, ensuring they bent properly, he touched the wall and felt his fingers adhere to the stone. When he pulled back, he felt a modicum of suction.

"I don't think it's enough," he said.

She reached out to hold his chin. "Listen to me: you can do this. You *will* do this. I estimate a ninety-foot climb to the window. It will be over in minutes. Don't look down, and follow my lead. Place your holds exactly where I place mine. Understood?"

He gritted his teeth. "Understood."

To his surprise, Mala leaned in and kissed him. The union of their lips was brief, but it was the first time she had ever initiated a kiss, and it lent him strength.

Without another word, she tucked her sash into her waist, scanned the ramparts to ensure no one was watching, and stepped onto the face of the castle wall beside the door frame. Will watched in awe as she began to climb the sheer vertical surface, using the minute dimples, bulges, and imperfections in the rough-cut stones as footholds and handholds. He wondered if she even needed the spidergel.

After ten feet, she stopped to let him follow. He put a foot and a hand on the wall and, with a deep breath, took the plunge and stepped out. The darkness helped shield the precarious nature of the climb, but it was still terrifying. The cold wind whisked into his face, threatening to dislodge him, and he cowered against the wall, clinging to his tenuous hold. Though the spidergel helped him stay attached, he knew that if he made a single misstep, the sticky substance would not arrest his fall.

"You're doing fine," Mala said quietly, then gave him instructions on where to place his hands.

A few lights were still on in various parts of the castle, though the window above them was dark. Will forced himself not to look down and, foot by laborious foot, followed her lead and climbed the castle wall in a zigzag pattern, searching out the best holds, following her every instruction. After thirty feet, his muscles started to burn, and after another thirty, he could barely keep his grip. He looked up and saw the window still fifty feet away, a distance that seemed like a thousand miles. A fierce gust of wind almost knocked him off the wall, and he pressed tight against the rough stone, afraid to move. "I'm not going to make it."

"You *will*," she said in a fierce whisper. "Try to relax your muscles so you don't expend so much energy."

Relax? he thought. *If I relax I'll plummet to my death.*

Digging deep within himself, finding that well of determination he always knew he possessed, he managed another twenty feet before both his biceps started to spasm. With a gasp, he pressed tighter with his toes, but he knew he was about to fall.

Before he could call out for help, the soft boom of giant footsteps shook the ramparts above them.

"We have to go faster," Mala called down, her voice barely traveling above the wind.

"I'm done," Will said, talking quietly so as not to expend any energy. "I can't move any further."

Mala looked down and saw how much he was struggling. The footsteps grew nearer, and Will knew the titan's head and shoulders were about to appear above the ramparts.

"Five more feet," Mala said, "and I can reach you with my javelin from the window."

Will took a few quick breaths and tried to move his right hand, but his arm almost gave out on him. "If I try to climb, I'm going to fall."

Her eyes darted from Will to the parapet above. "Hold on. Don't panic and don't look down."

"Hurry," he whispered, though he knew she couldn't hear him.

His eyes flicked upward, and he watched in awe as Mala started to climb much faster than before, almost as if she were walking up the wall. She reached the window in moments, and thankfully it opened with little resistance. Will felt his fingers slipping. He pressed his face against the cold stone, buffeted by the wind, straining to hold his position. *You can do this, Will. Pain is in your mind. Don't let go.*

His mental encouragement only took him so far. One of his feet slipped, and he almost fell before he found a crack in the stone a few inches below. As another footstep boomed above him, causing his stomach to bottom out in fear, he heard the gentle slap of fabric against stone. He looked up and saw Mala's blue sash dangling a foot above his head. The sash was tied to the end of her javelin, which Mala was holding in one hand as she leaned out of the window. She made a climbing motion with her free hand, then gripped the javelin tight.

With a final burst of strength, he reached up to grab the strong silk of the weighted sash with one hand, and then another, his heart leaping into his throat as his torso detached from the wall. As Mala braced him from above, he began to climb the wall with his feet, his hands moving higher and higher on the sash and then the javelin. Though exhausting, it allowed him to engage different muscles than before, and Mala pulled from above as well. She helped him through the window just as a leg of the titan came into view.

Mala put a finger to her lips as Will collapsed to the floor. She squatted beside him and stroked his cheek with a fingernail. "You've surpassed my expectations as a warrior, but you won't be joining the Thieves Guild anytime soon."

Unsure whether to laugh or cry at her clinical observations, Will closed his eyes as his body warmth slowly returned, happy to be alive.

"Catch your breath," she said, "because we have work to do before the sun rises."

The sheep's wool rug beneath him was soft and cozy. With a groan, he sat up and realized they had landed in a bedroom with Coffered paneling. Mala skirted the four-poster bed in the center of the room and approached a family portrait hanging beside the fireplace. "It appears my assumption was correct."

Will rubbed his arms to restore circulation as he made his way to her side. "Is that Lord Alistair?" he asked, pointing out a tall and handsome patriarch with a hawkish stare and a pronounced widow's peak. A silver-haired woman stood beside him, her arms on the shoulders of two young boys about three years apart in age.

"The style of this oil painting is now obsolete," Mala said, "and his wife died much younger than this woman, who I presume is his mother." She pointed out the taller boy on the left, who looked about fifteen years old at the time. "That's Alistair. I didn't realize he had a brother," she mused.

As Will's gaze rested on the smaller boy on the right, the blood drained from his face, and he realized why she had used the past tense. The clothes were different, but without a doubt, it was the same face they had seen on the ghost outside his cell.

"Curious," she said when he pointed that out, "but plenty of castles in Albion are haunted. It rather goes with the territory. Now come. There is little time and much to explore."

After lingering in front of the portrait, they crept out of the bedroom and emerged near the end of a wide hallway with a vaulted ceiling. Silk tapestries adorned both sides of the hall. Unlit glow orbs in emerald cages were spaced evenly along the wall.

"Shouldn't we be concerned about wards?" Will whispered as they began moving forward. The corridor was cool and smelled of old stone.

"Not on the inside of a keep. At least not in the common areas."

"What about the outside? Once we left the dungeon through the window and re-entered?"

"Are we not still alive? Is there anything we could have done about spiritmancer wards even if we had encountered them?"

"Not without Zariduke," he muttered, wondering what Alistair had done with the sword. Mala had lent him a dagger, but Will felt naked without his sword and buckler.

"The wards are likely set further out from the keep, especially with a titan roaming the ramparts. "'Tis not a strange thing to do. Now concentrate and thank the stars we have one less thing to worry about."

The entire floor was typical of European castles Will had seen in photos and always wanted to visit. Soaring ribbed ceilings in the great hall, dining rooms as large as gymnasiums, suits of armor and heraldic emblems decorating the walls. The exquisite furnishings of the Alistair abode reminded him of the royal castles from the Tudor era.

Yet it was also the keep of a prominent mage family. Books on magical theory and thaumaturgical history dominated the library, along with spellbooks in glass cases Will guessed were heavily warded. One of the rooms they encountered was a cross between an observatory and a lounge, complete with antique telescopes, buttery leather furniture, globes and astrolabes, and an interactive map of the dimensions on one wall that far exceeded virtual reality technology on Earth. Will gawked at the way his hand movements caused the three-dimensional map to shift through the planes of existence. He could have stood there and explored it for hours. *Are all those places real?*

Mala pulled him away, and they continued down a hallway with gold-framed oil paintings of family ancestors. Attached to the wall beside each portrait was a weapon, mostly staves or swords, embedded with a precious jewel of some sort.

"Wizard stones?" Will asked.

"Likely," Mala said, eying the gemstones with a greedy eye.

As they neared the end of the hall, the apparition from the dungeon appeared again. The dark-haired boy in the gray coat stared at them with eyes as mournful as a funeral dirge. He beckoned with one hand, then drifted backwards out of sight.

After exchanging a wary glance, Will and Mala reached the T-junction where the passage dead-ended at a set of stairs leading to a higher level. Coats of arms painted onto shields decorated the stone walls of the intersection. Down the hall to their left, they saw the ghost drift through a doorway.

"Choices," Will said.

"Choices," she agreed.

Her eyes followed the broad stone steps that led to the upper reaches of the castle. "If my orientation serves me, these stairs should take us to an occupied section of the keep."

"I think you're right. Most of the lights we saw outside the dungeon were to the left of our vantage point. You think it's too risky?"

"Not as risky as wasting time and being discovered."

"What about the ghost? Normally I wouldn't suggest following the lead of the main character in a horror movie, but this feels different."

"What?"

"Nothing. I meant it's foolish to see a ghost and follow it, instead of running in the opposite direction. But this is Urfe, where the abnormal is commonplace, and I can't help feeling that this spirit wants to tell us something. I know it's a bit clichéd, but on the other hand, clichés exist for a reason."

"What in Queen's Blood are you talking about?"

"What if we learned something helpful from him? Maybe even the location of the portal, if there is one? Surely after so long, the ghost knows the castle better than anyone."

"Now that," Mala said as she loosened her sash again, "is an intelligent observation."

"Plus, if he wished us harm, wouldn't he have done so already?"

"Not in incorporeal form. But he could be leading us into a trap, possibly of magical origin."

"A trap? Why?"

"So we can join him in eternal damnation roaming the castle."

"Oh. That. Yeah, maybe the stairs are better for—"

Mala was already striding down the hallway. Unsure if her last remark was a joke, Will hurried to catch up with her.

After inspecting the heavy wooden door the ghost had drifted through for traps, she eased it open. The ghost was nowhere to be seen. The walls were made of a smooth, milk-white substance that reminded Will of the crescent moon tip of Val's staff, as well as the nine dagger-sharp ends of Magelasher, Mala's cat o' nine tails she had recovered from the tomb of the sorcerer king. He wondered why she had left the weapon behind.

"Azantite," Mala murmured, confirming Will's guess. The ceiling and floor were made of the same substance. Throughout the room, black splotches marred the smooth face of the azantite, as if localized blasts of fire had charred the walls.

"What is this room?" he said.

Before she could answer, the ghost flew out of the wall right in front of Will with its spectral hands extended. Startled, he drew back in alarm, but the ghost was moving too fast to avoid. His dagger passed right through the transparent being, and Will flinched as the ghost flowed into him. He had no idea what sort of injury a ghost could cause, and he panicked thinking about Mala's warning of eternal damnation.

At first, when the room blurred and Will lost control of his body, he did think he had died and entered the afterlife. His vision cleared but the room retained a translucent, impermanent appearance, as if he were dreaming. Though the experience felt real, he also knew on some level that it wasn't.

Is this what it feels like to be dead? Living a half-life of self-aware frustration?

He looked down and realized his body was no longer his own. It was younger and thinner and dressed in archaic Victorian clothing. Though he couldn't see his own face, he assumed the ghost had inhabited his body somehow—until he realized the silver-and-black clothes he was wearing did not belong to the boy, but to a different member of the family. One he had just seen in a number of portraits on the wall.

"Alistair," said a youthful voice from behind him, confirming his suspicions that somehow, inexplicably, Will had assumed the boyhood form of the Chief Thaumaturge of the Congregation.

Will tried to respond, tried to shout to Mala that he was trapped in the past in a different body and had to get out, but he had no voice, and was not in command of his limbs. Terrified, he found himself turning to watch the new boy—the ghost they had followed into the room, presumably Lord Alistair's younger brother—close the door to the room and approach him.

But now the ghost was corporeal again, a boy of twelve alive in the world. Or at least he was in this weird tableau playing out before him.

What is happening? Am I trapped in a time warp, or in the ghost's memories? What if I can never get out?

Mala was nowhere in sight. The room looked the same as before, except the azantite walls seemed much less blackened than before. Only a spot here and there marred the surface.

"What are you doing?" Lord Alistair's brother asked in a curious voice.

Will-Alistair felt his face twist into a snarl. "Get out of here, Gavyn."

So the brother's name is Gavyn.

"Mother says it's dinner time."

"I told you never to bother me in here. It's too dangerous."

"Why?" the boy said eagerly. "Have you summoned Spirit Fire at last?"

"Get out!" Will-Alistair yelled, and Will somehow knew deep inside that Alistair was devastated because he had come of age and not yet produced a spark of Spirit Fire.

How am I feeling Alistair's thoughts? Or is it just Gavyn projecting what he believes his brother was feeling at the time?

Will-Alistair stalked across the room, causing Gavyn to scurry out. Using his mind, Will-Alistair slammed the door behind him, then turned, held his hands in front of his face, and tried to summon a flicker of Spirit Fire. A long time later, when the magic had still refused to appear, he hung his head and shuffled towards the door, drained of energy and resigned to another day of failure.

The room blurred and reformed into a similar scene, over and over, always in the same room: young Alistair trying and failing to produce a spark of Spirit Fire, roaring in anger, clenching his fists in desperation. Will felt waves of anguish course through him, bone-deep and all-consuming.

He lost count of how many times the scene played out. It was hard to explain, but it seemed as if months had passed in moments. Then he felt a different presence in the room, and his body stiffened. Will-Alistair turned as an older man with a stern bearing strode towards him, the same man in the family portraits.

"Father," Will-Alistair said, his eyes lowering. "I didn't realize you were coming today."

"There's been another uprising in the Second. The Conclave has called an emergency meeting, and I must leave for New Victoria."

"Can I go with you?" he said eagerly. "To New Victoria?"

His father crossed his arms. "Have you brought spirit forth yet?"

Will-Alistair hung his head. "No," he whispered.

"You're of age now, son. You know the family laws. I won't introduce you until you're able to command your heritage."

Will-Alistair's shoulders slumped even further.

"Look up, son," his father said sternly. "A spirit mage does not despair. He *cannot*. When you wield the black fire or travel the dimensions, the strength of your will is all that separates you from annihilation. That will must be encased in azantite. Never faltering, never doubting, never surrendering. There is no margin for error."

"Yes, father."

"Look at me."

Will-Alistair raised his head.

"Keep trying. Remember who you are. Bring it forth with the power of your heritage. It is your birthright. *Command* it to appear."

Standing tall before his father, Will-Alistair obeyed, clenching his fists at his sides and straining with every ounce of mental energy he possessed, reaching deep inside for the magic. It flooded his pores, infused his very being, and yet, while the magic came easily, the realm of spirit was deeper still, a door he had yet to unlock.

Not a spark appeared. As his father turned to leave, his disappointment a tangible thing, Will-Alistair had never felt such despair.

"Gavyn!" his father said in surprise.

Will-Alistair turned to find his younger brother watching by the door. *How dare he?*

"Never enter this room without permission," their father barked. "What if Alistair had lost control? You can't protect yourself yet."

"I'm sorry, Father."

The older man's face softened, which enraged Will-Alistair. Gavyn was a magical prodigy. Summoning Spirit Fire was still a few years beyond him, but he had mastered spells in many other disciplines, and their father treated him far more gently than he had ever treated Alistair. Though Will-Alistair wanted to love Gavyn, yearned to have a brother and a confidant, he couldn't get past his sibling's superior natural ability and their father's favoritism. It stung too deeply.

"Did you need me, Gavyn?" their father asked.

"I . . . wanted to show you something."

"In here? Now? What is it, boy?"

Gavyn's eyes shone with excitement. He held up both hands, furrowed his brow, and, after a moment, a spark of Spirit Fire danced between his palms. Gavyn's eyes watched the energy spark and flare, entranced, and then extinguished it. As Alistair gaped, Gavyn looked shyly at their father.

With a cry of joy, the patriarch rushed to embrace his youngest son. "But how . . . you haven't even completed your junior studies!"

Gavyn's eyes slipped guiltily towards Alistair. "I've been watching and listening."

"You must *never* summon this again without my presence," their father said in a sharp voice, though he failed to contain the notes of pride and excitement underlying his rebuke. "It's far too dangerous. I will teach you how to control it, beginning today."

"Yes, Father."

"Come!" he said, lifting the boy in his arms. "We must tell your mother of this extraordinary feat!"

As they left the room without a backwards glance, Will-Alistair felt a chasm of shame and sadness open up inside him. Yet it was a different feeling that caused him to feel dizzy on his feet, threatening to overwhelm him: the feeling that he had never hated anyone or anything so much in his life.

The room blurred again. Now Will-Alistair was alone in the azantite training room, late at night when the castle was asleep, infused with a rage that empowered him to reach deeper than ever before. At last he was successful: he shoved his way into the realm of spirit, and the magic welled inside him and burst free. For a moment, Will felt what it was like to be a mage. He experienced the sweet rush of power drawn from the essence of his being and pouring into his nerve endings, more intoxicating than any drug. He roared in triumph as Spirit Fire arced out of his fingertips and struck the walls with a fury, burning ugly black stains into the walls. The magic whipped wildly about the room, and he almost lost control. Panting, he managed to extinguish the magic before it consumed him. He almost wept in relief.

Another time warp. On a rainy Sunday afternoon, Will-Alistair entered the azantite room and closed the door behind him. Again Will knew young Alistair's thoughts as his own: that no matter what happened next, no matter how much he mastered his craft, his younger brother would always surpass him in his father's eyes.

"Alistair," Gavyn said, when he noticed his brother's presence, "watch!"

Twin arcs of Spirit Fire sparked from Gavyn's fingertips, entwining in a figure-eight pattern that wound slowly about the room like two snakes at play. The fire began to dip into and out of another dimension, blinking as it moved, providing a spectacular light show before dancing back to Gavyn's fingertips and extinguishing. It was an incredible display of control of the forces of spirit that Alistair could not touch, and which should have been years—maybe decades—beyond the young lad. Though Alistair's power had also grown, he was so embarrassed by his younger brother's prowess that he had not told anyone, not even his father, of his own success.

No one could know that he had summoned Spirit Fire before he had more command of the magic.

"Father says I'm to put on a display at the next Conclave!" Gavyn exclaimed.

Will-Alistair flinched as if struck by a physical blow. "He's taking you to the Conclave?"

"In a fortnight."

In the Realm's prominent mage families, tradition held that the eldest son stood at the right hand of the Father, with all the privileges that entailed. While Gavyn might be too young to fully grasp the ramifications of their father's decision, Alistair knew that if their father planned to introduce Gavyn to the Conclave before Alistair, his inheritance and titles would be stripped from him.

Gavyn would take his place.

"Do you think you'll go with us?" his brother said. "I won't be so nervous if you're there."

Spirit Fire crackled unbidden at Alistair's fingertips. Rage had become a trigger for his magic, and he had not yet learned to control it.

"Alistair!" Gavyn clapped his hands in excitement. "You've done it! Spirit Fire! And you haven't even told Father!"

Will-Alistair knew he could never match Gavyn's power, and their father's decision had been made. His tongue felt too thick for his mouth when he spoke. "Does he know you're in here? Practicing?"

"Oh yes," Gavyn said. "I told him I had to perfect my demonstration. Alistair, try the figure eight! It's easy once you grasp the concept. I'll walk you through it."

"In due time. I've a trick of my own to show you."

"How exciting! Let me see it!"

"Close your eyes and face the wall. I want it to be a surprise."

Happy to oblige, Gavyn clapped his hands in glee and turned his back to his older brother. Jealousy burned in Will-Alistair's veins like the fever of an infectious disease. As he raised his hands, Spirit Fire playing at his fingers, a flicker of long-buried love for his sibling caused him to hesitate.

Can I truly do this? He thought, right before the words of their father came to him, like a slap across the face.

But how . . . you haven't even completed your junior studies!

Will-Alistair raised his hands higher.

Come! We must tell your mother of this extraordinary feat!

The Spirit Fire sparked brighter in Will-Alistair's hands, a deadly dance of energy inches from Gavyn's back.

I will teach you how to control it, beginning today.

The final thin strand of humanity separating Will-Alistair from an unspeakable act unraveled as another phrase replayed over and over in his mind.

Father says I'm to put on a display at the next Conclave!

The next Conclave

The next Conclave

The next Conclave

The next Conclave

Will-Alistair's rage and humiliation at the loss of his heritance consumed him. He released the Spirit Fire, driving it into his brother's back. With no warning of the attack, Gavyn had no chance to erect a defense, and was slain by the magic.

Only a pile of ashes remained as Will-Alistair extinguished the black fire. Both thrilled and horrified by what he had done, he stumbled out of the room and fled down the hall, knowing his father would recognize the distinctive char of spirit on the remains of his brother. Believing that his eldest had not yet mastered the realm of spirit, his father would draw the only conclusion available: that Gavyn had lost control of his magic in the training room, and was destroyed by his own hand.

-6-

On a windy plateau in the heart of the Dragon's Teeth, overlooking a majestic vista of summits and valleys and frothy mountain streams, Caleb stood facing a line of one hundred warriors assembled at the edge of the cliff. These were the best fighters in the small army: ninety representatives from the Roma clans, nine Devla worshippers, and one veteran Marine from Earth. Though none of the Devlan were as experienced in battle as the Roma or Lance, selecting a handful of the Prophet's followers, Caleb knew, was an important gesture.

The rest of the camp had assembled behind Caleb, confused by the sunrise call to assemble, before the tents were collapsed or breakfast was served. Only Caleb and his inner circle knew what was about to happen. To preserve the shock value of the experience, even the elders had been kept in the dark.

The plummeting temperatures and the hardships of the journey had led to diminishing morale. Lance had come up with an idea to lift the camp's spirits. A former police officer and veteran of the Iraq War, Lance was the one hundredth warrior in line that morning. Will's best friend stood with his back straight and his chin high near the middle of the group, his gaze fixed on Caleb, betraying nothing.

The wind whipped Caleb's black cloak and ruffled his dark hair. Both Tamás and the Prophet had made symbolic suggestions about his attire, all of which Caleb had rejected. He stood before his troops as he always did: wearing his leather boots, vambraces, and black cloak with silver stitching. In his right hand, he carried his diamond-headed mace.

Not for one second had Caleb wavered in his purpose or forgotten why he had risked everything to trek across the breadth of New Albion. Every moment of every day the same memory throbbed within him: Marguerite and Luca lying dead on the ground beneath a Congregation mage who stood above their charred bodies with an amused, uncaring smirk.

That electromancer had received an order to retrieve the Coffer of Devla and kill anyone who stood in his way, and that order could only have been given by Lord Alistair, Chief Thaumaturge of the Congregation—the man Caleb had vowed to kill or die trying.

Whether anyone else joined his cause was not Caleb's concern. He had not asked for this army or this camp of followers. But since they were here, and had pledged their support, he would do his best to honor their decision.

The day was cold but beautiful. The morning sun glinted like gold off the mountain peaks, a rare clear day during the march. The Prophet, of course, viewed the emergence of the sun as a sign of approval from the heavens.

It was time. Caleb raised a hand in the air, quieting the murmurs from the crowd gathered behind him. When he spoke, Branyn amplified his voice so that everyone could hear.

"I have gathered you this morning to make an announcement," Caleb said, his gaze roaming the hundred men and women assembled before him. He had never made a speech in his life. "We all know that Zariduke has returned to Urfe. As you all know, legend claims the sword was made long ago for the Captain of the Paladins, a group of warriors loyal to the High Priests of Devla. Some believe the High Priests bestowed special powers upon their honor guards. While high priests and paladins have not walked among us for many centuries, what you may not know is that another totem from the past has returned to Urfe. The shield that Will Blackwood, my brother, recovered from the tomb of the sorcerer king was none other than the shield of Fieran Blackwood himself, Captain of the Paladins under High Priestess Nirela."

A murmur of excitement rippled through the crowd.

Caleb continued, "I'm told the paladins were the most powerful common-born soldiers in the history of our people. They were incorruptible, the bravest of the brave, and always at the forefront of battle. It's said that, when imbued with blessings from a High Priest of Devla, they even took up arms against mages. Are these stories from the past myths and legends, or are they true accounts? I have no idea. As most of you know, I'm not a believer in myths and legends, or gods and goddesses. Though I carry Roma blood, I'm not even from your world. But the Prophet, a man we all respect, tells me none of that matters. That Devla exists and acts among us whether I believe in him or not. That may or may not be true. No one can say for sure. That said, I know my position might leave you feeling uneasy about taking up arms behind someone who does not share your faith. You might be wondering what I *do* believe in—so let me tell you."

When Caleb paused to gather his voice, not a whisper could be heard from the crowd. Even the wind had died, as if nature itself had joined in the preternatural hush that had fallen over the plateau. He drew up tall and said, "What I believe is that all human beings, no matter their race or creed or ethnicity, should be able to worship, play, laugh, and love in the manner they see fit." Thinking about his next statement caused Caleb to choke up. He paused to gather himself. "I believe in the right of a child, a beautiful little boy who lost his parents and then his life to a senseless policy of violence, to live like other children and grow up to be a man." A tear fell from his eye and slid onto his cheek. With everyone watching, he stood very still and wiped the tear away. His face twisted into a snarl to mask his pain, and his voice rose to a shout. "Do you want to know what I believe in? I believe that men and women have the right to control their own destinies. I believe in brave souls who band together to overthrow tyrants and fight for their freedom." He thrust his mace skyward and roared the last line of his speech. "I believe in the power of all of us gathered here to march across this land, find a way to overthrow the cruel and unfeeling regime of an evil man, and secure a future for our families!"

The crowd erupted into cheers so loud they echoed off the mountain walls. United in a common purpose, driven by desperation, Caleb knew the men and women gathered on the plateau were giving voice to their hopes and fears and dreams, drawing strength from the words of their leader.

Though Caleb felt the heavy burden that all who lead others into war must feel, he also knew these people had lost all hope, were being hunted like dogs by the Congregation, and had made their choice to stand and fight for their dignity, if nothing else.

After the crowd calmed, Caleb turned to nod at the Prophet. The wild-haired leader of the Devla bent over, picked up a canvas bag lying at his feet, and carried it to Caleb.

"It is for these reasons," Caleb said, his voice still ringing through the camp as he reached into the bag to withdraw a buckler shield with a polished silver face, "that I have decided to bring the paladins back to Urfe."

As the crowd gasped at his words, Caleb held the shield high in the air, turning slowly so everyone could see the red rune on its face that resembled a squiggly line wrapped around a sword piercing a seven-pointed star. The night before, the Prophet had scrubbed the shield for hours and gathered enough flame berries to paint the symbolic rune that matched the one on Will's shield. After giving everyone a chance to see the marking, Caleb turned back to the line of one hundred men and women assembled before him. "This shield bears the personal insignia of Fieran Blackwood, as does the shield my brother recovered, and as will the shield that each one of you shall be given. After the Prophet anoints you this morning," he said, sweeping his gaze across the line of proud, shocked faces, "you will no longer go into battle as homeless survivors of Freetown, struggling to survive in the face of persecution, but as the heirs to a tradition that stretches back for centuries, and which will strike fear into the heart of all who stand against you. The next time we engage an enemy, you will fight by my side and lead us into battle as paladins of Devla!"

Caleb thrust the shield in the air again. This time, the roar of approval from the crowd was so loud it vibrated through his nerve endings.

They covered more ground through the mountains than usual that day. As Lance had predicted, the formation of the paladins had given everyone, not just those chosen for the elite group, a morale boost. The newly formed unit marched proudly at the head of the army, and during breaks in the march, Lance began teaching them what he knew about military tactics and formations.

The Prophet had asked his followers to collect any flame berries they saw along the way. Later that night, after camp was set, he instructed a contingent of Devla to dye the ninety-nine other shields which Tamás had collected with the insignia of Fieran Blackwood. Known for their staining qualities, the crimson flame berries would not last forever, but they should remain on the shields for the duration of the march.

The next morning, newly dyed shields in hand, the paladins resembled a uniform fighting unit. Spirits were high all around. Despite grumbles from a handful of elders that only a true cleric of Devla should anoint a paladin, most thought the return of Fieran Blackwood's shield was another sign validating Caleb's leadership.

By midday, the weather turned colder, and a freezing sleet began to fall.

The children and the elderly struggled to keep their feet on the slick mountain trail. An hour later, Caleb was forced to halt the march. The falling temperatures and icy conditions had exposed the camp's lack of proper gear. There was a shortage of blankets and tents, and almost everyone had a pair of gloves starting to unravel, or boots worn through on the soles, or an outer garment that offered little protection from the sleet, cold, and wind. Shielded from the elements by his magical cloak, Caleb tried to give it to someone in need, but everyone he asked refused.

He understood. Caleb had plucked the black cloak with silver stitching out of the Coffer itself. Like the artifact, it was a symbol of Devla's protection. No one dared provoke the faceless deity of the Roma people whose followers believed was responsible for all of creation.

Yasmina, using her heightened senses and knowledge of the terrain, led everyone down an overgrown footpath to a glade wrapped in a bowl-shaped depression among the peaks. It was good shelter from the weather, and the level ground was an ideal place to pitch camp.

Things went from bad to worse when Caleb heard eager shouting among the children while he was arranging his bedroll inside his tent. He stepped out to investigate the commotion and felt a wet blob land on his cheek. As he wiped his face and looked up, more snowflakes landed on his face.

As Yasmina had predicted, and everyone had feared, winter had come early to the Dragon's Teeth.

After dinner was served, and most of the camp was asleep, Caleb paced inside the command tent while Yasmina and the Brewer sat cross-legged in the corners. Lance had already retired, exhausted by the march and his training sessions with the paladins. Allira and the Prophet were tending to those in need, and Tamás was consulting with the mages on how to help people stay warm.

"Hey kid, good job with that speech of yours," the Brewer said. "I haven't had time to tell you, but now you *really* know what it's like to be a rock star."

Caleb flicked his eyes at his older friend, a former musician from New Jersey who had been magically transported to Urfe after playing a song on an ancient Sumerian lyre. "Not exactly what I had in mind."

"I know, I know. You were thinking all-night shows, screaming teenagers, and unlimited bar tabs."

Yasmina cast a warning glance at the Brewer which Caleb caught. Realizing his snafu, the Brewer lowered his eyes. He was huddled inside a sheepskin coat and rubbing his hands to stay warm. "Sorry, kid. You've been so clean I almost forgot you used to hit the bottle."

Caleb waved a hand in dismissal, barely registering the comment, which he could tell caused Yasmina even more distress than the Brewer's slip of the tongue. The old Caleb would have cracked a joke in response, or told some wild story about a night at the House of Spirits.

Yasmina stood and walked to the front of the tent. She lifted the flap and peered outside. "There's a foot of snow out there, and it's not even midnight."

Due to the lack of dry wood for a fire, the inside of the tent was freezing. People were suffering throughout the camp, but Yasmina had refused to take one of the blankets offered to the children, women, and the elderly.

"We can't keep going, can we?" Caleb asked.

The Brewer shook his head. "Not a chance until this snow melts. Even if we manage to keep people warm, the trails will be treacherous."

"Yaz?" Caleb said. "Any ideas?"

When she turned to regard him, her hazel eyes met his for the first time in a long while. Caleb was surprised by the strength reflected in her gaze. He knew she was a wilder now, a steward of the Realm, but he had not taken the time to sit down with her and talk through what it all meant. But one thing was clear: she was not the same carefree young woman he had known and loved for many years.

I guess that makes two of us who have changed.

"The animals have sought shelter," she said. "They're not expecting the weather to improve anytime soon."

Caleb cursed and slammed a fist into his palm.

"Bono never had to deal with freezing temperatures and trails clogged with snow," the Brewer muttered.

"Or the lives of thousands of people in his care," Caleb said.

"Yeah. That too."

"We can't keep going," Yasmina said. "We won't make it through. But once the sun comes out and melts the top layer, it won't be too late to turn back.

It might be dangerous, but the paths we've taken so far are navigable even in wintry conditions. The high mountain passes are another story."

Caleb continued pacing the tent. "I don't see another option," he said, in a voice bitter with disappointment.

The Brewer rose with a yawn. After a weary goodbye, he bundled up and left the tent. Yasmina decided to follow suit. She wrapped her pewter-colored cloak tight around her throat, approached Caleb, took him gently by the hand, and said, "They follow your lead. Take care with them."

Before she could disengage, Caleb gripped her hand and held it tight. Her eyes lifted to meet his, and for a moment, he felt as if he were back in New Orleans, and they were about to go out on the town after his shift, and none of the horror of the last year had ever happened. She took a step closer, lifted her other hand to his cheek, and caressed his face. He wanted so much to hold her in his arms and let her take the pain away. But then a vision of Marguerite floated in his mind's eye, laughing in the river after they had exchanged vows, teasing him as they made love, snuggled together by the campfire. Yasmina's eyes became Luca's trusting gaze, her hand became his small and brown one, and a sob of rage and despair bubbled out of his throat. He pushed Yasmina away. The hurt and confusion on her face made him feel even worse. When she left the tent, he sank to his knees and buried his head in his hands, hating himself almost as much as the man he had sworn to kill.

The next morning, as Caleb lay on his back on his cot and thought about how to break the news to his followers that they had to turn back, Lance called out softly from the other side of the tent flap.

"Hey buddy, you awake?"

"No."

"There's something you need to see."

Caleb didn't like the note of warning in his friend's voice. "What is it?"

"Better just come."

After donning his wool pants and shirt, stepping into his boots, and shrugging on his cloak, Caleb moved the tent flap aside and stepped into the crisp dawn air. The snow had stopped falling, but his boots sunk knee-high into the fresh flakes, and it was freezing outside.

Caleb remembered Lance as an easygoing former Marine with a crew cut, a square-jawed grin, and a muscular physique that had drawn attention from plenty of women. During the fight with Zedock, Lance had lost a kidney and collapsed a lung, ruining his career as a police officer and driving him into depression. Swollen with fat and self-pity when he arrived on Urfe, his decision to join the Revolution and the march through the mountains had done wonders for his self-esteem. The weight had fallen off him, and the confident glint in his eyes had returned.

Dressed in a long-sleeved leather jerkin and a brown woolen cape, Lance held out a *Semper-Fi* tattooed forearm and pointed to his right, towards the hidden footpath the army had taken between two mountain peaks to arrive in the bowl-shaped glade. Caleb followed his finger and felt the blood drain from his face.

The little footpath no longer existed. In its place was a mountain of snow that must have reached two hundred feet in height, obliterating the gap between the sheer peaks on either side.

"Jesus Christ."

Lance grimaced. "There must have been an avalanche during the night."

"Can we tunnel through it?"

"It'll take days, maybe weeks, to clear out something like that. Assuming no more snow falls."

As the camp came alive around them, gasps arose as people stepped outside and saw the blocked pass. Caleb turned in a slow circle, taking in the jagged peaks that surrounded the little depression in which they had camped. "So we're trapped here?"

"With a week's worth of supplies at best," Lance said. "We can melt snow to drink, but if we can't hunt or fish soon, people are going to starve."

By afternoon, despair gripped the camp as tightly as a mouse caught in the talons of an eagle. Tamás coordinated an effort to try to dig through the avalanche, but as Lance had predicted, every time they made progress, the tunnel soon collapsed. It became too risky and they had to give it up.

The mages tried their hand as well, but none of them was a pyromancer, and they couldn't find a good solution. As a last resort, they could fly everyone over the snow blockade one by one, but the draining effort would take days or more, separate the army from the supplies, and wouldn't solve the food shortage. Still, that seemed like the best solution—right until the snow began to fall again.

"Even if we manage to move half these people in a few days," Lance said to Caleb, "there's no good place to set camp in this weather, and we'll still have no food."

Yasmina and Tamás had no answers. Allira was unfamiliar with snowy climes and had no silent advice to offer. Even if they managed to escape the glade, Caleb realized the high mountain passes would be clogged with snow.

The elders who had questioned his decision to anoint the paladins began to grumble and cast dark looks Caleb's way. He didn't blame them. He had led their people into this nightmare and had no solution. He was furious with himself, and horrified by the lack of options. *We'll save the children, and as many others as we can. The mages can fly the most vulnerable people to lower ground.*

Through it all, the Prophet remained maddeningly calm. His solution was to sit cross-legged in his tent and pray, though even his followers had begun to mutter and glance uneasily at their prison of snow.

As the sun began to sink behind the mountains, the temperature plummeted even further. The snow was unrelenting. The paladins coordinated an effort to redistribute the food and blankets to those most in need, but Caleb knew that some of the elderly shivering on the cold floor of the tents might not see the morning.

Distraught, he wandered through the camp with Yasmina, trying to provide comfort where he could. After fixing the tent of a single mother with three children that had collapsed under the weight of snow, Yasmina gripped his arm and pointed to the north, towards the highest peak in view.

"What is it?" he said, noting her look of concentration.

"I don't know yet. But something large is flying towards us."

Fearing a dragon or some other predator, he tensed and called for Tamás. She hushed him and said, "Wait. I don't think . . . the way the wings are outstretched . . . could it be?"

Impatient and on edge, he waited as she tracked whatever she was watching with the superhuman sight imbued by her owl staff. And then he saw it also:

a crimson speck in the distance that drew steadily closer, flying over the peak she had pointed out.

"It's a simorgh," she said, "with a rider. I believe it might be a Yith."

Soon Caleb saw a sinuous feathered bird about half the size of a dragon, with gorgeous crimson wings and a long tail that fluttered in the wind. As people began to point to the sky in awe, the simorgh drew nearer, circling above the camp as the men and women below cleared a space for it to land.

The simorgh swooped in to a graceful landing on four taloned limbs. A Yith woman dressed in the traditional dress of her people, baggy canvas trousers and a white fur jacket with feathered shoulders, dismounted and removed a plumed headdress. Caleb's companions gathered around as Tamás approached the woman.

"Well met, rider of the Simorgh," he said, exchanging a ritual handclasp. "As you can see, we've been caught by the early snows."

The Yith were descendants of the Romani people who had long ago taken to the Făgras and the Dragon's Teeth, intermingled with the native people, and tamed the gargantuan wild avians that dwelled in the peaks and crags of the mountain ranges.

The woman absorbed the condition of the camp. "One of the mages who left your army arrived at a Yith outpost this morning. We know what happened at Freetown, and of your mission, and of your journey through the mountains." She swept a hand towards the mountain of snow blocking their way. "More snow will fall. The mountains will be impassable by foot for many moons."

"Tell us something we don't know, lady," Lance muttered to Caleb.

More gasps rose throughout the camp, and people began to point at the sky again. Caleb looked up. This time he saw a horde of black specks approaching in the failing light, inky pinpricks of movement that slowly materialized into birds with bodies as big as houses and wingspans that dwarfed even the largest of dragons.

"Rukhs," Yasmina breathed. "Dozens of them."

Flying close on their heels was a phalanx of amber simorghs in tight rows that extended far across the sky. The sight of them induced ripples of awe from the crowd.

"Our peoples have long been aligned," the woman said. "The Yith know of the Congregation's designs on the Ninth, and that our way of life is threatened. If you will allow us, we'll ferry you across the mountains, and offer sanctuary to your children and infirm. Fearing you were unprepared for the early winter, we've also brought provisions and blankets. We advise leaving at first light."

Everyone who had heard her speak whooped with joy. Barely able to believe the turn of events, Caleb let out a deep breath and ran his hands through his hair, relieved beyond measure. As he strode forward to accept the proposal and thank the Yith Rider, he glanced back and saw, in the midst of the laughs and hugs and tears of joy throughout the camp, the Prophet standing alone by his tent, eying the approaching legion of rukhs and simorghs with a small, knowing smile.

-7-

As Val flew inside the Sanctum, the midnight blue pyramid in the center of the Wizard District which served as the headquarters of the Congregation, he took a moment to absorb the surreal nature of his surroundings: both the inside of the Sanctum itself, and the prestigious guests attending the yearly Mage Day celebration.

The unofficial holiday commemorated the anniversary of the Battle of Londyn, when a small faction of wizards led by Myrddin the Defender defeated a force of over sixty thousand soldiers and druid warrior-priests, ending the Pagan Wars and the Age of Sorrows and establishing the Congregation as the true power in the Realm. Though celebrated by everyone as a day of victory over oppression and prejudice, the mage-born in particular celebrated the holiday with vigor, often throwing all-day parties and producing elaborate mageworks that transformed the night sky into celestial lightshows.

Every year, the Congregation hosted a Mage Day party and invited high-ranking wizards from an array of countries and kingdoms, even those with shaky relations to the Realm. This year, Val noticed the guest list mostly included high-ranking members of the Queen's court in Albion, along with a smattering of elder mages from countries in close alliance with the Congregation. Noticeably absent were the Battle Mages of the Mayan Kingdom.

Lord Alistair, it seemed, was making a statement.

Beneath the soaring black marble ceiling that rippled and shone with localized mageworks for the party, Val clutched his father's staff and made his way around the cavernous lounge filled with wizards dressed in the latest fashions, displaying their chosen disciplines on weapons and jewelry. The first-time visitors to the Sanctum gawked at the artwork on display: exotic taxidermy that felt real to the touch; bronze urns with elaborate bouquets arranged by a floramancer; slivers of disembodied waterfalls that plunged through the floor; enchanted multimedia art installations that probed the limits of the imagination.

For a moment, the splendor of the scene distracted Val from the realization which had consumed his every waking thought over the last few days.

A father. I'm going to be a father.

The out of town guests had arrived through portals on the lower levels. Most would return home that night. The entire Conclave was in attendance, along with important mages from across the Protectorates. Val felt lucky to be invited. Adaira was also there, and while they caught each other's eye from time to time, they had decided to use the opportunity to mingle. Val was no slouch at that sort of thing, and was accustomed to rubbing shoulders with important people from his time at the law firm. Still, the power and influence of Manhattan's finest paled in comparison to a gathering of elder mages and heads of state.

Dressed in a tailored silver-and-black suit, Alistair cut a handsome figure as the consummate charming host. When he saw that Val had arrived, the Chief Thaumaturge introduced him to a circle of Londyn mages. Val spied Braden watching him from nearby, the cuerpomancer's jaw tightening with jealousy.

As Lord Alistair put his guests at ease and shored up alliances, Val took mental notes of the cultural differences. He also watched in admiration as Adaira worked the room, flitting from group to group, drawing even the most taciturn of mages into conversation. One day she would be her father's best political asset. Perhaps, Val mused, that day had already arrived.

There was a woman standing near Lord Alistair whose beauty rivaled Adaira's. Not in Val's eyes, of course, but he noticed the rest of the men could not stop looking at the curvy young woman with pillowy lips and curls of blond hair that spiraled to her waist. Val knew her as Melina, a Roma sorceress who had left her homeland to seek her fortune in New Victoria. Like Val, she had taken the oaths and pledged her loyalty to the Realm, and gained the favor of Lord Alistair.

Melina wore a lavender gown that matched her eyes, and even more jewelry than Mala, but Val did not see a wizard stone that might indicate her discipline. When she extended her hand to let him kiss it, the diamonds on her fingers sparkled, and her perfume, the scent of cherry blossoms in the spring, swarmed his senses. He felt slightly dizzy, unmoored by her presence.

"Enchanted," she said, with a smile that could break apart clouds.

"Likewise," he replied weakly. He let her hand go and forced himself to look away. She turned to someone else, and Val felt the need for a stiff drink. He might be physically attracted to a temptress like Melina—who wouldn't be?—but the true path to Val's heart had always been through his head. Adaira was the only woman for him, there was no doubt in his mind about that.

After leaving Lord Alistair's side, Val made sure to greet Kalyn Tern, Professor Azara, Jalen Rainsword, and the other members of the Conclave. Kjeld Anarsson was the only non-mage in attendance. Val avoided the Head Don of Majitsu and instead wandered over to a group of mages in steel-gray cloaks with black runes on their sleeves, quaffing granth around an emerald table. The distinctive cloaks belonged to members of the Queen's Wizard Guard, and Val recognized a face he had not seen since leaving Londyn.

"Cyrus!" Val called out, offering his friend a warm forearm clasp.

The stern-faced mage allowed his lips to crease with a smile. "Well met, Valjean! It appears your star continues to rise."

"Yours as well," Val said, eying a new set of gold runes on the breast of Cyrus's cloak.

"During your mission to the alternate Urfe, I supported you when others lost faith. Upon your return, our stars rose together. I've been promoted to Captain of the Wizard Guard," he said proudly.

Val gripped his shoulder. "A well-deserved honor. Congratulations. By the way, is the Queen in attendance? I'd like to pay my respects."

"She couldn't come." After a troubled glance about the room, Cyrus topped off his granth and said, in a low voice, "Walk with me."

Keeping a calm demeanor, Val refilled his own glass and followed Cyrus to one of the alcoves recessed into the amber walls of the lounge, where Cyrus pretended to admire a set of magical drums from Kalingaland. Val knew that not everyone approved of Lord Alistair's assumption of war powers, and wondered if this was the reason the Queen had declined the invitation. He asked Cyrus as much.

"No," Cyrus said. "One of her cousins died last week, and she had to attend the funeral."

"I'm sorry to hear that. What about you?" Val asked.

"Eh?"

"Do you approve?"

Cyrus leveled his gaze at Val. "It is not my place to approve or disapprove of the Queen's decisions, or Lord Alistair's, or anyone else not under my command. I follow orders as they are given."

"I didn't mean to put you in an awkward position."

"It's fine." Cyrus stepped out of view and waved a hand towards the entrance to the alcove. Val felt a shimmer of power. "There," Cyrus said. "We're shielded now, in case anyone is listening. Don't be fooled by the revelry. There is plenty of chicanery at play tonight, on both sides."

"I understand," Val said, and indeed he did. Back home, even the closest political allies spied on each other when given half a chance.

"The Queen has mixed feelings concerning Alistair's ambitions. I do not believe she approves of him personally, or of his petulant persecution of oath avoiders. And yet, the continents across the Great Ocean are a different creature from the Old World. There is more opportunity for expansion of the Realm. The Queen knows this, and is a politically expedient woman. I believe she's willing to let Alistair . . . explore options . . . in the New World. But that is not why I called you over."

Val sensed there was more to the story, and that Cyrus had his own opinion despite his demurral to the Queen.

"I've heard murmurs of disapproval about your sudden rise in the hierarchy of the Congregation," Cyrus continued. "Murmurs from powerful people."

"Is that so?" Val said, crossing his arms. He had an idea as to the source. "Braden?"

Cyrus gave a curt nod. "He has many allies in the Congregation."

"So do I," Val said grimly. "Chief among them Lord Alistair."

"That is true, and why Braden will not confront you directly. But you should watch yourself, Valjean. Even in the court of Londyn we know of his demotion in standing, and that Lord Alistair favors you as his successor. That is a wound to Braden's pride he will not suffer lightly."

Val's eyes flicked towards the room full of mages, wondering who else might be aligned with the ambitious cuerpomancer. Braden hailed from the Third Protectorate, which was closely aligned with the First—home to Kalyn Tern, an extremely talented aeromancer from a prominent wizard family. Kalyn's family was closely allied with that of Braden's, and their friendship was no secret.

"Do you know of a specific plan?" Val asked.

"I do not. But you should avoid a private confrontation with Braden."

"I can take care of myself."

"You're a powerful mage, but a young one, and not yet a match for an elder mage of any discipline."

Val pursed his lips; he knew Cyrus was right, despite his mastery of Spirit Fire. "Who told you these things?"

Cyrus gave a cynical smile. "You know better than to ask."

After a moment of contemplation, Val gripped him by the arm. "Thank you for telling me. Are you returning to Londyn tonight? If not, perhaps we could meet for breakfast?"

"I'm here for some time. A regiment of the Wizard Guard has been assigned to New Victoria until the uprising is quelled."

"Really?" Val said, amused. "I hardly think we'll need your help."

Cyrus chuckled as well. "I would hope not. It's a gesture of political support for the Congregation, nothing more. But we'll have plenty of opportunity to talk in the coming weeks. In fact, I've never been to New Victoria. I'm looking forward to seeing the city."

"I've got a pub or two to recommend, if the renowned Wizard Guard are allowed to have any fun."

"Only on the third Tuesday of the month," Cyrus said with a straight face. As Val exchanged a parting arm clasp, the gray-cloaked mage gave a sharp intake of breath. "That ring—where did you get it? I don't remember seeing it."

Val glanced down at the bluish white ring in the shape of an ouroboros—a serpent swallowing its own tail—that he had found hidden in Myrddin's Tomb in the alternate dimension of Urfe. He had kept it in his pocket when he returned to meet the Queen. "A traveling merchant," he said, deciding to conceal the truth until he knew more about it. "Why? Do you recognize it?"

Cyrus peered closer. "Ah, perhaps not. At first I thought the ouroboros seal belonged to Myrddin of Demetae, but the face of the serpent is not quite right, and that would be . . . most astonishing."

"Why?"

"No artifacts from Myrddin of Demetae remain unclaimed on Urfe. They are among the most powerful ever made, and the few that remain are closely guarded." Cyrus smirked. "I'm sorry to say, my friend, that you've been sold a forgery. I hope you didn't hand over too much coin."

After lifting the shielding spell, Cyrus rejoined the Wizard Guard, leaving Val twisting the strange ring around his finger as he wandered back into the room. He mingled for a while more, until even he grew weary of small talk and political maneuvering.

Adaira had a commitment in the morning and had already left. Deciding he had stayed long enough, Val decided to tell Lord Alistair he was leaving. He found the Chief Thaumaturge standing by a zelomancy board, talking to an older couple with sharp Scandinavian features. They were both very pale and wore cloaks lined with thick ermine fur. Lord Alistair asked if he could have a word with Val before he left, then dismissed the couple after a promise to consider whatever proposal they had been discussing.

Half of the zelomancy set was made of diamond, the other half obsidian. Similar to chess, zelomancy had a nine-by-nine board instead of eight-by-eight, and utilized different rules of movement. A traditional board had nine knights or foot soldiers—pawns—on the second row. On the back row, pairs of giants, dragons, and kethropi represented the forces of land, air, and sea. In place of the traditional king and queen in the center of the row, a pair of majitsu protected a wizard or wizardess who was the key to victory.

As Val stood across the table, Lord Alistair reached down to grasp the obsidian wizard on his side, tilting it idly back and forth. The zelomancy board brought back a vivid memory of Leonidus's keep and the dungeon Val had fought through with his brothers. A journey that seemed like yesterday in some ways, and a lifetime ago in others.

"Have you had time to adopt our world's version of chess?" Lord Alistair asked.

Val failed to hide his surprise. "Not yet. You've played chess before?"

"The Congregation has catalogues describing the customs and pastimes of thousands of worlds. I've always thought the greater complexity of moves in zelomancy reflected a fundamental difference in a magical society versus a technological one. The deeper levels of reality of which we are aware. It leads to a richer life experience, in my opinion."

Val couldn't disagree.

"I find it quite remarkable," Lord Alistair continued, "that one such as you, born into a world bereft of magic, has been able to embrace your father's heritage and adopt the customs and mindset of this land so rapidly. Not just adopt, but excel. One would never know you were not born here."

Val tipped his head at the compliment. "I confess it didn't come easily. I couldn't accept the truth for some time."

"It is your adaptability, Valjean, that I find most impressive. That is the hallmark not just of a survivor, but of a leader. And what do you think of our Mage Day celebration? Does it serve to divide us from the common-born or bring us closer together?"

The switch in topics caught Val off guard. After a moment, he said, "Both."

The corners of Alistair's lips twitched. "Elaborate."

"Like the Oaths, the purpose and history of the holiday brings us closer to those common born who embrace the rule of wizards. But it tears us further apart from those who do not."

"And is that a positive thing, or a negative one?"

"It is a necessary one."

Val could tell by the twinkle in Lord Alistair's eye that he was pleased. The Chief Thaumaturge reached down to move one of the kethropi who, like knights in chess, are able to 'swim' through other pieces. "There is something difficult I must ask of you."

"Of course."

"I need you to intervene with your brother, Caleb."

Val tensed, uncertain what he meant.

"I know you're preoccupied with the progress of his army. No, not preoccupied: worried. Distressed. Because you know full well what must eventually happen."

"I do," Val said quietly. "I just don't see why . . . he doesn't know what he's doing."

"He's hurting, and his mind has been poisoned with lies by those around him. He blames us, and perhaps me personally, for what happened to his family. Yes, this tragedy occurred during a confrontation with one of our mages, but it was a confrontation provoked by the gypsies when we sought only discourse, after a long history of refusing to take the Oaths, pay taxes, or live like responsible citizens. War is a terrible thing, and this misguided revolution . . . he's going to get himself killed," Lord Alistair said.

Val looked away, knowing the truth of the last statement.

Lord Alistair laid a hand on his shoulder. "I don't want that to happen," he said gently. "I always prefer diplomacy to war, and if Caleb comes to his senses, we can avoid a great deal of bloodshed. He will never listen to me, or anyone else from the Congregation—save, perhaps, you."

Val looked up.

"I want you to go to him soon," Lord Alistair said. "Bring him here, to New Victoria, and I will send Caleb home as I did Will."

"I would love to," Val said, "but how? Do you want me to journey to the Ninth?"

"We'll open the Pool of Souls. It will be a dangerous proposition—he'll have to bring you through, and you'll be at his mercy—but you'll have a chance to convince him of the error of his ways. If you can bring him to New Victoria, I believe the Prophet will lose the faith of his followers, and this so-called army will disperse."

"And you'll send Caleb home, if I bring him here?" Val said. "Just like Will, with no repercussions?"

Lord Alistair's hand slipped to the zelomancy wizard as he looked Val in the eye. "You have my word of honor."

Late that night, after the revelry had ended and Val returned home to Salomon's Crib, he stood on the rooftop balcony and gazed at the rows of golden orb lights illuminating the streets of New Victoria. Higher up, under the dark of a new moon, he beheld the spires of the Wizard District, candles to the heavens that evoked every ounce of magic and mystery this world of his father possessed.

And now I will raise my own son here, and his innocent eyes will gaze on these glorious spires and marvel at the wonders in the world. What a strange thought, that my firstborn child will know nothing of Earth except for the bedtime stories I tell. Or will I, like my father, carry my child through a portal of time and dimension one day?

As much as Val loved his father, Dane Blackwood had made one mistake Val did not plan to repeat: the decision not to tell his sons about their heritage. Maybe Val's father was afraid his sons couldn't handle the truth, or would spend their lives longing for a place they could never visit. Whatever the reason, Val vowed not to risk a surprise announcement that could shatter the worldview of his own children. No, they would understand, as soon as they were old enough to hear stories, that their father was from a land across the stars, and had chosen to call Urfe home.

Perhaps he judged his own father too harshly. Urfe was a land where magic and monsters were commonplace, where spirit mages and portals bridged the gap between worlds. If Val's father had told him of Urfe before Val saw it for himself, would he really have believed him? Or would Val have questioned his sanity and put a strain on their relationship?

He realized that his father's decision, right or wrong, sprang from love. Already Val felt an ineffable tenderness for his future child pouring forth, and the one thing he knew deep down, a greater truth than he had ever discovered, was that he would do anything, absolutely anything, for his child.

This knowledge made him think of Caleb, and the pain he must be suffering. Val knew why his brother had chosen this path, and, if he was anything like Val, why he would never stand aside.

Which made it all the more imperative that Val sent him home before Caleb got himself killed.

Val lingered on the rooftop for a very long time, simply staring at those spires and absorbing the view with a soul-searching reflection his driven personality did not usually engender. As he stood there, mesmerized, pondering the beauty and pain in the universe, the two worlds he had known, and the family he was about to have, an unfamiliar feeling fluttered in his chest, like an exotic bird glimpsed in the foliage. After more reflection, he realized what it was.

Despite his grave concern for his middle brother, and his sharp pain of longing for his youngest, Val realized in that moment that, against all odds, he had never felt so content.

-8-

Will felt a wrenching sensation, a release somewhere deep inside, as if his soul had been freed from a suction. He shuddered as the ghost retreated from his mind, the spectral vision of Lord Alistair's past disappeared, and the azantite-lined room in the castle returned to normal.

"Will," Mala said. "Will the Builder. Can you hear me?"

She pressed a hand to his forehead. Will realized he was lying on his back on the floor. He sat up in time to see the ghost of Alistair's younger brother, Gavyn, drifting backwards into the wall. A note of satisfaction had softened his forlorn expression, and Will wondered if the troubled spirit would move on to a better place.

Mala helped Will to his feet. "What happened? You collapsed as he flowed into you, and I feared the worst."

"He killed him, Mala. He killed his own brother."

"What? Speak plainly."

After he described how Lord Alistair's jealousy had led him to murder Gavyn in a fit of rage in that very room, she grimaced and said, "So the Chief Thaumaturge's rise to power began with fratricide. A worthy prelude for one such as he. Are you certain the vision can be trusted?"

"It felt as real as anything I've ever experienced."

"His family must have never suspected, which is why no one has heard of his brother."

"I don't follow," Will said.

"A suicide to a house of such renown is a disgrace. They would have tried to erase him from the family tree."

Will felt off-balance from the visceral experience of inhabiting another body. "How can a ghost do that? Take me into the past in someone else's mind?"

"I don't believe a normal one can. But the lost soul of a spirit mage . . . who knows what happens to the residue of magic from someone with power like that, especially in the circumstance of an untimely death. Perhaps the magic itself survived, imprisoning Gavyn in his own memories."

"Hopefully he's found some relief."

"Come," she said sharply, as if bothered by his comment. "Morning approaches. I fear our time is short before someone realizes you've escaped."

After glancing into the rest of the rooms in the hallway and finding nothing of interest, they backtracked to the stone staircase leading to the second floor of the castle. Once they reached the next landing, they noticed a hint of illumination seeping out from a closed doorway near the middle of the corridor.

"What if it's a wizard?" Will whispered.

"More likely it's a servant or a mistress. I doubt Alistair would trust another mage in his own home."

"Not even to guard it?"

"A titan on the ramparts is not guardian enough for you? Between him and the spirit wards around the keep that are most assuredly in place, Alistair has little to fear. Few mages on Urfe could contend with either."

"Then we see what's behind Door Number One?"

"I think we must. If someone is inside, we'll restrain them as quickly as possible, and force them to tell us where the portal lies."

"What do you mean, *force* them?"

He didn't like her wolfish smile in response, but decided they would cross that bridge when they came to it.

The walls of the hallway were adorned with furnishings even more exquisite than on the lower level. Ensorcelled tapestries that enacted battles from centuries past. Three-dimensional wizard paintings by Urfe's version of Renaissance masters. None of the rooms on the left had doors, and they peered carefully into each one, revealing a series of showrooms for objects d'art from around the world. Her eyes gleamed as she beheld crowns inlaid with gemstones; wands and scepters suspended in glass cases; amulets and girdles and crystal balls and scores of other items that exuded a magical, priceless aura. When she started wandering through one of the rooms, checking for traps beneath a silver-framed cabinet showcasing a set of lifelike porcelain miniatures, he reminded her of the possibility of magical traps and the peril of their situation.

"Yes," she said, her fingers twitching as she stepped away from the cabinet. "Yes, I suppose you're right."

There was only one door on the right side of the hallway: the one they had noticed with a penumbra of dull yellow light seeping through the edges.

The oaken door inlaid with sapphire tile was wider and taller than the others they had seen in the castle proper. Mala stepped close and put her ear next to it. After listening for a spell, she sprinkled a fine green powder on the surface, then ran her hands along the frame. Satisfied no traps of the non-magical variety stood in their way, her hand slipped to the iron handle. Will gripped the dagger she had lent him, feeling grossly unprepared.

The door opened without a sound. Her sash twirling silently in one hand, her curved dagger in another, Mala moved swiftly into the room. Will followed on her heels, his eyes absorbing the room lit by glow orbs hanging on long silver chains. The rectangular hall was vast, with a ceiling that tapered to a peak far above their heads.

While it might have once housed a banquet hall or an auditorium, the space now resembled a giant workshop, and stank of sulfur and formaldehyde. In the center of the room, five azantite pods, each large enough to hold a human being, stood in a circle. On Will's left, a row of obsidian helms hung from the wall on bronze hooks. More pods were spaced throughout the room and along the walls. Unlike the azantite pods in the center, the other pods varied in size and shape, and were constructed mostly of cast iron and copper. All of the pods were bolted to the floor or chained to the wall, had a single translucent window on the door, and were paired with wooden tables blotted with dark stains. Will spied movement in a few of the pods, the shadow of some unfortunate creature imprisoned within.

A gleaming assortment of knives and other tools of vivisection hung from hooks arranged neatly on the walls. Will knew what this place was. He had seen one like it before, in the Valley of the Cursed.

"Does Lord Alistair have menagerists in the family?" Will said uneasily. Outside of the pods, they had seen no sign of movement in the room.

"Not of which I know. And I find it highly doubtful."

"There's always a black sheep," Will muttered. "And there goes your theory about no mages inside the keep."

As tense and alert as a cat on the prowl, Mala explored the room beside Will.

When they passed near the ring of azantite pods in the center, he couldn't help peering inside. The pods were empty, with no blood stains or other signs of a former occupant. He wondered at their purpose.

As they drew closer to the far wall, Will heard footsteps behind them. He spun as a middle-aged bald man dressed in a brown smock entered the room. The man was gingerly holding a sword a foot out in front of him, as if he had never held a bladed weapon before. He was so tall and thin that his jutting knees and elbows reminded Will of a stork posing as a scientist.

The man noticed them at once and stopped moving. "What are you doing here? How did you get out?"

At first glance, his subdued voice and his unassuming, almost docile face made Will think he was a custodian or an assistant to the menagerist who used the lab. But then he noticed the crooked tilt to his thin lips, and the gleam of cruelty in his eyes.

Will glanced behind him and saw no sign of Mala. *Where is she*?

"Do you understand where you are?" the man continued.

He took a shuffling step forward, allowing Will to get a better look at the silver hilt of the broadsword he was carrying. Will sucked in a breath.

"I see you recognize Zariduke," the man said with a pronounced lisp. "Did you think you'd sneak in here and retrieve it? I still don't understand how you escaped." He shrugged. "No matter. Now that you're in my workshop," he said, rubbing his hands together eagerly, "perhaps we should peer inside your—"

The menagerist dropped the sword and doubled over in pain as a *swoosh* came from Will's left. He glimpsed a blur of sapphire fabric, the weighted ends of Mala's sash spinning through the air. The menagerist was far more aware than his addled appearance let on, because millimeters before the sash smashed into his face, he cocked his head to the left and caused the weapon to strike an invisible barrier and fall harmlessly to the ground, blocked by a Wizard Shield.

Yet the menagerist had failed to stop the dagger she had thrown. The blade was sticking out of the left breast of his frock, right through his heart. As Mala had often preached, the only way to harm a mage was to attack on multiple fronts in tandem.

The menagerist reached down, plucked the dagger out, and tossed it aside with a sneer. The blow to his heart seemed to have had no effect. Mala raced towards him anyway, her short sword raised, screeching a battle cry Will was unaccustomed to hearing, but whose purpose he understood. She was risking her life to distract the mage, giving Will a chance to go for the sword that lay twenty feet away on the floor.

He took a few steps and dove, sliding across the floor, hands extended for Zariduke. Mala withdrew another dagger strapped to her side and threw it at the menagerist's head, distracting him just long enough for Will to reach his sword. As the menagerist blocked the dagger and thrust his hands forward, sending Mala crashing into one of the azantite pods with a powerful Wind Push, Will's fingers closed around the hilt of Zariduke.

With a roar, he leaped to his feet and held the sword out in front of him. His opponent was three feet away and vulnerable. Confident no Wizard Shield or other magical defense could stand in his way, Will stepped forward and thrust with both hands, aiming for the center of the menagerist's chest.

Inches before the sword penetrated, two green reptilian arms burst through the sides of the menagerist's brown frock, just below his other arms. The long and scaly appendages shot forward with incredible speed, like two snakes striking, and seized Will by the waist. Dagger-sharp talons pierced his side, causing him to scream in pain and drop Zariduke as the menagerist lifted him into the air.

"Do you think I've not performed a few experiments on myself over the years?" the menagerist said, his lisp even more pronounced than before.

Holding Will aloft with one reptilian talon, he extracted the other from Will's side and used it rip off the brown frock and reveal a torso that caused the bile to rise in Will's throat. The patchwork skin and appendages had been fused together from a bevy of different creatures. There were patches of thick muscle in some places and orange fur in others. A band of spiked ridges encircled his waist, and instead of a belly button, a third pair of long-fingered hands with black nails clutched the air. With a proud smile, the menagerist turned to showcase a trio of huge oval eyes on his back surrounded by interlocking plates of saurian body armor. The eyes opened and closed at different times, as if each belonged to a separate consciousness.

"The lady's aim was true, but I long ago surrounded my heart with the pericardial membrane of a basilisk. Few weapons can pierce it. It is a tricky thing to work with an organ, but with the gracious patronage of Lord Alistair, I've had the opportunity to advance my art far beyond my predecessors."

"You're a freak show," Will whispered. Out of the corner of his eye, he noticed Mala pulling herself to her feet, dazed from slamming into the azantite pod.

"I call it evolution of our species." The eager look returned to his eyes. "I'm not allowed to kill you yet, but since you're here, Alistair won't notice a few minor experiments I've had in mind for my next human subject. How gracious of you to stop by. And for your friend, well, the sky is the limit."

The menagerist waved a hand, causing the latches on two of the azantite pods to lift. The pod doors flew open, and with a whispered word, he raised Mala into the air and forced her towards one of the pods. She cursed and struggled in vain as the menagerist kept Will suspended by the talon thrust into his midsection. He struggled to keep focus through the pain.

"Perhaps we'll attach the wings of the owl shrike first," he said to Mala, "and proceed from there. Have you ever wished to fly?"

Will tried to break the talon off in his side, but it was too sturdy. In desperation, he bit down on the scaly flesh of the appendage, thinking it looked softer than the talon. It tasted like rancid alligator and he almost broke a tooth.

Once Mala was inside the pod, the door slammed shut. Will knew if he could break the wizard's concentration for just a moment, she might have a chance to flee before the door was latched and her fate sealed.

"Hey!" he roared at the top of his voice, holding up his left arm to showcase an iron bracelet engraved with a grotesquely lolling tongue. "You see this armband? I took it off an ogre-mage. It allows me to understand the speech of any living creature. How would you like one of these, you creep? You can listen to the curses of your victims as you mutilate them."

"Intriguing," the menagerist said, "if you speak the truth. I do sense a confusing magical aura around the item. But you are hardly in a position to bargain for your—"

Behind them, the door to the azantite pod flew open, and Mala stepped out. The menagerist frowned. "Get back in there," he said, flicking his hand to push her back inside and close the door.

"Mala," Will said. "Catch!"

Zariduke was still lying on the ground at his feet. Will had no way to reach down and grab it, but the menagerist had lowered him enough that he managed to extend his leg and give the sword a swift kick as soon as the pod opened, sending it sliding in Mala's direction.

It wasn't enough. She was still ten feet away, the door to her pod about to shut. But the menagerist had made a mistake. Instead of focusing on Mala, Will saw him concentrate in the direction of the sword, as if trying to arrest its movement. Caught up in the moment, he had forgotten about its power, and the sword did not respond to his magic.

Mala took advantage of the distraction. Her hand slipped to her pouch and produced a silk lasso. She tossed it at the sword, looped it expertly around the tip, and jerked hard. The lasso caught on the hilt and brought the sword right to her. It happened so fast the menagerist was caught off guard. He tried to force the door closed but it caught on the silk cord. Before he could recover, Mala had the sword in her hands and was stepping out of the pod.

"Let him go," she said, stalking towards the wizard.

The menagerist yanked his talon out of Will's side and drifted out of reach, high above their heads. "You have nowhere to go," he said. "I'll call the guardians to put you right back in the dungeon."

"By the Queen you will," she said with a snarl.

"Don't let him leave the room," Will said, holding his sides to staunch the blood flow.

"I don't plan on it."

As the menagerist started flying towards the exit, Mala raced to one of the other pods and broke the latch with Zariduke. The menagerist turned as the door opened, and the corpse of an emaciated elf fell out.

"Stop that at once!" the menagerist cried. "My creations!"

Mala ignored him and raced across the room, her eyes roving the pods and selecting the only other one made of azantite. The pod was double the size of the others, and through the tinted glass window, Will glimpsed a monstrous form lurking inside.

A look of fear crossed the menagerist's face. "Ah, I wouldn't—"

Using both hands, Mala raised the sword above her head and struck the azantite padlock with a precise blow. The lock shattered, the door swung open, and a winged creature burst out of the pod that caused Will to lurch backwards in terror. Over ten feet tall, the thick humanoid body was as black as midnight and striated with bands of muscle. Two wicked horns curved back from the top of its head, and orange flames flickered in the oval of its mouth and the sockets of its eyes.

"Fesoj," it roared, stretching night-black wings that unfurled eight feet on either side, lifting the creature into the air with a gust of wind so strong it rippled Will's hair. "I've waited a long time for this."

"Oh dear," the menagerist said.

"An ember demon," Mala whispered, transfixed by the terrible being.

With a shriek, the wizard tried to fly out of the room, but the demon caught him from behind with a massive clawed hand. "You'll be coming with me," it said, and inscribed a doorway in midair with its other hand. As Will and Mala peered out from behind a pod, they watched a jagged portal open, revealing a realm of fire and torment echoing with the screams of the damned. Fesoj howled as the ember demon laughed and carried him through, right before the portal disappeared.

Will stepped out from behind the pod, shaken by the encounter. "That was abrupt."

"He got what he deserved," Mala said with a shudder. "Fusing others against their will."

"I guess the ember demon didn't like it either. Why didn't he just open a portal inside the pod?"

"The azantite would prevent it. A more curious question is how Fesoj trapped the beast in the first place."

"I wonder what the Congregation would think of Alistair working with a menagerist?"

"About as highly as if they knew he had killed his own brother."

"We have to warn Val," Will said. "He has no idea what he's doing."

"We'll do nothing unless we find a portal. You're bleeding quite badly. Let me see your wounds."

Wincing in pain, Will lifted his shirt to expose the deep gouges in the sides of his abdomen where Fesoj had grabbed him.

"I'm out of healing salves," Mala said, "but let me clean and dress it."

"We don't have time. I'll live."

"Not if you get an infection or lose too much blood."

Mala withdrew a jar of brown paste that Allira had given her. Though the smelly paste did not close the wound like a healing salve would have done, it stopped the bleeding, helped ease the pain, and allowed Will to breathe easier. Mala applied a rudimentary bandage to the wound and patted his cheek. "How does it feel?"

He raised his arms above his head, testing the pain and his mobility. "I can still fight."

After holding Zariduke lengthwise in her hands, as if contemplating its power, Mala held it out to him. Will stared down at the blade, wondering what gave him the right to wield such a powerful weapon. "Maybe you should have it," he said quietly. "You're a better swordsman than I am."

"Foolish boy," she said, thrusting the sword into his hands. "This is a blade for heroes, and as I've told you many times, I am anything but."

"You seem to be pretty good at it, whether you admit it or not. Without you and everything you've done, the Revolution would have no hope at all."

"It still doesn't." Mala sheathed her dagger, pocketed the jar of brown paste, and retied her sash around her waist. "Now let's find that portal."

Will looked around the workshop, noting the lack of doors besides the one through which they had entered. "Why was Fesoj carrying such a valuable sword around? He clearly didn't know how to use it."

"Aye. Good question."

"Lord Alistair must have thought it was safer here than in New Victoria, and he's probably right about that. But why not lock it up somewhere? Or was Fesoj disobeying orders?"

Mala considered the question. "It's possible there's a phrenomancer here, and Fesoj took the sword for a consult."

"A phrenomancer? I thought they could only read the minds of people?"

"They don't read minds, Will. They travel the pathways of spirit."

"Oh," he said, his eyes slipping to his ensorcelled blade. He wondered for the first time if Zariduke was sentient, alive somehow.

"I believe you're on to something, though," she said. "There are no other exits in the room, so where was he going with the sword? Perhaps to the same place the portal lies."

They decided to give the room a better search. Nothing stood out until Will examined the portion of the broad stone wall opposite the entrance. Ever since they had entered, he had found it strange, from a construction perspective, that this wall had no doors or other openings. It was a very long wall for the interior.

"Mala, come here," he said, running his hands over the stone.

After a moment, she stepped beside him and frowned. "I see nothing untoward. Wait—it's almost unnoticeable, but the stone isn't quite as worn in this section, is it?"

"And there aren't any cobwebs along the bottom."

The stone felt cool to the touch, sturdy and ancient. Nothing odd about it. Mala detected no traps or secret hinges. After studying it a moment longer, Will raised Zariduke and pressed the tip of the blade to the wall. It gave a little, as if sinking into mud, and he pushed as hard as he could. Finally a snip of blue-white light appeared, brighter than any he had seen before. A door-size section of the wall dissolved into an opaque rectangle of blackness set into the stone.

A doorway of impenetrable gloom and unknown origin.

"Those were powerful wards," he said, waving the sword back and forth through the opaque opening. "Why isn't this weird black wall disappearing? It has to be magic."

"Perhaps not," Mala said, studying it with a thoughtful air. "It could be a dimensional door. I've heard spirit mages and some bibliomancers can create them. They're born of magic but permanent once created, in a way I don't understand."

"What's their purpose?"

"Usually to shield a room they don't want anyone else to enter."

After exchanging a glance, Will poked the sword all the way through, and then his arm. "Shall we?"

With a leap of faith, they stepped through the void together.

Will's foot landed on solid ground. Mala came through beside him and shook out a glow stone to reveal a tiny, cube-shaped room made of azantite, similar to the room where Gavyn had died except for the lack of stains on the walls.

At once Will noticed a familiar pair of items lying on a crystal table in the center of the room: a teardrop buckler shield marked with platinum runes, and a worn leather scabbard attached to a sling he had retrofitted to wear on his back. He walked over to pick up the shield, slipped Zariduke inside the scabbard, and strapped the sling on his back. "I feel better already."

Disappointingly, there was no portal in the room, but Mala's eyes widened as she studied the assortment of treasures on the velvet-lined shelves built into the wall. Among those items was a crown made from a substance that resembled the key Salomon had once given Will; a collection of elaborate glass containers he assumed were potions; and a row of spellbooks with a range of bindings, from jewel-encrusted tomes to vellum pages so old they looked ready to crumble.

Will pointed at the single shelf on the far wall, where a dozen bottles the size of mason jars aligned in a neat row. The bottles were made from a shiny black gemstone, obsidian or onyx or even black jade. "What are those?"

"Soul jars," Mala said grimly. "Most likely belonging to the owners of the spellbooks on display."

"Soul jars? Um, is the meaning literal?"

"I'm afraid so. This must be Alistair's sanctum sanctorum, the place where he hides his most valuable possessions from prying eyes. Most often, soul jars are used to trap the essence of an enemy and transport them to jail or wizard prison. It's illegal to keep someone imprisoned in a soul jar for long, even the worst of criminals, for obvious reasons."

"Eternal torture and all."

"Yes."

"Why is he keeping them here?"

"Why else? To break their will and steal their knowledge, or for leverage, or for some other nefarious reason."

Will walked forward to examine the bronze plaques on the wall above each jar, engraved with the names of what he assumed were the unfortunate occupants of the containers. "Should we free them?"

"Their bodies would be long dead, and their souls . . . it's quite possible they've gone mad, or will mistake us for their captors. If these are powerful mages, then we can't risk raising their ire."

"We shouldn't just leave them here like this," Will muttered, and then stood very still, as if pole-axed to the ground, when he reached the jar at the end of the line.

"Mala," he said, his voice coming out as a croak.

"Yes?" she said, in a distracted voice. She was standing by one of the spellbooks and chewing on her bottom lip.

He tried to speak again but couldn't find his voice. Drowning in emotion, overcome by horror and confusion, he could only point his finger at the name engraved on the face of the plaque.

Dane Maurice Blackwood

-9-

Early in the morning after the Mage Day celebration, still awake and pleasantly numb from the granth, Lord Alistair watched Melina wander through the observatory atop his tower in the Wizard District. After marveling at the celestial maps on the walls drawn with magical dyes that rendered them three-dimensional to the human eye, the sorceress gazed up at the stars through the glass ceiling, then walked to the lone window to absorb the view of the colored spires hovering in the sky around the tower.

"What do you think?" he asked. Melina had never visited the observatory at night.

"Magnificent," she breathed. "The best view in the city."

He felt his blood stir as Melina meandered through the room, her array of rings, bracelets, and other charms jingling and glittering in the light of the glow orbs. She was still wearing her slinky lavender gown from the party but had removed her shoes. The effects of the long night of revelry, the disarray of her blond curls and the smudge of lipstick around her mouth, made her even more ravishing. She was the first woman who had moved him since his wife had died.

Melina drifted across the artistic renditions of the planes of existence that wrapped the support columns and flowed onto the silver floor tiles, letting her fingertips trail across an antique telescope. "Should we contact Fesoj?" she asked, stopping in front of a line of obsidian Spirit Helms hanging on the wall. "See if the probabilities attached to that cursed sword have sunk even further?"

"Tonight?" he said, amused. "You're even more vigilant than I."

"I'll cease to worry when the prophecy is extinguished."

He waved a hand. "The probabilities are negligible now. The sword and the Blackwood boy are secure. Come," he said, wrapping her in his arms from behind and inhaling the sweet intoxication of her perfume. "There is a time for war and a time for love."

"My people are very superstitious," she said without turning, stretching like a cat in his arms. "It's one of the few vestiges of my heritage I have yet to shed."

"I find the concern for my welfare quite charming."

She reached back to run a hand through his dark hair, sending currents of desire arcing through him. In the corner, streaks of silver light pulsed across the shadowy form of the sole remaining Spirit Liege. Alistair wondered what it felt as it watched them, if it retained any human emotion. Since it was a new class of being altogether, one he and Fesoj had brought to life, perhaps it had a new and unclassified emotional palette.

At times, Alistair pondered the wisdom of revealing his secrets to Melina. Besides Fesoj, she alone knew about the Spirit Liege, the location of the sword and the Coffer, and the prophecy that had plagued him ever since those cursed items had returned.

Of course, desire had played a part in loosening his lips. He was well aware of this. Yet he also knew that Melina desired him as well, that her ambition rivaled his own, and that she would never jeopardize her new standing in the Congregation. He valued her insight, she had no proof of anything, and if she did betray his trust, he could snuff her life as easily as taking a breath.

And, of course, Melina did not know all of his secrets.

She walked over to admire an azantite case showcasing a collection of magical artifacts. "I still think you should kill the brothers as soon as possible. Two are already in your grasp. Why leave the prophecy to chance?"

"Chance is leaving threads untied, my dear. Will is secure in my stronghold, Val is under my thumb, and I will use them both as tools, if needed, to reach Caleb."

"Can you not reach him in other ways?"

"Of course—but all the better if Valjean convinces him to come to me. Caleb will think he is returning home through a portal, I will kill all three brothers in secret, and there will be no outcry from the people. The foolish Devla think Caleb Blackwood is their savior, their redeemer. The gullibility of human beings never ceases to amaze me. In any event, what better way to defuse a revolution than if their leader chooses to return to his home world, slinking away to a safer place, rather than lead his followers into war?"

"And you're certain you can convince him?"

"I'm certain *Val* can. Caleb will listen to his older brother and realize the only possible outcome of his march to New Victoria is certain death. He will choose the portal home—or at least so he will think."

"And what of Adaira, when she learns of Val's death?"

Lord Alistair looked away. "Yes, that is most unfortunate. I admit I'm fond of Valjean myself, and were circumstances different, I would welcome him to our family. But things are what they are, and I fear Adaira will take his death poorly. I plan to give her a task to occupy her mind."

"Such as?"

"I'll send her on a mission to the protectorates to facilitate the revival of true cuerpomancy. Establish healing centers available to the common born. That will not only heal my daughter's heart and keep her grief at bay, but bolster my own reputation among the people."

"I see," Melina said demurely, reaching up to cup his face in her hands. "Your wisdom and breadth of vision is unparalleled."

"You flatter me."

"Of course I do. It's part of my magic. Yet the secret to my charms is that I speak the truth as well."

Though Melina had studied sylvamancy at the Academy, Alistair knew her true talents lay in seduction and persuasion. The tinkling jewelry that bewitched men's eyes, the heady perfume that lowered inhibitions, the mesmeric sway of her hips when she walked, the magically sweet honey in her voice: it was all a calculation, practiced and perfected, her natural abilities enhanced by her magic.

He knew this, and still he had no defense.

"And when the prophecy is no longer a worry?" she asked, swaying closer until their bodies were touching, locking her arms around his waist.

"What do you mean?"

"What becomes of the sword and the Coffer? Will you dispose of them?"

He had not told her, or anyone, that he had tried to force the Coffer open with magic and had failed. A troubling fact. Yet he was certain that, with time, he would unlock the Coffer's secrets. Then the artifacts would become the problem of his enemies.

With Zariduke in hand, and the Coffer at his side, no mage on Urfe would dare stand against him. The queen would lay her crown at his feet.

"Dispose of them?" His mouth curled into a smirk. "Why ever would I want to take such a foolish action?"

Her eyes narrowed. "You seek to wield them yourself one day."

"But of course."

As the Spirit Liege flickered in the corner, Melina disengaged from his embrace, slipped out of her gown, and began drifting towards the wizard chute in the corner. Her gleeful laughter was like swans gliding across water as Lord Alistair flew to meet her, caught her in his arms from behind, and carried her down the chute to his bedroom.

-10-

The rukhs and simorghs flew all through the night and into the morning. They took more than half the camp—the infirm, the elderly, children and their mothers— to the ancient home of the Yith in the uppermost reaches of the western mountains. There, they would be kept safe and warm, provided with food and shelter during the long winter. Relief poured through Caleb as he watched them disappear.

The Yith Riders guided the rest of the great avians across the snow-clogged peaks of the Dragon's Teeth, ferrying the Devla and Roma to the jagged green foothills on the other side. They landed at dawn beneath a plateau streaked with lichen, surrounded by old-growth evergreens and a river snaking through the forest.

The Yith left after feeding and watering their mounts. They left behind as many provisions as they could spare. Everyone, Caleb included, was overcome with gratitude for all they had done. The Yith had elected not to join the march to New Victoria, since they rarely ventured outside their homeland, but as the great birds wheeled into the sky to return across the mountains, the cheers from the camp resounded throughout the forest.

After the evacuation, around three thousand Devla and Roma remained. Now that the camp was pared down to fighters and mages, Caleb began to truly think of it as his army. It was a strange feeling. Though the burden of leadership weighed heavy, everyone remaining had made the choice to continue. It felt good, for once in his life, to take a stand for something. Lord Alistair was a tyrant and a bully, and these people had reached the breaking point. They were doing the right thing.

Or at least this was what he told himself as his eyes roamed the gathering of three thousand souls in his care.

After a long day's march, they set up camp beneath a rocky cliff with a waterfall plunging right down the center. As the sun dipped below the horizon, the last fiery rays caught the cascading water at just the right angle, transforming it into liquid fire. The Prophet led a worship service at the base of the natural phenomenon, and many of the Roma joined the Prophet's followers in song and praise to Devla. Caleb watched the celebration with hooded eyes, both dismissive of their beliefs and envious of their faith.

After the evening meal, he stood alone on the eastern edge of camp, facing the direction of New Victoria, just inside the wards that Branyn, Elaina, and the other mages had set. The woods smelled of fir trees and loamy soil. Now that they had crossed the Dragon's Teeth, he planned to head sharply southeast, to avoid the much larger range—the Rockies, back home—to the east. Once they traveled far enough south, they would head into the dry Southwest, until they reached the central plains. According to his advisors, crossing the great plains of the Ninth would be exceedingly perilous, even without an attack by the Congregation. And the journey would take so very long. Months. Caleb could barely contain his yearning to confront Lord Alistair, and wished there were some way he could take a portal straight to him. Yet not even he was rash enough to confront the Chief Thaumaturge without the Coffer by his side.

The Coffer of Devla.

How was he going to get it back?

Perhaps someone would help him, or he would think of some insane plan to retrieve it once they neared New Victoria. He knew only that he had to find a way. From the moment he had raised the lid and peered inside, and felt its mysterious power course through him, he had known, in a manner that he could not explain, that it was *his*.

A grim smile creased the corners of his lips. He supposed he had faith after all.

Faith in the power of revenge.

On his way back to camp, he noticed Lance sitting in his tent with Allira. They were warming their hands by the fire and enjoying the mutual silence. He had seen them together on other occasions. Curious. Perhaps they had forged a common bond after leaving their homelands so far behind.

Caleb knew why Lance had come back. He had seen it written all over his face as Lance told him what had happened to him after the battle with Zedock. The former Marine and police officer had lost a kidney, and then a career, and finally his pride. Lance was a warrior, no matter which world he called home. He needed something to fight for. A cause to believe in.

One kidney or not, by joining in the cause to overthrow a tyrant, even if that cause seemed futile, Lance had found his purpose.

Reclaimed his self-respect.

When Caleb wandered by Yasmina's tent, hoping to catch a word, he found her engaged in quiet discussion with Tamás. It was no secret to anyone the revolutionary had fallen in love with the beautiful wilder. Caleb had noticed them talking more and more during the journey, and each time Tamás seemed to sit a little bit closer. But Caleb knew Yasmina almost as well as he knew himself, and he could tell by her body language she did not return the interest.

The Brewer was entertaining a large crowd in the center of camp, strumming his lyre and belting out Roma folk tunes overlaid on chords from rock songs back home. Everyone was in high spirits from the miraculous escape. Caleb no longer thought he was capable of experiencing joy, but he did feel relief they had crossed the mountains, and that the most vulnerable among them were safe. He was on the verge of joining the crowd and enjoying the music when something inside him, something broken and powerful and infinitely sad all at the same time, like some ruined statue of a pagan god lying forgotten in the jungle, caused him to return to his tent alone.

The next day, after continuing along the river until midday, the wide bank disappeared and they were forced to cut east into a forest of spruce and pine. The paladins led the march, and the army made better time without the children and the elderly. So far the game was plentiful, but they knew an early winter on the plains would spell trouble almost as much as in the mountains. On the other hand, they had a better chance of finding settlements and wandering caravans on the plains.

They camped in a forest glade without incident and made good time again in the morning. After lunch, the forest broke and they entered a geologically active area marked by rocky plains, black soil, and the blasted cones of ancient volcanoes. Judging from a map Tamás brought out, Caleb thought they might be somewhere east of Yosemite. He could not recall from the pictures back home whether the national park had such a bleak landscape, but not everything from Urfe correlated to his own world. Judging by the desolation, it looked as if a couple of warring mage armies had once waged a battle here, and the prophecy in the Roma Canticles came unbidden to his mind.

The one who unseals the Coffer as he breaks the will of the world.

Maybe, he thought grimly, *New Victoria will look like this one day.*

They slogged up and down long, uneven slopes filled with boulders and scrub grass that had clawed its way to the surface. When the ground leveled out, they found themselves traipsing through a valley rife with bubbling fumaroles, geysers, and hardened lava flows.

The afternoon air was damp and still. Breathtaking views of the mountains appeared in the distance. Another feast for the eyes were the red, green, and orange lichens that grew on the rocks, atop the lava beds, and in the pools of water that spilled outward from the geysers. At first Caleb enjoyed the novelty of the scenery, but as the fumaroles and thermal hot springs grew more numerous, the smell of rotten eggs stuffed his nostrils, and the sulfur in the air stung his eyes.

So far, they had not followed any one trail, but wound their way through the dangerous geysers as best they could. When the only way forward became a trail of hardened lava that snaked between two hot springs as big as lakes, Caleb called a break to consult with his advisors.

"Aye, I don't like the look of this place," Tamás said. "'Tis so barren and devoid of life. And the smell . . ."

Yasmina rolled her eyes. "You'll survive the smell. And there's more life here than you realize." A loud caw caused her gaze to lift, and she watched her harpy eagle land on the branch of a twisted juniper tree. "I think it's quite beautiful."

Tamás looked down, embarrassed by the rebuke.

"So you don't think it's dangerous?" Caleb asked.

"I didn't say that," she said. "I've seen no sign of a malevolent creature, but this terrain is new to me."

"I don't like how strung out we'll be," Lance said, eying the narrow path that wound between the shallow hot springs. "We can go five abreast at most. On the other hand, something would have to wade through acid and boiling water to reach us."

"Or attack by air," Branyn added. The geomancer was leaning on a walking stick and drinking from a leather canteen. "I've flown high a few times to scout the terrain. There's a good place to camp a few miles away. A hilltop with enough space to pitch tents. "

"Darkness falls in two hours, by my estimation," Tamás said.

"Aye. We'll need to hurry."

"Is it smart to keep going," Lance said, "if we don't know for sure where the trail leads? What if it's a dead end?"

"According to the map," Tamás said, "the trail spills into an open stretch of grassland about fifteen miles away."

"Does your map mention the nightmarish trek through Volcano Alley?"

Everyone looked to Caleb to make the final decision. Mist from the spray of a geyser landed on his cloak, stinging his eyes, and he glanced uneasily at the steaming pools of bright blue water on either side. Even if they turned back, they might not make it to higher ground before nightfall. "I say we push through. Let's get to that hilltop and aim for the grasslands by tomorrow night."

"Aye," Tamás said with a slow nod. "I don't like our choices, but I agree that backtracking is not ideal."

Instead of keeping the paladins at the front of the army, Caleb decided to intersperse them throughout the troops. He remained at the front with Tamás, Lance, Yasmina, and Allira. The two women used their tracking skills and knowledge of the land to help guide the way and detect threats.

The army made good time at first. The Brewer started a marching tune, and they proceeded in well-ordered lines. The ground was flat and covered in moss that did not slow them down. Geysers and shallow basins of water persisted on both sides, infusing the trek with steam and mist and the stench of sulfur.

Half an hour into the march, the ground turned spongy. At first it was a minor annoyance, an inch of squishy muck that coated the bottoms of their boots. But soon the loose soil became so deep the suction tugged at their feet and slowed them down. A layer of moss still covered the ground, so he could see why Branyn had not noticed the change in terrain.

Caleb took a step and sank to his calves in mud. "I don't like this."

The temperature had started to drop, causing Yasmina to wrap her cloak tighter as she eyed the sinking sun. "We have half an hour of light at most. At this rate, we won't make the clearing before dark."

"Unfortunate," Tamás said, "but we've seen no sign of danger. Unless you sense something we cannot?"

"Not yet," she said. "But as I said, this is unfamiliar land. And not all dangers can be sensed in advance."

Caleb ran a hand through his hair. "I guess we have little choice but to keep going."

The union of approaching dusk and mist from the pools had cut their visibility to less than twenty feet. Thankfully, the mud did not get any deeper, but as they feared, it slowed them down enough that by the time darkness fell, they still had not reached the clearing. Branyn had decided to conserve his remaining energy, so they had no way to tell when they would arrive.

"It can't be that far," Caleb muttered, lifting his leg for yet another labored step through the mud.

A scream pierced the air behind him.

"What was that?"

Another scream, followed by shouts of alarm and confusion all through the ranks. As the paladins called for order, Caleb noticed something bulky on the ground moving towards him in the darkness, less than ten feet away.

"Branyn! Light!"

The mage flew forward, drawing amber light from the sickle of moon overhead to illuminate the path in a wide radius around Caleb and the others at the front of the march. The form Caleb had glimpsed coalesced into a mottled, slimy brown body slithering out of the pool of water on their left. About eight feet long, the grotesque creature resembled a squashed seal, and the front of its body broadened into a wide circular maw lined with needle-like teeth. Caleb watched in horrified fascination as the segmented body advanced in the manner of an earthworm, lengthening and contracting like some antediluvian species pulling itself out of the primordial muck.

He whipped around to see another emerging on the opposite side. A quick glance behind him revealed that a third had swallowed a man halfway to his waist. The unfortunate man's legs kicked wildly as the men and women around him hacked at the creature. Neither edged nor blunt weapons seemed to have an effect. Nausea welled in Caleb's throat, and he saw that yet another of the creatures had attached itself to a Devla worshipper's back, feeding as she screamed.

"Leeches," Lance said from behind Caleb. "Those disgusting things are giant leeches!"

"I can't believe their size," Yasmina whispered.

With a surge of terrified adrenaline, Caleb ran to the nearest leech and struck a heavy blow with his diamond-headed mace. The weapon bit deep into the creature, opening a wound that spilled brown ichor and caused it to retreat. Caleb let it disappear beneath the water and turned to find Lance, Tamás, and Yasmina attacking another leech to little effect. Only Yasmina's owl staff caused it to flinch, but even that did not stop the thing from creeping forward.

"Branyn!" Caleb roared.

The mage had a wild look in his eyes. "No spell of mine affects them. I can push them back with a Wizard Wind, but they crawl forward again, and I grow weaker."

"Take me up," Caleb said. "I need to see."

Branyn looped an arm through Caleb's and flew them high above the path, to the limits of their visibility. Below them, as far as they could see down the line of the embattled army, leeches emerged from the hot springs and stagnant pools surrounding the muddy pathway. The leeches did not move very fast, but there was nowhere for anyone to run. Sensing fresh blood, the loathsome creatures had emerged ahead of and behind the army as well, trapping them on all sides.

"Jesus," Caleb said. "There's nowhere to go. They'll devour the whole army."

"What do we do?" Branyn said.

"I don't know."

They descended to find panic on the faces of the soldiers.

"Yaz," Caleb said, "how do you kill leeches?"

"Salt, chlorine, lemon juice. Dry them out."

"I don't think that's going to help us here," he said, as he beat back another with his mace. "What else do you know about them?"

"I'm not an expert on invertebrates, but I know they don't have ears, can barely see, and sense vibrations through their epidermis. They can go a year without food, have advanced taste receptors, and communicate through chemicals secreted through touch."

"Great. They might have been waiting twelve months for this meal. Let me rephrase: do you know anything that might help us in this particular life or death situation?"

Instead of responding, she leaped to the side to avoid the maw of another leech, then twirled her staff and smacked it on the back, causing it to writhe backward.

As Caleb searched for an answer, the screams of the wounded and the dying rang through the night. Allira provided a brief ray of hope when she tossed a handful of yellow powder from one of her pouches on the back of a leech attacking Lance. The thing shuddered, obviously in pain, then slithered backwards to the water as fast as it could.

Caleb ran over to ask how much more of the powder she had. Maybe Branyn could weaponize it. He could tell by her doleful expression, even before she showed him the pouch with only a few pinches of powder left, what he needed to know.

Caleb saw the Prophet moving among the soldiers, praying and offering words of encouragement. But when they locked gazes, Caleb saw a rare look of doubt in the holy man's eyes.

With no solution except to go on the attack, Caleb howled and tore into as many of the leeches as he could, keeping those around him safe. Yet the screams from further down the line grew more frequent, and for every leech he drove back, two more seemed to appear.

Yasmina caught his eye. While she remained outwardly calm, he knew her well enough to spot her quiet desperation. Before she looked away, her face crumbled into a chasm of sadness and regret, and he knew, in that moment, that the look was for him, and that a part of her, perhaps a large part, still loved him. He wished he could return the sentiment, but the only thing he felt in the moment was that his journey was about to end, and the deaths of Luca and Marguerite would go unavenged.

A flare of crimson light appeared in the corner of his eye. Confused, since they didn't have any pyromancers, he turned to see a fiery missile the size of a tennis ball launch into the darkness.

Thinking they were under attack by yet another enemy, he was about to race back down the line until he heard a familiar chorus of ululating cries that made him stop in his tracks, stunned, and call for Branyn again. The mage, who had not strayed far, flew over to lift his leader into the night sky once more. When Caleb got a better look at what was happening, his jaw dropped in disbelief.

On both sides of the path, creatures that resembled giant pink salamanders were springing through the shallow waters, unbothered by the heat and acid. The creatures had long narrow heads, similar to a crocodile, and strapped to their backs were saddles bearing seven-foot tall humanoids with bright red skin and a pair of long curved horns atop their heads. The powerfully built beings were holding long gray tubes out of which they launched balls of molten lava at the leeches.

Darvish on the backs of darrowgars. Holy Mother Mary, those are darvish warriors!

All along the pathway, the palms of hundreds of darvish warriors glowed bright as they used their internal heat source to power their strange weapons. Lava ball after lava ball slammed into the leeches, causing them to ignite, curl, and wither on the spot. The darrowgars joined the fray as well, biting the leeches in two with their massive jaws and flinging the severed halves into the water. The agile darrowgar had no problem avoiding the gaping maws of the leeches. Before long, the entire mass of loathsome invertebrates—maybe due to those chemical secretions Yasmina had mentioned, transmitting a communal message—decided to wriggle back into the fumaroles and hot springs from which they had emerged.

The darvish lowered their weapons. Once the Devla and Roma fighters realized the fearsome newcomers who looked like devils weren't going to attack them, but had instead come to save them, a great cheer rose up, a pent-up roar of collective relief.

All the ululations had ceased except for one voice: that of a female darvish who was on the back of a darrowgar running swiftly through a shallow pool towards the head of the army. In contrast to her male counterparts, she had three-inch nubs instead of horns, and was only as tall as Caleb. His friends and advisors surrounded him as she approached, but he waved them off and stepped out to greet her with a stunned expression.

"Lisha!"

With a swish of black hair, the beautiful young darvish attached her gray tube to her saddle, hopped off the darrowgar, and walked towards Caleb. Tight-fitting black boots and a full-length, satiny jade cloak helped protect her from the colder temperatures of the surface world. The cloak had an arched collar and flared cuffs, reminding Caleb of the whimsical architecture of the darvish city he had glimpsed at the bottom of the Great Chasm far beneath the surface of Urfe.

Everyone parted to let Lisha through. He could feel the heat emanating from her crimson skin as she approached.

"What a dish," the Brewer said in a low voice to Caleb. "I never thought I'd live to see a darvish."

"We meet again," Lisha said in halting English, which surprised him. In the Darklands, they had not been able to communicate other than through Will and his armband—if one did not count the time Caleb and Lisha had made love as communication.

"Uh, yeah, thanks for popping by. Were you just swinging through the hood?" She blinked in confusion at the vernacular, and he wrapped her in a fierce hug. "Thank you, Lisha. You saved all our lives."

Her skin seemed to turn even redder, if that was possible, as she peered at him through her long lashes. "You're most welcome."

"I don't understand—what are you doing on the surface? How'd you know we were out here?"

She swept a hand. "This is an area of great seismic activity. Entrances to the Darklands abound."

"I can see that, but your people live miles underground."

"Times have changed since you freed me. The delver mining operations have pushed closer and closer to our homeland, causing great disquiet among our people. We fear there might be war. We are not ignorant of surface affairs, and we realize the Congregation is paying the delvers to mine tilectium. I also know of your mission to petition the Congregation for peace, and about your family. I'm . . . very sorry."

Caleb looked down.

"I was on my way," she continued, "to offer you my assistance."

Stunned, his eyes lifted to regard her. "You were?"

"We, too, suffer from the actions of the Congregation, and would like to lend our support to your cause. Therefore," she said proudly, "I and nineteen of our finest warriors have come to offer to accompany you through the Ninth Protectorate to help ensure a safe arrival."

"Twenty," he said softly.

"We would send more, but we only possess twenty of our special surface skins that allow us to survive the direct sun and cold nights."

He took a deep breath and infused as much gratitude into his voice as he could muster. "Thank you, Lisha. Your help is very much appreciated. But you should know we aren't marching to New Victoria to make a petition. We march to force our demands to be met."

"Force? But how . . ." she saw the deadly look in his eyes, swallowed, and said, "I see. We will still accompany you through the Ninth, but I do not believe . . . I do not know how . . ."

"It's okay," he said, taking her by the shoulders. "We don't either."

After they locked gazes for a moment, she broke away and called out a series of commands in her own language. The darvish warriors helped collect the dead and wounded, and the Prophet approached Caleb as they prepared to march again.

"It seems another timely intervention has occurred," the Prophet said. "Yet another miracle beyond human understanding."

"Something like that."

The Prophet gazed at the stars and crossed his hands over his chest with his fingers splayed, a common gesture of Devla worship. "Praise be to Devla for his grace, benevolence, and wisdom."

Caleb eyed the bodies of the fallen slumped across the backs of the darrowgars. "Tell that to the families of those who just died."

An hour later, with the darvish guarding the army's flanks against the leeches, they reached the hilltop Branyn had spied. They had to navigate a rocky slope in the darkness to reach the clearing but were glad to be on higher ground, safe from the dangers of the mud flats.

With their remaining energy, the mages channeled the moonlight so the army could set camp among the boulders, weeds, and jumbled rock formations. By the time the motes of light began to dissipate, the wards had been set, the corpses of forty men and women cremated in a funeral pyre lit by the darvish, and dinner had been served.

Caleb was the last to leave the funeral pyre. Weary to the core, devastated by the loss of life, he trudged back to the center of camp, ready to eat and collapse in a heap. Yasmina had avoided him ever since Lisha had shown up, and he couldn't bring himself to care. *All that is behind me. I'm sorry for all the hurt I caused, but my heart belongs to someone I can never hold again.*

After washing down his dried beef with a flagon of water, he mumbled good night to his friends and headed to his tent. On the way, he heard a disembodied voice calling his name, faint at first and then louder.

"Caleb! Caleb, can you hear me?"

It was a voice he would know anywhere. He froze as a spectral image of his older brother appeared in front of him, standing waist-deep in a pool of shimmery silver-blue liquid. The image was transparent. Caleb could see right through Val to the boulder behind him.

Stunned by the appearance of his brother, Caleb heard a crowd gathering, murmuring in awe and unease at the strange apparition. "Val?" he said. "Is that really you? Where are you?"

His brother held out his hands, palms upturned. "It's really me, Caleb. I need to talk to you urgently. I'll explain everything. Now reach out and bring me through!"

-11-

Emotions surged through Will as he stood in front of the soul jar below the placard bearing his father's name.

"Careful," Mala warned.

"You think it's warded?"

"Doubtful. But the person inside the jar . . . might not be your father. Not as you knew him."

"When he died searching for Zariduke, they found his broken body at the bottom of a cliff. I saw him myself at the funeral. What does that mean?"

"It means that if he's truly inside, then only his essence survived. I've no idea what it's like to exist inside a soul jar for so long."

Will's hands clenched at his sides. "I'm not leaving him in there another second. So whatever happens—" he took the soul jar off the shelf and held it in his hands "—happens."

"Perhaps you should consult a proper—"

With a snarl, Will uncorked the jar and set it down on the azantite floor. Almost at once, a fine silver mist flowed out and began to coalesce. He took a few steps back, joining Mala in the center of the room, his heart thumping against his chest.

Moments later, the swirling mist assumed the shape of his father. Though not as transparent as the ghost of Alistair's brother, Dane Blackwood's form was not quite corporeal, either. His build and facial features were clearly defined, but it was as if he were looking at his father in a darkened room, though plenty of light existed. Something more than a shadow and less than a human being. It made Will wonder why his physical form was present at all. Perhaps the body and soul were linked forever in ways no one understood.

He had a million questions, but all he could manage was a single croak. "Dad?"

At first his father stared right through him, but then he blinked a few times and said, "William? Is it really you?"

Though the shade's voice was more of a spectral whisper, it possessed subtle inflections in tone that drew Will sharply back to his childhood. He had no doubt this was his father, or his father's spirit.

Will started forward to embrace him, then stopped himself, unsure what to do.

"It's okay, son," his father said. "I understand. I want nothing more than to hug you too. But my my, how you've grown! Even if I had my body, I'm not sure I could wrap you in my arms anymore! How old are you?"

Choking with emotion, Will said, "I'm twenty now, Dad. You've been gone almost ten years."

Though his father didn't speak or move towards him, Will could see by the stillness of his insubstantial form how much the words affected him.

"I'm just glad you're okay," Will said. "We weren't sure if . . . how the soul jar would . . ."

"I'm not sure I would call this *okay*," his father said gently. "The body you see is but a projection of my mind. Which, by the way, is still intact. Though not without a struggle. I've been . . . dreaming, Will. For such a very long time."

"Dreaming about what?"

"About your mom and this moment, mostly. Seeing you and your brothers a final time."

Will looked away. He had the sudden overwhelming urge to kill whoever had done this terrible thing to his father.

Except I don't have to speculate.

I know who did it.

"I see that you have Zariduke," his father said. "That's very good. Where are your brothers?"

"I'm not sure, but they're on Urfe somewhere. Last I knew they were safe. We got split up and . . . it's a long story."

Will didn't have the heart to tell him that Val was working hand in hand with Lord Alistair, and that Caleb was leading an army on a suicidal march to New Victoria.

His father gave him a sharp look, as if he knew that Will had withheld the truth. "Where are we? I presume Alistair imprisoned me in a soul jar, but how did you find me? And who is this lovely young lady? Your wife, I presume?"

Mala snorted, and Will laughed to break the tension. "There's so much to tell you, Dad. After you died, a necromancer from Urfe came to New Orleans. Charlie gave us our inheritance, but the necromancer killed him. Val, Caleb, and I came to Urfe with no idea what to do, and we hired her—Mala—to help us. She taught me how to fight and we found Leonidus's Keep and then—"

"Slow down, son. Charlie's dead?"

"Yeah. He is."

His father's eyes lowered. "He was a good man. He kept my secret all those years. I probably shouldn't have . . . there were so many hard choices."

"Don't blame yourself. And Charlie saved us. He watched over us all those years, and gave me the sword, and helped us fight the necromancer as best he could."

"So you found my journal? And took the portal in New York?"

"Portal? What portal? Zedock stole the journal, and some old wizard named Salomon gave us a key that brought us to Urfe."

"Salomon?" the shade of his father said. "Who is that? I don't understand."

"Neither do we. Whoever he is, he provided a home for us in New Victoria, and weapons, and money, and then disappeared. He pops up every now and then, like he's playing some kind of game with our lives."

"How very odd," his father whispered, in a faraway voice.

Mala gripped Will's hand. At first he thought she was providing moral support, but then he saw what she must have noticed: his father's ethereal form had started to break apart.

"Dad?" he said. "What's happening? You don't look as . . . substantial . . . as before."

"Yes. I can feel it." He hesitated. "I don't have much time, Will."

Will felt a familiar twinge of panic clawing at his chest, one he had not experienced for a long time. *You can't leave me again, Dad. Not after I just found you.* "What do you mean?"

"Souls do not live forever," his father said gently. "At least not in this plane of existence."

"But you just got here. You can't . . . I can't . . ."

"Will," his father said firmly. "Look at me. I love you, son. I love all three of you, more than anything else in the multiverse. I consider it a miracle that I'm able to tell you this in person one more time."

"One more time? Dad!"

"*Listen*, son. We have to get through this. I have a very short amount of time."

A lump formed in Will's throat, and he felt dizzy with emotion, unmoored by anguish. He picked up the soul jar and stepped forward. "Let me put you back in. You'll last longer in there. You can—"

His father laid a hand on his son's shoulder, though Will did not feel the touch. "No, son. I'm sorry. I wouldn't go back in there even if it would help."

Will looked down at the floor, feeling as if his world was crumbling. He fought to corral his grief, and slowly lifted his head. "What do we need to do?" he said, in a voice barely above a whisper.

"Is my assumption correct that we're in Alistair's stronghold?"

"That's right. He sent me to his dungeon, and Mala freed me."

"Then you know the danger you're in. When Alistair found me, we did battle in another dimension, a place where only our kind can go. I took him there to lead him away from you and your brothers and mom. I held him off as long as I could, and jumbled the spirit pathways to Earth, but in the end he defeated me."

"Can you help us kill him?" Will said grimly.

"No. My magic is no more. I don't know why. I don't understand where magic derives from any better than I ever did, or the concept of the soul, or the source of all things. I do sense there's another realm . . . a place where I will soon go . . . I've been on the frontier of this place for a long time now, waiting to enter, glimpsing it in my dreams. Bah. That's a discussion for another time, when we're all together one day." His father's voice sounded further and further away, and his spectral form was crumbling into silver mist.

"Dad, do you have any idea how we can get out of here?"

"I've never been to Alistair's castle, but mages often keep portals in the uppermost reaches of their strongholds, usually at the top of a wizard chute. I'm sure Alistair has one somewhere. Don't delay, son. Go now!"

Will took a step closer to his father. "I have to know something first. When you were on Urfe, were you part of the Revolution?"

"I . . . it was complicated. I didn't hate the Congregation. In fact, I joined it, and rejected the plea from my kinsmen to support their cause. I thought I could stay neutral to both sides. But Alistair made me choose, and I . . . I decided to leave my home world. How I ended up on Earth, the planet harboring Zariduke, is another story—I now believe I was led there by another agent. But I always knew someone might come for me and my family, so I took steps to protect you. I never imagined Alistair would find me so quickly. He had to have used a talented gazer, or somehow implanted a tracking spell before I left. Looking back on my youthful choices, I can admit I was seduced by power on some level. Val and I are alike in that way. But the freedom of belief should never be restricted. Militant religion, atheism, magic or common-born: one form of tyranny is the same as another. And somewhere along the way, I don't know when, Alistair chose the wrong path."

"I think I know," Will said grimly.

As his father's form continued to dissolve, his hand lifted in a final goodbye, and his lips formed a warm, familiar smile that seemed to encompass Will's entire childhood. "Goodbye, son. Always remember how much I love you. Tell your brothers the same."

And then he was gone.

Will let out a cry of anguish and sank to the floor. After a moment, Mala approached from behind to lay a hand on his shoulder. Wanting only to lie down and give in to his grief, Will shuddered, squeezed her hand, and forced himself to think of all the people depending on him. After murmuring a final goodbye to his father, he stuck the soul jar in his pocket, stood, and turned his energy towards escaping Lord Alistair's stronghold.

"We need a portal," he said grimly.

"Aye."

"What if Dad's right, and it's at the top of a wizard chute we can't reach?"

"One thing at a time," she said. Her eyes swept the treasure of the artifact room with a greedy spark.

"It's not worth the risk," he said.

"You're right, of course," she murmured, then led the way back through the invisible door and into Fesoj's workshop.

Will had so many questions, but he thrust away his doubts, fears, and love for his father as he and Mala raced through the workshop and returned to the wide stone staircase. They climbed with only Mala's light to penetrate the gloom, surprised to find that the stairs continued on to the fourth level, and then a fifth, with no end in sight.

"We must be in the tower now," Mala said, peering out of an iron-barred window overlooking the ramparts.

"Someone had to have figured out we're gone by now. Maybe Lord Alistair himself, if he checked in with Fesoj."

"Aye," she said, and took the next set of stairs two at a time.

On the sixth-floor landing, Will heard a boom outside the window, followed by another. The tower vibrated beneath his feet, and the window beside him shook in its pane. Cringing, he whipped around to look out the window.

What he saw made his knees turn to jelly. Walking swiftly across the ramparts, covering twenty feet or more with a single step, was the guardian of the castle. Seeing the storm titan at its full height—at least thirty feet tall, with limbs like oak trunks and a shaggy head the size of a boulder—caused Will to stop and stare at the gigantic being in stupefied awe.

Boom.

Boom.

Boom.

It was heading right for the tower, iron club raised, the icicles clinging to its beard as long as Will's sword and waving in the wind.

"Will!" Mala said, but he couldn't stop staring at the fascinating spectacle of the titan stomping across the ramparts. It was like something out of a Greek myth, a god on Mount Olympus approaching a puny mortal who life was his to command—

Mala slapped him hard on the face, breaking his concentration.

Boom.

Boom.

Boom.

When she raised her hand again, he blinked and caught her arm. "Okay. I'm fine."

"The titan awed you. Don't look right at him."

"I won't. Sorry."

"Now *run*."

Unsheathing Zariduke and gripping his shield, knowing they would not do much good against a being of that size, he followed Mala as she sprang up the staircase, wondering how high the tower reached.

On the next level, Will glanced out the window, careful not to look directly at the titan. It had covered half the ground to the tower and was coming right for them.

Boom.

Boom.

Boom.

The titan's footsteps continued to shake the floor. They sprinted to the next landing. Just as they reached it, Mala pushed Will against a wall as a bolt of lightning streaked through the window and blackened the stone beside them.

"Stay low!" Mala screamed as she dove onto the floor. "Electromancer!"

She belly-crawled beneath the window to the stairs, jumped to her feet, and began climbing again. When Will passed the window, he couldn't help glancing outside. He saw a cloaked figure hovering like a mosquito beside the titan's head. Sparks crackled in the air, followed by twin bolts of lightning that shot down from the clouds, flowed through the mage's outstretched arms, and missed Will by inches. He was unsure how much the bolts of lightning were magic-infused, as opposed to a pure natural phenomenon, and whether the sword could stop them. He didn't want to have to test it out. He could feel the heat from the blast as he dashed up the stairs behind Mala, crouching behind his shield as he ran.

Boom.

Boom.

All of a sudden, the pounding of the titan's footsteps ceased. Will had a surge of hope when he saw the staircase had ended.

They had reached the top of the tower.

"It's here!" Mala cried, pulling him out of the landing just before a blast of lightning arced up the stairs and struck the ceiling. The electromancer must have flown through the window in pursuit.

Without a backward glance, Will took in the top of the tower, a hexagonal stone room with no windows and a hole in the middle of the ceiling protected by a glass window. *Some sort of retrofitted wizard's chute*. In the center of all six walls, except the one with the stairs, was a doorway framed in azantite, with a familiar bluish-white substance filling the center.

Spirit mage portals.

"Which one do we take?" Will shouted. He could feel the energy gathering in the air behind him, another bout of deadly electricity about to be unleashed. A looming mass of shaggy beard and icicles appeared above the window in the ceiling, blotting out the sky, just as a cloaked figure flew up and out of the staircase and into the landing, a pale woman with haughty eyes and bolts of lightning in her hands.

"This one," Mala said, grabbing Will's arm and pulling him through the nearest portal as the wizardess threw the lightning.

-12-

Caleb reached for the translucent image of his older brother, trying to pull him out of the shimmering pool of liquid in which he was submerged waist-deep. Caleb realized the silvery-blue substance in the basin had more viscosity to it than water, and that it did not cling to Val's body.

"Not like that," Val's faraway voice said, when Caleb's hands passed right through him. "Concentrate with your mind. You have to *want* me to come through."

Caleb tried to do as Val said, willing his brother to be there with him. Almost at once, Val assumed solid form. Behind him, the three-dimensional image of the pool remained in place, hovering in front of the boulder.

As Caleb embraced his older brother, his presence and familiar smell evoked a lifetime of memories from a world Caleb had all but forgotten in recent months. While the two brothers had very different personalities and often clashed, especially since their father had died and Val felt responsible for raising his younger brothers, the two loved one another deeply. Caleb harbored a deep respect for Val's determination and accomplishments, especially since Caleb struggled in those areas.

"I wasn't sure I'd ever seen you again," Caleb said.

Val grinned. "I'd say the same to you. Let's make sure one of us isn't a ruse or a double. What's my favorite cocktail at the House of Spirits?"

"Boulevardier, Four Roses bourbon, twist of orange. But you drink red wine unless you're having a bad day, or you're in the mood to party. With a preference for Paso Robles Cabs and Washington Shiraz."

"Passed with flying colors."

"And that time Will and I drove all the way to New York to visit you?" Caleb asked. "Where did we meet when we arrived?"

"On the New Jersey turnpike, after the Honda Civic broke down and I had to come get you."

"I guess it's really us."

"I guess it is."

A crowd had gathered behind Caleb. Yasmina rushed forward to embrace Val, and after they parted, Lance stepped up to give him a firm handshake.

Val was stunned to see Lance. "I didn't know you were on Urfe again. What happened? How did you get here?"

"Salomon brought me."

"*Salomon*?"

"I saw him in New Orleans and ran him down. He gave me another of those . . . keys . . . and since I didn't have much else going on, I decided to use it. When I stuck it in the door of my apartment, it brought me to Freetown. I guess the rest is history."

"Playing games again," Val muttered, his eyes narrowing. "I know about your injury and your career. I'm sorry. I made sure you got to the hospital that night, then flew straight to New York. I had to try to help my brothers."

"It's fine," Lance said. "Thanks for doing what you could." With a nod, the former soldier crossed his arms and joined Yasmina behind Caleb.

"Who is this mage?" Tamás asked, striding through the crowd with a hand on his sword. "Where has he come from?"

Caleb turned and held out a palm. "It's my brother."

Tamás stilled, his face darkening. "The one rumored to be a spirit mage? We can't allow—"

"I'll handle it," Caleb said sharply.

Tamás stopped moving, his hand still grasping his weapon, looking from Caleb to Val with a grim expression. The Prophet, standing at the entrance to his tent, calmly watched the events unfold. By now, everyone had heard Yasmina's story of how she had arrived, and that the eldest Blackwood brother had joined the Congregation and helped Lord Alistair retrieve the Coffer.

Caleb turned back to Val. His brother did not look much different from the first day they had landed on Urfe, when they had found the stash of clothes in Salomon's Pad and scurried down Magazine Street to the Minotaur's Den. Val was still carrying their father's staff, still had the same trim haircut, and was wearing similar clothes to that day: dark wool pants and a high-collared white shirt beneath a traveling cloak of soft lambskin. Looking closer, Caleb noticed two rings he had never seen before: a silver signet ring on Val's left hand, and a bluish-white ring on his right.

"That weird basin is still behind you," Caleb said. "What does that mean?"

"It's called the Pool of Souls, and it's waiting for me to return. I tried to reach you through it once before, in Freetown, and the effort landed me in Wizard's Prison."

"It won't do so again?"

"I have permission this time."

Caleb's mouth tightened as he absorbed the import of his brother's words. "Can other wizards come through?"

"Only if you accept them, as you did me. But there's no one else waiting."

Caleb peered intently into the pool but saw no sign of life in the shimmery depths. "So it's true you joined the Congregation?"

"It is."

"Then why should I trust a word you say?"

"Because it's me, Caleb. Your brother. I would never betray you, not for any prize in any world. I've come to do the opposite, in fact. I've come to save you."

A faint smile appeared on Caleb's lips. "Save me."

"I heard about what happened to your family. God, I'm so sorry. I wish . . . I just wish I could turn back time. I failed you. I wasn't there for you. I didn't do enough in the cemetery, I didn't get control of my magic soon enough, I . . ." Val swallowed hard. "None of this would have happened if I was stronger. Let me make it right, Caleb."

"Right?" Caleb said, with a snarl. "Make it *right*? This isn't a business negotiation. Can you bring the dead back to life, Val? Restore a heap of charred ashes to a pair of human beings that I loved more than life itself? Because that, my brother, is the only way you can make it *right*."

"I'm sorry. It was a poor choice of words." Val stepped forward with his hands out, as if to embrace him again. Caleb took a step back, out of reach, and Val's hands slowly dropped. "I won't attempt to speak to your pain or their memory. Just know that, as your brother, I would do anything, *anything*, to make it better."

Caleb stood rigid. "Then join us. Help me kill the monster who gave the order."

"There was no order," Val said gently. "No one meant for that to happen.

Things spiraled out of control, and Alistair had no idea your wife and adopted son had been killed."

"What are you talking about?" Caleb said with a snarl. "The electromancer came right to me. He was after the Coffer. He killed four guards and then my family."

"That was never supposed to happen. That mage was out of line and took matters into his own hands."

"Out of line? *You think*?"

"I promise you he didn't want your family to die."

"I promise you he did!" Caleb roared.

He took a step forward, fists clenched, and Lance took him by the elbow. "Just calm down, buddy. Remember who this is. Hear him out."

"He's a member of the Congregation," Tamás said. "He's extremely dangerous and not to be trusted."

Caleb shrugged out of Lance's grasp and turned to the crowd. "Get back! All of you! I'll speak to my brother alone!"

Tamás reluctantly obeyed, and Lance moved the crowd back fifty feet, giving Caleb and Val space. Yasmina gripped Caleb's hand before she left, and the Brewer gave him a sympathetic look.

Once Caleb was alone with Val, he said, "Why are you here? What do you want?"

"Only to help. I came to send you home."

"Home? Where is home? It's not Earth any more. For me, home is where my wife and son are."

Val's hand strayed to his silver signet ring, and a conflicted expression creased his brow. "I have someone to think of now, too. A fiancé and an unborn child."

"I didn't know that."

"I haven't told anyone. Her name is Adaira, and I just found out about the child."

Caleb pressed his lips together. "I'm happy for you. So you understand, then, why I'm doing what I'm doing."

"My heart is breaking for you, Caleb. But getting yourself killed will serve no purpose. It will not honor their memory. Worse, you're leading all these people into certain death."

"I didn't tell them to come."

"Doesn't matter. They're following you. They think you're their savior."

"I've told them I'm not. Over and over. I'm not responsible for their choices."

"You keep telling yourself that," Val said.

"Are we done here?"

Val held his gaze for a long moment. "I'd heard the rumors, but . . . you've changed, Caleb."

"Seeing your wife and child murdered right in front of you has a tendency to affect people."

"Turn your newfound purpose in a new direction," Val urged. "Work for peace. Disperse this army and let me send you back to New Orleans."

Caleb's laugh was harsh. "You were never a gullible person, Val. In fact, you're the opposite. Your desire for power is clouding your vision. Do you really believe Alistair wants peace?"

"No," Val said after a moment. "I don't. He's intent on exploiting the resources of the Ninth, and maybe more than that. That's what countries do, Caleb. The United States expanded to the Pacific and made our country what it is. It's the way of the world. Things change. Empires rise and fall. You can't win this war. Let's not repeat the mistakes of the past and cause any more bloodshed. Surrender peacefully."

"That's what they told the Native Americans to do, and look what happened. They're slaughtering us already."

"The only slaughter I've seen was by the Black Sash gypsies. If you convince these people to stand down and take the Oaths, the Congregation will welcome them." Caleb snorted, and Val continued, "I've seen things, Caleb. I've seen what happens when prejudice and ignorance take hold. They used to kill wizards here for sport, just for being wizards. My fiancé was strung from a tree and almost murdered for using magic in a village—and that was after she healed a little boy about the same age as Luca."

"Don't use his name like that!" Caleb shouted.

"I'm sorry, but you need to hear it. Countless lives can be saved. More grief averted for mothers and fathers who will be hurting just like you, if you don't turn aside."

"You're living a lie, Val. A sanctimonious lie."

"And this little revenge mission of yours is selfish beyond belief. Can't you see that?"

"Leave."

Val took a step forward. "Blaming the Congregation for the ills of this world is not only foolish, it will get you killed. They'll massacre you."

"Then why haven't they yet?

"Because they're giving you a chance to call it off," Val said through clenched teeth. "That's why they sent me."

"You want to avert some bloodshed? Convince the Congregation to stop the death squads, clear the Fens, and offer the Roma and oath avoiders the citizenship and freedoms they deserve."

"I'll do my best, I really will. But that's out of my hands."

A breeze carried a whiff of ashes from the funeral pyre to Caleb's nostrils. To him it represented more blood spilled by the actions of the Congregation.

Friends he had lost that very night.

"I'm sorry I have to do this," Val said softly, when he turned back at Caleb. "You're my little brother, and I want you to always remember how much I love you."

"Do what?" Caleb said, as Val raised his palms and caused a cage made of blue-white bars of energy to manifest around his brother. Caleb gripped the bars and did not receive a shock, but when he tried to bend them, they felt as strong as iron.

"I'm taking you with me through the portal," Val said, "and then I'm sending you home."

Shouts arose as Caleb's body lifted a foot off the ground, still surrounded by the magical cage, and began to levitate towards Val. Without looking behind him, still staring at his brother, Caleb thrust a fist in the air and called Lance's name.

"It won't hurt you," Val said. "But there's no use resisting. We'll go through the portal together."

"You might want to rethink that plan," Caleb said.

"I wish that were an—"

"Look behind you."

Confused, Val turned and saw that a dozen mages had silently levitated through the darkness to land in a line behind him, cutting him off from the

Pool of Souls. The mages spread out, standing ten feet apart, with Branyn and Elaina in the middle. Caleb's magical prison stopped moving, and he heard the sound of booted feet and bristling weapons approaching from behind. He glanced back to see the paladins, marching in orderly rows of twenty under Lance's direction, form a phalanx beside the magical prison holding Caleb. The front row of paladins all had a distance weapon pointed directly at Val: spears, axes, bows and arrows.

"I don't know much about magic," Caleb said, "but I know you can't hold a spell and fight a battle at the same time. If you move me an inch closer to that portal, I'll order an attack from all sides. I've heard you're powerful now, but can you fight them all?"

"Don't do this, Caleb. Let me help you."

"I won't ask again."

With a snarl of frustration, Val made the cage disappear, dropping Caleb to his feet. "You don't know what you're doing."

"Where's the Coffer being held?"

"I have no idea."

Caleb did not think his brother was lying, but even if he was, Caleb wasn't going to force the information out of him. Instead he drew up tall and pointed a finger at the Pool of Souls. "Go back to your new friends. And when you arrive, tell Alistair I'm coming for him, with or without an army."

At a signal from Caleb, the mages standing in Val's way parted to let him through. Gripping his azantite staff, eying the impressive gathering of a hundred paladins standing to attention at the front of the army, Val slowly backed away. As he neared the shimmery basin, his form grew more and more transparent, and he locked eyes with Caleb until both pool and spirit mage dissolved into the night.

After Val returned through the portal, the mood in the camp turned exuberant. A Congregation mage had appeared right in their midst, and they had forced him to tuck his tail and flee. Not just any member of the Congregation, but a *spirit* mage. The most powerful of all wizards.

Caleb stalked to his tent by himself without saying a word to anyone, while most of the others began talking excitedly in small groups. Some of the Devla began to sing and dance and celebrate. It was a marked change of tone from the funeral pyre that had stained the sky earlier that same night.

During the commotion, one of the Devla worshippers, a man who had spoken to no one that evening, strode to the edge of camp with his face tucked deep into the cowl of his robe. Once no one was looking, he stepped past the string of glow orbs and the geomancer wards and into the darkness of the hillside. As he walked, his form began to morph, his posture shortening and becoming more stooped, the flesh of his hands and his face now spotted with age, his eyebrows elongating until the hairs jutted out like broken springs.

"Well," Salomon remarked to himself, once the transformation was complete. "That was a curious turn of events."

He kept walking, noting the wisps of magic lingering in the air from the Pool of Souls. He pondered the appearance of Valjean and what it portended, as well as the absence of a spirit signature surrounding Caleb whenever he wore the cloak he had retrieved from the Coffer of Devla.

Would one of these children from another world, these three brothers whose lives he had followed so closely for so very long, unearth secrets of the multiverse that had eluded Salomon himself after two thousand years of effort? Even if they did it unwittingly?

Knowing as he did some small bit about how the gears of the multiverse worked, it would be a fitting, and not unexpected, irony.

Only time will tell, he mused. He had grown quite fond of these quite different siblings who threatened to upend the fabric of Urfe. In fact, he had observed them for so long he had almost come to think of them as his own sons. Was that perhaps the ultimate purpose of his quest? That instead of finding the answer to the mystery of his lost son, he would find a replacement? Three of them, in fact?

No.

One did not replace such things as a son, no matter how many eons passed. That much he knew.

Or perhaps, now that he had observed human affairs from afar for a thousand and more years, and pledged not to intervene except in the rarest of times, Salomon had become less of a human being and more like the Great Architect of the multiverse, who, like Salomon's son, Salomon had sought but never found.

Intriguing. Perhaps *that* was the purpose of his link to the Blackwood brothers. Perhaps *Salomon* was the guinea pig, and the three brothers his proving ground, and that if he grew powerful enough and passed whatever test was being given, then he would be granted his own world or multiverse and become an apprentice to the Great Architect, or even ascend to become one himself.

That last thought caused him to cackle out loud as he walked. *Mad, you've gone mad, old boy! Purely and truly raving insane!*

Realizing it was time to go, for he had somewhere else to be, the edges of Salomon's form blurred into a fine mist as he walked, turning a silver-blue color and becoming less and less substantial, until he had become a thing of pure spirit and was racing through unseen realms towards the stars.

-13-

Will thought he must be dreaming.

That, or he had died and gone to an afterworld designed by a madcap intergalactic committee led by Einstein, Gaudi, and Willie Wonka.

After blinking a few times, he realized he was awake and floating, or drifting—he wasn't really sure—through a multi-dimensional, polychromatic landscape that his mind had trouble absorbing. Surrounding him on all sides were all the colors of the rainbow, and a hundred thousand more, preserved in solid state as if light itself had been split into every conceivable hue and molded into the bridges, loops, pathways, spirals, tunnels, wormholes, archipelagos, honeycombs, grottoes, and other incredible shapes for which he had no name. There was no sky or ground, no up or down, no left or right—just polyhedral dimensions of color stitched into the fabric of reality.

"Oh my God," Will said, as a sense of awe overcame him, deeper and more profound than he had ever experienced.

"Perhaps, Will the Builder," Mala said from somewhere behind him. "Perhaps."

"Where are we? Did we die?"

"We're in the Place Between Worlds, and I feel as alive as I ever have. I suppose it's possible that we die here, only to be resurrected when we re-enter our world or another. You'd have to ask a philosopher that question, though I'd wager that whichever conclusion you draw for yourself is as good as another."

"Oh my God," he said again, causing her to laugh.

When he attempted to turn to see where she was, he realized he couldn't move his neck, or any part of his body. He started to worry until he saw her drift past him, turn, and cock her head.

"Coming, Will the Builder?"

"I can't seem to move."

"That's because you think you're still on Urfe. You move with your mind here, and not with your body."

He tried to do as she said, and *thought* about moving closer to her. Just as she had promised, he found himself drifting nearer. He concentrated harder, gained steam, and plowed right into her, sweeping her up by the waist and carrying her with him as he whooped in delight. "The Place Between Worlds?" he said.

"That's what the wizards call it. Do you see what looks like a cave mouth behind us?"

He turned and saw, scattered on the horizon, circles of darkness that were oddly one-dimensional. "Those flat discs that look like eclipses?" He kept turning and realized there were more of these objects, dozens of them, though they seemed quite far away.

"I don't know what those are," she said with a shiver, "except they feel dangerous."

"Yeah. I know what you mean. Just looking at them makes me feel uneasy."

"I meant that." She pointed to her left, at a semi-circular patch of darkness that indeed resembled a cave mouth, looming beneath a pink and fuchsia overhang a mere stone's throw away. Unlike the one-dimensional circles in the distance, the cave mouth had streaks of green and blue and brown, and he got the distinct impression it existed in multiple dimensions, though he couldn't say why.

"I see it," he said, turning in a lazy circle. "What is it?"

"Urfe."

He stared at the cave mouth beneath the overhang as the implications of her words sunk in. All around him, the bizarre dreamscape of the Place Between Worlds was riddled with similar formations. He saw them tucked beneath bridges and arches, clinging to the sides of spiral tunnels and wormholes, imbedded into the honeycombs and dunes and tessellations. They were everywhere, as far as he could see, each of the occluded openings dappled, speckled, or streaked with the same mindboggling array of hues as the landscape stretched out before him.

He said, "You mean if we go in there, we'll be . . . back?"

"You're a fast learner."

"So then all these other cave mouths . . . those are *worlds*? And we can go *inside* them?"

"Does the name of this place not speak for itself?"

"Um, yeah, I didn't think it was *that* literal."

"You truly did not know of such a place?"

When he realized she had posed a serious question, he laughed. "No. I didn't. How do you know so much about it?"

"Everyone on Urfe knows of it, or at least has heard the legend. As for me, I've been here once before."

His eyes widened. "When?"

"Do you remember when I battled the majitsu outside Zedock's stronghold?"

"I always wondered how you survived that."

"I couldn't beat him in a fair fight, so I used an amulet to transport us here. It was . . . an experience I'd rather not dwell upon. Suffice to say we entered a strange world—one I hope never to see again—where I found a way to kill the majitsu, return here, and re-enter Urfe."

"Kill a majitsu? How?"

"With the use of powerful and strange magic endemic to a world I don't profess to understand."

"I knew you'd seen most of Urfe, but this place—" he swept his arms in a circle, still overcome with wonder at what he was seeing, "makes you an interstellar adventuress."

"A what?"

He grinned and pulled her into a kiss. She didn't resist, and they sank into each other's arms, drifting through the phantasmagorical landscape. When he disengaged, reeling as always from her heady perfume that never seemed to lose its potency, he found her looking to the side with a wistful expression. In the past, he might have been bothered by her apparent indifference to the kiss, but now he knew that Mala was too complex to pigeonhole, and that while he loved her very much, his own moods no longer swung so wildly with every bat of her eye or teasing comment.

Somewhere along the way, he had discovered a confidence he had never known before, and that confidence extended to alluring and deadly mercenary babes.

"What is it?" he said, stroking her hair.

"Nothing," she murmured.

"It's something."

She laid her head against his chest as they spun in a slow looping circle. "I was just thinking of what my life might have been on another world, even yours perhaps, and whether there is a world . . ."

"Just like Urfe, but where things are different? Maybe even with another Mala?"

When she looked up at him, he saw through her dark smoky eyes and into the wilderness of her soul.

"You're a very perceptive person," she said.

"It's hard not to have those sorts of thoughts here." He hesitated, wondering if she was thinking about a lover on that other world she had mentioned. *I might have more confidence, but I haven't kicked the green-eyed monster to the curb.* "Were you talking about something specific? Or someone? Maybe it's better if we just get it out in the open. Is it Gunnar?"

Her face wrinkled in confusion. "Who?"

He blinked. "Uh, your former boy toy with the twenty-inch biceps who, I have to admit, turned out to be a really good guy?"

"What on Urfe are you talking about?"

He stared at her, uncomprehending.

After a moment, her expression slowly crumbled, and he saw a look of understanding riddled with pain that took him aback. "I'm sorry. I didn't mean to open—"

"It isn't Gunnar," she murmured. "That's another story . . . Will the Builder, I've never told you much about my past."

"That's the understatement of the century."

They were still drifting in a lazy orbit around the portal to Urfe, as if caught in a gravitational pull that applied only to the Place Between Worlds. Two specks of sentient dust inside a kaleidoscope with infinite patterns. It made him think about the physics of this place, why they were able to breathe and speak and how far they could travel if they tried.

"When I was a little girl, traveling through the Albion countryside with our caravan, we were attacked by a band of fighters led by majitsu. Though disguised as mercenaries, it was a gypsy extermination squad sent by the Congregation."

Will sucked in a breath. "How old were you?"

"Ten."

"Against majitsu? You would have . . ."

"Stood no chance? We didn't. I survived because my father hid me in a latrine. They slaughtered everyone else, my entire caravan, my family, like chattel."

"Mala, I'm so sorry—"

She held up a hand. "I'm not telling you to induce pity, nor will I accept it. But I want you to understand my motives."

"I'm listening," he said.

She told him of the leader of the majitsu, the giant one they called the Despiser, who took great pleasure in the killings, snapping her mother's spine and torturing her father to death as she watched. By the time she finished the awful tale, Will felt as if he might vomit. Mala was staring straight ahead, the emotions buried deep inside. He squeezed her hand and shuddered away his own horror, unable to conceive what seeing that would do to a child.

"The wretched Despiser still walks the face of Urfe. Not just walks, but commands the Order of Majitsu that protect the wizards of the Congregation. He is Head Don, Will, and worthy of the title. Some say he is as powerful as a full wizard, and I can attest to that fact. I saw him do things . . . no matter. Suffice to say he is a fearsome foe, and one I've sworn to destroy. It's the only goal I've ever had. You know where I stand on these matters. I do not work for causes or subscribe to foolish quests. But this is my fight. My destiny. To best this monster in battle or die trying. I've avoided him all my life, because to do otherwise would have been suicide."

At last Will understood. "The Sorcerer King's tomb . . . that's why you went with us. To find Magelasher."

"Aye."

"And now you have a chance to beat him."

"Kjeld might be so powerful that his Wizard Shield can withstand the lashes. I know not. But I'm duty bound to try."

"Duty bound? Don't be absurd. That's a repudiation of every principle you've ever espoused."

She whirled in his arms to separate them, furious. "What did you say?"

"You heard me," he said. "That's a very traumatic story, and thank you for confiding in me. I can't express how sad it makes me and how much I want to alleviate your pain. But don't you see? We all have principles, touchpoints, that make us want to be a hero. And you're right. Most of it is reckless pride. This is exactly the sort of thing you've always shunned, and if you continue chasing this monster, you'll be a starry-eyed fool like me, and it will probably get you killed."

"I see what you're trying to do," she said coldly. "The sentiment is appreciated."

"It's the truth."

"And I don't disagree. I'm as foolish as you are. I just thought you might have understood."

After a long moment, he pulled her closer, and she allowed him to hold her at arm's length. "I had to say it. And if you have to do this, then we'll be foolish together. I have a weapon that *will* overcome his Wizard Shield, and I'm making a vow right now to use Zariduke to the best of my ability, to help you avenge your parents."

"Don't make another ridiculous—"

"Did I stutter? Just like you, my foolish promises are my own to make and keep."

She glared at him, and then her mouth was pressing into his, kissing him long and deep and with more passion than ever before. Will lost himself in the kiss, adrift in a different sort of realm entirely, until he heard a high-pitched moan in the distance, like a teapot starting to boil. His eyes opened and he saw, approaching rapidly on their left, a fluttery shadow as long as a dragon in flight. The shadow had an amorphous shape that kept changing, as if responding to the hues of light in some mysterious way.

Mala disengaged and gripped him by the front of his shirt. "The astral wind . . . the wraith!"

"What?"

"Come! There's no time!"

She was already floating away, towards the cave mouth she said was Urfe, dragging him along. During their kiss, they had drifted further from the portal than he had realized.

The long shadow drifted closer. He worked on moving his body with his mind, though it was hard to concentrate through the fear. It was going to be close. The wraith was moving much faster than they were, but Mala was picking up speed, and Will did his best to help her. He unsheathed Zariduke, but she shouted at him to put it away and concentrate. He ignored her, not convinced it wouldn't help them.

The howling wind drew closer, faster than he would have thought possible. The keening whine hurt his ears. Stray gusts from the astral wind buffeted them forward, putting them closer to the portal, but when he looked back, he saw the Wraith riding the wind like a kite, gaining ground so fast he did not think they would make it in time.

"Faster!" he roared at Mala. "It's almost here!"

He had no idea what would happen if that thing touched him, but it couldn't be good. The portal to Urfe was twenty feet away, and he noticed from up close the "cave mouth" was a filmy opening that seemed less substantial than its surroundings, as if they could slip right into it.

Mala extended her hands as if flying. Will followed suit, and it helped him move faster. He looked back and saw the Wraith right behind him, one of its fluttery appendages just inches from his back.

The cave mouth was right in front of them, much bigger than it had appeared from a distance. It seemed to expand the closer they drew, as if it could hold anything and everything that went through.

Behind them, the astral wind screamed its fury, threatening to shatter his eardrums. He was no longer flying of his own accord but caught in the terrible gale, thankful it was propelling him in the right direction but knowing the wraith was moving even faster.

Just before they entered the portal, he looked back and saw one of the long coils of the wraith wrap around his ankle. He felt a hard tug and an icy pain worse than anything he had ever experienced, causing him to scream as he reached in vain for the cave-like entrance to Urfe.

The astral wind had died, but the shadowy appendage of the wraith wrapped tight around Will's ankle, pulling him back. He could feel its frigid touch sinking deeper into his calf, as if the wraith was somehow worming its way inside him. He looked back and saw in horror that where the bottom of his leg should be, he could only see the inky tendrils of the wraith.

Reacting on instinct, his sword arm reared back to take a swipe at the thing. He had to try something, even though Mala said it would have no effect.

"No, Will!" she said. "Reach out with your arms! You must reach the portal!"

Glancing back, he saw that she had stopped moving a few feet ahead of him, inches before the filmy cave mouth that led to Urfe.

He hesitated, his instincts screaming at him to attack the wraith.

"Please!" she said, flying back to grab him by the wrist. "You must trust me."

The wraith flowed deeper inside him, imparting a numbing sensation that terrified him even more than acute pain, as if he was being subsumed by the awful being. He sensed he had moments to decide what to do, one last decision to make—and the wrong choice would be deadly.

He hesitated a moment longer. He couldn't feel his body below the waist. Finally, instead of thrusting Zariduke at the otherworldly creature, he did as Mala asked and pointed his sword arm at the portal to Urfe, willing his body to move forward. The numbness caused by the wraith had spread to Will's chest, but he began to inch toward the portal again, and Mala pulled hard on his wrist. Together they passed through the filmy surface, and then he and Mala were lying on a sun-kissed wooden floor beneath a canopy of lush vegetation.

-14-

The morning after Val appeared through the Pool of Souls, Caleb was helping Tamás break down the administrative tent for the day's march. As they toiled in silence in the weak dawn light, before the mist had lifted, the Prophet appeared, his wheat-colored hair and beard more disheveled than usual.

"I've had a dream," he said, his voice breathless as he approached them. Although his eyelids drooped from lack of sleep, his irises gleamed with an intense light.

Caleb and Tamás exchanged a glance. Rarely did the Prophet exhibit any emotion other than supreme equanimity.

"A dream?" Caleb said. "Me too. Quite a few last night, and none of them very pleasant."

"Not just a dream." The Prophet raised his head to the sky. "A vision."

Tamás set down the tent pole he was holding. "What did you see?"

After a spell of feverish contemplation of the heavens, the Prophet fixed his gaze on Caleb. "Your brother is still alive. Though I'm sorry to say he is not in your home world as the unbeliever promised."

"What? You mean Will?"

"The wielder of Zariduke. I saw him quite clearly in the Place Between Worlds."

Caleb went back to taking down the tent. "So he was in your dream, too. Cool. Say hi to him next time."

Tamás gave Caleb a sharp glance. "The Place Between Worlds is not a metaphor for the dream world. It is a separate realm altogether."

"You've been there?"

"No, but—"

"Let me know when you have."

Tamás gripped his arm. "Seers, shamans, and spirit mages throughout history have reported its existence and described its contours."

The Prophet looked taken aback, as if Caleb's comments were shocking to him. "You truly do not know of the Place Between Worlds? Did you not travel through it to arrive on Urfe?"

"The first time we came, we touched a magic key to a door. For Act Two we jumped through a hoop of darkness."

"Mage portals. I suspect they, too, utilize the Place Between Worlds in some way or another. I know not. But your brother . . . he was indeed there, and he carries the sword born of spirit with him."

Tamás clenched his fists. "You saw Zariduke? You're sure of this?"

"To lie before Devla is a sin."

Caleb wanted to discount what he was hearing in the same way he always did, when it came to matters of faith. But on Urfe, it was undeniable that magic was real, and he knew firsthand that more than one world existed.

"Maybe he was on his way home to Earth," Caleb said.

The Prophet shook his head. "No. I saw them just outside the entrance to our world, though I sensed great danger."

"What kind of danger?"

"There are many perils in the Place Between Worlds. Chief among them the wraiths and the astral wind."

"Those don't sound good."

"Let us pray to Devla they will escape unscathed, so the sword can return to us once again. This must be the meaning of the vision—it is a sign from Devla!"

"Or a bad dream," Caleb muttered.

The Prophet switched to the paternal tone he used when offering Caleb advice, and which grated on Caleb's nerves. "I thought you should know. It might inspire the others to know the sword is on the way."

"I'll tell them when I see it for myself, and leave the hope and prayers to you."

"As you wish," the Prophet said with a submissive bow, before walking away. Caleb glared at his back as he left.

"If it's true," Tamás said to Caleb, as they continued taking down the tent, "the return of Zariduke and your brother from the clutches of the Congregation would inspire clans across the Realm."

"*If* the vision is true," Caleb said, "and *if* Will safely finds his way here. Like

I said, I'll believe it when I see it. And don't get too excited. Zariduke won't give us a chance against an army of Congregation wizards. We still have to find the Coffer. Come see me when our wild-haired friend has a dream about *that*."

The day's march saw Caleb's army leave the mud flats behind and enter a region of deep blue lakes, towering firs, and freestanding granite monoliths that rose above the landscape like sentinels set in place at the beginning of time.

A stiff wind with a frosty bite warned of winter days to come. After lunch, the army followed a footpath that wove around a series of small lakes and through forests strewn with pine straw. Though easy to navigate, the path was only wide enough to march three or four abreast. As the line snaked forward, Caleb knew it would be a race to reach the southern climes before the snows caught them once again. Maybe they wouldn't be trapped on a high mountain pass, but they would be marching through wintry conditions while short on supplies, shelter, and food.

After the midday break, the trail narrowed even further as it led between two thimble-shaped granite outcroppings that stood so close together it seemed from a distance as if they were one giant thumb. On either side of the trail, a slope covered in evergreens pitched sharply upwards.

They were forced to proceed two at a time between the giant rock formations. Caleb and Branyn led the way, followed by Tamás and Yasmina, then Lance and the Brewer. A contingent of paladins came next, and another contingent guarded the rear flank with a trio of mages. At Lisha's request, she and the darvish traveled at the rear of the army. Though no complaints were voiced, Caleb suspected her warriors did not feel comfortable interacting with surface dwellers, and he agreed it was best to cut off tensions before they arose.

If I were a monster or a mountain troll chieftain, Caleb thought, *I would choose this exact spot for an ambush.*

He had sent Branyn on a scouting mission before they entered the pass, and Yasmina was carefully watching for signs of danger, but neither of those measures had protected them from the leeches, and they likewise failed to detect the indigenous woman standing alone in the center of the path as they rounded a bend.

Startled, Caleb put up a hand to halt the march, wary the woman's appearance signaled the presence of others nearby. On closer inspection, he noticed her eyes were completely white, and the edges of her body were shimmering and slightly blurred. The dappled light streaming through the trees did not seem to fall on her copper skin. Besides that, she was a beautiful young woman with straight black hair that fell to her waist, a hooked nose, and sharp cheekbones. Only a splotchy white burn scar on her right arm marred her comely figure.

"Hail, travelers," she said as they approached. She was barefoot and wrapped in a vermilion cotton shawl that did not seem warm enough for the clime. "You need not fear me."

"That wasn't really on my mind," Caleb said, though her cold, confident smile in response unnerved him. "We're just passing through this land. I'm Caleb, and—"

"I know who you are, Caleb Gideon Blackwood, and what you represent."

A chill ran down his arm. No one had called him by his full name for years. "How do you know my name? Did Val send you?"

"I know many things. I am Nicill, keeper of the energies and shaman to the Cahuilla people."

Beside him, Branyn sucked in a breath, and Caleb heard Tamás gasp. "You know of her?" Caleb asked them, too low for the woman to hear.

"The Cahuilla shaman is a legendary figure, rumored to have all sorts of mystical abilities," Branyn whispered back. "Their ancestral homeland is far to the south. I've never heard of one, or any of their tribe, appearing this far north."

"Are we in danger?"

"The Cahuilla are known as a peaceful tribe, though a shaman . . . I suppose it depends on why she is here."

"I am not *a* shaman, but *the* shaman, successor to the one who came before me and herald of the one who will follow. And my intentions this day are indeed peaceful."

Caleb had no idea how she could have heard their whispered discussion from so far away. "Why are you here? Are you alone?"

"My people are in grave danger. We know of the Congregation airships and their plans to subdue our lands. We also know of your quest and the opening of the Coffer. It is perhaps the only hope for our people, however small."

Does everybody and their sister know about our mission?

"After consulting the energies and communing with the One Soul," she continued, "I've come to believe it is our duty to guide you on your journey to the Great River. While our territory is now but a shadow of the past, our ancestral routes once extended from this land of stone towers, which we know as the Garden of the Gods, all the way to the Great River."

"Garden of the Gods? Didn't you just say there was only one soul?"

The hint of a smile appeared on her stoic expression. "There is one soul, and many gods, as it has always been and always will be."

"Listen, we appreciate your offer, but could you be a little clearer? Are you going to guide us, or give us a map?"

"Not I, but those I have sent. I needed to judge your intention before I called them."

"And?"

Nicill's body began to shimmer and blur, not just at the edges but all over. When she spoke, her voice sounded faraway, filtered through space and time. "Farewell, Caleb Gideon. May your troubled spirit find rest one day."

As the shaman disappeared, indigenous people began slipping like phantoms out of the fir trees on both sides of the steep slopes. When not in battle, Caleb's diamond-headed mace hung from a strap attached to his belt. He reached beneath his cloak to grip the handle of his weapon when he saw that the Cahuilla were carrying bows and arrows, axes, and small clubs—though as far as he could tell, the newcomers numbered less than thirty, and their weapons were sheathed.

He removed his hand from his weapon, knowing Branyn and the other mages could take defensive action as needed. "Yasmina," he said without turning, "how'd they get here without you knowing?"

"Either the shaman brought them, or they're better at woodcraft than I. Perhaps both."

"Tamás? Lance? Brewer?"

"As I said, the Cahuilla are known as a peaceful tribe," Tamás said. "Though they will defend themselves as needed."

Lance grunted. "Be prepared, but don't escalate unless you need to."

"All you need is love," the Brewer sang.

The corners of Caleb's lips upturned at that last comment, and he called out to the nearest Cahuilla, a lean man almost as tall as Caleb with nut brown skin, a long face creased by the elements, and an eye patch over his left eye. Deerskin clothing and fur-lined boots helped protect him from the cold.

"Hail, leader of the Devlan Crusade," the man replied in heavily accented English.

The Devlan Crusade? Is that what they're calling us? "Hail right back at you," Caleb said. "And it's not a crusade. It's a mission of justice."

"As you wish," the man said, with a tip of his head.

Secure in his cloak and bracers, carrying his mace at his side, Caleb walked out alone to greet him, offering a hand clasp. The other Cahuilla stayed back as the two met, just off the forest path.

"My name is Naxan," the Cahuilla said, accepting Caleb's gesture.

"Caleb."

"The shaman asked us to guide you to the Great River. Will you accept our offer?"

"Hell yes."

"I am pleased to hear that. We are thirty in total, and at your service. You head south, towards the Cahuilla lands past the mountains, and then you will venture east?"

"That's right."

"And speed is desirable?"

"I can taste the snow on the air."

Naxan tipped his head again, then whistled to his followers in a birdsong cadence, causing them to file onto the path behind him. "Come. We know the fastest ways through."

Over the next three days, the Cahuilla impressed everyone with their knowledge of trails and woodcraft. Led by Naxan, they veered onto overgrown, barely visible footpaths that cut through dense swaths of forest; navigated hills and ridges that seemed impassable; and even led the army down a steep gorge to follow a rushing river for half a day, cleaving miles off the journey. They were expert trackers and hunters, and helped teach the Roma warriors, who knew the land well themselves, how to better feed the troops from the forest. When Naxan learned that Yasmina was a wilder, Caleb saw him bow in deep respect, and the two could often be seen together at the front of the march, deep in conversation.

Along the way a curious thing happened. More and more people began to trickle in and join them, sometimes from the towns and villages and homesteads the army passed, and sometimes travelers who had ridden great distances to seek them out. They were farmers, wanderers, Devla converts, Roma from the clans who lived nearby. Even a few renegade mages trickled in. Somehow, word of Caleb's army had spread throughout the Ninth, a spark of light in the darkness. By now, everyone knew of the Death Squads and the Congregation airships, and had either gone into hiding or decided to march to New Victoria to fight for their freedom.

At first, Caleb didn't understand it. He understood his own motives; he had nothing left except revenge. But gradually, as he talked to more and more of the new arrivals, each of whom had a horror story about the suffering they had endured, their own version of the raid on Freetown, he understood they had all lost hope and desperately wanted something to believe in. With nothing left to lose but their lives, they had decided to place their faith in the intervention of Devla.

More specifically, they had placed their faith in *him*.

It made him increasingly uncomfortable. Each night the worship service grew larger and larger, converted more and more believers. Every time the Prophet proclaimed that Caleb was the appointed agent of Devla on Urfe, a roar of approval rose from the crowd, and Caleb wanted to scream in frustration from inside his tent. Sometimes he did it right in front of them. Yet nothing deterred them. He grew to realize that, ironically, the faith of his followers in his leadership had nothing to do with him at all. It was like being in love, he thought. The people we choose to love often don't deserve it or return it; and that has no bearing on the fact that we're in love.

A responsible lover lets them go gently, he told himself.

Something I've never been.

But why, he shouted in his mind every night as he closed his eyes to sleep.

Why did that stupid Coffer open for the most unworthy person who has ever lived?

* * *

Caleb couldn't sleep that night. As the camp started to quiet, he decided to sit cross-legged around the dying bonfire and absorb the stars. When he and Marguerite had traveled the Ninth together, she had loved to stroke his hair and make him chuckle by inventing her own constellations and myths to explain the absurdities of the cosmos. *You see that one up there, Caleb? That there is the grandma pushing the oxcart off a cliff, though I suppose if you're on the other side of the world, she's pushing it* up *the cliff. So which is it? Methinks it's both, of course! That's the meaning of the world, a grandma going up and down a cliff with an oxcart!*

And she would laugh, and wipe her eyes at her own joke, and tuck her warm body more tightly into his.

With a snarl, he snapped a stick in half and threw it into the fire.

"Caleb?" Yasmina said, startling him. She could move as quietly as the Cahuilla, even through the crowded camp.

"Yeah?"

"Want some company?"

She put a hand on his shoulder. It felt so nice and warm and human. He closed his eyes and, for a moment, imagined it was Marguerite's hand, and they were in the Blackwood Forest once again, and Luca was sleeping peacefully beside them, and the universe had not yet imploded. He wanted to give in to the feeling and invite Yasmina into his tent.

"I was just going to bed," he said as he rose, causing her hand to fall away. "I'll see you tomorrow."

"Dream well," she said softly.

Caleb's inner circle had begun holding a morning briefing session in the administrative tent to prepare for the day. Just before dawn the next morning, when Caleb was the last to arrive as usual, the entire inner circle was there: Tamás, Yasmina, the Brewer, Lance, Branyn, Elaina, and the Prophet. Naxan had joined them as well.

"How long before it snows?" Caleb said roughly as he swept into the cozy confines of the tent. He blew into his hands to warm them and noted the frosty exhalations in the air.

Yasmina and Naxan exchanged a glance. "Days," the Cahuilla warrior said.

"And once it starts, how long before we slog through it and reach your homeland?"

"A month. Maybe more."

"And how long from there?"

"To the Great River? At least another month, perhaps two, depending on conditions and how often we must take a side route to avoid the hill troll tribes."

A few days ago, Caleb had asked why there were not more indigenous tribes like the Cahuilla in the Ninth Protectorate. Naxan had told him that many had been slaughtered in the troll wars centuries earlier, that many had moved east, and that the few who remained did their best to avoid contact with outsiders.

"So we're looking at a minimum of two months, and more likely three or four? With no guarantee we won't run into major problems or lose half our people on the way? That isn't good enough. There has to be another way."

"Another way?" Tamás said. "What do you mean?"

"I mean Urfe is full of magic and miracles and flying giant birds and . . . I have to believe there's a better way for us to reach New Victoria. A portal or something. A magical conveyor belt."

"No portal is large enough to hold an army," Branyn said gently. "Not even an elder spirit mage could transport as many as we are now."

"What's the latest count?"

"Four thousand," the Prophet said. "Praise be to Devla."

"It doesn't do us any good if we're stuck in the Ninth Protectorate. Can we steal an airship?"

Tamás snorted a laugh, saw that Caleb was serious, and then frowned.

"There is something," Naxan said slowly. "A legend among my people."

"What kind of legend?" Caleb said.

"That of a forest which exists in a world parallel to our own. It's said to appear only if the proper rites are invoked during a full moon."

"There's a full moon tonight," the Brewer said. "But I don't understand. A disappearing forest? How does that help us?"

"According to legend, this place—*Temmenily Ayawet*, or Forest of the Moon Dead—not just appears, but can be entered. *Temmenily Ayawet* is very dangerous, a domain of madness and wayward spirits, but it's said that if one enters the forest and manages to return, one will emerge in a different place from where one entered."

"A different place? What do you mean? Where?"

"Of that I'm unsure."

"Even if the legend were true, we could end up further from New Victoria than where we started. It could be halfway across the world."

Naxan hung his head as if ashamed. "I am sorry I do not possess more knowledge. It is only a legend. As far as I know, no one alive has entered *Temmenily Ayawet*."

"Thank you for bringing it up," Tamás said, in a tone that signaled the matter was closed. "Now let's discuss the terrain we might encounter today, and the food supply—"

"What about the shaman?" Caleb said, taking a step towards the Cahuilla warrior. "Does she know anything more about this place?"

Naxan shrugged his shoulders. "If anyone does, it is she."

"Are you able to contact her?"

He hesitated. "We've been instructed to invoke her spirit only if we are under duress or have a pressing need."

"Then do it."

"I . . . as you wish. When would you like to reach her?"

"Right now."

Feeble morning light seeped through the trees, illuminating the mist saturating the valley in which the army had set camp. Caleb inhaled the loamy smell of the forest as he watched Naxan carefully extract an object resembling a silver bird's egg out of the pouch at his side. The rest of the inner circle had joined them in the copse of evergreens at the edge of camp, still inside the wards.

Naxan held the egg at arm's length and crushed it. Instead of releasing a yolk, it crumbled into a silver powder that hovered in midair, swirling and eddying in the mist. Soon the fine particles began to spread out and coalesce into the outline of a head and torso. The bottom half remained a funnel of silver powder, like a genie half-escaped from its bottle, as the top portion assumed the contours of a woman's breasts and narrow waist, followed by the facial features of the Cahuilla shaman.

"You have summoned me from my sleep," she said, in a voice filtered through the ether.

Naxan's eyes slipped downward, as if embarrassed by her nakedness. "I am deeply sorry, *Ni-ye*."

"Look at me. Do not be ashamed." When he raised his eyes, she continued, "Are you in peril?"

"No, *Ni-ye*."

"Then what do you desire? Knowledge?"

"Yes."

"Speak to me."

Naxan told her about the conversation in the tent, and Caleb's desire to reach New Victoria more swiftly. Except for faint shifts with the breeze, the silver outline of her figure remained unmoving throughout the narrative.

"*Temmenily Ayawet*," she said at last.

"Is it real?" Caleb asked.

Naxan looked shocked by the interruption, but when his shaman turned to respond directly to Caleb, the Cahuilla leader stepped back in deference.

"It is real," she said. "Though I have never traveled there myself."

"Then how do you know?"

"Because I am *Ni-ye*. I am imbued with the knowledge of my forebear, and the one who came before her, and every *Ni-ye* and *Ne-na* since the beginning of our people."

"I guess I'll have to take your word on that. So it's true we can move faster through this moon forest?"

"You cannot move faster, but you can reach a destination more quickly. My knowledge is limited. I know that *Temmenily Ayawet* can appear in many different places, because we have summoned it from across the ancestral lands. How far its dominion extends, I know not. Yet always, without fail, when one enters *Temmenily Ayawet*, one leaves from a different place, often far from where one began."

"How does it work? Is it another dimension? A worm hole kind of thing?"

"I am unfamiliar with those terms, and I know not why or how things are as they are in this place. I know only that our reality does not exist in the same way in *Temmenily Ayawet*."

"I've got some experience with those sorts of places. Is there a choice in the matter?"

"What do you mean?"

"I mean where you end up."

"This place once belonged to a living deity, a goddess who roamed the lands on which we stand and loved the people who inhabited them. It is said the goddess appears to some who venture to *Temmenily Ayawet*, and grants desires, though no Cahuilla shaman has ever met her. Or perhaps the memories are shielded from me."

"Is she a good living goddess or an evil one?"

"She belonged to a people who lived and died long, long before the Cahuilla planted their first crop. Except for the ritual and the legend of *Temmenily Ayawet*, no knowledge of the goddess or her people remain."

Caleb did not understand any of this, and he asked more questions the shaman was unable to answer. The Prophet observed the conversation with a small and infuriating smile, as if to say, *Do you see, Caleb? It is not so hard to believe.*

When the shaman's form began to shimmer, Caleb knew their time was drawing short.

"How many of those silver eggs do you have?" he asked Naxan.

"Two more."

"I assume they're pretty hard to make?"

"They were given to us by *Ni-ye*."

Cale turned to the shimmery form of the shaman. "I want to try the ritual. Tonight. Can you help?"

"If this is your desire."

"What do we need to do?"

Before the silver powder dissipated into mist, the shaman issued a very precise set of instructions. Caleb made sure to remember every word.

Many hours later, long after the moon had risen, Caleb stood knee-deep in a forest stream they had found near the end of the day's march, holding his boots in one hand and a live dove in the other. The water moved swift and pure across the bottom of his cloak, though the ensorcelled garment repelled the water and kept him dry, except for his bare feet.

Surely this is supposed to be a summer ritual.

Beside him, the Brewer stood on a flat-topped boulder, ready to play his part. According to the lore of *Temmenily Ayawet*, a single person was supposed to sacrifice the dove and complete the ritual, and it could take months to perfect the right tone and words to the ancient song of summoning. When the full moon was high in the sky, the Cahuilla shaman was supposed to appear and guide Caleb through the song. Since the shaman could only appear in spirit form, and the Brewer had perfect pitch, and Caleb couldn't hold a note, they had decided to attempt the ritual together, unsure if the improvisation would work. They had little choice in the matter unless Caleb wanted to let the Brewer go it alone, which he wasn't about to do. This was his wild idea, and Caleb wasn't going to put his friend in danger without standing by his side.

The little stream was only ten feet wide. According to the ancient ritual, the banks had been cleared of brush on either side to form a perfect square. On each of the four corners, a fire burned inside a cairn of stacked stones. The most tedious part of all had been arranging sticks from the forest into five strange symbols on both sides, over and over in repeating patterns atop the soil, which the shaman had inscribed for them in the air with the silver powder from the crushed egg. The Brewer said the symbols reminded him of the wedge-shaped cuneiform that formed the notes to the magical song inscribed on the ancient Mesopotamian tablet that had transported him to Urfe long ago.

Beyond the borders of the square, the rest of the army crowded in to observe the events. By this time, everyone knew what Caleb was attempting, and a few people had left the camp, afraid of being killed or trapped forever in the Forest of the Moon Dead. Yet the vast majority had stayed, trusting Caleb and the Prophet in this as in everything else.

As usual, Caleb's friends and closest supporters were at the front of the group. He caught Tamás's eye, and then the Prophet's. Yasmina folded her hands in front of her chest, prayerlike, to convey her support. Lance took his place at the head of the paladins, and Lisha stood next to the commander of the darvish warriors.

The dove squirmed in Caleb hands, and he held it tighter, uncomfortable with the requirement of a sacrifice. Not only did he consider it barbaric, but Old Caleb believed so deeply in pacifism that he had avoided killing insects. Also, standing in the stream made him think of Marguerite and the day of their wedding. She, too, had revered all life, and would frown at what he was doing for her sake.

The forest was thick and dark around them, alive with the sounds of the night, sentient and watching. Caleb looked up in time to see the last of the cloud bank covering the full moon slip aside to reveal its gleaming bauble. It must have been a supermoon, because it seemed twice as large as normal, dominating the sky like a fat grey eye peering down on the stream and the puny humans far beneath it.

"You ready for this?" Caleb said to the Brewer, as the shaman materialized in front of them.

"I was born ready, kid."

"That's my man."

"Actually, I feel more nervous than my first time onstage. Hopefully I won't vomit this time. You?"

"Just another day at the office," Caleb said grimly.

Like the first time she had appeared, on the path between the rock formations, the shaman looked almost human except for the shimmery, indistinct edges of her form. She observed the preparations they had made, then gave a satisfied nod. "All appears to be in order. Which one of you will complete the ritual?"

"We both will," Caleb said. "We did everything you asked, except my friend is going to sing."

She turned to regard the older man. "Very well, if this is your choice."

"Oh," Caleb said, as he released the dove into the air, watching the poor creature's wings beat in a frantic rhythm as it sought the freedom of the sky, "and screw it. I'm not going to kill the bird."

"Good for you, kid," the Brewer murmured.

"I know not the effect your unorthodox choices will have on the ritual," the shaman said.

"Duly noted," Caleb said. "Now let's rock."

After meeting his gaze with a neutral expression, the shaman bowed her head, folded her arms across her chest, and began to sing. The words were in a language unfamiliar to Caleb, though he knew it was not Cahuilla. These sounds came from deeper in the shaman's throat, more guttural, more ancient.

Every few seconds, whenever there seemed to be a natural pause, she would stop to let the Brewer parrot her words. Caleb listened in awe as his friend mimicked every sound in perfect pitch, his deep baritone ringing through the forest. Even Caleb began to recognize the same words and phrases repeated over and over, and as the Brewer gained confidence, the shaman sang faster. They sang together for a long while, until Caleb began to lose track of time and wondered how long they could keep this up. As the stream gurgled at his feet, he realized the fires in the four corners of the square were blazing far higher than they should have been, halfway up the trees, and the stick symbols on the ground were now glowing bright orange to match the flames. Stunned, Caleb realized the shaman had disappeared, and that the Brewer had stopped singing.

As the fires subsided, and the blazing symbols on the ground returned to being normal sticks, Caleb realized that *everything* around him had changed.

"Uh, kid?" the Brewer said, looking around at the eerie, unfamiliar forest.

"Yeah?"

"Where are we, and what happened to your army?"

-15-

After Val described his meeting with Caleb to the mages and luminaries gathered at Lord Alistair's mansion in the Garden District, a combination of the War Council and Alistair's most trusted advisors, Val fielded questions from around the long table.

"How many mages were present?" asked Kalyn Tern.

"I saw at least a dozen," Val said.

The aeromancer gave a contemptuous sniff. "A dozen?"

"There might have been more."

"Were you not tasked to find out?"

"I didn't get the chance. As I said, things happened quickly."

"Or maybe you didn't try hard enough," said Braden Shankstone. "He is your brother, after all."

"Yes, he is," Val said evenly. "I assure you that did not affect my efforts."

Braden stood, set his palms on the table, and leaned forward. "How could it not?"

"Don't be foolish," Val said, tired of the cuerpomancer's insinuations. "I *want* to send him home."

"Then I'd have to think a Congregation spirit mage could accomplish a task as simple as that."

As Val bristled, Lord Alistair cut in. "You weren't there, Braden, and you heard his account. Are you questioning my decision to send him?"

The rebuke caused the cuerpomancer to utter a chagrined "No, milord," and sit down. After Lord Alistair turned away, Braden's eyes cut across the table to glare at Val.

The questions came rapid fire after that.

"How many warriors do you estimate were present in the camp?" asked Yasir Ookar, a reptilus whose genius for battle strategy had propelled him to First General of the Protectorate Army.

"Did you note any unusual spirit signatures?" Professor Azara chimed in.

"What about majitsu?" Kjeld Anarsson added in his booming baritone. "We've only had a handful of defectors over the last decade—disgruntled rejects all—and I'd love to round the lot of 'em up." He cracked his knuckles to emphasize the point.

"Did you see any evidence of intervention by foreign powers?" Alaina Whitehall asked. The common-born Governess of the Protectorate was a shrewd, powerful woman, and in Val's estimation, always asked astute questions.

"Was the Prophet with Caleb?"

"You saw a woman with red skin and horns? A *darvish*?"

Val patiently answered their questions for over an hour, relaying every detail of his brief visit. At last Lord Alistair held up a hand from the head of the table, quieting the room. "I've heard nothing in this narrative which gives me cause for concern. As we suspected, the Roma *army* is nothing more than a ragged collection of criminals, oath avoiders, and superstitious peasants. I cannot explain the presence of a darvish in their midst, nor do I care. In fact, the only thing which troubles me in the slightest is the potential for negative attention if this situation is not handled correctly."

After the meeting adjourned, Val strolled arm-in-arm with Adaira down St. Charles Avenue beneath a canopy of gnarled oaks dripping with Spanish moss. On both sides of the street, stone mansions loomed behind spiked iron fences and towering hedgerows. Val inhaled deeply, enjoying the saccharine aroma of decaying vegetation that always made him think of home.

Pairs of majitsu floating on both sides of the street accompanied Val and Adaira on their walk. The day was cool and misty. As was his custom, Val had chosen dark woolen pants, a white shirt, and brown leather riding boots; she, a casual silver-and-crimson outfit with a golden circlet in her hair.

"When did you tell him that you're pregnant?" Val said quietly.

She gave him a sharp look. "How did you know?"

"You weren't at the meeting. He would have invited you, in your own house, unless he was protecting you."

"You're so perceptive, my dear. I told him last night, after dinner. I was going to tell you this morning. I'm sorry I didn't discuss it with you first. My father and I were talking and it just . . . felt right."

Val tensed. "And?"

She stopped walking and frowned, which caused his heart to skip a beat, before curling her lips into a radiant smile and kissing him on the mouth. "He gave us his blessing, and wants to know the wedding date."

For a moment, Val had worried the next place he laid his head might have been on a cold azantite floor in wizard prison. "Who said anything about marriage?" he quipped, which earned him a playful smack on the cheek.

"I told him what we discussed, that we'd both feel more comfortable once Caleb is safe in your home world, and this unpleasant business is behind us."

Val's face darkened. He and Adaira had not had a chance to talk since his visit with his brother through the Pool of Souls, and he updated her on the encounter. She stayed quiet for an entire block, prompting him to stop in front of a manor with marble steps and beautiful stained-glass windows.

He put his arms around her waist. "You're worried I'll return to my own world."

Her hand strayed to her belly, barely swollen with child. "It's your brother. I know how much you love him."

"Yes, he's my brother, and yes, I love him very much. But you're my wife-to-be," he said, placing his hands atop hers, "and this is my son or daughter. I won't leave you, Adaira. Not for my home world or any other. Ever."

"Be wary of promises you won't keep."

"I never make them if I can't."

"Good," she whispered, and squeezed his hands.

He pulled away, both anxious and thoughtful. "Your instincts are right. I'm worried sick about Caleb. He's just . . . I've never seen him like this. Caleb doesn't like to swat flies, and now he's leading an army? He blames your father for what happened. The Congregation sent the airship to Freetown, and your father is the Chief Thaumaturge." He shook his head in anger. "Terrible things happen in war, and they'll happen to him if he doesn't stop what he's doing, no matter how much I try to protect him."

"What if he refuses to listen?" she said.

"Then I'll find a way to force him to go home."

"And if you can't?"

"I don't know," he said, starting down the street again with a troubled hunch to his shoulders. "I just don't know."

-16-

After plunging through the portal to Urfe in the Place Between Worlds, Will and Mala found themselves lying on a sun-kissed wooden floor beneath a canopy of lush vegetation. He realized they were in a treehouse with three-foot walls but no roof. A crow's nest in the forest.

Cringing, he whipped around but saw no sign of the astral wraith or the mind-bending colors and shapes of the Place Between Worlds. Instead he glimpsed a moody dusk sky through a mass of bougainvillea, wisteria, and tree branches looming twenty feet overhead.

Fearing the worst, he looked down in a daze, but found his legs intact and the pain gone. He was able to stand with no problem.

"While fatal in the Place Between Worlds," Mala said, "the dangers of an astral wraith do not translate to this plane. Or so I've read. Thank the Queen I have not had opportunity to test that particular bit of lore, but you seem to have confirmed it."

He released a shuddering breath. "What would have happened to me?"

"It's said the astral wraiths devour the souls of travelers. Seeing that you're uninjured, I suspect our minds or souls are fully present in the Place Between Worlds, but our physical form is just a projection."

"But how can that be? Our physical bodies moved from there to here."

"You would have to ask a spirit mage that question."

"It did feel like it was . . . devouring me. As if I would have ceased to be. And the wind? What was that?"

"The fabled astral wind, buffeter of souls. It flings travelers through the Place Between Worlds like leaves in a hurricane, to other dimensions or realms or universes. It's said those whom it catches never find their way home."

"Why did it slack off?"

"Who's to say? You now know as much as I about that place. Perhaps the dangers are sentient, and the wind believed the wraith had caught its prey.

Perhaps it was luck. I suspect we'll never know. Count your blessings we survived, as spirit mages prepare for years to navigate that realm."

Will paled. "You were pretty nonchalant about the whole thing."

"Since the portal to Urfe was so close, I admit I let my guard down. It was . . . unwise."

"Did you just admit you made a mistake?"

He didn't see the dagger until it was under his chin, pressing painfully upwards. "Tell anyone," she said, "and it will be the last secret you divulge."

He grabbed her wrist and pulled it away at the same time he leaned in to give her a kiss. She lowered the dagger and kissed him back, and he could see the edges of her lips upturned, smiling that mocking smile.

"It's good to be alive," he said when they parted, "but where are we?"

She peered over the side of the treehouse. "Home."

"You mean back on Urfe?"

"I mean *home*, or the closest thing I have in New Victoria."

He joined her in peering over the wall but could not see through the canopy. "You live in a treehouse?"

Laughing, she moved to the center of the structure and pressed hard with her foot on one of the planks, causing a trap door to spring open and reveal a rope ladder.

"Come," she said, stepping onto the first rung. "Close the door behind you."

Will marveled at the seamless construction of the trap door as he pulled on the handle to close it. He would never have noticed its existence, and he was pretty good at spotting hidden doors and seams.

The rope ladder led to a stout branch fifteen feet below the treetop perch. He realized they were climbing down an enormous live oak, perhaps the largest specimen he had ever seen. The long limbs stretched into the canopy like a petrified octopus, adorned with swaths of Spanish moss hanging like curtains throughout the tree. Using steps built onto the trunk, more rope ladders, and a series of smaller platforms, she led him down to the flat-topped roof of a house.

She spread a hand. "My jungle palace in the city."

Peering through the foliage, just a short distance away, he caught a glimpse of the spires of the Wizard District, catching his breath once again at their beauty and mystique. He wondered if Val was somewhere nearby.

"Where are we?" he said.

"The Live Oaks District. It borders the Thieves Quarter."

"Yeah . . . we don't have one of those back home. Or at least not an official one. How did we arrive here from the Place Between Worlds? I mean, I'm glad we didn't end up in a dragon's mouth, but it seems kind of convenient."

"If you concentrate on the place you seek, The Place Between Worlds will carry you to your heart's desire. I chose the safest place I could think of."

After she opened another trap door with her foot, he followed her down into an upstairs hallway. A collection of knickknacks from around the world decorated stone walls framed with timber. He admired a tapestry of knotted cords that looked Incan, a pair of crossed samurai swords, and a line of tribal masks. To his left, he glimpsed the open door of a bedroom.

Curious as to when she had acquired the place, and why she had never told him about it, he started to ask her when she silenced him with a sharp look and a raised finger.

"What is it?" he whispered, but she wagged her finger and motioned for him to follow. She led him down the hall away from the bedroom, past two closed doors and a tight staircase in the center that descended to the first floor. At the end of the corridor, a sunroom with an open window overlooked a clearing surrounded by dense vegetation. He marveled at how isolated her bungalow was, though he realized the isolation worked both ways in case of an intruder.

Then again, who would scare Mala?

She strode swiftly to the window and peered outside. The light was failing quickly, and the hum of insects had begun.

He stepped beside her, not liking the tenseness in her brow. "What is it?"

"I never leave the windows open."

"Are you sure? Not even if you run down to the—"

"*Never.*"

She turned to study the room, snarling as she picked up a hardbound book lying in an armchair. Will read the title over her shoulder.

Principal Flora and Fauna of New Albion.

"That's not even mine," she said. "Someone's been here."

Before he could respond, she drew her short sword and lifted her weighted sash off her belt, then crept soundlessly to the staircase and down to the first floor. He followed behind as quietly as he could, Zariduke in hand, his buckler shield at the ready.

The downstairs had a more open floor plan. A cozy sitting area spilled into a kitchen with windows overlooking the garden. To his left, a short hallway ended at a wooden door reinforced with iron bands.

"Could it be a neighbor?" Will asked. "Stopping by to check on the place?"

She crept towards the kitchen, taking everything in, searching every shadow. "No one knows I live here."

"Maybe Allira came back? Another friend?"

Her voice turned sharp. "I said no one." After a moment, she inhaled and said, "Do you smell that?"

He had never had a good nose. "Um, not really. It smells like . . . house?"

"It's a man's scent, only different. A little musky, almost like an animal." Her face paled, and she hurried to a standing wooden cabinet and threw open the doors. Inside was a dry larder stocked with dried fruit, bags of grains, strips of dried beef, and hard-rind cheeses. "Untouched," she whispered.

"What's that mean? I don't understand."

Her eyes flew to the window, and then she was racing outside, around the back of the house to a standalone brick structure the size of a walk-in closet. She tried the doorknob and cursed as it twisted, as if expecting it to be locked. As soon as the door opened, frigid air seeped out, plus a gamey smell that wrinkled his nose and reminded him of the time Lance had taken him rabbit hunting.

She opened the door wider, revealing a frost-rimed pantry with shelves stocked with vegetables, lard, and portions of uncooked meat such as sausage links and chicken legs. He wondered how the pantry stayed cold, guessing magic was involved. But what caught his eye was the line of hares hanging from hooks from the ceiling, their necks twisted at unnatural angles. They had not been skinned, and, except for the broken necks, were otherwise intact. He counted five in total. Mala was staring at the hares with a grim set to her mouth.

"I'm guessing those aren't yours," he said, backing away from the door and gripping Zariduke tighter.

"We might not have much time. Do you remember outside Takros's Keep, when I came to warn you about the dhampyr twins? How Nagiro came after me, and how I feared Ferala, his twin sister, was after the Coffer of Devla?"

He swallowed. "The half-woman, half-vampire assassin you told me about? I believe your exact words were 'she's the most efficient killer I've ever met?' Why would she be at your *house*?"

"Perhaps because I dueled with Nagiro, won, and turned him over to the Thieves Guild. The last I knew, he was their prisoner—with a very somber outlook on his future."

"His sister can't be happy about that."

"She must have tracked my scent here, waiting for me to return. From what I remember of her habits, Ferala sleeps most of the day, prefers to dine at dusk, and walks again at night. I don't know why she left, but she could return at any time. Those rabbits were fresh kills."

"So what do we do? What's the best way out of here?"

A rare moment of uncertainty creased Mala's brow. As she glanced into the canopy, and then back at her house, her jaw firmed, and she twirled her sash in her hand. "Ferala will never leave me in peace. You should go. Run into the city. I'll show you the way out. I'll have a better chance against her here, in my own home, than anywhere else. I doubt she's found all of my surprises."

"You can show me the way," he said, though when she started to point out a footpath leading into the vegetation, he grabbed her hand and said, "The way to where I need to stand and fight so I can help you."

After meeting his gaze with those unreadable eyes, she gripped his hand tight. "Here's what you need to know. Even without a weapon, a dhampyr is a fearsome opponent, more than our match in battle. But Ferala carries an ensorcelled dagger imbued with a poison whose touch is certain death. We have no hope to defeat her as long as she holds the dagger. She's far too fast."

"Is she like a vampire? Can she turn to smoke, hypnotize us, call upon the creatures of the night?"

"A dhampyr is a hybrid with no fear of sunlight. They can take the form of an avatar, and are marked by a spur on their left wrists. Beware Ferala's fangs and her spur, for they are dangerous indeed. She's also my equal in swordplay, and much faster and stronger than I. But most of all, we must account for the dagger."

They fled into the house as Mala concocted a plan on the fly. After pouring him a mug of ale, she disappeared up the stairs, and he returned to the garden to await Ferala's return. Mala said Ferala would see and smell him long before he saw her, and the only chance to catch her off guard was to feign nonchalance and distract her from Mala's unseen presence.

With a pit of fear opening in his stomach, Will sipped the mug of ale by the firepit as the sun sank beneath the tress, casting the garden into darkness and bringing a nip to the air. Minutes later, just as he realized he had never asked Mala about Ferala's avatar, he heard the flap of leathery wings, and a giant bat swooped into the garden by the silver light of the moon. The creature's five-foot wingspan dwarfed any bat Will had ever seen, and sent a shiver of fear whisking down his spine. Just before it hit the ground thirty feet away from him, right at the edge of the clearing, it made a seamless transformation into a tall and slender woman with clipped dark hair and sharp, haughty features.

"What are you doing here?" Ferala as she approached. She was wearing boots and swathed in black clothing made of silken material. Her orange eyes shone like hot coals in the darkness.

Will was backing away, and didn't have to feign his terror. "What are you . . . how did you . . ."

"Answer the question!"

"I'm a friend of Mala's. Her boyfriend. I just returned from a trip. She gave me a key."

Ferala had closed half the distance and was walking towards him in a focused manner, slow and sure, a predator stalking her prey. He caught a whiff of exotic spice wafting off her, clove and cinnamon, and found her cold beauty as seductive as it was deadly.

Seductive? Beauty? What is it with me and dangerous women?

She moved like a panther, sleek and powerful, as quiet as the night. He kept backing towards the door, stumbling to make sure Ferala paid attention to him and not the canopy of trees.

"There's no need to run," Ferala purred, showing the tips of her inch-long fangs. "You're a handsome lad. Why don't we have some fun before dinner?"

When Will reached a stone planter by the front door, he threw the mug of ale to the side and slid Zariduke out of its sheath. "I know what you are," he said, allowing his voice to tremble but holding his sword steady. "I know what you want."

A dagger with a wavy blade and a black hilt slid out of Ferala's sleeve. "A duel, is it? My favorite kind of play."

Just a few more steps.

Will wove Zariduke in a figure-eight pattern, a showy technique designed to buy time. Ferala's lips curled as she advanced, mocking his amateur defenses, the dagger held loosely at her side. He stopped weaving and pointed the blade at her. "A dagger against a broadsword?"

Her grin expanded, and she raised the blade higher, letting him appreciate the fine-edged steel. "A very special dagger. One that will—"

Without warning, the blade flew out of her hand and into the bushes, as if jerked by an unseen hand—or Mala's invisible lasso.

Ferala jumped back, staring at her hand in shock. "By the blood of—"

The dhampyr's words turned into a gurgle as her fingers clawed at her neck. Mala had repurposed the lasso as a strangling cord, as they had planned. Will sprang into action, thrusting Zariduke at Ferala's midsection and hoping for a killing blow. Just before the blade pierced her skin, the dhampyr jumped into the air and spun to the side like a twisting tornado, an incredible maneuver, and kicked him in the face. As he stumbled back, dazed by the powerful blow, she used the spur on her wrist to cut the invisible cord.

Ferala bared her fangs and drew another dagger out of her boot, whipping around to determine where the attack had come from. Seeing no one, she came for Will.

He watched her navel as Mala had taught him to do, ready to react when she moved, but her thrust was so fast it caught him flat-footed. She slid like water past the tip of Zariduke, and the dagger struck like a cobra, right at his midsection. Just before it pierced his skin, he noticed a blur in the darkness above, and Mala somersaulted down from a branch to drive her dagger into the dhampyr's back.

The blade sank deep. Ferala released a shriek and stumbled away. The fall had taken the wind from Mala, not allowing her to follow up on the blow. As Will prepared to launch another attack, Mala struggled to her feet and screamed at him. "Fall back! Inside!"

A guttural growl issued from Ferala's throat as she bounded after them. *How did she recover so fast?* She would have caught them if Mala hadn't turned and released her spinning sash. Though Ferala ducked at the last moment, just avoiding the weighted ends, the maneuver gave Will and Mala a chance to escape into the house.

Will slammed the door in Ferala's face. The dhampyr kicked the door down, splintering the frame. From across the room, Mala tossed a handful of fire beads as the dhampyr stepped inside. Ferala slid to the left, narrowly avoiding the beads as they burst into flame against the wall.

"I knew you would return, gypsy. How kind of you to bring the wielder of Zariduke. I'll hang you both in the icehouse and kill you slowly to avenge my brother."

Blood dripped from the dhampyr's back and onto the wood floor as she advanced with a cruel smile. Will and Mala fled through the sitting room and into the hallway, aiming for the stairs. Ferala was a blur as she streaked across the room in pursuit. Mala watched over her shoulder, and as soon as the dhampyr entered the hallway, Mala pressed hard against one of the stone blocks on the wall, causing two spears to punch through the floor beneath Ferala. One of them stabbed her through the leg. She fell against the wall and clutched her thigh, her face twisted in agony. She broke off the shaft of the weapon and left the barbed tip in her leg.

"I'll take your tongues first," Ferala said through clenched teeth as she limped after them, blood pouring from her new wounds. "And then your eyes and ears."

How much damage can she take? Will wondered, dashing up the stairs after Mala to the second floor, where he threw a bookshelf they had planted earlier across the top of the stairs. Mala flung open the trap door and pulled herself onto the flat-topped roof. Will followed her up, careful not to disturb the bundle of fire sticks around the edges. Mala left the trap door open and bent to pick up Magelasher, her cat o' nine tails with azantite tips. Will's buckler shield was also on the roof, right where Mala had left it. He retrieved it as he heard Ferala tossing the bookshelf aside below them.

Footsteps on the stairs. Will started to jump for the bottom of the rope ladder that led into the canopy, an essential part of their escape plan. Mala grabbed his arm and pulled him back. "There's no time."

She was right. Ferala would catch them from behind if they tried to climb. Left with no choice, they backed towards the closest edge of the roof instead. After an ominous moment of quiet, he heard a chittering sound from below.

He pulled Mala down and threw up his buckler to protect them as the sleek brown body of a bat, its membranous wings folded tight, flew like an arrow through the square opening in the roof. The trap door exploded, releasing a ball of fire that engulfed Ferala as it shot skyward. The blast was so intense it almost knocked Will and Mala off the roof. While the buckler protected their faces and vitals from the flames, he could feel the heat through his boots and exposed clothing.

The vampire bat was aflame and wobbling in flight. Afraid she would disappear into the canopy, Will leaped as high as he could and caught one of her wings with the tip of his sword. Though it was only a glancing blow, the touch of the blade caused Ferala to revert to human form. With a shriek, she fell and crashed on the roof, just beside the jagged hole caused by the blast. Her hair and most of her clothing had burned away, leaving her face and body terribly singed and blackened. The wounds in her legs and back were grotesque. She tried to rise but could barely move.

"You'll never escape the Grandfather," Ferala managed to say as Mala approached her with Magelasher.

"Maybe, maybe not," Mala said, raising the scourge above her head. "But it won't be you who does his bidding." She whipped the cat o' nine tails onto Ferala's prone form, and the azantite tips bit deep. The dhampyr shuddered and lay still, her eyes open in the stare of death.

With a grimace, Mala dropped Magelasher, drew her short sword, and used both hands to sever Ferala's head with one clean blow. "We have to be sure," she said, using the blade to lever the corpse off the roof. "We'll burn the body in the fire pit."

Will took a deep breath and retrieved Zariduke. "I'd think that would do it."

"It's necessary. Dhampyrs are poorly understood and very hard to kill."

Mala sank to a sitting position on the edge of her roof. Earlier, before she had climbed into the canopy to await Ferala's arrival, Will knew she had retrieved a pair of magic items from her almost depleted private stash. One was an invisible lasso; another was a movable ward with a magical remote detonator she had used to trigger the explosive fire sticks.

He detected a pensiveness in her gaze, along with relief. He also saw a deflated look as she eyed the hole in the roof. "I can fix that, you know. I just need a few materials."

A smile played at her lips. "Thank you for the offer. I'd be most appreciative. But first things first, Will the Builder."

He wasn't quite sure what she meant by that.

After building a fire and reducing the remains of Ferala to ash, they trudged wearily inside and fixed a dinner of cheese, bread, and ale.

"What did Ferala mean when she said you would never escape the Grandfather? Who is that?"

"A story for another day," Mala said, with a nonchalant wave of her hand that Will could tell was forced.

"I'll hold you to that," he said. "Sooner rather than later."

She stood and held out a hand. "Come."

"Where are we going?"

She gave a deep-throated laugh and swayed closer, tilting her chin to look him in the eye, hair unbound and framing her face, her smell as intoxicating as ever despite the overtones of ash and sweat from the battle. "Foolish boy." She trailed a finger across his cheek as she walked past, and turned to look over her shoulder. "Upstairs. That is where we are going."

"I may be foolish sometimes," he said, sweeping her off her feet and carrying her into the hallway. "But I learn quick."

As he started up the stairs, a rap on the door caused Mala to jump out of his arms and whisk a dagger out of her boot.

"Mala?" a male voice called out from behind the oak door. "Oh Mala dear, are you in there?"

-17-

A moment earlier, Caleb had been standing at night in a shallow stream surrounded by a forest of old-growth fir and spruce, the full moon hovering overhead, the Brewer perched on a rock beside him and the rest of the army anxiously awaiting the outcome of the ritual to summon *Temmenily Ayawet*, the Forest of the Moon Dead.

Now, as Caleb stepped out of the stream and onto the rocky shore, he saw that everyone had disappeared except for himself and the Brewer. There was no sign of the cleared space on the banks of the stream, the sticks arranged into symbols, or the cairns in the corners. They were still in a forest, but unlike any Caleb had ever seen. At first he thought the trees were made of silver, but on closer inspection he realized they were made of wood that shone with an eerie whitish light in the semi-darkness. The moon was obscured behind a film of violet twilight that had a tangible quality, as if he could take a knife and rip a hole in the atmosphere. It was like he had entered a dream but was fully awake, the veil between worlds a literal one.

After exchanging a confused glance with the Brewer, Caleb approached one of the trees and rapped on the bark. Hard and smooth. None of the limbs had any leaves. He spun in a slow circle and observed that the forest stretched in all directions as far as he could see.

"*Temmenily Ayawet*, I presume," said the Brewer.

Caleb bent to study the grass, which possessed the same metallic sheen as the trees. He broke a blade in half and studied it. It felt normal. He stuck a hand in the stream and it came back wet. "Yeah. Wherever and whatever that is."

"What do you want to do?"

Caleb stared at the unchanging sky. Like the rest of the forest, it was as still as a painting. No insects chirped, no breeze stirred, and when Caleb inhaled deeply, expecting fresh air and loamy soil, he detected no scent at all. Besides himself and the Brewer, the only sign of life was the stream, which flowed and gurgled as it would on Urfe.

"I'm sorry I got you into this," he said to the Brewer. "I wish I'd come alone."

"You can't carry a tune, kid, so that wasn't an option. Hey, personal experience makes for stronger ballads. Consider this a quest in the service of great art."

Caleb peered into the forest, trying in vain to distinguish one direction from another. "I think we should follow the stream," he said finally. "We'll just get lost otherwise."

The Brewer gathered a handful of sticks and stuck them in the ground in a line. "So we can know where we started, if we decide to head back."

"Good idea. What do you think about drinking the water?"

While their clothes and weapons were intact, they had not expected to come alone, and had not brought any provisions. *That was an oversight.*

"Bad idea. At least for now."

"I feel the same. Let's hope we figure something out before we don't have an option."

They decided to head downstream, what would have been south on Urfe. The carpet of stones and low undergrowth along the bank was easy to navigate. They walked in silence for some time, weapons at the ready, peering into the trees with every step. Although the stream twisted and turned through the strange forest, nothing else in the environment seemed to vary. The moon and stars stayed in the same position, the trees never rustled, not a single creature stirred.

"Do you think we're making any progress?" Caleb asked, stopping to kneel beside the stream and poke through the dirt. His search for an insect, anything to reassure him that life existed here, was in vain.

"Beats me. My legs are tired, though. And I'm thirsty. So I guess we're still alive, unless the afterlife is a trial of deprivation."

When they started up again, the Brewer sang folk tunes to pass the time and lift their spirits. After Caleb estimated they had walked for at least three hours, and still nothing had changed except the course of the stream, he stopped again in frustration. "Maybe the shamans know a better way to travel here, but I get the feeling all we're doing is tiring ourselves out."

"You're reading my mind, buddy."

After holding his head in his hands, Caleb said, "Screw it" and scooped a handful of water from the stream into his mouth. Bracing for the worst, a burning sensation or a magic spell that turned him into a rainbow trout, he was relieved to find the water cool and refreshing.

The Brewer sat with his lyre on his lap, strumming a few chords. "I see you decided to drink the water."

"I had to try something. It's the only variable I can see."

"And?"

"It tastes delicious." After waiting another minute to see if anything unusual would occur, he dipped his hand back into the steam and let the water flow over it. "But maybe I'll leave it at that for now."

With a grunt, the Brewer pushed to his feet. "Keep walking? I'm not sure what else to do."

"Let's give it another half hour. We have to get somewhere eventually," he said, trying to convince himself it was true.

They continued following the stream as it wound around a low hill covered with the same silver trees. Soon after, Caleb saw a flicker of movement in the woods to his left. He whirled and caught a human-sized shadow flitting through the trees. He could not make out the features or even the gender. "Bruce—did you see that?"

"What?"

"A shadow running through the trees. There!" he said, pointing further in the distance. "Another one!"

"I can't see anything. Maybe your vision's better than mine."

"It wasn't that far away." Caleb stared in the direction he had seen the shadow figures, but they seemed to have disappeared. Both unnerved and optimistic something else lived here, they kept walking until he saw another figure race out of the forest right in front of him, leap across the stream in a single bound, and disappear into the trees. "Surely you saw *that*?"

The Brewer was looking at him strangely. "Uh, kid? Saw what?"

Caleb waved his arms in disbelief. "It was a shadow person. A woman, I think. She ran out of the woods and jumped the stream right in front of us!"

The Brewer looked down at the water, and then back at Caleb. "I'm not sure I'd drink any more of that water."

At first Caleb agreed with him, but then he realized there was another way to look at it. He bent down to the stream and gulped a few more handfuls of water as the Brewer watched in shock.

"Are you crazy?"

"Maybe," Caleb said grimly. "But what if the water somehow heightens our perceptions? Allows us to see this place as it really is?"

"And what if it's messing with your mind?"

"I'm already the guinea pig, so I thought I'd double down."

The next time Caleb saw movement in the trees, he glimpsed a pair of boys with skin and hair the color of captured moonlight racing through the forest, wearing loincloths and headbands made of woven leaves. As they ran, the boys laughed and tossed a ball back and forth between them.

"I guess you don't see that, either?"

"Not a thing," the Brewer said.

Caleb waved a hand. "Hey! Over here!"

One of the boys turned without breaking stride. He looked right at Caleb but gave no sign of recognition. Caleb kept calling and waving his arms. The boy looked confused for a moment, but kept running until he disappeared into the forest.

After describing the encounter, Caleb said, "I don't think those shadows I saw earlier or these boys are the ones who aren't fully real here. I think it's *us*."

The Brewer scratched his beard and bent to twirl a finger in the water. "So do we both take the chance? Or keep one of us as a control, in case you're wrong? And what about you? Do you drink more and see what happens?"

After debating the issue, they decided the Brewer would not drink the water yet, and Caleb would wait before drinking any more. Half an hour later, still with no sign of birds or insects or animals, Caleb slowed when the stream widened as it wound into a dale with a small village spread along the bank.

The settlement was a collection of fifty or so triangular dwellings made of logs and woven grass—and every single one was on fire.

An inferno of orange flames rose from the roofs and licked the sky. The odor of ash and wood smoke hit Caleb's nostrils, the first smell since their arrival. One of the dwellings collapsed as he watched.

Caleb stopped moving, stunned by the devastation.

The Brewer strained to see into the distance. "What are you seeing?"

A scream came from the village, piercing the eerie silence of the forest. "Someone's alive in there!" Caleb said.

"What? Who? I can't see a thing."

Without bothering to explain, Caleb sprinted towards the village as the terrified screaming grew in volume. It was a little girl, of that much he was sure. His feet pounded on the small stones lining the bank, and as he drew nearer, he had to cover his nose to combat the stench of charred flesh. At first he didn't realize he couldn't feel the heat from the flames, but when he kicked down the door of the first hut and saw a family of six lying dead on the floor with their throats cut and their limbs dismembered, he realized the fire had no effect on him. He backed away, suppressing the urge to vomit, and considered his immunity a positive as he raced through the village to see who he could help.

It was a charnel house. Everyone he encountered was already dead, slaughtered in the same manner as the occupants of the first house. Everyone, that was, except for the source of the screaming: a little girl of perhaps six, wearing deerskin clothing and similar in appearance to the boys in the forest.

The girl was lashed to the bottom of a thick, twelve-foot pole carved with runes in the center of the village, screaming over and over as the village went up in flames around her.

"I'm coming!" Caleb said. "Hang on!"

A circle of conical huts ringed the pole, all of them on fire. As he drew closer, he realized the ground around the pole was strewn with sticks and thatch, and that soon the fire would find its way to the girl.

She didn't seem to notice him. He ran right up to her, drawing his mace as he ran. As she shrieked in terror, he ran around to the back of the pole, swung the mace—and stumbled forward as the weapon passed through the wood as if it wasn't there.

He ran to face the girl and tried to grab her hand. The same thing happened.

No no no.

"Can you hear me?" he yelled, right in her face. "I'm right here!"

She stopped screaming for a moment, blinking in his direction as if confused, just like the boys in the forest. By the time she resumed screaming, Caleb was already racing out of the village and back to the stream by the Brewer.

"What are you doing?" the Brewer asked, as Caleb bent to shovel water into his mouth, trying to make himself more corporeal.

"No time," he said, realizing the Brewer hadn't seen any of the horror in the village. "There's a girl about to die. Got to save her."

The Brewer watched him for a moment, stunned, then bent down and started drinking from the stream. "Who wants to be the only sane person in the asylum?" he said as he followed Caleb back into the village.

Caleb outpaced him, arriving at the pole in the center of the village well ahead of the older man. The fire had spread to the ground and had almost reached the girl. She was frantic now, her eyes rolling back from fear. She still didn't seem to notice him.

He tried to take her hand, shake her, and even yell into her ear.

It was like he was a ghost.

"No!" he roared, trying to shove against the pole but falling right through it. The Brewer didn't fare any better, and Caleb raced back to the stream to find more water. He drank until he could drink no more, feeling bloated as he stumbled away from the stream and raced down to the village again.

When he returned to the girl, her screams had stopped, and she was choking to death as her lungs filled with smoke. Still he couldn't help her.

He tried one more time to drink from the stream. By the time he returned she was dead.

Caleb collapsed to his knees, shaking, and put his head in his hands. The Brewer put an arm around him. "If it's any consolation," he said quietly, "I don't think it was real, at least not in the way we think of reality. I'm beginning to think this place is some kind of collective dream from the past, like a . . . a trapped memory. I don't know how or why we're here, or what it all means, but you did your best, kid."

When he had gained control of his emotions, Caleb passed a hand across his eyes and stood. "It was real enough to her."

They followed the stream past the village and saw two more like it, in valleys not far away.

All the dwellings on fire. People massacred in their homes, and always a young child tied to a rune-covered pole in the center.

Nothing Caleb or the Brewer could do.

Despite the futility of their efforts, Caleb kept trying to save the sacrificial children, hoping something would change. But no matter how much water he drank, he could never affect the outcome. He even tried eating grass and acorns and a few mushrooms he found beneath a tree. Nothing helped. They walked further and further into the strange land, reeling from the death and violence, the screams of dying children a soundtrack of the damned in his head.

"Sing the song again," he said grimly to the Brewer as the stream skirted a hill and delved into yet another valley, this one mercifully free of habitation.

"Which one? The Stones tune I was humming? The Who—"

"The song from the ritual. The one that got us here. Let's see if she listens."

"Who?" the Brewer said gently. "You mean the girl?"

"Not the girl. The goddess."

After giving him a curious look, the Brewer nodded, gathered himself, and began to sing. As before, the harsh syllables and intonations of the guttural language grated on Caleb's ears, and he gritted his teeth, wondering what sort of deity these people had worshipped, and who was behind the genocide.

When the Brewer finished singing, Caleb scanned the valley for a sign that something had changed. "Sing it again," he said, seeing nothing.

After pursing his lips and staring into the distance, the Brewer tried once more, louder this time, his powerful baritone ringing through the valley. He sang again, and again, and again. Caleb began to shiver as he listened to the dark and eldritch hymn, not from the cold, but from some effect of the music. He was unsure whether it was the eerie language itself or the visceral power of the Brewer's voice, or a combination of the two. While he couldn't explain how he knew, he felt in his gut the chant was not purely a ritual of summoning, but an ancient dirge that spoke of the terrible events that had occurred, a lament for the slaughter of the people with skin like captured moonlight.

Still following the stream, they left the valley and entered a forest that was darker, denser, and more foreboding than any so far. As the Brewer continued to sing, the trees began to twist in upon themselves until they became parodies of living things, branches crooked and grasping, trunks withered like old crones, root systems clawing out of the ground as if trying to escape their graves. Caleb felt a heaviness descend, as if the air itself had more weight, or gravity was denser. He clenched his fists as they continued walking deeper into the consciousness of the forest, through the scar that covered the wound.

The stream rounded a bend and passed into a grove surrounded by the largest trees Caleb had ever seen. They appeared untouched by the devastation in the landscape, and were the same varietal as all the others in *Temmenily Ayawet*, silvery and sparse of branch. They soared hundreds of feet into the air, wider at the base than the oldest swamp cypress back home.

Entering the grove gave Caleb the impression of being inside a mammoth natural cathedral. Lounging and cavorting on the bed of soft grass were forest animals, a small group of indigenous people like the others he had seen, and a host of mythological creatures such as satyrs, centaurs, and nymphs floating on diaphanous wings. In the center of the clearing, sitting upon a throne carved into the trunk of the largest tree of all, wearing a garland of vines and leaves, was the most beautiful being Caleb had ever laid eyes on. She was voluptuous and a foot taller than he, with skin and hair similar in color to that of the native people, except hers was far more luminous, truly moonbeams made flesh. Her lips were red as berries, her eyes as delicate and white as snowflakes. A sleeveless gown of gossamer material, silk straight from a spider's web, cascaded from her shoulders to her bare feet.

The Brewer's voice cut off abruptly. When Caleb looked over at him, he was shocked to find that a vine had wrapped around his face and sealed his lips. The Brewer's eyes were open very wide, and his fingers couldn't pull the vine away.

"Who dares to disturb this lovely afternoon," the woman on the throne said, in a lazy and contemptuous voice, "with such a horrid ballad?"

Caleb realized she had spoken in English, and that he was staring at her face—gawking, actually. He had to blink a few times to remind himself who he was and where they were. "My name is Caleb Blackwood, and I've come from very far away to meet you. Are you the goddess I was told about? Of the Forest of the Moon Dead?"

"The Moon *Dead*? Whatever do you mean, child? As you can see, my people are here with me in my grove, safe and happy for eternity."

At a glance, her words appeared to be true. Though some of the creatures and people eyed the newcomers with interest, most had returned to relaxing on the grass or frolicking in the stream.

"What about the others?" he said, pointing towards the edge of the grove. "Out there."

The eyes of the goddess narrowed as she leveled her gaze at Caleb. "What others? Out where?"

All of a sudden, he realized the occupants of the grove had grown very still.

Careful now, Caleb. She's a few fries short of a Happy Meal.

He got the sense the Brewer was right, and that this place, *Temmenily Ayawet*, was trapped in a powerful spell, or inside a bubble of this being's consciousness, in a way he could never hope to understand. He wasn't sure if any of it was real, or what *real* even meant anymore. What if those poor people in the villages were doomed to repeat their fates forever?

His instinct was to try to help them by showing the goddess the truth. But that could be exceedingly dangerous, judging by the way she had silenced the Brewer. He also had a sudden thought—what if the goddess had gone mad and killed all her people herself?

The Brewer laid a hand on his arm, as if sensing his thoughts, but Caleb took a deep breath. He had to try. "I saw people who need your help beyond the borders of this grove. Villages were burning, hundreds slaughtered. They looked just like the people in here. *Your* people."

The goddess rose on her throne as her face twisted in anger. "You lie, mortal! I would never let this happen to my children! We have loved each other, they and I, for eons and eons, and so it shall ever be! Since before these forests took root in the soil, since the snow and ice of ages past covered these hills! *Laurius! Thethalos!*"

Two centaurs near her throne responded to the call, beating their chests as they reared on hind legs. The larger of them had arms as thick as Caleb's waist, and must have weighed over six hundred pounds.

"Tie these two to the rune pole," the goddess commanded. After issuing her order, the goddess sank into her throne, watching as a pink-and-blue butterfly landed on her arm. She gently lifted the creature and set it free.

In the corner of his eye, near the edge of the grove, Caleb noticed a rune-covered totem similar to the ones he had seen in the villages. As the centaurs thundered over to grab him and the Brewer, Caleb chose not to draw his mace, knowing there was no way out of this place even if he managed to defeat them, which he doubted he could do. Instead he raised his hands, palms out, hoping to inspire calm. "My apologies, goddess. I must have been mistaken about what I saw. I had a fever last night and perhaps it affected my perception."

She looked up. "Yes," she said primly. "I'm quite sure it did."

The centaur had a firm grip around Caleb's waist, but had not yet picked him up. Caleb could smell the musky, equine scent of the man-beast and feel the enormous strength in its hands.

"The reason we came here," Caleb said hastily, "is because we're travelers searching for a faster route to our destination. We've heard you can . . . grant a swifter passage, if you so desire."

"Within the boundaries of my domain, yes, this is true."

"Could you help us, then?"

She stretched like a cat and then curled up in her throne, her expression softening as she watched two children playing at the base of a tree. "A reasonable request, I suppose." She unfurled a hand and held it out towards the Brewer. "I will help you, but not him."

Caleb glanced over at the Brewer, who started to blink rapidly.

"No can do," Caleb said to the goddess. "I'd never leave my friend behind. Surely you, who takes such good care of her people, can understand?"

She plucked at the hem of her sleeve. "You're very persuasive, and a most comely man indeed. Perhaps you could stay, and he could go?"

"You're very comely yourself, but I'm sorry. We have to leave. *Both* of us."

"Yes," she said, her gaze suddenly intensifying. "I see your heart belongs to another. I've no doubt that in time I could persuade you otherwise, but I have an edict to never interfere with love." She sighed. "The price for such passage, then, shall be as it always was. Double, to free your friend as well—and he must agree never to sing those horrible lies again."

"Let him speak," Caleb said, "and I'm sure he'll agree."

"If he doesn't, the rune pole awaits. And my mind will not be changed again."

"Understood."

With a flick of her wrist, the goddess caused the vine sealing the Brewer's lips to slither free and fall at his feet. He worked his jaw back and forth a few times, checking to make sure it still worked. Caleb noticed lines of blood where the vine had bit into his skin.

The Brewer bowed deeply. "I thank you sincerely, fair goddess. And I apologize deeply if I have offended you. I pledge never to commit such a grievous error again, and to always keep the memory of your generosity and benevolence foremost in my mind."

"Well then," she said, mollified by the speech. "See that it is so."

"What's your price for this transaction?" Caleb asked, nervous she would ask for his mace or his cloak. He wasn't sure what he would do if she did, though he supposed he had little choice in the matter. "I don't have any money with me, but you're welcome to all that I have."

"And mine," the Brewer chimed in.

Her laughter was like a breeze through a field of sunflowers. "Coin? Silly mortals, what need has one such as I of worldly affectations? The price, of course, is your soul, to be collected immediately."

Caleb swallowed. "My soul? I . . . what do you mean?"

"What do I mean?" She looked around the grove, and this time her followers joined in with the mirth, filling the grove with giggles, snickers, raucous laughter, and frenzied snorting from the centaurs. "Now that is one question I've never received in response to that demand. I would think it's rather obvious. Normally I require half a soul, but since your price is doubled to save your friend, I must take it all. Or at least almost all—no one, not even *Arawn Kewwet,* can claim an entire soul."

"Take half of mine," the Brewer said, stepping forward. "We'll both pay."

She wrinkled her nose. "I'm afraid not. I desire only his."

Caleb felt as if he were back in the Tower of Elarion, having an absurd metaphysical conversation with Humpty Dumpty, or Jim and Huckleberry Finn. Yet not even in the tower had such a grave threat loomed. He looked over at the Brewer, who gave a quick shake of his head.

"Don't risk it, kid," he whispered.

Could this mad goddess really do as she claimed? Caleb wondered. And if she did take his soul, what would that mean? Would he cease to exist? Be a mindless slave for eternity? Was that why all these poor creatures were trapped in the grove with her?

Caleb had never even believed in the concept of the soul, not to mention goddesses stuck in a time warp in some weird dimension. He thought the universe had started with the Big Bang, though he had no idea how *that* had happened or what had come before it, and the theory had always seemed pretty incomplete to him. Regardless, he thought everyone and everything would return to stardust one day, and the universe would wind down and be cold and still forever, and that would be that. Earth, Urfe, universe, multiverse, who the hell cared? It was all part of the same big pointless random chaos monster.

Or was it?

Despite his best intentions otherwise, the opening of the Coffer and all of the unexplainable events he had witnessed on Urfe had caused him to doubt his own militant belief in the Theory of Nothing.

If this lady was a goddess, could Devla be real, too? He had no idea. He hadn't had time to think about it. No, that wasn't entirely true. He didn't *want* to think about it.

Because that would mean trying to ascribe rhyme or reason to the murder of Marguerite and Luca, and where would that get him?

No, the Tao of Caleb was firmly intact.

He didn't want to know and he didn't want to care.

Besides, even if he did have a soul, it was a tainted one, far more undeserving of life than the people on Urfe being harmed by the actions of the Congregation.

If by standing up to the Congregation I can save even one innocent person, or sway one prejudicial viewpoint, then this lady can have my stupid worthless soul.

He waved a hand in dismissal. "Take it."

As the Brewer's face fell, the goddess smiled, and a great cheer rose up from the crowd. They began to chant a phrase over and over, in the same language as the ritual, something ancient and somber. The goddess rose off her throne and strutted towards Caleb, mesmerizing him with the radiant splendor of her beauty.

"Wait!" he said, forcing himself to concentrate. Beside him, the Brewer gripped his sword and took a step towards the goddess, causing one of the centaurs to restrain him.

"You've already agreed to the bargain. It's too late for second thoughts."

"But you never asked me where I wanted to go."

She was standing over him now, causing him to swoon from the intoxicating fragrance of her skin. "I already know that, of course." She reached out with her silver arms and placed her hands on his head, breathing deeply in pleasure, and he prepared for the worst as his knees buckled and his skin tingled at the pleasure of her touch.

Will it hurt? Will I even know it's gone?

After a long moment in which he experienced no sensation, the goddess drew back with a shriek. "What trickery is this?"

Caleb blinked. "What?"

Her face twisted into a snarl, and she stamped a foot on the ground. "Who is protecting you, knave? Is it *Arawn Kewwet?* No, I would know if it were he. Who, then?" Her voice rose to a shout, causing her followers to cringe around the grove. "Who!?!"

Caleb pointed a finger at her, not understanding but realizing he had nothing to lose. "Ah, that would be the great and powerful Oz. I forgot to tell you. He's a serious, grade-A badass deity. I'm under his protection—we both are—and I wouldn't mess with him. Nope, he won't like that one bit."

The goddess stopped ranting and pulling at her hair. "I know not of this deity. From where does he hail? Who are his people?"

"You'll have to ask him. Listen, lady, we had a bargain. It's not my fault you can't take my soul. But if you don't fulfill your side of it, right this second, I'll tell Oz to come down here and destroy this grove."

The centaurs reared and approached Caleb again, but the goddess stopped them with a raised hand. "He speaks the truth," she said through clenched lips. "I am duty bound to fulfill my bargain. I know not of this Oz, but if he is powerful enough to stay my hand in this matter—" her face softened as it swept across the grove—"then I cannot risk the harm that might befall all of you. No, I must do as I promised. But first," she said, shaking her head in confusion, as if to clear it from a fog, "I would ask a favor."

"What?" Caleb said. "We really have to get going."

The goddess stared at the boundary of the grove for a long moment, the devastation on the other side invisible from her vantage point, before turning to a satyr holding a lute with silver strings. She snapped her fingers and held out a hand. The satyr rushed to hand her the instrument, and the goddess in turn offered it to the Brewer. With a trembling voice, she said, "Sing your song for me one more time, and use this as you do." She turned back to Caleb. "When I touched your head, I saw . . . I fear that . . ." Her lips continued to tremble, but her jaw firmed and she stamped her foot again. "I must know the truth."

Caleb and the Brewer exchanged another glance. This time Caleb gave a slight nod in affirmation. Maybe they could help that little girl after all.

The Brewer solemnly accepted the instrument, strummed it a few times to get in key, and concocted a chord scheme on the fly as he sang the song that had brought them to *Temmenily Ayawet.*

As the words poured forth, the goddess grew deathly still at first, and then stumbled away from the Brewer as if her skin were on fire. Her followers watched in horror as she retreated to her throne, curled into a ball, and put her head in her hands. When he finished singing, she was shaking, and her violent weeping echoed throughout the grove.

"What has been done?" she cried. "What have they done to my children?" She tilted her head back and released a wail of such utter despair that Caleb bit his lip and turned away. It reminded him of his own distraught state when his family had been slaughtered before his eyes.

I lost two people, and this goddess lost an untold number.

Unable to help himself, he stepped forward to comfort her, but she jerked the crown of laurel off her head and threw it at his feet. "Go! Leave us be and never return!"

Before he could respond, she swept a hand through the air and began to wail again. The edges of the grove blurred in Caleb's vision, and then everything in his line of sight did the same, as if he had taken a powerful hallucinogen. As he reached out for the Brewer, the light of the moon expanded to fill the grove, turning the world into a canvas of silver-gray light, and then Caleb was standing in a different forest under a normal moon and full of familiar trees, pine and spruce and oak. It was not the forest they had left behind in the Ninth Protectorate, but he was definitely no longer in *Temmenily Ayawet.*

The Brewer was beside him, and Caleb exhaled with relief. He was afraid the goddess would not have remembered—or chosen—to send both men home.

"Where are we?" Caleb asked.

Before his friend could answer, a familiar voice called out their names. Still reeling from the transition, Caleb turned to see Yasmina running towards him, followed by Lance and Tamás. In fact, he saw all of his inner circle, as well as his entire army, filling the forest. He was going to pose the question again, until he saw everyone looking around with the same look of disoriented confusion he knew was on his own face, as if they, too, had just awakened from a dream and found themselves in a new location.

"Uh, kid?" the Brewer said.

Caleb noticed the older man was still holding the lute with silver strings from the grove. "Yeah?"

"I think I know where we are. And it's, um, well, you might just want to take a look for yourself."

Troubled by the odd note in his friend's voice, a mixture of astonishment and trepidation, Caleb turned to follow the Brewer's outstretched finger. He was pointing to their left where, in the distance, a field of glowing, multicolored spires pierced the night sky like a thousand celestial lances.

-18-

Ever since Val's conversation with Cyrus the night of the Mage Day Celebration, he had scoured the libraries in town, including the extensive collection at the Abbey, searching for information on his bluish-white ring in the shape of an ouroboros. He had seen plenty of references to other artifacts created by Myrddin, and Cyrus was right: Myrddin's personal seal was quite similar to the one on Val's ring, but with distinct differences, such as the smoother shape of the scales on the entwined serpents.

Was the ring a forgery? Or was it possible that, in the alternate dimension Val had journeyed to, Myrddin had a different seal?

Early one morning, he wandered into a rare bookseller on Magazine Street around the corner from Salomon's Pad. Inside a dusty old tome on magical relics from the early days of the Congregation, soon after Myrddin the Defender had led the wizards to victory in the Pagan Wars, Val was shocked to find a drawing that matched his ring.

He purchased the book at once, and took it to the Minotaur's Den to peruse over a late breakfast. He learned that many of the artifacts in the tome were unverified or apocryphal, belonging to myth or legend. A little disappointed, he sipped his coffee while he read the passage beneath a drawing of a ring almost identical to the one on his hand, and bearing Myrddin's true seal.

The Ring of Planar Orientation, it was called. A fabled artifact crafted by Myrddin to aid him on his journeys through the Place Between Worlds. During his time at the Abbey, Val had heard of such a place, a bridge to other worlds and dimensions said to have formed at the beginning of the multiverse itself. Not only was the ring supposed to act as a sort of compass in the Place Between Worlds (though the book did not explain how), it was also said to provide protection from the astral wind and wraiths, as well as the ability to open and close dimensional doorways. No one knew what happened to the artifact, if it had ever existed in the first place. Some speculated Myrddin had lost it during one of his many journeys beyond the stars.

Curious. Val had never been able to get the ring to work, but maybe he needed to be in the Place Between Worlds. He filed the information away as Synne rushed into the tavern alongside another of her black-robed brethren. The newcomer, a majitsu ten years her elder, and who Val recognized as one of Lord Alistair's personal majitsu, hurried over to Val's table as Synne trailed behind her.

"I bear an urgent summons," the woman said. "The Chief Thaumaturge requests your appearance in the War Room of the Congregation with utmost haste, to attend a personal briefing."

Requests, Val knew, meant *command.* After glancing at Synne, who appeared just in the dark as he was, he took a final swallow of coffee and stood. "I'm on my way."

The War Room.

A musty, gray-walled chamber in the lowest level of the Sanctum, barely used over the last century. It was protected from prying ears by its underground location, a permanent ward of silence, and the all but impenetrable defenses of the Sanctum itself.

With his staff by his side, Val sat around a polished wooden table, waiting for Lord Alistair to arrive, wondering at the purpose of the meeting. Professor Azara had just drifted in, claiming the last remaining seat, and Val took stock of the other attendees.

Yasir Ookar, First General of the Protectorate Army.

Kjeld Anarsson, Head Don of the Order of Majitsu.

Kalyn Tern, the most powerful aeromancer in the Realm, and Lord Alistair's most influential advisor.

Last but not least, Cyrus Ravensill, Captain of the Wizard Guard in Londyn, and the queen's representative in New Victoria.

It was a small but highly distinguished group, one that made Val question the utility of his own presence. Earlier, Synne had accompanied him to the entrance of the Sanctum, where Val had continued into the atrium, taken a wizard chute to the lower levels, nodded to the guards, and followed the signs to the War Room. So far, except for small talk with Cyrus, none of the other attendees had spoken to him, though each had greeted him with a nod or an arm clasp. This did not bother him. He knew by the nature of the invitation that it was not a backslapping kind of meeting, and everyone present was too savvy too give away how much or how little they knew.

A notable absence to the meeting was Braden Shankstone. The cuerpomancer would not be pleased by the snub.

Val glanced at the portraits of monarchs and past Chief Thaumaturges on the walls, interspersed with detailed maps of New Victoria, the Protectorate, and the Realm at large. With the wave of a hand, the maps could expand to three dimensions in the center of the room, with the option to add geographical features, supply lines, troops, and other helpful variables.

It was always fascinating to view the similarities and contrasts between Urfe and back home. He had a memory flash from the first time he and his brothers had viewed a map of the Protectorate of New Albion—Urfe's name for North America—as they had crowded around a kitchen table in Salomon's Pad with Lance, not yet convinced they had traveled across time and space. Their collective shock and disbelief seemed so long ago, and yet so visceral. It induced a sharp pang of longing for his brothers.

"I see we're all assembled," Lord Alistair boomed as he and his mistress, Melina, flew into the room. Melina took a seat next to Val, while Lord Alistair settled onto the dais of congealed spirit floating a foot above the floor at the head of the table.

The Chief Thaumaturge eyed each of the attendees in turn. "I know the summons was inconvenient, and you're curious as to the nature of the meeting. So let us proceed without ceremony. Just after sunrise this morning, I received word that a Protectorate patrol had spotted the rebels gathered in the Lafitte Forest, a mile from the Fifth Protectorate byway—and less than a day's march from New Victoria."

Yasir lifted a gloved hand. "Excuse me, milord, but of which revolutionaries do you speak?"

"The only ones of any consequence. The so-called army being led by the Prophet and Valjean's brother, Caleb Blackwood."

Though everyone in the room was too professional to give voice to their surprise, Val could sense the collective gasp in the room, and see the tightening of hands around the table. Even the unflappable Yasir Ookar evidenced his shock with a shift in his posture. Only Kalyn Tern seemed unaffected, making Val wonder if Lord Alistair had confided in her before the meeting.

The news caused Val's stomach to clench with fear and worry. *Caleb is less than a day's march from the city? How is that possible? More importantly, how will the Congregation react?*

Though his brother's involvement already weighed heavily on Val, the last he knew, Caleb's army was over a thousand miles away, on the far side of the Ninth Protectorate. It should have taken him months to arrive, giving Val far more time to figure out a way to extricate his brother.

"I don't understand," said Professor Azara, with her precise diction and lilting accent. "The entire army has crossed the Ninth overnight? *Lah*, how can this be?"

Lord Alistair leveled his gaze at her. "I was going to ask you the same question."

The striking professor of spiritmancy opened her mouth and then slowly closed it. Val still sweated over the fact that he had assaulted her son, Gowen, during his search for the Pool of Souls. But Professor Azara had never mentioned the incident, and Val assumed Gowen was too embarrassed to tell anyone.

Or maybe he had told her, and she was biding her time for revenge.

"Could it be a mirage?" Cyrus asked. "A magical projection?"

"The rebels' physical presence was confirmed by hyena wolves and close observation by our scouts," Alistair said.

"What if they used rukhs or simorghs?" Val asked, remembering his own experiences with the giant avians. "Could they fly that far?"

"Not overnight," Kalyn said, though her tone was not disapproving. "Besides, we have airships along the Great River. The spymasters would not have overlooked the passage of such a large group."

"Not even if cloaking magic was involved?" Yasir asked.

"No spell or artifact of concealment could shield a group that large. Nor has a single such mount been seen with the rebels."

Yasir grimaced as he leaned back in his chair.

There was a long period of silence. At last Professor Azara said to Lord

Alistair, "You said the entire army appeared this morning. Approximately how many people?"

"The estimate is now upwards of five thousand."

"Five *thousand*? I don't need to tell you that not even a spirit mage could accomplish such a task, nor any known portal."

"What about a theoretical one?"

"*Neh*. The ability to move so many people that far in such a short time . . . would require godlike power." She gave a thin smile. "Assuming, of course, one believed in the existence of such beings. The only possibility I can imagine seems extremely unlikely."

"Which is?"

"They found a portal to the Place Between Worlds, proceeded through it one by one, and returned to Urfe in the Lafitte Forest instead of the Ninth Protectorate."

Lord Alistair stroked his chin as his bi-colored eyes, one black and one pale blue, stared across the room. "The only two physical portals to the Place Between Worlds of which I'm aware are here, in the Sanctum, and in the Queen's Keep in Londyn. Unless you know of another?"

"Not in the Realm. Though as you know, it's possible for a spirit mage of sufficient power to construct one. It would take decades, and the only two wizards in the Realm who could possibly manage such a feat are . . ."

She trailed off, as if unwilling to continue.

"Lord Groft and I," Lord Alistair finished.

"We can investigate this question ourselves, after the meeting, by traveling to the Place Between Worlds and studying the spirit signatures."

He pursed his lips. "I consider that avenue extremely unlikely for many reasons, not the least of which because the presence of such a large group would attract the wraiths and the astral wind. I suppose it's possible Groft has such a portal in his possession, or the rebels have acquired one from some unknown source." He pursed his lips. "Still, see what you can uncover, and consider alternate theories as to how this feat might have been accomplished. I want no more surprises, and I'll be very cross if I wake up tomorrow to learn the rebels have relocated to the Gypsy Quarter and are marching through the city."

"*Leh*. Understood. I will do my best."

Val found himself wondering how Caleb and his followers *had* managed to cross such a large distance overnight. While Lord Alistair was a more powerful mage than Professor Azara, she was the scholar, and had more knowledge of the ways of spirit than anyone in the realm besides Groft.

Was it possible the former spiritmancy dean with the sad eyes was behind this? He had always been kind to Val, but from long experience, Val knew that people could react in radical ways when their principles or livelihood were threatened.

Lord Alistair swept his imperious gaze across the table. "Regardless of how this was done, we must deal with the gnat that has come to flit about the window of our house."

"This is an act of aggression," Kjeld rumbled, folding his massive arms. "The law is clear that no armed group may gather within a hundred miles of the city. "I say we arrest the lot of them—or if they refuse to surrender, solve the problem once and for all."

"It is indeed an unlawful act, and the course of action you propose is sound. The question becomes, when and by what manner?"

Prim and proper as always, Kalyn interlaced her bejeweled fingers on the edge of the table. "We need to narrate the tale."

"Precisely. If there must be a revolution, let it play out—and end—on our terms. I can only assume their plan is to attempt a peaceful march on New Victoria and insist we meet their demands. They have no hope of defeating us. By forcing us to stop them, which we must before they enter the city, they will try to frame our actions as an act of wizard aggression, in an attempt to unite the common born and raise sympathy for their cause."

"So we convince them to provoke us instead," Kjeld said, stroking his long red beard. "Or force them to do it."

"Yes."

Yasir leaned forward. "What do you have in mind?"

"I leave that to you, though I advise using a contingent of the Protectorate army. If the Congregation is involved too early, a successful provocation by the rebels will not be credible. Not only that, it's best if *common born* soldiers are threatened or wounded. This will enrage the populace. We accept a very minor loss, secure the will of the people, and end the twin annoyances of the oath avoiders and the Devlan once and for all."

"The people of New Victoria will not be hard to convince," Kalyn said.

"The Black Sash have demonstrated the malice of the oath avoiders, and the vast majority are inured to the standard of living and protection from invasion that has resulted from wizard rule."

"What about the pockets of Devlan worship that have sprung up across the city?" Yasir said. "I'm told these heresies grow in number by the day, and consider Caleb an agent of the divine."

Alistair's face tightened in fury. "Then perhaps we challenge their prophet to display the power of their non-existent god, or to feed the poor with their convictions."

"The common born will always be gullible," Kjeld said with a sneer, then clapped Yasir on the back. "Present company excluded. You're far from common, my scaly commander."

"No offense taken," the reptilus general said coolly.

"As I've said before," Alistair said, "the so-called revolution has given us the perfect opportunity to crush the scourge of religion in New Albion once and for all, so we can focus on the threat of the Mayan Kingdom, whose battle mages continue to gather at the border."

"Is there talk of war from the spies?" Yasir asked.

"The Arch Governors have long held designs on the Ninth, and I fear they'll use this distraction to establish a foothold."

Kjeld snarled. "The governors are not to be trusted."

"No," Alistair said, "they are not. Within a week, I'd like you to present a plan to secure our southern border, even if it means an incursion into Mayan territory."

"With pleasure."

Lord Alistair folded his hands in front of him. "As Professor Azara explores this mysterious method of travel—perhaps it is something we ourselves could use?—I'd like Kalyn and Yasir to coordinate the strategy for dealing with the rebels. Kalyn and I spoke already this morning, and she suggested a wise course of action."

He opened his palm towards the aeromancer, and Kalyn took the floor. "Right from the outset," she said, "I'd like to give the rebels a chance to lay down their arms and surrender. This, of course, we know they will not do. But to please the people, we must try—and in a very public manner. I believe it's best to send an emissary aboard an airship, along with a viewing portal displayed in a public square for all to see. This will allow us to extend an olive branch while observing the activity of the rebels from a safe distance."

"Excellent," Alistair said. "Does anyone dissent to this course of action?"

No one did.

"Cyrus, would you please inform Londyn, and communicate any response from the Queen?"

"I shall."

"Excellent."

Val noted that while Cyrus voiced no opposition and had maintained a neutral expression throughout the discussion, Val got the distinct impression he was not thrilled by the turn of events. *He knows it's all a power grab by Lord Alistair.*

Val knew it was above his pay grade to meddle in the politics of Urfe, but he had a personal consideration, and the conversation had left him terrified at the implications for Caleb. He had to find a way to reach him before he got himself killed. As if reading Val's mind, Lord Alistair looked right at him for the first time during the conversation.

"That leaves you, Valjean, for the final task I have to assign. None of us wish for your brother's involvement to end in a tragic manner. I believe you alone have the best chance of defusing the situation, convincing Caleb to return to his home world, and avoiding unnecessary bloodshed. For these reasons, I'd like you to be our emissary aboard the airship."

Val bowed his head in assent, as well as to conceal his roiling emotions. He had one day to figure out a way to deter his brother while pleasing Lord Alistair, and, judging by the last meeting between the two brothers, it might be an impossible task. "Thank you," he said, looking up. "I'll do everything in my power to convince him."

"I have no doubt. Along with the typical airship crew, Professor Azara will also accompany you, since until we learn the whereabouts of Dean Groft, we must proceed with caution. You'll receive further instruction, but I anticipate you will set out at dawn tomorrow."

-19-

"Mala?" the man called again from behind the door to her cottage. "I sense you're listening. I'd like to come inside."

The cultured, intelligent voice had a New Victoria accent. Will detected a note of wariness but also confidence, as if the speaker understood how dangerous the owner of the bungalow was, but knew Mala would not attack him.

Will couldn't believe it. Not only had the visitor interrupted his first night with Mala, but from the sound of things, a former lover had decided to show up.

Then again, Mala was frowning as she unlocked the door and took a few steps back with a hand on her sash.

"Do you know him?" Will whispered.

"Aye."

"Who is he?"

She held up a finger for silence as the doorknob turned. When Will started to draw his sword, Mala shook her head in warning. Frustrated, he kept his hand on the hilt of Zariduke, waiting by her side as the door opened to reveal a sinewy, tall man of Asian descent. From the crow's feet around his eyes, Will guessed his age around fifty, though his black hair bore no trace of gray. The man was dressed in a fashionable silver doublet and hose with crimson trim, padded shoulders, and buttons of ivory. Rings adorned every finger, diamonds studded his ears, and a gold necklace draped his chest. A rapier hung at his waist, though his palms were open at his sides as he entered.

Will remained wary, but he was certain of one thing: there was no way this aging dandy could be one of Mala's boyfriends. The feeling was reinforced by the way the man ran his eyes approvingly, and boldly, over Will.

"You can ease your hands off your weapons," the man said, closing the door behind him and then raising his eyebrows as he surveyed the interior. The cottage was a wreck from the battle with Ferala. "Lover's spat?"

"How many men are outside?" Mala asked.

"Only a few dozen."

Will gawked, but the answer didn't seem to surprise Mala. "How did you find me?" she said coldly.

"Funny that. We knew there was a dhampyr active in the city, quite probably Ferala on the hunt to save her brother. We also suspected she was living near the Thieves Quarter. A sentinel happened to be walking close to your property when he spotted a fireball shooting above the tree line. His curiosity aroused, he approached the wall and noticed a bonfire that smelled suspiciously like . . . dhampyr."

Her eyes narrowed. "Is that so?"

"Unsure what had occurred or who owned this property, we thought it prudent to investigate a disturbance so close to our border. I was notified, and swiftly assembled a team. When I, ah, traversed the wall, I noticed a certain short sword through the kitchen window."

"The same one you once gave me."

"I'm quite flattered you've kept it."

"Don't be. It's an excellent blade. Didn't you learn to ask permission to enter someone's property?"

"Didn't I teach you how to avoid it?"

Confused by that last comment, as well as the one about Mala's sword, Will was looking back and forth between the two when the man said, "And who do I have the pleasure of meeting? Your latest consort, I presume?"

Mala's hand slowly fell away from her sash. "Will, meet Guild Lord Dashi, my former mentor and the second highest ranking member of the New Victoria Thieves Guild."

Will worked to conceal his surprise. "I'm William Baggins," he said, deciding he did not want such a powerful man to know his last name. "From Freetown."

"Is that so?" Dashi gave a thin smile. "Your accent is quite unusual for the Ninth Protectorate."

"I was raised by wolves."

"Ah," Dashi said. "That explains it, then."

Will responded with a tight smile of his own.

"What is it you want, Dashi?" Mala said. "I don't appreciate unannounced visits."

"I understand, my dear, though *I* do not appreciate those who keep secret residences right next door to my territory."

She waved a hand. "I just like the neighborhood. I'm no threat to you, and have no interest in the guild. You know this."

"Do I? I'm unsure I trust any mercenary with a professed lack of ambition—and I've certainly never considered you someone of that ilk."

"I have ambition. Just not for the backstabbing, double-crossing, insular life of the guild. That's why I left, as you well know. I'll take my oath-avoiding freedom, thank you very much."

"I do miss your quick hands and quicker wit, my dear. No one has come close to replacing you."

"And I miss your sense of style and avuncular charm."

Dashi threw back his head and laughed. "Avuncular. Only you, Mala. Only you."

Mala folded her arms. "I'd provide a refreshment, but I've only warm ale on offer. We just returned from a long journey."

"I appreciate the gesture, and it's no bother. I've just finished dining. I won't take much of your time, as I'm sure you have . . . duties . . . to attend to, especially if you've been away." After winking at Will, he wagged a finger and said to Mala, "I've been curious for some time, you know, as to where you reside in the city."

"And now you know."

"'Tis a pity. I've a feeling the property will soon be up for sale."

"Of course it will," Mala said with a snarl. "I won't have the Guild looking over my shoulder. Do you know how long it took me to find this place and secure it to my liking?" She took a deep breath, and Will could tell her temper was on the verge of exploding. "Your visit tonight must be of some importance, if you've decided to approach me yourself. So what is it, Dashi?"

"As intuitive as always," he murmured. "Shall we get some fresh air while we chat? It's a bit stuffy in here. Understandable, when a dhampyr takes up residence. I'm quite familiar with the odor, you know, from my interrogation of Nagiro."

Mala gave Will a meaningful look, as if sharing a secret, and held it long enough to ensure Dashi saw it. "We won't be conducting this discussion outside," she said. "And you should know that trying to exert undue influence inside my house, or bringing any more men inside, would be very unwise."

"Ah," Dashi said, with a nervous glance around the room, the first crack in the façade Will had seen. He smiled to himself; Mala was a very good bluffer. "Most impressive, by the way. The two of you slaying Ferala. Of course, one assumes the addition of Zariduke to the battle—" he turned to face Will "—likely had a positive effect."

Will was stunned by the comment but recovered quickly. "Zariduke? You mean the legendary sword of spirit? Here? I don't understand—"

"Don't bother, old chap. I know who you are and what you carry. Your likeness has been circulating in the guild for weeks."

Before Will could respond, Mala gave him a barely perceptible head shake that he interpreted as *don't worry, he already knows*.

Two silver groats appeared in Dashi's fingers as if from nowhere. As Will watched in amazement, the coins began flipping, spinning, and dancing across Dashi's knuckles faster than Will could follow. He quickly looked away, wary the guild lord was trying to mesmerize him. "Now," Dashi said, not even looking at the coins, "while it's true I was troubled by a member of the storied Alazashin Zashiri camping on my doorstep—and I'm *most* appreciative of your assistance in alleviating this threat—I confess I've been looking for you, Mala."

"I don't like the sound of that," she said.

"Hear me out. Your ingenious capture of Nagiro both inspired me and got me thinking . . ." he stopped speaking and glanced at Will. "Perhaps it's best if Mala and I continue this discussion alone."

"Whatever you have to say," she said evenly, "can be said to us both."

The guild lord showed his teeth. "Even if it's dangerous for his health?"

Mala seemed to reconsider, but Will stepped forward. "Now you've *really* convinced me to stay."

"Ah," Dashi said, "the sweet ripe fruits of love."

Mala waved a hand. "Enough of this banter. Say what you came to say."

The coins disappeared, and Dashi spread his hands. "Fine. Though I warn you—" he turned to Will "—that if you repeat anything I say in this room, I'll deny it to the grave and slit your throat ear to ear."

Will's hand closed tighter on the hilt of his sword. "You mean you'll *try*."

"A loyal and spirited lad," Dashi said with a chuckle, though his eyes betrayed no mirth. "I understand what you see in him, Mala." He clapped his hands. "Now to the business at hand. I've a proposition for you."

"A terrifying thought," Mala said.

"Tsk tsk. As I was saying, I've been pondering my own ambition in light of your skillset and your relative anonymity to the guild. There is one thing I desire above all else in life—I think you know what it is—and you happen to be uniquely positioned to help me obtain it."

Mala stared at him for a moment. "Now I understand why we're talking here instead of the guild. You want help killing the Maven."

"As I said before, you haven't missed a beat."

Will had heard Mala mention Ilianna Nightwing, maven of the New Victoria Thieves Guild, on another occasion.

"I'm no assassin, Dashi," Mala said. "You of all people should know that."

"Consider it a public service instead. Ilianna has become drunk on her own power, and places her political ambitions above those of the guild."

"Neither of those is my concern."

"She helped the Congregation rid the city of the Black Sash. Your people, Mala."

"Even less of my concern."

Dashi nodded as if he expected her answer. "I'm pleased to see you haven't changed. It's comforting that at least one person in the world adheres to her principles, or lack thereof."

"Are we finished?"

"I rather anticipated your response," he said, "and planned accordingly. You should know the vast majority of the guild is behind me, by the way. If I seize power, they will renounce Ilianna at once. There will be no fear of reprisal, to me or to you, if that is your concern."

Mala yawned.

"Did you know, my dear, that Ilianna once aspired to be a majitsu?"

"I've heard the rumor."

"It's the truth. Her, ah . . . principles . . . saw her dismissed from the training grounds during the admission period. This was many years ago, of course, and there is no record of her attendance. The story is all but forgotten. Ilianna's reflexes and prowess in battle are legendary, and she works hard to hide her past."

Mala's brow knitted in sudden understanding. "You didn't come for me. You came for Magelasher."

Dashi rested a hand on the hilt of the rapier hanging at his side. "Soulskein has many attributes, as does Ferala's dagger one of my men found in the bushes, but neither blade will assure that I can overcome the defenses of a majitsu. Especially as Iliana has now claimed the Mirrorcloak that *I* procured."

"Magelasher is not for sale," Mala said. "At any price."

"*Everyone* has a price, my dear. Are you not a paid mercenary, a retriever of magical items? I will pay you so handsomely for the scourge you can buy ten items of equal power."

"If you could do that, you wouldn't be standing here right now."

He grinned. "Fair enough. But while a formidable weapon, surely the scourge has no special meaning to you . . . it has no chance of defeating a true wizard, as does Zariduke, and to my knowledge you're not in the business of hunting majitsu."

"Your knowledge is not as extensive as you think it is," she said softly. "As I said, Magelasher is not for sale." She walked to the door and put a hand on the knob. "I believe we're done here.

Dashi stiffened. For a moment, Will wondered if he would reach for his rapier or call out for his men. Instead the guild lord's gaze darted about the room, as if searching for something to grasp onto. At last his eyes came to rest on Will, where they gleamed with a look of cunning so fierce and intelligent Will was taken aback. *Behind that polished exterior is a cobra ready to strike.*

"Perhaps nothing I have to offer will sway you," Dashi said, "but let's test those bonds of love. I have good reason to believe a certain Coffer is being held in a secret vault in New Victoria. The location of which I, and I alone, can give you."

Will tensed. "The Coffer of Devla?"

"Aye."

The Coffer . . . could he really know where it is? That's invaluable knowledge to the Revolution.

Will could tell by the sudden uncomfortable look on Mala's face that she knew full well the value of that information. He also knew how important Magelasher was to her, the one chance she had to fulfill her lifelong mission to avenge her parents.

The corners of Dashi's lips upturned. "I thought that might leave a mark."

Will was torn. Should he try to sway her? The Coffer represented the only true hope that his people, and a host of others suffering on Urfe, had to protest the authoritarian rule and threat of genocide from the Congregation.

On the other hand, how could he ask someone for such a sacrifice, especially the woman he loved? Under different circumstances, he might have offered Zariduke to Dashi instead. But the sword born of spirit, like the Coffer, was a relic of great power that belonged to his people. The Revolution needed them both. He didn't feel right offering it up, especially not to help a guild lord assassinate his superior.

In the end, he said nothing at all, because he knew that Mala also knew all of this, and it was her choice to make.

"That's a heavy price for a rumor," she said finally.

The two coins had returned to Dashi's knuckles, the measured nonchalance to his voice. "But such it is," he said, "for I desire Magelasher alone. Unless, of course, you prefer to offer the sword?"

Mala's eyes met Will's for a moment, unreadable as always, before she turned back to Dashi. "That is not mine to give. What I can offer you is this: in exchange for this information, I will lend you Magelasher for one year, after a period of one month that commences today, no sooner and no later. That is my final offer."

Will gaped at her, stunned she had agreed.

"Ah, she loves him indeed, to make such a sacrifice! The great and heartless Mala brought to heel at last! I commend you, my dear, for reaching for that brass ring of happiness. May I ask why you chose a month in particular?"

"That is my business."

"And if you die in the interim?"

"Then you have a better chance at retrieving the weapon from my corpse than anyone else. That is the price for a rumor, Dashi. And if that rumor proves to be false, our agreement is null and void."

Still reeling by her acquiescence, Will could only watch as Dashi's coins disappeared. He held out his forearm to Mala. "A strange proposition, to be sure, but one I can agree to under the circumstances." Mala met his arm in a forearm clasp, but Dashi didn't let her go when she tried to pull away, causing Will to tense. "Given this contract is one of performance, I'm sure you won't mind if I secure your end of the bargain with an aegis?"

Mala grimaced. "I mind very much. But do as you must. I've no intention of breaking it."

With his other hand, Dashi reached into an inside pocket of his doublet to retrieve a tiny green vial. He unstopped it with a deft twist of his nimble fingers, causing a stream of silver vapor to issue forth. The vapor swirled around Mala and the guild lord as he repeated her promise to deliver the weapon in one month's time, in exchange for the location of the relic.

When it was finished, Dashi clapped his hands again and bowed to them both. "A pleasure doing business," he said to Mala. "The current location of the Coffer of Devla is beneath the Sanctum, in Lord Alistair's personal vault. Normally, retrieving it from there would be an impossible task, and I might feel guilty about our exchange, but you do have the benefit of Zariduke, and, well, remorse after a transaction is not an ailment from which I suffer. Personally, I suggest abandoning this foolish quest and retiring to a Cretan isle. But in any event, do try to stay alive over the next month, or at least not incinerate yourself. Even a freshly deceased corpse can complete an aegis."

With a dramatic twirl of his wrist above his head, Dashi opened the door and left the cottage, leaving Mala cursing in his wake, and Will gawking at the sudden turn of events. He took her by the shoulders and said, "Thank you. I can't tell you how much that means."

She turned away. "Don't flatter yourself, or me. The only reason I agreed to that devil's bargain was because I fear . . . I fear that otherwise, I would never have gone through with it."

"I don't understand."

She looked away. "I would never have confronted the demon who killed my parents."

"Oh, I see. Wow, what a genius solution! It had nothing to do with me or the Revolution at all. You couldn't have, you know, just told Dashi to go to hell and imposed your own deadline." He took her by the chin and turned her head back to his. "As I've always known, there's a noble soul in there, and one I love deeply. I said *thank you*, and I meant it, and I wasn't looking for a reply. Now I've got to figure out a way to get inside the Sanctum, which I have to agree does sound pretty impossible. While I don't expect you to go with me, I'll be happy to solicit any advice you might have."

As she stared at him in disbelief, almost as if he were another species, he could see her hands trembling at her sides, though he wasn't sure what it meant. "Foolish boy," she whispered so softly he could barely hear. After closing her eyes for a long moment, she shuddered and expelled a deep breath. When she opened her eyes again, the old gleam had returned. "Zariduke might allow you to cut through the wards, but without inside help—magical help—we'll never get inside the Sanctum on our own."

He decided not to ask if her use of the first person plural meant she had agreed to go with him—or why. She would reveal her decision, and her reasons, when she was good and ready.

"Dozens of wizards will be present at any one time," she continued, "and I have no idea what's inside. There are *colossi* guarding that building, for Queen's sake. What we need, to have the slightest chance of success, is a wizard with inside knowledge. Of course, convincing a Congregation wizard to help us do such a thing might be more of an impossible task than the thing itself."

"Maybe," Will said grimly. "But I do know where to find one."

-20-

After returning from *Temmenily Ayawet*, Caleb met with his advisors in a bower of live oaks. The morning sunlight barely penetrated the canopy, and sheets of Spanish moss hung from the muscular branches of the trees. A startling variety of bird life chirped in the forest. The damp air smelled of moss and ferns. Though winter, it was still warm enough in the southern clime of the Fifth Protectorate to wear a light cloak.

No one knew what to make of the strange and mystical journey from the Ninth Protectorate to a forest less than two dozen miles from the city limits of New Victoria. Not in his wildest dreams did Caleb imagine they would end up that close.

On the one hand, he considered it a gift. His ultimate goal—making Lord Alistair pay for his actions—was now within reach.

Or was it? Being within spitting distance of the Congregation scared the bejesus out of him, not only from the imminent peril to his own life, but for the lives of those who had followed him across a continent.

"We've traveled too far, too fast," Tamás said. The revolutionary was pacing back and forth, his long hair unbound and his face dark with worry. "I was counting on gathering support along the way."

"Enough support to fight the Congregation?" Lance said. "A few thousand more oath avoiders are hardly going to make a difference. From what I've heard, maybe a few *hundred* thousand won't."

"Truth," the Brewer said, strumming a chord on the silver-stringed lyre from *Temmenily Ayawet*. The instrument had the purest sound Caleb had ever heard.

"Are you advocating for a retreat?" Yasmina asked Tamás. A yellow songbird was perched on the wilder's shoulder while her harpy eagle stalked the canopy.

"What purpose would that serve?" Tamás muttered. "It's genocide in the Ninth, and genocide here."

"Not when the Coffer returns," The Prophet said calmly, sitting cross-legged on a bed of moss in the center of the grove.

"Maybe, maybe not," Tamás said, his voice rising, "but the Congregation has the Coffer!"

The Prophet pushed to his feet. "Have faith, my brother. Have you not born witness to the events that have befallen us on this journey? A divine hand is surely at work." He turned to Caleb. "I need to attend to my followers and calm their nerves with prayer. I trust you will send if you need me?"

Caleb waved a hand in dismissal. Since the beginning of time, to further their own interests, people had claimed to be special, or favored by their god—right until a stronger army or civilization wiped them off the face of the planet.

After the Prophet left, Tamás stopped pacing and crossed his arms. "The Congregation surely knows of our presence by now. They'll never tolerate an armed force so close to New Victoria. The only question is whether they'll arrest us all and shove us in the Fens—or kill every last one of us."

"But you knew this when we started," Yasmina said. "What changed, other than the proximity of the enemy?"

"We had more time for a miracle. I just . . ." Tamás trailed off and put his hands to his forehead. Caleb sympathized with the Roma leader. From the start, there had been no good course of action. Tamás was just trying to help his people. The clans had chosen to fight because there was no better option.

Or was there?

All of a sudden, Caleb knew what he had to do. He couldn't lead these people into a senseless slaughter. The fight was over, or at least it was for them. "Change of strategy," he said, drawing the immediate attention of the group. "Maybe we *have* been given a gift. I agree attacking the city is foolish. But that doesn't mean we can't march— peacefully—and make our demands. We're so close, and if we can get a little bit closer, maybe we can reach the hearts of the people of New Victoria and force the Congregation to listen to our demands." He glanced at Yasmina and the Brewer. "On my world, there was this guy called Gandhi, who broke the back of an empire with a hunger strike. The Congregation may take some of us prisoner, or even kill some of us, but if they slaughter us in full view of the citizenry . . . what is the public's appetite for mass murder?"

"For oath avoiders and the Roma?" Tamás said grimly. "I'm not sure it has a limit. Are you really proposing a peaceful march on New Victoria? After all that's happened?"

"I'm proposing that, without the Coffer, anything else is suicide."

By the end of the day, after an endless series of heated discussions, they still had not decided on a course of action. The wasted day gnawed at Caleb like an itchy mosquito bite, a constant reminder of the peril of their position.

When would the Congregation appear? Why hadn't they already?

In case of an attack, Lance and Tamás had issued battle instructions. They might be able to fend off a small, advance company of Protectorate soldiers—maybe—but they had no hope of defeating a contingent of Congregation wizards of any size.

Which was why, first thing the following morning, Caleb had decided to order everyone to join a peaceful protest march to New Victoria—or flee across the Great River.

They didn't have the Coffer. They had no way to fight the Congregation.

He saw no middle ground.

The thought of losing his army made him feel numb, but he would press forward, find a way to reach the Coffer and Lord Alistair on his own.

There must have been something in the air that night, or perhaps the warmer southern clime and the sultry embrace of the live oaks had stirred people's libidos, because Caleb saw far more couples together than usual. Maybe everyone had realized they might not have long to live, and decided to make the most of it.

He noticed Branyn and Elaina, the two most powerful Roma mages, drifting hand in hand into the forest. A pretty Devlan woman laid her head in the Brewer's lap as he sang near the fire. Deeper into the night, when most were asleep, Caleb watched Allira slip into Lance's tent. Tamás must have given up on wooing Yasmina, because he disappeared with a statuesque farmer-turned-swordswoman who had joined them in the Ninth Protectorate.

On the darvish side of camp, Caleb guessed Lisha was entwined with her lover, a handsome darvish prince. Earlier in the journey, she had entered Caleb's tent late one night, and he feared her youthful infatuation had remained. Instead she told him she was betrothed to the prince, and planned to marry when they returned. He could see the love in her eyes, and the news made him happy.

And, finally, he had seen the Prophet return to camp from the forest deep in prayer, faithful as always to his beloved Devla.

When the camp was quiet at last, Caleb entered his tent, slipped out of his shirt and shoes, and laid on his back on his cot, trying to clear his mind enough to sleep. Not long after, a familiar voice whispered through the canvas. "Caleb—are you awake?"

"Unfortunately."

"Can I come in?"

"Sure."

The flap of the tent parted, and Yasmina slipped inside. She was dressed in boots damp from the forest, leather breeches, and her pewter cloak. After slipping off her boots and setting them by the entrance, she sat on the floor next to his cot.

"Where've you been?" he asked. "It's late."

"In the forest with Naxan."

Caleb cocked a grin. "I see."

She blushed. "It's not like that. We were . . . learning about the forest."

"And?"

"For my PhD studies, I studied the ecosystem around New Orleans extensively. This forest is a lot like back home. Similar flora and fauna. Except for the monsters, of course."

"You saw one?"

"No, but I could sense them. It's hard for me to explain, but it's there in the way the animals react, the smells, the sounds."

"Wilder stuff."

"Yeah."

"Gotcha. Was there something you wanted? Take your cloak off, you look hot. Er, you look flushed, I mean. Not that kind of hot. I mean, not that you're not hot . . ."

"Why Caleb, I've never seen you at a loss for words. At least not around women."

"I just didn't want you to think—"

"It's okay," she said gently, slipping out of her cloak with a sad smile. Underneath was a beige cotton shirt adorned with a slender necklace and an emerald charm he knew had belonged to her mother. Yasmina's skin glowed like warm caramel in the soft light of the lamp. While she had always been fit, her travels as a wilder had toned her lithe figure even more.

Caleb swallowed as she laid her cloak across the foot of his cot. His physical attraction to Yasmina had never been the problem.

She leaned back on her elbows and tilted her face towards his.

"What happened in the Forest of the Moon Dead?"

He blinked. "I told you. I met a goddess."

"I know what you told the group. I know you, Caleb. Something happened you didn't tell us. Something painful. It's okay if you don't want to talk about it."

After a long moment, he said quietly, "Those burning villages I told you about? There was a child tied to a pole in the center of each one. A sacrifice to some stupid god. The first one was a little girl. I tried to save her, but I couldn't, no matter how hard I tried. I had to watch her die, burning to death right beside me . . ."

She leaned closer and took his hands in hers. "How terrible. I didn't know."

He shuddered, taking strength from her familiar presence. "It's so much, Yaz. The misery, the death, the pointless suffering. Not just here but everywhere. Back home, too. It always has been for me. I've never known what to do."

"I know, Caleb. I always have."

"What do you mean? I never said anything about it, and I sure as hell didn't *do* anything. I've always been such a coward."

She stroked his forehead. "It takes far more courage to love than to hate."

He shook his head side to side, unwilling to accept the compliment, knowing deep down he was selfish and weak and cowardly, no matter what she said. The only thing that had spurred him to action was seeing his loved ones murdered, and who wouldn't be moved by that?

"You won't be going with us, will you?" she said.

He released her hands and sat up on the cot. "What do you mean?"

"You're going to tell everyone to surrender, but you're not running away. Am I wrong?"

He looked away as the memory of Luca and Marguerite fell on his chest like a collapsing building. "No," he whispered.

"You're going after Lord Alistair."

"I have to."

"That's suicide."

"It's the only chance I have to help these people. I led them here, Yaz. This is on me."

"The only way? Haven't you been advocating for a peaceful solution all day?"

"We both know that's a long shot. I just . . . I just can't send them to war without a prayer of victory."

"Then lead them back to the Ninth. Go into hiding, as you said."

"I can't live like that."

"Yes, you can."

"Fine. I *won't*."

"You don't have to seek revenge, Caleb."

"I already told you I did."

"It's not your fault—"

"Shut up!" he snapped, and then regretted it at once. He released a deep breath and slumped on his back again. "I'm sorry. I know you're only looking out for me, but Alistair has to pay for what he did. He'll pay, or I'll die trying to make him. And I'm fine with that choice. I *want* it, don't you see?"

She leaned over to cup his face in her hands, staring gently into his eyes, her hair falling across his bare chest. "And what will that solve, besides getting you killed?"

"It will make this pain go away, one way or the other. I can't take it anymore, Yaz. Their memory . . . it hurts too much. I can't breathe."

Her closeness and the familiarity of her touch, combined with the constant stabbing pain of the memories, made something snap inside him. For the first time since the night Marguerite and Luca had died, he began to weep, great wracking sobs that consumed him from head to toe. He did his best to keep quiet so no one would hear him, curling into a ball on the cot, his body shaking as Yasmina cradled him in her arms and whispered soothing words into his ear, stroking his face and hair, wiping his tears as her own spilled gently forth. The combination of her kindness and her unrequited love for him, added to the loss of his wife and child, made him feel as if his soul was ripping apart, that nonexistent paradoxical soul in which he didn't even believe. He knew he couldn't relieve his own pain, but maybe he could at least relieve hers. He pulled her on top of him, and she let her body sink into his, the salty sting of their tears mingling with the passion of their kiss.

When they finished making love, he lay wordless on his back, still flush with pleasure but more ashamed of himself than he had ever been. Yasmina stroked his face for a long time, kissed him softly on the forehead, then dressed and slipped out of his tent.

After lying awake half the night, Caleb slept later than usual the next morning. Normally he was up before dawn, but as the first rays of morning slanted into his tent, the flap opened and Yasmina ducked inside. Prepared to have an awkward discussion, Caleb reached for his shirt and sat up in bed.

"Get dressed and come quick," she said. He noticed she was breathless and her boots were muddy. "The others are waiting."

"They are?" he said. "Why?"

"Because an airship is approaching from the east."

Caleb's face fell. He slipped on his boots, leather vambraces, and cloak as fast as he could. After grabbing his mace, he hurried out of the tent and looked up. Sure enough, approaching slowly in the sky from the direction of New Victoria, was the unmistakable bulk of a Congregation airship. The sight of the floating instrument of death caused his stomach to clench in fear.

"Sweet Jesus," he whispered. "We're out of time."

"Maybe, maybe not," she said, tugging on his arm. "There's something else."

"What?" He broke into a jog, following her towards the bower of oaks on the periphery of camp where he had met with his advisors the previous day.

"When I was in the forest before dawn, I was approached by a Battle Mage."

"A what?"

"Wizards from the Mayan Kingdom. When I traveled there with Will, searching for the Coffer, we ran into one. It was a rather terrifying experience, but we survived. Will almost killed the Battle Mage, but spared his life and earned a friend instead. The name of the battle mage was Aahpo. He's the one who approached me in the forest."

"What? Why is he here?"

"He wants to help us, Caleb, and he brought friends. Twenty Battle Mages!"

"Help us? Why?"

"I'll let him tell you himself."

Just before they entered the grove, Caleb stumbled backward in shock. At the entrance, sprawled around the trunk of a live oak, was a twenty-foot snake with green scales, its body as thick as a barrel.

Yasmina laid a hand on his arm. "It's okay. The Battle Mages use them as mounts. It won't hurt you."

"Jesus, Yaz, you have to warn me about these kinds of things."

The reptile's yellow eyes watched them approach. After giving the monstrous serpent a wide berth, Caleb swept aside a curtain of Spanish moss and saw that everyone had gathered in the bower, plus a slender young man wearing a feathered headdress and a loin cloth, his body was covered head to toe in leopard body paint. The mage's left hand gripped a hooked iron staff, and he stood in the center of the grove with an imperious bearing, facing Caleb as he entered.

"I hear you knew my brother," Caleb said.

"My name is Aahpo Hun-Ahpu, and I am a Battle Mage of the Third Order of the Kukul—"

"Got it," Caleb said. "Sorry to cut you off, but I just saw a Congregation airship heading this way. I heard you came to offer help. Is this true?"

Aahpo gave a curt nod. "The Congregation has massed troops along the border we share. It's obvious their next target is the Mayan Kingdom. We prefer to begin the battle here, on their territory. We know of your army and your mission, and thought it advantageous to join forces."

"We don't have much to offer at the moment," Caleb said.

"We understand. My advance force is small as well. But you know the city and the customs better than we do, and we are fighting the same war: to curb the ambitions of Lord Alistair."

"Fair enough. We can talk politics later. Yasmina said you have others like you?"

"My fellow mages await in the forest nearby."

"Is twenty enough to have a chance against an airship?"

"It depends who is onboard. If the Congregation believes they are only engaging ground troops, with a few Roma mages unschooled in the art of war, they might have only sent a few wizards."

With Yasmina by his side, Caleb pressed his lips together and searched the faces of his friends and advisors. Lance and Tamás and Branyn looked tense and ready to jump into action. The Prophet was deep in thought as always. Lisha, who joined his inner circle now and again, stole a curious glance at Aahpo. The Brewer was staring grimly down at his lyre. Though everyone was processing the new information in their own way, Caleb knew they were looking to him to decide.

He glanced up and caught a glimpse of the airship through the canopy. Judging by the speed of the dirigible, they had little time before it reached them.

Still watching the sky, Caleb said to Aahpo, "Is it your opinion this ship has come to destroy us?"

"I see no other reason to send such a powerful message."

Caleb turned to his advisors and asked them the same question. No one could dispute the obvious conclusion. With a deep breath, he gripped his diamond-headed mace, looked at the ground, and then raised up with a hardened expression. "Then I say we go to war."

-21-

Val clutched the railing of the airship as it sailed over the swamps and low-lying forests to the west of New Victoria. Somewhere in that morass of water-soaked terrain, Caleb and his ragtag army of oath avoiders were waiting like ducks in a pond surrounded by hunters.

The cool wind rushed through Val's hair and rippled his cloak. Looking down from his bird's eye view was a dizzying, surreal experience. He had never ridden a hot air balloon before, but he imagined it felt somewhat like this—except the airship was a gigantic vessel, as big as an aircraft carrier back home. Tilectium rods and panels supported the wooden exoskeleton, and two sails manned by aeromancers caught the wind and propelled the ship forward. From the ground, the airship resembled a cross between a blimp and a colossal flying sailboat.

To the south, Val spied a small lake. The Great (Mississippi) River was a few miles north of his position. To the east, the soaring spires of New Victoria were aglow with the rising sun. According to the airship captain and the Protectorate scouts, they should reach Caleb's position within the next thirty minutes. Val was rehearsing in his mind the speech he had stayed up all night preparing to convince his brother to return home.

Surely, when confronted with the overwhelming might of an airship loaded with soldiers and Congregation wizards, he'll have no choice but to surrender.

Protectorate soldiers lined the guard rails on each side of the vessel. It was a light crew; the airship did not plan to land or engage, merely intimidate. Along with the aeromancers powering the sails, eleven more Congregation wizards stood on the front deck with Val, their high-collared shirts and cloaks popping in the wind. A masthead topped by an octopus cast in bronze and painted with the colors of the principal wizard disciplines—the symbol of the Congregation—rose proudly at the prow of the ship.

Fifteen Congregation wizards in total. More than enough to squash any aggression from the rebels, especially since their handful of mages would have to fly up to attack the airship. Only suicidal fools would attempt such a feat. Not just that, but there was another spirit mage on board, standing right beside Val, and she was even more experienced and powerful than he—at least in this stage of his development.

"Are you prepared?" Professor Azara asked, leaning close to be heard above the wind, dressed in a full-length midnight blue cloak with silver stitching.

"I am," Val said.

"Do you think your brother will surrender?"

"I hate to say it, but I'm no longer sure I know the answer to that question. He's not the same person I knew before." He shook his head and swore softly. *Caleb, Caleb. I can't believe it's come to this. Please don't do anything stupid today.*

As Professor Azara looked over at him, her stern expression softened a fraction. "*Leh*, this must be hard for you."

He gripped the railing and looked down at the terrain to hide his emotions. "If he won't listen to reason, I'll appeal to the lives of his followers. Maybe he doesn't care about his own life anymore, but the Caleb I know would never condemn others to die."

She didn't respond, and they both knew the truth: if the rebels didn't surrender, Lord Alistair wasn't going to try to arrest five thousand people or throw them all in the Fens.

This could only end one way.

A shout from the spymaster announced the rebels were in sight. Minutes later, as the airship began its descent, Val began to make out a collection of tents and people clustered around a forest glade surrounded by tracts of swampland.

"You're still committed to flying down alone?" she said.

"I fear it's the only way he'll agree to talk."

She gave a curt nod. "Ensure your Spirit Shield is intact, and release the flare when you're ready to return."

He nodded as the camp slowly came into focus. Val was surprised by the number of people that had poured into the glade to watch the airship descend. Using a pair of spyglasses attached to the railing, he strained for a glimpse of his brother but saw no sign of him. There were just too many people. Val released the glasses and began building his Spirit Shield, an advanced spell far more powerful than a simple Wizard Shield made of hardened air. A Spirit

Shield was more draining, too, though not nearly as much as Spirit Skin, the strongest of all magical barriers, able to withstand dragon fire and attainable only by the most powerful of spirit mages. Spirit Skin was still beyond Val's powers, and he wondered if Professor Azara could pull it off.

No matter. Once prepared, he could hold Spirit Shield for long minutes, and summon it again at a moment's notice. He couldn't use any more spells while it was in place, but once Caleb agreed to talk, he planned to relax the invisible barrier as long as no threat presented.

The airship slowed to a stop two hundred yards above the ground, just out of longbow range. Val took a deep breath and prepared to depart. Though not expecting to fight, the Protectorate soldiers were lined up along the metal railing with weapons in hand.

"I'm ready," Val said to Professor Azara.

"Be safe," she said, as she levitated him above the railing so he would not have to expend his own magic.

As Val drifted into open air, an aeromancer named Rendor pointed to the tree line west of camp. A shape could be seen rising rapidly towards them on an angle.

"Spymaster," Rendor called out, "what approaches from the west?"

Before he could answer, shouts of alarm rose along the sides of the ship. Val had drifted far enough out that he could see the open sky beneath the ship, and all around them, he saw shapes that resembled golden bullets speeding out of the trees towards the airship.

"Mages!" the spymaster roared. "Those are mages in flight! Prepare your defenses!"

The warning came too late. The attacking mages were flying faster than any wizard Val had ever seen, and the nearest one had drawn close enough for him to see a woman with her arms extended, wrapped in a golden cloak that streamed behind her and gave the sleek appearance of a speeding missile. Before anyone could react, the attacking mages—he estimated two dozen—released rays of yellow light from their palms that shone as bright as sunbeams. The rays slammed into soldiers up and down the airship, as well as the structure of the ship itself. A few of the sunbeams struck the Congregation mages clustered at the prow of the ship, and one hit Val as well. Though his Spirit

Shield held firm, the blast threw him out of the sky and against the wooden side of the pilothouse.

"Battle Mages," Val heard Professor Azara utter in a shocked voice.

His Spirit Shield had absorbed most of the impact. Dazed but uninjured, he struggled to his feet and tried to get a handle on the situation. A few feet away, Rendor was lying on his back with a hole through the center of his forehead. Another mage was dead from a wound to the chest, and half a dozen others had injuries ranging from burned limbs to the loss of an eye. While the attack had come on fast and hard, these were experienced Congregation mages, and Val knew they could erect a Wizard Shield at a moment's notice.

Which meant, if their defenses had been up, that the attacking mages were at least as powerful as they were.

All along the side of the ship, soldiers cowered beneath the iron railing, afraid to expose themselves to the terrible rays. Despite the wards protecting the hull, the ship itself was lurching and starting to descend.

Another sunray hit Val in the chest. This time he planted his feet, his back braced against the pilothouse wall. The blast felt like a punch to the gut, but he stood his ground. The Battle Mage who had attacked him, a husky Amerindian man wearing a feather crown, was closing fast. His arms were extended, palms out, ready to release another sunbeam.

Val didn't know what to do. Using an offensive spell would mean releasing his Spirit Shield, which could mean his death. But he did not know if his defenses would continue to hold. He had never tested them like this before. Judging by the impact of the last two rays, he had a feeling the next one might get through.

All around the ship, the Battle Mages were closing in, firing at the ship itself and anyone still standing. Before he could decide on a course of action, Professor Azara appeared out of nowhere beside him—she must have gone invisible in some way—and discharged twin blasts of Spirit Fire into the Battle Mage closing in on Val, turning him to dust. Wielding the Spirit Fire like controlled lightning, she whipped the bolts into the next Battle Mage over, fifty yards away, and then the one beside him. None saw it coming—or lived long enough to scream.

Two nearby Battle Mages sent sunrays arcing towards Professor Azara too fast for her to turn her Spirit Fire around. Yet somehow, in the blink of an eye, the Spirit Fire extinguished and the professor disappeared.

"Stay down!" she called out to Val from a few feet away, though he couldn't see her.

"I want to help!"

"*Leh*, you'll just get yourself killed! Tend to the wounded!"

Val was no healer and had nothing to offer the injured. Instead he rose to a crouch, kept low to the railing, and tried to assess where he could help. His Spirit Shield was draining him too quickly, and he was forced to let it go. He knew how much energy Spirit Fire took to wield, and as he watched Professor Azara appear and disappear at random along the railing, unleashing the dark energy to devastating effect, he wondered how long she could last.

The Congregation mages who had survived the initial onslaught, and were not too injured to fight, had finally joined the battle. After Professor Azara, the highest-ranking mage was an aeromancer named Baltyr. A slender man with iron-gray hair, he was Kalyn Tern's first cousin and a first commander in the Congregation's wizard battalion. A very powerful mage.

After seeing that Rendor was dead, Baltyr roared at the two remaining aeromancers. "Go! Tend to the sails with Alyk! Take us back to the city!"

With a nod, the other aeromancers raced through a pilothouse door and disappeared. Val could only hope the sails were salvageable and escape was an option.

A pyromancer used a bronze firestick to send Fire Spheres whooshing into the sky. One caught a battle mage looking in the other direction and sent his charred corpse plummeting to the ground. A geomancer sent deadly iron spheres darting to and fro in the air, cracking skulls if a battle mage did not erect his or her defenses in time.

It would have been a fascinating battle if Val had time to watch. Instead he was racing up and down the railing, trying to find an opening while erecting his Spirit Shield whenever he thought an attack from a deadly sunray was imminent. He stopped another blast and felt his shield start to waver.

The soldiers clung to anything they could find—vertical railings, pieces of splintered wood—as the ship continued to lurch around so it could return to New Victoria. The Battle Mages outnumbered the surviving Congregation mages at least two to one, but the ship itself helped protect the defenders, and it was slowly picking up speed.

Despite the ferocity of the attack, Val did not seriously consider the possibility the airship could go down—right until all the Battle Mages flew beneath the ship in tandem, disappeared for a long moment, and the hull of the ship exploded beneath his feet.

Stunned, Val went into free fall as the ship broke into pieces, colossal hunks that began to plummet from the sky along with the crew, the Protectorate soldiers, and the remaining mages.

Val's first thought was *ohmygod, they've destroyed an entire airship.*

His second thought was a split-second decision on whether to arrest his fall with magic or use his waning power to summon a Spirit Shield.

He went with the latter, and it proved to be a wise decision. A sunray hit him in the chest as he fell, spinning him around and coming dangerously close to breaking through. When he regained his equilibrium, he looked up and saw the Battle Mages forming a loose circle, beaming their deadly rays at any Congregation mages they could find. The mages were easy to spot because everyone else—the crew and soldiers—were plummeting towards certain death.

Horrified, Val realized his decision might have saved his life. He let himself keep falling, far beneath the circle of death unleashed by the attacking mages, to all appearances a doomed soldier with no magic to stop his fall. Beneath him was an army of men and women armed with swords, spears, and bows and arrows. It was death above and death below.

As the ground rushed up to meet him, Val let his Spirit Shield go and stopped his descent thirty feet before he hit the ground. Without pause, he flew upwards on a diagonal as fast as he could, weaving and spinning to avoid any missiles sent from below. He looked up to find the remaining Congregation mages surrounded and outnumbered, using Wizard Shields and other magical defenses to fend off attacks. A few were hiding behind levitated pieces of the ship. Every now and then someone would send out a spinning tornado, fireball, or other spell into the midst of the enemy, with little success.

After every attack by the Battle Mages, Val noticed a slight dip in their position, which they quickly regained. The Mayan warrior-mages seemed to have perfected the art of using their sunrays and Wizard Shields in tandem with flying. He also noticed the sunbeams seemed weaker than before, though it wasn't going to matter. There were too many of them, and too few Congregation mages remaining. Professor Azara was among them, but either her power was spent, or she couldn't find an opening to attack.

The Battle Mages had not yet noticed him. Should he engage? Fly down and attempt to kidnap Caleb?

Joining the fight would make little difference, and he doubted he would get through to his brother. Not right now. Trying to escape seemed the wisest course of action, but Val couldn't leave his fellow mages to die in this buzzsaw.

With a roar, consumed with adrenaline, he reached deep into his well of power. Instead of summoning twin arcs at his fingertips—which he expected—the magic he brought forth coalesced into a ball of black energy he could barely control. Startled, worried it was about to consume him, he sent it spinning towards the nearest Battle Mage. With a whoosh, as if sucking in the air around it, the hula-hoop of energy slammed into the back of the mage and disintegrated him in an instant. It kept going, scattering friend and foe alike as it tore across the sky and dissipated.

As the enemy mages worked to regroup, Professor Azara screamed into the wind and chaos. "To me, wizards!"

The other Congregation mages were close to her position. Heeding her shout, they flew to her side as the professor of spiritmancy raised her arms with her palms facing down, her waist-length black hair streaming behind her. The closest two mages, one on each side of her, extended their arms towards the professor to hold her in place in midair—a modified Wind Push, Val knew—allowing her to cast her spell.

Two of the Battle Mages had pinpointed Val as the source of the attack. They turned to blast him as Professor Azara dropped her arms. At once, Val felt as if a three-ton stone was attached to his back. He could no longer sustain flight and started plummeting towards the ground, along with every Battle Mage beneath Professor Azara's position. Val tried to stop his fall by flying away but nothing he did had any effect. Terrified, the ground rushing up to meet him, he prepared to die when Professor Azara reached an arm towards him and curled her fingers. At once he was yanked in the opposite direction, flying towards her and the other Congregation mages as fast as he had plummeted towards the ground just moments ago. Whatever spell she had used on him had no effect on the Battle Mages.

The Professor swept her arms across her body as Val neared her position. It felt as if he had bungee-jumped almost to the ground and ricocheted even faster into the sky. But he was now in control and could fly, though the ball of Spirit Fire he had summoned had drained him to the very limits of his constitution. It was all he could do to maintain flight.

A rectangular black doorway as tall and wide as Val appeared in the sky beside Professor Azara. She dropped her arms and swooned, her magic depleted. A downward glance told Val the enemy mages had stopped falling just before they hit the ground, released from whatever spell she had cast by the appearance of the black doorway.

No one wasted any time. The portal was already breaking apart. Baltyr scooped up the unconscious professor in his arms as he flew through the opening, followed by the remaining Congregation mages. Val came last, slipping into the rectangle of darkness just before it dissolved.

The next thing he saw were the spires of New Victoria.

After translocating high in the sky above the Wizard District, Val and the surviving Congregation mages touched down near the infirmary. Only Val and Baltyr were uninjured. After leaving Professor Azara and the other three wizards with a team of shocked cuerpomancers, Baltyr shrugged off their attempts to check him for wounds, snarling as he gripped Val by the elbow and led him towards the Sanctum.

Unsure what was happening, too exhausted to resist, Val could barely sustain flight as they neared the looming black pyramid. The commotion around them grew, wizards and bystanders who had noticed their arrival. By the time he and a grim-faced Baltyr had reached the Sanctum, they were surrounded by people clamoring to know what had happened.

At Baltyr's command, a pair of majitsu cleared the entrance. Synne tried to get through to Val, but Baltyr stopped her in her tracks with a palm and a harsh word. As Val and the high-ranking aeromancer entered the Sanctum, Baltyr called out for someone to bring them food and drink, ordered a wizard guard posted around the entire city, and summoned the War Council.

Braden Shankstone was clustered with a small group of mages by the fountain in the atrium. As Val and Baltyr passed by, Braden's eyes narrowed, and he noticed Baltyr's grip on Val's arm.

After hustling Val down a Wizard Chute and into the War Room, Baltyr finally let him go. Val assumed the older mage had been trying to protect him and reach the Sanctum as fast as possible. They both greedily consumed the water, bread, cheese, and plate of cured meats brought to them by a majitsu. Yet after the light meal, instead of speaking, Baltyr glared at Val with crossed arms as the others arrived one by one: Kjeld, Yasir, Cyrus, and Kalyn Tern.

Confused but not wanting to appear weak, Val said nothing as Lord Alistair flew into the room and, with a twirl of his finger, caused the heavy oak door to fling shut. "Is it true? They destroyed an airship?"

With a slow and determined nod, Baltyr confirmed the impossible.

Lord Alistair slammed his palms on the table. "How? *How* could this happen?"

"They had Battle Mages, milord. Twenty of them."

Everyone looked shocked by the information. The Chief Thaumaturge's face turned white with fury, and for once, he was speechless.

"*Battle* mages?" Kalyn said. "Here? On our doorstep?"

Baltyr gave a weary nod. "They launched a surprise attack we had no hope of defending. As you know, we had half that number of mages aboard the ship, and were not prepared for that such a concerted attack."

As Baltyr recounted the details of the disastrous battle, Lord Alistair grew angrier and angrier, until Val worried he might accidentally vaporize the entire room.

When Baltyr neared the end of his tale, he said, "None of us would have survived without the intervention and quick thinking of Professor Azara, who I can only hope will recover in due course." The aeromancer pointed at Val. "None of us would have survived, that is, except *him*, who somehow managed to be near the rebel camp and outside the ring of enemy mages after the ship exploded. I wonder, if the professor's Spirit Whip had not brought him back, if he'd be dining with his brother tonight? Perhaps he knew of this surprise attack beforehand?"

Val couldn't believe what he was hearing. He jumped to his feet as everyone in the room stared at him. Kjeld's neck turned a dangerous shade of purple,

Kalyn's eyes were frosty, Yasir clenched a gloved fist atop the table, and even Cyrus's eyes tightened with suspicion.

"Valjean," Lord Alistair said in a measured but rigid tone, "kindly *sit* and provide an explanation of how this course of action came to be."

"Of course," Val said, sinking back down. "I had no idea—"

The door flung open, causing Lord Alistair to whirl around, furious at the intrusion. Instead his eyebrows lifted when he saw Professor Azara standing in the doorway, looking as if she was about to collapse. He hurried to help her inside, but she shooed him away and approached with an unsteady gait.

"*Leh*," she said. "I'm fine. Depleted of magic for some time, but able to walk on my own two feet." Her pallor was gray as she shuffled towards the table. As she eased into the seat, Val wondered just how close to death she had come by expending so much magic.

"Val was just about to tell us," Lord Alistair said icily as she sat, "how he came to be on the wrong side of enemy lines before you reeled him in."

"On the wrong side—" Professor Azara looked taken aback, blinking a few times as she stared at the Chief Thaumaturge and then Baltyr. "But of course," she murmured. "You wouldn't have understood." She turned back to Lord Alistair. "Since he is not yet privy to Congregation defensive battle tactics, when the ship exploded, I assume Valjean let himself fall instead of joining us in the circle of protection—"

"That's right," Val said. "I had no idea—"

Still looking at Professor Azara, Lord Alistair raised a finger to silence him.

Professor Azara continued, "It was *Val*, not I, who summoned the ball of spirit that scattered the Battle Mages."

Baltyr scoffed. "Impossible. I'm no spirit mage, but everything I know about the discipline suggests he is not ready for such a powerful release of energy."

"I would have said the same," the professor said, "had I not witnessed it with my own two eyes. Not only that, *leh*, but that much power leaves a mark. I saw the signature, and have no doubt it came from him."

As all eyes turned to Val, he noticed a smile of pride creeping on to Lord Alistair's lips, before he snuffed it. "Valjean? Is this true?"

"It wasn't a conscious decision," Val said. "I was reaching for spirit, and full of adrenaline, and that . . . ball . . . came out."

"You're lucky it didn't consume you," Professor Azara said frankly, and turned to Lord Alistair. "We've been remiss. He needs to complete his education."

"I agree—as soon as this unpleasant business with the rebels is concluded."

Baltyr's eyes slipped to Val. "It appears I owe you an apology."

"It was an honest mistake. If I was in your position, I would have thought the same." Out of the corner of his eye, Val noticed Lord Alistair gave a barely perceptible nod of approval at the decision not to humiliate Baltyr.

"Valjean saved our lives," Professor Azara said. "Or those of us who are left. Had he not distracted the enemy, I would not have had the window to cast Gravity Hammer and open the portal."

Gravity hammer? That feeling of weight when I fell . . . dear God, can she do that?

"Quite impressive," Cyrus murmured, with a glance of approval at Val. "Both of you."

"The effort almost killed me," the professor said with a shrug, "but, *leh*, it did not. Though I fear I'll need a week of rest to return to full strength."

Lord Alistair levitated off the ground and onto the raised dais of spirit. He rubbed his chin in thought and, after a moment, crossed his arms. "We've lost an airship, an entire regiment of Protectorate soldiers, and almost a dozen Congregation mages. Needless to say, after this massacre, we no longer need to worry about a justification for war." He regarded them each in turn. "The only decision that remains is how soon, and in what manner, we move to destroy them."

After a morning engulfed by meetings, including presenting another recap of the battle for the Conclave, Val spent the rest of the day with Adaira, recovering in his lover's arms. They had dinner together at her father's mansion on St. Charles, and though Lord Alistair was not present, he arrived home late that night and surprised Val by summoning him to his private study for a glass of granth. Adaira decided to turn in for the evening. Val placed his hands on the swell of her stomach, kissed her softly on the forehead, and bid her goodnight.

Lord Alistair handed Val a glass of fine granth as he entered the study. Val sank into an armchair next to the alabaster fireplace, above which hung a three-dimensional painting of the Wizard District. Those born with the gift of spirit could shift the perspective of the painting with their minds and view the wondrous spires, parks, and architectural marvels from whatever angle one chose.

The last time the Chief Thaumaturge had summoned Val to a private meeting, he had asked him to join the Congregation, and given him permission to marry his daughter.

The price? Recover the Coffer of Devla, which Val had helped him do.

Still flush with excitement from the battle, worried about Caleb, and proud of his own role in repelling the enemy mages, Val sipped the fiery granth that smelled of warm butterscotch as he waited for Lord Alistair to speak. The Chief Thaumaturge seemed lost in his thoughts, a rare occurrence. Normally he cut to the chase.

Finally Lord Alistair crossed his legs and set down his granth on the table beside his armchair. "Given what occurred today, Yasir tells me it would be wise to assess the strength of the rebel army—particularly the number of Battle Mages who have joined them—before we engage."

"How many enemy mages are there?"

"Less than a thousand Battle Mages in the entire Mayan Kingdom. Even if the Arch Governors sent every single one to New Victoria to fight, which they would never do, we could still defeat them. Quite easily, on our own soil. That said, I prefer not to waste lives or Congregation resources. I plan to send a powerful force into the field and strike a decisive blow. Yasir tells me the scouting report should arrive sometime tomorrow, and our march will begin the next day. I would like you to lead it, alongside Yasir and Kjeld."

Val took a long drink. *Lead the march against my own brother.* "I'm hardly qualified for that."

"No, you are not. Nor should you be. Yasir and Kjeld will handle the logistics for the ground forces, and Baltyr will marshal the wizards. We will send many more mages, of course, enough to guarantee a swift victory. But though I am enraged at the butchery that occurred this morning, I still believe we have a chance to end this war without undue bloodshed. And that chance, Valjean, is you."

Lord Alistair leaned forward and unfurled his left hand, revealing a small onyx bottle the size of a saltshaker. Tiny runes covered the wooden stopper, and Val's breath caught in his throat as he realized the nature of the object. He had seen one of these—and tried to use it—on one other occasion.

He swallowed. "A soul jar?"

"Just until we send him home. It is your final chance to save your brother." The Chief Thaumaturge's expression softened. "At the moment, he'll be safer inside there than anywhere. You will ride at the vanguard of our forces, but only as a figurehead. If you can convince Caleb to meet you on the battlefield, and draw close enough to use this, the Revolution will lose its leader—and the war will be over before it begins."

Lord Alistair leaned into the heat of the fire, reaching across the space that divided them, and offered the soul jar to Val. "Bring your brother to me, and I will send him home."

When Val left the Alistair mansion, he found Gus waiting by the curb to pick him up. This night in particular, Val felt comforted by the presence of his oldest friend on Urfe. As the horse-drawn carriage clacked down St. Charles, Val gazed out at the city with a deeply troubled heart. The fog-drenched moonlight and heaps of Spanish moss obscuring the view could leave one feeling unmoored, lost in time and place, and that was how Val felt when he thought about Caleb.

What hadn't been said by Lord Alistair—because it didn't need to be—was that if Val failed to reach his brother, then no one, neither Val nor anyone else, could save him.

Not only that, but if Caleb refused to stand down, Val would be joining the charge on the opposite side of the battlefield.

Against his own brother.

Did he have a choice? If he couldn't get Caleb to surrender, Val could hardly stop the war. Then again, he didn't have to participate.

But if you run away and leave the city, you'll never see Adaira again, never see your unborn child enter the world.

The carriage turned onto Magazine Street and stopped outside Salomon's Pad. As Val exited, Gus called out to him. "Everythin' all right there? Not sure I recall seein' you so pensive, not even on the first day of wizard school."

Val wanted to lay bare his soul and get his driver's wise opinion on the dilemma, but he knew he couldn't trust anyone with that kind of information. Not even Gus. "I'm fine. Thanks for asking."

Gus spat a gob of tobacco on the curb. "Ye be in need of anythin' laddie, anythin' at all, ye let old Gus know, ye hear?"

A melancholy smile crept to Val's lips. "Thank you, my friend. Now go get some sleep. I'll need you very early tomorrow, an hour before dawn."

"Aye."

Gus clicked to get the horses moving. As the carriage clacked down the street, Val trudged to his front door with footsteps that had never felt so heavy. Inside, he set his staff by the door, shrugged out of his cloak, and knew he was too wired to sleep. Deciding to visit the roof for a nightcap, he experienced one of the greatest shocks of his life when he saw who was waiting on him in the kitchen, mug of ale in hand, his feet kicked up on the table.

Will raised his mug in greeting. "Welcome home, big brother."

-22-

After a moment of stunned silence when Val entered the kitchen of Salomon's Pad, Will saw his brother's intelligent green eyes whisk to Mala, who was sitting at the table next to Will, toying with a string of Fire Beads as she watched Val's every move.

For just a moment, Will experienced a sliver of doubt as to how his brother would react—right before Val rushed over to pull him out of the chair into a fierce bear hug in the middle of the kitchen. It was the greeting they had not had time for on Takros's Isle, when Lord Alistair had interrupted their reunion. The familiarity of his brother's embrace, after being apart for so long and in such mortal peril, overwhelmed Will with emotion.

Val finally pulled away and held him at arm's length. "I don't understand. Why aren't you home? What are you doing here?"

"If by *home* you mean a rat-infested dungeon in a cloud castle in Scotland protected by a storm titan as big as this house, then, well, we decided to try a healthier climate."

"Don't forget the wayward revenant and the menagerist," Mala added. "Or did you know about those already?"

Val looked back and forth between the two. "What are you talking about?"

Mala sneered. "In Macedonia, you watched Alistair open the portal. You're a spirit mage. Did you really not know?"

"Mala—" Will started.

"Let him answer."

"Know what?" Val said. "I thought Will was going back to New Orleans, as Alistair and I agreed."

After Will told him the truth about where Alistair had sent him, Val's jaw slowly dropped, and he sank into his chair and steepled his fingers against his forehead. "I can't believe I let him . . ." With a snarl, he pounded the table.

"Why would Alistair do that? If he's going to break our agreement, why not just . . ."

"Kill me?" Will said.

Val compressed his lips and looked away. "I'm so sorry, Will. Of course I had no idea." His face darkened. "But I do now."

Will glimpsed a strangely troubled look on his brother's face. He brushed his long hair off his forehead as he leaned over his beer. "I've been thinking this over. What if Caleb's use of the Coffer to kill that electromancer spooked Alistair more than we realize? What if he's keeping you around—and keeping me alive—for insurance against Caleb?"

Mala's slender fingers tapped a slow rhythm on the table, her bracelets jingling softly. "I suppose that's possible." She fixed her gaze on Val. "Or is there something else in play?"

His eyes narrowed. "Like what?"

"You tell us."

Just as Will thought his brother's temper might flare, Val took a deep breath and lowered his head. "I'm in a relationship with his daughter," he said, as he looked up at Will. "I wanted to tell you, but we haven't exactly had time for a family chat. It could be that Alistair is . . . protecting her from being hurt."

"By keeping you alive?" Mala said. When Val gave a somber nod, she laughed. "Now *that* I find highly improbable."

"Whatever his faults," Val said, "he loves his daughter very much."

"Everyone loves something in this world. Perhaps he thinks you're truly loyal to him—and maybe, indeed, you are."

"Not anymore," Val said in a low voice.

Mala sneered. "Regardless, it does not explain the decision to keep Will alive once he arrived at Alistair's stronghold. I can see no good reason for this."

"Nor I," Val murmured. "But there are things you should know."

Will exchanged a glance with Mala, and she gave a subtle shake of her head *Don't tell him yet. Let's see what he has to say.*

"We have more news also," Will said. "But go ahead."

After refilling their ale and pouring one for himself, Val gave them a brief recap of his adventures since they had parted so long ago in the cemetery in New Orleans. This included his time at the New Victoria wizard school, the journey with his companions to the strange world of mist to earn his freedom, his agreement with Lord Alistair to find the Coffer and join the Congregation, and finally the events of that very morning, the arrival of Caleb's army outside the city and Val's participation in the disastrous mission.

"So as you can see," Val said, "things have escalated."

"Caleb's that close to the city," Will said, "and he still wants to kill the most powerful mage in the Realm? We have to get him out of here."

"I fully agree," Val said grimly. "Lord Alistair does, too—or so he says. Just before I came here, he asked me to lead the next attack, and try to bring Caleb home before the battle."

"I'll bet he did," Will said. "Surely you saw right through him?"

Val looked embarrassed. "I . . . I just never saw Caleb as a threat worthy of that kind of deception. You, either. Not that someone with Alistair's power would take seriously."

"Not even after what happened at Freetown with the Coffer?"

"That was one electromancer, with a sliver of the power of Lord Alistair. And Caleb doesn't *have* the Coffer. If he did, I would have looked at it differently."

"I don't understand. How *do* you look at it?"

Val tipped his head and shook it. "I don't know, Will. I'm still processing it, trying to figure out Alistair's motive."

"It will be difficult to move against him and risk one's standing in the Congregation," Mala said. She folded her arms and stared at Val. "Sitting at the right hand of the Chief Thaumaturge, no less."

"I admit I enjoy being a wizard," Val said, "and was probably blinded by ambition. But none of this changes the fact I've come to believe the wizards are *right* to suppress the Revolution, though I don't always agree with their methods."

Will could hardly believe what he was hearing, but Mala retorted first.

"How lovely that you don't agree with mass murder and oppression," she said.

"Mass murder?" Val said calmly. "Oppression? You mean the very things the Pagan Wars were fought to prevent—against wizards?"

"That happened hundreds of years ago."

"The black sash gypsies are here today, in the city. I personally saw them slaughter a dear friend, and try to kill me and many others."

"What?" Will said. "Who?"

"It's a long story, but they've committed atrocities all over the city, up and down the Protectorate." He looked at Mala. "Or do you deny this?"

"The Black Sash is a small and violent faction of the clans," Mala said. "Are you trying to argue the wizards are an oppressed class?"

"No, but they are in the vast minority. They could not stop a concerted revolt by every citizen, nor would a world without the support of the common born be a world in which the wizards would want to live." His eyes went distant. "I saw for myself what the future could be, in that other world I told you about. It was an alternate reality of Urfe where the mages lost the Pagan Wars, and were still being persecuted. Hunted down and treated like dogs. Sacrificed to demons. They tried to hang Adaira from a *tree*." He shuddered. "Like I said, I do think the Congregation's tactics are oppressive, and Lord Alistair has gone too far. But it's not black and white. I know plenty of honorable wizards. Most of them, in fact. And why not just take the oaths and become law-abiding citizens? Is it really that hard?"

"I suppose giving up your principles comes quite easily to a slick-tongued schemer like you," she said.

"I would say the same to a mercenary with no ethics."

Will jumped to his feet. "Stop it—both of you! Val, I—" Will put a hand to his forehead. "I don't know everything that's happened to you, and I understand it might be more complicated than we realize, though you'll never convince me the wizards are in the right. I saw them destroy Freetown with my own eyes. But that doesn't matter right now. Lord Alistair imprisoned me for some reason, and we have to put aside our differences and help Caleb. Do you agree?"

"Absolutely."

"Good."

Mala gave Will a sharp glance, as if to say *careful whom you trust here*.

Val set his beer down. "But there's a problem. While of course I agree in theory, if we can't trust Lord Alistair, I don't know how to help Caleb, unless he agrees to call off his vendetta. I don't see any portals to Earth lying around."

After a moment, it dawned on Will what he meant. "Alistair offered you the same deal with Caleb, didn't he?"

"Yes. He did."

"And obviously that's off now? Right?"

"Of course," Val said, looking so wounded that Will felt bad for having to say it. "What do you think . . ." Val put his hands to his temples as if a great weight bore down on him. After a moment, he got up, went into the hallway, and returned with a small onyx bottle the size of a saltshaker. He set the bottle on the table. "When I meet Caleb on the battlefield, I'm supposed to use this to bring him back. It's a—"

"Soul jar," Will said.

Val gave him a sharp look. "How did you know that?"

Will glanced at Mala, who was still seething from the argument with Val, and then back at the onyx bottle. "It's my turn to talk, and you're not going to like what I have to say."

"Okay," Val said slowly.

"From what I've seen, I don't think we're going to be able to convince Caleb to go home."

"Me either. I met with him already and he used his army to kick me out."

"You met with him?" Will said. "When?"

"A few days ago. I'll tell you all about it." He waved a hand. "Go on."

Will took a swig of ale and looked his brother in the eye. "If we can't convince Caleb to stop what he's doing, Lord Alistair is going to imprison or kill him, and I've no doubt we're next on his radar. In my mind, that leaves us with only one option."

"Which is?"

"Help Caleb win."

Val stared at him. "You can't be serious. You have no idea of the power Alistair wields."

"With the sword and the Coffer, if we can surprise him somehow, we might have a ghost of a chance. And I don't see any other way."

As Val continued to shake his head in disbelief, Will described their ordeal after landing in the dungeon, including the encounter with the ghost of Alistair's brother, but leaving out the conversation with Dane Blackwood. They also filled Val in on the conversation with Dashi, and their belief the Coffer of Devla was being kept in a vault beneath the Sanctum.

Val grew more and more distraught as he listened. By the end of the tale, his hands were clenched atop the table, his mouth was rigid, and Will knew from the dangerous glint in his eye that his brother was about to explode.

Yet there was a shadow behind his gaze as well, that same troubled look that Will wasn't sure how to process, and which surely involved the woman he had mentioned. Could Val's loyalty truly be divided? After what he had just heard?

"Your brother speaks the truth," Mala said to Val. "Every single word."

"There's one more thing," Will said. He went into his bedroom, retrieved the item he had carried back from the cloud keep, and set it on the table beside the smaller but similar onyx bottle Val had brought.

"Is that another soul jar?" Val said, his eyes widening.

"It is."

"Who's inside it?"

"No one anymore. But it used to be our father."

"Excuse me?"

"I saw Dad, Val. I *talked* with him."

After a long period in which Val did not move or even seem to draw a breath, he leaned forward, his voice low and hard. "What are you talking about?"

"He was in there, and he was alive—or at least his spirit was. He was more of a shade, I think. We found him in Alistair's stronghold. He stuck Dad in there after they fought all those years ago. He's been inside for years, maybe decades on Urfe. He was so far gone he only lasted a few minutes when we released him."

"He's been imprisoned in a bottle all that time? All alone?"

As Will nodded, Val looked as if someone had pole-axed him through the chest. Will repeated the conversation with their father as best he could remember, as well as the terrible secret the shade of Lord Alistair's brother had revealed to them.

"He killed his own brother?" Val whispered.

"Still pondering that last shred of loyalty?" Mala said.

Val looked down at his hands. "Did Dad . . . did he say anything about me?"

"He said to tell you he loved you. More than anything else in the world."

Val's face took on a greenish pallor, as if he might be ill right there on the table. With a snarl, he jumped up and began pacing the room like a trapped animal, his neck and face so splotched with rage Will worried he might have a stroke. Even Mala's suspicions seemed to melt as she witnessed the palpable fury on his face.

Just thinking about what Lord Alistair had done to their family caused Will's blood to boil as well. To find Zariduke and further his own ambitions, Lord Alistair had kept their father in a soul jar, stripped their mother of her sanity, indirectly killed Charlie, ruined the brothers' lives, and was almost assuredly trying to kill all three of them.

When Val finally stopped pacing, his hands had stopped shaking, and his face was deadly calm. He took a seat across from them and laced his fingers atop the table. "This plan to retrieve the Coffer—what did you have in mind?"

Later that night, after Mala claimed exhaustion and retired to one of the bedrooms, Will found his brother on the roof, staring at the colored spires of the Wizard's District rising above the city. The last time the two of them had beheld that magnificent sight together was the night before all three brothers and Lance had departed with Mala for Salomon's Pad. At the time, they had barely believed Urfe was real.

Not in Will's wildest dreams could he have imagined the incredible series of adventures that would befall all three of them, and how entangled they would become in the events of the Realm.

Things weren't so complicated in my papasan chair, playing video games and reading fantasy novels and munching on Cool Ranch Doritos.

And they certainly weren't so dangerous.

A light breeze carried the sweet stench of dying vegetation. Will had always enjoyed the transformation of the seasons in New Orleans. Summer was his least favorite, but fall meant relief from the crushing humidity, the rustle of leaves in a cemetery, and the whisper of all things dark and mysterious on a foggy night among the oaks. Winter was a short and bitter affair, surprisingly cold when the sea winds blew, but a time to reflect and yearn for the warmth of spring, and celebrate Mardi Gras.

Would he live to see a new year dawn?

Would any of the brothers?

"Lord Alistair's daughter," Will said as he stood beside Val. "Your girlfriend. What's her name?"

"Adaira," Val said. "And she's my fiancé."

Will threw his arm around his brother's shoulders. "You're engaged? Congratulations!"

A small, contented smile crept to Val's lips. "Thanks."

"What is it with my brothers pulling the trigger over here? First Caleb, who I never thought would settle down, and now you?"

"It surprised me, too."

"How long have you known her?"

"Long enough," he said quietly.

An expression of love and contentment swept across Val's troubled expression, softening his features. It lasted but a moment, but it was so powerful Will could tell his brother was in love. He wanted to say *I hope I get to meet her*, but from the darkness that quickly smothered the love, he knew they were thinking the same thought.

That the father of Val's fiancé was the man who was trying to kill them.

Val forced a smile. "From the looks of things, the women of Urfe have your number too. I saw you and Mala before she turned in."

"It took me a while, but yeah. Things are looking up on that front."

"You're not worried she might stick a knife in your back?"

"Only if she's had a really bad morning. Hey, there's something I need to know. Back when we fought Zedock in the cemetery . . . is Lance . . ."

"He's alive, Will. No longer with the police, I'm sorry to say, but he survived. Not only that—I saw him, and Yasmina, with Caleb."

Will was thunderstruck. "Lance is here? How?"

"No idea."

"Thank God he's alive, but . . ." Will put a hand to his forehead. It had been a *very* long day.

They reminisced about home for a while, tacitly agreeing to avoid discussing the impending trials and decisions that hung over their heads like the sword of Damocles. Not until Will could barely keep his eyes open, and he was ready to turn in, did he ask his brother if he had any more thoughts on how to reach the Coffer inside the Sanctum.

Val slowly shook his head. "Only that we're going to need help."

Will was too tired to press him on that. They embraced, and Will pulled open the trap door that led to the kitchen. Right before he descended the drop-down ladder, he glanced up to find Val staring at the spires with his arms folded, wrapped in his wool cloak, looking as if he might stand there all night. Will knew there must be a million thoughts racing through his eldest brother's mind, thinking through all the angles, brainstorming solutions that did not end in disaster.

Trying to find a way out.

-23-

As the Congregation airship fell from the sky and the smoking pieces crash-landed in the swampy forest, Caleb's army watched the spectacle in stunned disbelief, followed by a roar of victory. The cheers grew even louder as the surviving Battle Mages swooped down from the sky in their golden capes and landed in the center of the glade.

The army surrounded their Mayan saviors, weapons raised, adrenaline surging through the camp like wildfire. Caleb joined them, thrusting his diamond-headed mace into the air, shocked to the core by their victory.

We just destroyed a Congregation airship. With Congregation mages aboard.

He barely had time to enjoy the moment before the harsh reality registered. Not only had the war started in earnest, but they had bloodied an enemy they thought was invincible. There was no turning back now. No marching in peace to new Victoria. No fleeing to the Ninth Protectorate.

It was win or lose—and he had no doubt the Congregation would do everything in its power to destroy them.

The thought was terrifying. His army might have drawn first blood, but they had launched a surprise attack with powerful Battle Mages on their side, and the Congregation had sent a tiny fraction of its forces.

Still, they had *won*. Caleb would let his army savor the moment while he and the inner council plotted the next course of action.

After making a lap around the camp on his stallion with his fist raised in the air, providing a further boost to morale, Caleb returned to the bower of live oaks to meet with his friends and advisors. Aahpo slipped away from the celebration to join them, his face drawn with fatigue as he sat cross-legged on his golden cloak. The day was sunny and pleasant, the grove filled with birdsong.

Tamás approached the Battle Mage and rested a hand on his shoulder. "Thank you, my friend. That was a sight I shall never forget. The Congregation forced to flee like a frightened cur!"

Overcome by emotion, the Roma leader turned away and clapped a hand over his chest, his eyes misty. Caleb remembered that Tamás had lost a brother in the same Darklands mines which the Congregation used to produce tilectium for their airships. Watching one of them fall must have been a powerful moment for him.

"I need to rest," Aahpo said, "but not until we decide on the next course of action. We have a saying among my people: if you stick a hand into the hole of the snake, prepare for it to be bitten."

"And bitten fast," the Brewer said, echoing everyone's thoughts. "They won't let this stand for long."

Lance rested a muscular forearm on his knee. "You know them best," he said to Tamás. "How long do we have before they return?"

"I'm unsure," the revolutionary said slowly. "After what just happened, they'll want to respond swiftly to save face. But they will also want to reassess our strength. They will send spies," he glanced up at the canopy as if one of the birds might be watching, "possibly in familiar form. Most of all, the Congregation will want to know how many Battle Mages will join in the next attack."

All eyes turned to Aahpo. Caleb, too, was keen to know the answer to that question.

The young Battle Mage lifted his weary head. "Most of our mages are posted on the border or along the Great River, where the Protectorate has amassed forces. I can petition the arch governors of our kingdom for reinforcements, but even if they agree, that will take time."

"How long?" Caleb said.

"Days, at the least."

Caleb swallowed. He doubted they had that long. "And how many more will come?"

"It's hard to say. The border must remain protected."

"It's not enough," Tamás said slowly. "Not *nearly* enough. And I do not think the Congregation will wait three days to attack."

"Nor I," Aahpo said grimly.

Lance waved a hand. "Why did your . . . arch governors . . . bother to send so few mages? Don't get me wrong, I'm extremely grateful, and you saved our lives, but they must've known the Congregation would retaliate."

"Our orders were to act as scouts for the greater force along the river,"

Aahpo said. "Your appearance out of nowhere surprised us as much as the Congregation."

"And your orders now?" Caleb said.

"To return to the river, unless I see fit to stay. Which I . . . your brother saved my life once. Now I have saved yours. My debt to your family is repaid. Yet the threat to our kingdom remains. If we can threaten or even distract the Congregation, it would help give our people time to prepare for war. That is an honorable goal."

"What about sanctuary?" Yasmina said. "If we could reach the border, would your arch governors provide shelter to these people? Maybe even relocate them?"

"I wish that we could," Aahpo said. "We have a strict policy against immigration. An exception can be made for families or individuals, but never for a group this large. I am sorry."

"It is as it has always been," Tamás said quietly. "Our people are on their own, and must forge their own destiny."

Instead of being offended, Aahpo looked pensive. "We, too, were once persecuted. We, too, had to carve a home from lands that belonged to stronger tribes. I can make no promises, but our interests are aligned, and I will help you if I can. That said, I will not lead my mages on a mission of suicide."

By dinnertime, as the descending sun dappled the forest glade with shadows, Caleb sat alone in his tent with a ration of stew he had barely touched. Despite endless meetings, no decisions had been made, no viable plan of action proposed. The thrill of victory had receded, replaced by a growing awareness, a dread, that the response from the Congregation would be swift, sudden, and overwhelming. Aahpo and his battle mages had saved their lives, but for how long?

The Prophet, of course, had no qualms about leading his people into another battle. He believed their god would reach down with a divine hand to smite their enemies.

Caleb knew it didn't work that way. If so, then omnipotent beings wouldn't let bad things happen to good people. They wouldn't let children die in accidents or from hunger or struck dead by sneering electromancers.

A voice called his name from outside the tent. "Hey buddy, can I come in?"

"Sure."

The flap of the tent parted, and Lance poked his head in. A short bearded now covered his thick neck and strong jaw. "You're not gonna believe who just showed up in the forest."

Caleb wasn't in the mood for drama. "Just tell me."

"You remember Hashi?" Lance said, with a catch in his voice.

The name evoked a sharp memory. Hashi was a Chickasaw warrior who, along with Akocha and Fochik, had guided the Blackwood brothers on their journey to Leonidas's castle when they had first arrived on Urfe. Over the years, many Chickasaw warriors had joined the Revolution on behalf of the eastern protectorates.

Though less than a year had passed, the adventure with Hashi seemed a lifetime away. He was a good man and one of the fiercest warriors Caleb had ever seen. Near the end of the journey, he had sacrificed himself by using his magical cudgel to shatter a dungeon floor, saving everyone from a terrifying monster known as a stone golem. Caleb would never forget watching Hashi sink into the lake of acid without making a sound, proud and calm to the end of his life.

Hashi and Lance, both products of a warrior culture, had grown close on the journey. The selfless sacrifice of the native man had hit Lance hard.

"Of course," Caleb said quietly. "What about him?"

"His son is here—and he's requested to see you."

Caleb followed Lance down a game path on the northern side of camp. The area was a low-lying, inaccessible part of the forest, marked by saw palmettos and pecan trees rising out of the dense undergrowth.

"How much further?" Caleb said, after they had walked a few minutes down the path.

"Almost there."

"Who found him?"

"He tripped one of the wards on purpose—somehow he knew where it was set—and waited for someone to come. Branyn and Yasmina are there with him now."

"Are you sure he's one of the good guys?" Caleb said, his pace quickening at the thought of Yasmina on the edge of camp with someone unknown. He knew she roamed the woods all the time, and had mad wilder skills. But he didn't trust this world and never would.

"Yaz and Branyn promised to stay behind the wards until you got there."

"What if he has mages with him? Or is one himself? Why did you leave her?"

"It's Hashi's son, and he came to meet us alone." Then he said, more quietly, "I care about her too, you know."

"I'm sure you do," Caleb said curtly.

"Plus that harpy eagle with claws as long as a grizzly bear's is watching from a tree." He shuddered. "I wouldn't mess with that thing. I don't think Yasmina needs me or anyone else looking out for her."

"It's not about that. I'm not losing anyone else I love."

"Hey buddy, I'm just saying—"

Caleb raised a hand to cut him off as they rounded a bend and the terrain shifted to a cypress swamp marked by brackish water and lichen-draped trees. Twenty feet ahead, Caleb saw Yasmina and Branyn standing where the path ended at the edge of the water. Ten yards past them, squatting on a mound of roots and grass beside a cypress tree, was an indigenous man in leather breeches who was unmistakably Hashi's son. Like his father, he had a stern and proud bearing, hands the size of baseball gloves, and a blacksmith's shoulders. Intricate tribal tattoos swarmed his arms and torso. Though not quite as large as his father, he was still in his late teens, and already bigger than Lance. In a show of good faith, his cudgel was on the ground, leaning against a tree.

"I hear you want to talk to me," Caleb called out as he walked up to join Branyn and Yasmina.

"His name is Chooshe," Yasmina said in a low voice. "He hasn't said a word since we sent the runner for you and Lance.

The Chickasaw warrior stood. "You are Caleb?" he said, with a thick Common accent.

"In the flesh."

"Then aye, I've come to exchange words. I was sent because you knew my father. Are you aware you've entered our lands?"

Caleb exchanged a glance with the others, and then made a rash decision. He handed his mace to Lance and stepped into the water.

Branyn grabbed his arm. "You're about to leave the safety of the wards."

"Then be ready to cover me."

"What are you doing?" Lance said. "Let me go with you."

"I'm going alone," Caleb said in a tone that left no room for discussion. He glanced at Yasmina, but unlike the two men, who were watching Chooshe with wary eyes, she met Caleb's gaze with a calm expression, as if she knew what he was doing and approved.

With Chooshe looking on, Caleb waded through the cypress knees and calf-deep water, walking slowly to keep his balance. When he reached the mound Chooshe was standing on, Caleb stepped onto dry ground, bowed deeply, and offered a forearm clasp. "Your father gave his life for me, as well as my friends and brothers. He was a brave man and a great warrior. I'm proud to have known him."

Chooshe's face tightened with emotion as he accepted the arm clasp. "Thank you," he said, looking at Caleb with respect.

"You said we're on your land. We didn't know. Is that going to be a problem?"

"Where did you come from?"

"That's . . . complicated. A portal, of sorts, from the Ninth Protectorate."

Chooshe digested the information. "We witnessed the battle this morning. You oppose the Congregation?"

"We oppose anyone who wants to kill us and our families. The Congregation has left us no choice."

"We too are being hunted, as well as our brothers and sisters in all our lands. Alistair does not honor the old treaties."

"I'm sorry to hear that," Caleb said. "So where does that leave us?"

"What do you plan to do next?"

"I'm sort of figuring it out along the way. My goal is to get the Coffer of Devla back and use it to force the Congregation to listen to us. Don't ask me how we'll do that. I don't know. Right now, to be honest, our goal is to stay alive. The Congregation is going to want payback for this morning, and my guess is they'll want it soon. Again, I'm sorry we've brought this to you."

After considering Caleb's words, Chooshe glanced into the trees and folded his massive arms. "On behalf of our tribal council, on which I have taken my father's place, I am able to offer you not just passage, but safe harbor for as long as you remain on our land."

"Thank you. What does that mean exactly?"

"It means we will view an attack on you as an attack on our tribe." He whistled long and loud with a mellifluous, birdsong melody. In response, tribal warriors emerged from the swamp behind Chooshe, stepping out from behind trees and canoes and mounds of grass hidden in the vegetation. As Caleb gawked at the hundreds if not thousands of armed tribesmen that had appeared, Chooshe picked up his cudgel and slapped the heavy end into his palm. "Maybe we cannot defeat the Congregation in battle, but we can make their life very difficult in the swamp."

Late that night, after Caleb and his advisors met with Chooshe to formulate a plan of action, the Prophet approached Caleb around the bonfire. While warming his hands, Caleb thought about his brothers, the risky plan they had devised with Chooshe, and all the lives in his hands.

The Prophet's animal-hair tunic smelled of sweat, honey, and the damp forest floor. "How fortuitous the arrival of the native people. I see the hand of Devla at work again."

"Chooshe's offer is the sins of the Congregation coming back to bite them."

"I see the gentle hand of faith has still not found its way to your side. Such is it written: *Faith is required of Devla's prophets, but not of his warrior*. Scholars have long debated the singular noun of that verse in the Canticles, and most consider it a mistranslation. But it must refer to *the* warrior. The Templar."

Caleb snarled. It didn't matter to him what the Prophet chose to believe. The Tao of Caleb supported all viewpoints, all personal choices that did not harm others. What infuriated him was the constant insinuation that Caleb was some sort of chosen one, and that a divine force was intervening on his behalf. *If Devla gave a damn about me, he would have saved my wife and child.* "You do realize how this will probably end? Are you still going to be carrying on about Devla if a pyromancer burns the camp alive?"

"You mistake my intent," the Prophet said, with a sad smile. "My goal has never been to lead us to victory. That is not my place." He laid a hand on Caleb's arm, his eyes shining with the fervor of belief. "My goal is to fulfill the will of Devla."

The next morning, as Caleb was breaking down his tent, a bird the color of fresh blood flew high above the camp, hovered overhead, and then plummeted straight downward. As everyone pointed and shouted, it became apparent the bird was aiming for Caleb. The bird was similar in size and shape to an eagle, but the flames trailing from its feathers reminded Caleb of a phoenix.

Branyn and Elaina tried to arrest its flight with funnels of wind. The bird flew right through their spells. The arrows that were launched fared no better. Just before the creature reached Caleb, Yasmina's harpy eagle screeched and swooped down from a tree, trying to take the smaller creature in its claws. Caleb marveled at the speed and power of the harpy eagle even as its talons failed to arrest the flight of the flame bird.

Instead of running, Caleb stood in place with his mace raised, not wanting to endanger anyone else, poised to take it on. At the last moment, the bird-creature transformed into a humanoid the same blood-red color as the bird, and landed on its feet in front of Caleb. The facial features of the strange being were only half-formed, as if made of magical clay. It began to speak in a toneless voice. "The forces of the Congregation approach. At noon today, your presence is requested by your brother, Val Blackwood, at the vanguard of the battle. He seeks a parlay to avoid bloodshed and gives his oath no harm will come to you. Meet him atop Oyster Knoll at the appointed hour. Do not be late."

Before Caleb could respond, the crimson being dissolved into beaded fragments that looked for all the world like droplets of blood. Like a bleeding wound without a host, the droplets fell to the ground and soaked into the soil.

Branyn was the first to reach Caleb, his eyes wide as he stared at the wet patch on the ground. He bent to touch his fingers to the substance, sniffed it, tasted it. "A blood missive. I've heard rumors of such a thing, but have never witnessed one."

Caleb folded his arms. "What is it?"

"They're made by a haruspex, a rare specialty of wizard who studies the entrails of animals, including human beings. Often they're called to reconstruct a sequence of past events. But they have other talents."

"Can this . . . message . . . be trusted?"

Branyn looked back up. "Once formed, the contents of such a missive cannot be altered. It can only be sent by using the blood of a family member of the intended recipient. If no blood tie is found within range, the spell dissipates without activating."

"So my brother sent this? You're one hundred per cent certain?"

"That or someone else in your immediate family. There is no other way."

-24-

Oyster Knoll was a patch of raised grassland a mile east of the clearing that Caleb's army was using as a home base. Thought to have once been a fortification built by indigenous peoples, the elevation of the "knoll" was only slightly higher than the surrounding forest, rising to a height of fifty-five feet at the center. The knoll acquired its name when the Protectorate Byway—the only one for hundreds of miles—had divided the raised plain into two halves that resembled the shape of a cracked oyster shell.

Caleb whispered soothing words to Margo, his young stallion, as he left the safety of the trees and trotted onto the Byway. The roiling leaden sky mirrored the color and temperament of his horse, as well as Caleb's mood.

There was nothing but swampland and dense forest surrounding the knoll for miles. Nothing, that was, except for the lone figure at the apex of the hillock, and the thousands of mages and Protectorate soldiers massed behind him. The Protectorate forces stretched the width of the grassland—at least two hundred yards—and continued back into the forest as far as Caleb could see. A chill swept through him at the sight of dozens of mages hovering in the sky above the ground troops, surveying the terrain. During the night, an airship must have ferried them all from New Victoria.

The cloaked figure on the hill carried a staff in his right hand. Caleb drew closer and recognized the crescent azantite tip. He raised a hand in greeting, and Val raised one back. Margo snorted as Caleb dismounted and left her to munch on the grass.

Wrapped in his black cloak with silver stitching, the diamond-headed mace concealed at his side, his vambraces prepared to counter an arrow or spear attack, Caleb slowly approached his brother, watching the troops behind him for a sign of any movement.

The breeze fluttered the high collar of Val's cloak of fine gray wool that he wore clasped at the neck. When they met, neither moved to embrace the other, remembering how the last encounter had ended. "Thank you for coming alone," Val said.

Caleb's voice was cold. "I see you didn't."

Val glanced over his shoulder at the Protectorate forces. "You have my word they won't try to harm you. Not until an hour after we part."

"Your word?" Caleb gave a harsh laugh. "You mean like the last time, when you tried to shove me through a portal?"

"I apologize. I thought I was doing the right thing."

"So you've changed your mind? What is it now, turn myself in and you'll do your best to make it a swift death?"

Val snarled. "Caleb, *listen*. Do you realize what you've done? Your army destroyed an airship and embarrassed the Congregation. They'll never forgive you for that."

"Don't you mean *we'll* never forgive you? You're one of them now, brother."

Val shook his head. "Do you think I'd sell out my own brother?"

"To be honest, I don't know what you're capable of."

"I'd have to say the same of you now."

"Are we done here? I was under the impression you had something to tell me."

"I came to offer you one last chance to surrender. You would have to go home to Earth, and the Prophet would have to stand trial, but if you agree, the rest of the army will be given the chance to take the Oaths and start the path to citizenship."

Caleb stared at him in disbelief. "Why should we trust Alistair? More likely he'll kill the men and throw the women and children in the Fens."

"You can't win, Caleb. The Congregation will squash you like a bug. A handful of Battle Mages won't save you this time. The Congregation has power you wouldn't believe."

"This is what you came to tell me? Surrender or die? Yeah, we got that one covered."

"Please, Caleb. Take the offer. Go home."

"Go to hell."

After staring at him with pursed lips, Val began speaking in a low voice that sounded ominously like an incantation. Caleb took a step forward, reaching beneath his cloak for the handle of his mace. "You better not be casting a spell."

Val held up a finger but kept speaking. Caleb was forced to decide between attacking his brother—and risk breaking the spell of protection the Chickasaw shamans had cast—or let Val finish whatever he was doing. Despite his misgivings, he couldn't bring himself to raise his hand against his own flesh and blood. With a snarl, he turned to leave.

Val lowered his hand. "It's done. A spell of silence surrounds us, in case the Congregation wizards are listening."

Caleb stopped moving. "What do you mean?"

"Everything I just told you—while true—was for show. I knew you'd refuse, but I had to say it again, in case someone was listening."

"Won't they be suspicious of the sudden silence?"

"Not if we embrace and pretend it's our last moment together. But we should act quickly."

As Val approached and threw his arms around him, Caleb remained stiff. He could not deny that it felt good to feel his brother's embrace, but he had not forgiven him for trying to send him home—or for joining the Congregation.

"Things have happened," Val said softly in his ear. "Major things."

"Like what?"

Val spoke quickly and urgently, describing his meeting with Will and the bombshell revelation that Lord Alistair had stuffed their father in a soul jar and left his mind to rot. "It looked something like this," Val said, pulling a small jar out of the inside of his cloak and reaching for the stopper.

Caleb shoved Val away, backpedaling from the jar.

"Thank you," Val said. "That's exactly the reaction I needed them to see. Alistair sent me here today to trick you into the jar."

Caleb looked down at the horrible little vessel, still unsure if he could trust what he had just heard. "So? This adds to Alistair's list of sins, but my mind was already made up. It doesn't change anything."

"It does for me," Val said softly.

"Really? You'd give up all of this?" Caleb swept a hand towards the Congregation forces, and the city of spires unseen in the distance. The power and wealth it represented.

"Alistair ruined our lives and lied to me. He destroyed our *father*, Caleb. He imprisoned Will, and I've no doubt he wants to kill the two of us as well. He thinks we're a threat in some way. Maybe it's the sword, or the Coffer, or both. I'm unsure, and I don't care." He looked away. "Alistair has to pay."

"So what are you going to do?"

"Help Will get the Coffer. We think it's being held beneath the Sanctum. He has the sword already. If we can use them to kill Alistair or even hold him off, I think there's a chance the Congregation will back down. Alistair has supporters, but some think he has gone too far."

"So you think it's possible? To kill him?"

"Not really. But I'm going to try."

Caleb stared into Val's penetrating green eyes for a long moment. "Why should I trust you?"

"What do you mean? After what you've just heard—"

"Which could be a lie."

"It isn't. Swear on my life I'm telling you the truth, Caleb."

"Like I said, I don't know what you're capable of anymore."

Val grimaced in frustration. "Listen, we've had our differences over the years, but our family means more to me than anything else. It always has and it always will. Let me help you, Caleb. Please. Surrender, and I'll find a way to free you. I swear it. We'll get the Coffer and fight Alistair together."

"Why the hell should I surrender?"

"Because I can't keep you alive otherwise."

They locked gazes. Caleb took a step back, still eying the soul jar.

"We won't do it that way," Val said. He returned the jar to the pocket of his cloak. "I'll fly you to the city myself, and come for you as soon as I can. The Sanctum is almost impossible to sneak into and I need a few days to make a plan."

"You want to help me? Fine. But like I said, I can't trust you anymore."

Val threw up a hand in frustration. "Caleb, *listen*."

"Find a way to get the Coffer. That's how you can help. Bring it here and then we'll talk."

"We don't have that much time," Val whispered. "They'll kill you today."

Caleb backed away, his hand on his mace and his eyes locked onto his brother's. "Bring me the Coffer, Val."

* * *

After Caleb left Oyster Knoll, he joined Yasmina and Tamás on a footpath just inside the tree line. Yasmina ushered them deeper into the forest, watching carefully for signs of pursuit.

Though Caleb could not see or hear them, he knew that Chickasaw warriors surrounded them in the forest, ready to secure a safe return. But Val kept his word and no one followed. Caleb was afraid it had all been a feint, and his brother was going to try one last time to send him home. He had prepared for that contingency before the meeting, and did not think Val had suspected the full-sensory illusion, even when they had embraced.

"How did it go?" Tamás asked, once they felt safe enough to speak.

"Not as expected. I'll update everyone when we return."

Yasmina gripped his arm. "I'm glad you're safe, and that was useful. I was able to get a good look at their forces."

"And?"

Her hand fell away. "Thousands of soldiers, a regiment of majitsu, and at least a hundred mages. Easily enough to overwhelm us."

"Good thing our plan isn't to stick around to be overwhelmed."

After rejoining the army, Caleb met with his advisors and the Prophet in the grove of live oaks. When Caleb relayed Val's message, the Prophet murmured a prayer of thanks to Devla, and Tamás's eyes sparked with hope. "Do you think your brother can do it? Reach the Coffer?"

"I've no idea. Both my brothers are resourceful, but if the Coffer is secure in the Sanctum . . ." He took a deep breath and didn't finish the thought.

My first worry is keeping these people alive for another day.

"Did he suspect the illusion?" Branyn asked. "If so, and his intentions are not as they say, it could impact our plan."

Caleb shook his head. "He didn't bat an eye."

"We should go," Lance said, pushing off the low branch he was sitting on. "The shamans are in position."

"Good," Caleb said, with a curt nod.

On his way out, the Prophet touched his elbow. "A prayer before you leave? Today above all days, we will need Devla's blessing."

Caleb didn't even bother with a reply as he swept out of the grove. Yasmina, Lance, and the Brewer followed him out, while Tamás, Branyn, and even Aahpo stayed behind to kneel with the Prophet in prayer.

Half an hour later, Caleb crouched on a spongy patch of swamp grass, preparing for the onslaught of Congregation forces, smelling of a foul paste the Chickasaw used to ward off insects. He slapped at the occasional reckless bug that made it through to gnaw at his skin.

"I can see them," Yasmina whispered from beside him. She was clutching her owl staff and peering through a gap in the trees. "A line of wizards at the front are dismantling the wards. They'll be here in minutes."

"What's the advance formation like?" Branyn asked.

"Majitsu at the vanguard to protect the wizards. A line of cavalry is right behind them. After that, it's . . . it's a lot."

"With any luck, the advance wizards will float right over the trap," Tamás said.

"Go time," Lance said, jumping to his feet. "The paladins are in place."

The Brewer strummed a chord on his lyre. "See you on the other side. One way or another."

The inner council dispersed to lead their respective divisions. Three regiments would head immediately into different sections of the swamp and begin the half-day journey to the rendezvous point. The fourth regiment, led by Caleb and Tamás and the Prophet, was supported by a large group of warriors and paladins waiting in the forest south of the camp's main clearing. This was the main front they would present to the enemy.

A front that would disappear like fog in bright sun.

Soon the air rang with the march of booted feet. The crazed laughter of hyena wolves floated on the wind, guarding the flanks of the Protectorate forces, making Caleb's skin crawl. He calmed his nerves by taking deep breaths of fresh air and gripping his leather thong necklace with Marguerite's wedding ring attached. He tuned his mind to the soothing cadence of the shamans chanting in a ring around the clearing, maintaining the illusion by linking their minds in a way he did not understand. One of the shamans, a woman named Posha with a braid of hair so long it almost brushed the ground, stood next to Caleb and Tamás. She was the conductor of the orchestra, and told them she would be invisible to the enemy.

Just before the first Congregation wizard floated into view, Posha stood to face Caleb and his army. She swept her hands upwards, signaling for everyone to rise. Caleb drew his mace and adopted a battle stance. Tamás was right beside him, gripping his sword with both hands, his long hair secured in a ponytail. The Prophet remained on his knees, head bowed in prayer, right until the wizards appeared. After letting them see him, a carrot for a very large stick, he melted back into the army.

After dismantling the wards, most of the wizards at the front of the Protectorate forces dropped back to let the cavalry lead the charge. Caleb suspected the wizards were waiting for the Battle Mages to appear. Though not ideal, the plan remained the same. As the shamans continued to chant, Posha whipped her arms forward, inducing a roar from the army. The Protectorate forces yelled in return and surged forward to meet them, swords and halberds raised, spurring their steeds into a thunderous gallop meant to break the spirit of the enemy.

The clearing was wide enough to allow fifty riders abreast. As the first wave of cavalry poured through, and the hard ground turned to mush, their horses passed right through the illusion and plunged into a swamp full of crocosaurs and giant water snakes just south of the clearing. The horses fell or simply stopped, confused by the sudden presence of water. Many of their riders plunged into the swamp. The second line of cavalry was charging too fast to stop, and plowed right into their own forces.

Caleb and his army added to the confusion by racing forward as the shamans kept chanting, the projected illusion making it seem as if they were charging right into the enemy's midst. They added to the pretense by cutting and slashing and feinting, throwing the enemy forces into further confusion.

The shamans' spell worked as planned. A hundred Protectorate cavalry were lost to the swamp or trampled in the initial rush. By the time they realized they were hurtling into a swamp they could not see, and the soldiers they were battling were not real, Caleb's army had closed in from the flanks and unleashed a furious attack with spells and ranged weapons. Between the longbows, the deadly sunbeams of the Battle Mages, and the handheld lava cannons shooting fireballs from the palms of the darvish, the front ranks of the Protectorate forces—including the majitsu and a handful of wizards—were annihilated. Further back, Caleb could see wizards rising high above the ground, trying in vain to determine what was happening, listening in horror to the sounds of battle and thrashing crocosaurs tearing apart men and horses.

Caleb did not keep up the attack for long. His army couldn't risk engaging the bulk of the Protectorate forces. Now it was time to continue to Phase Two of the strategy: getting the hell out of Dodge.

"Fall back," Caleb shouted. "Fall back!"

The command was picked up by those behind him and passed through the ranks. While the army retreated into the forest, the shamans maintained the illusion, disguising the deadly terrain and making it impossible to follow. The plan was to flee on paths and shallow swamp channels known intimately to the natives, twisting and turning through the low-lying forests before meeting at a designated fall-back position. There, deep inside the wilderness, they would camp for the night and live to fight another day.

If they could escape the Protectorate forces in time.

The Congregation wizards couldn't seem to dispel the illusion, perhaps confused by the unusual residue of the shamans' spell, but they had started counterattacking by sending fireballs and lightning bolts in the direction of the retreating army. Many of them found a mark, tearing through the ranks of the revolutionaries until the Battle Mages began counterattacking and focusing on the wizards, forcing them to erect Wizard Shields. Though outnumbered, the Battle Mages were still under the cover of the illusion, able to send their deadly rays with impunity. The frustrated Congregation wizards closed ranks and shouted imperious commands for reinforcements.

The camp's horses were waiting in the trees behind Caleb's regiment. Caleb and Tamás, now at the rear of the army, were the last to reach their steeds. Caleb had seen no sign of Val and hoped he had not been killed or injured in the ambush.

The plan was to take the widest path through the forest. With two riders per horse, they had enough mounts for everyone. More now that casualties had been sustained.

Destroying the cavalry would hamstring the Protectorate's ability to pursue the rebel army in the unfamiliar terrain. The wizards could take to the air but would have a hard time seeing through the thick canopy, especially with shamans cloaking the forest. Thinking they had successfully escaped the gauntlet, Caleb swung onto Margot just as a fireball exploded into the poor horse next to him, which Tamás was about to mount. Whirling, Caleb saw a small group of Protectorate forces that had ranged ahead of the others. Along with a wizardess, a dark-haired pyromancer with a cruel mouth and hands full of glittering rings, there was a small group of foot soldiers with fancy gilt-edged shields, led by a tall and stern reptilus commander wearing forest-green armor and a gleaming bronze helm.

"As always, your instincts were unfailing, Yasir," the wizardess said to the reptilus. "Not only did we skirt the illusion, it seems we've found two of the three prize pigs."

The wizardess used a flame stick to ignite another Fire Sphere, while the soldiers advanced towards Caleb and Tamás. The reptilus commander raised a crossbow and fired two bolts in quick succession. The first struck Tamás in the chest and expanded into an igloo-like web trapping him inside. On instinct, Caleb spun to the side, just avoiding the bolt streaking towards him. He turned and used his diamond-headed mace to smash through the web enclosing Tamás, allowing him to step out.

Shouts came from behind them. Someone had noticed their predicament. Yasir heard the shouts and barked an order to the wizardess. With a smirk, she threw the Fire Sphere at Tamás, only to watch it slow and then dissolve in midair. Posha, the Chickasaw shaman, stepped out of the trees behind Caleb, followed by five horses bearing two paladins apiece.

A pair of snakes summoned by Posha slithered out of the bushes and leapt at the pyromancer. The pyromancer caught the snakes with hands that had turned into tongs of fire and burned the serpents alive. Caleb turned away, forced to sidestep a sword thrust, and attacked on an overhead diagonal with his mace. His opponent raised his shield in time, but the diamond head of the mace shattered the wooden buckler like it was glass. The soldier had no time to react as Caleb swung again and smashed through his armor.

Taking a moment to catch his breath, he turned to see Tamás stab one soldier and begin a furious parry with another. The rest of the Roma warriors weren't faring so well. It was obvious the golden shields signified some type of elite force, and they were cutting down paladins like a scythe through tall grass. Yasir joined the battle as well, wielding a huge, two-handed broadsword in his gloved fists. He swept the sword to and fro as agilely as most men wield a dagger, barely pausing as he cut down the first two revolutionaries who engaged him.

With a grimace, Caleb faced off against a soldier with a golden shield who circled him warily, aware of the power of the mace, trying to stay to Caleb's left. Caleb let his opponent gain the angle he wanted, tricking him into thinking he had a clear path to strike. When the soldier lunged, Caleb used his magical vambrace as a shield, shattering the blade with his left arm while he swung the mace like a tennis racket and crushed the man's ribcage.

The fighting raged around Caleb. Looking for a new opponent, flush with battle lust, he turned to see Posha trapped inside a sphere of fire that was rapidly shrinking. The shaman was trying hard to keep the flames away, but the smell of charred hair and flesh had already reached Caleb's nostrils. He ran to save her, calling out for help, but was forced to watch, helpless, as Posha's defenses collapsed and the Fire Sphere consumed her.

Caleb roared in fury, sidestepping the next soldier who tried to engage him and rushing straight at the pyromancer.

"Caleb, no!" Tamás shouted, but Caleb was too enraged to back off. He did not think either his cloak or his vambraces would protect him from a pyromancer, but he didn't care. He couldn't stand there and watch her burn alive more of his people.

The Congregation wizard watched in amusement as he approached, forming a cage of fire between her palms that expanded to human size. She sent it rushing towards Caleb right as a sunbeam slammed into her back and burned a hole through her chest.

Stunned, Caleb watched the cage of fire dissipate as the pyromancer slumped dead to the ground. He looked around and saw the ground littered with blood-stained golden shields.

A Battle Mage named Ikal flew out of the trees and landed beside Caleb. The Mayan ended the fight with twin sunbeams that burst through the armor of the final two Protectorate soldiers.

"Go!" Ikal said. "The main force approaches. We'll hold them off as best we can and join you later."

As Caleb raced to leap onto Margot, devastated by the losses they had suffered, he scanned the carnage and noticed the reptilus commander was nowhere in sight. He must have fled, or used a magical item to escape, but there was no time to search for him.

Tamás sprang onto Margot behind Caleb, causing the spirited stallion to snort in annoyance. Caleb soothed her only to see her spooked again as a giant green snake with a bronze-and-rope saddle emerged from the underbrush. Ikal descended to his mount as the surviving Roma soldiers joined Caleb and Tamás, fleeing to the shelter of the forest.

An hour after Yasmina's regiment left the base camp, guided by Chooshe and his Chickasaw warriors down a series of game paths invisible to the naked eye, she stopped the procession with a raised hand. Though she did not know the dark and murky swamp forest as well as the natives, her owl staff and wilder instincts allowed her to see further, hear better, and sense subtle changes in the terrain in a way that a normal human could not.

"What is it?" Naxan whispered from beside her.

She held up a hand to quiet the Cahuilla leader, listened for a long moment, inhaled deeply, and wrinkled her nose in distaste. On a current of air, she had caught a rancid, oily, spoiled-meat odor she would never forget, from a race of creatures she loathed above all others.

"Tuskers," she said quietly. "A large group."

Naxan and Chooshe exchanged a worried glance. Like Yasmina, they would not be concerned about surviving an encounter with the filthy humanoids. The worry was that the tuskers would sound one of their pigskin horns, which carried for miles, and alert any Protectorate troops who were searching the forest for them.

The Brewer stepped to Yasmina's side. "I might be able to handle this. Which direction are they?"

Yasmina pointed to her left.

"East? And they're marching this way?"

After she nodded, he began shouting in a guttural language that grated on her ears. The shouts turned into a conversation he carried on in three distinct voices, one of them higher pitched and more feminine, if such a thing could be said of that horrible language.

Chooshe's eyebrows lifted. "You speak mountain troll?"

"Enough to fool a tusker," the Brewer said as he waved everyone forward. The march resumed as he kept up the shouted conversation, adding in more voices now and again. It was a virtuoso performance, and Yasmina marveled at his linguistic prowess.

She knew tuskers were terrified of mountain trolls. While she also knew that no mountain trolls lived within a thousand miles of these swamp forests, the tuskers were too stupid to realize that, and would be too scared to investigate further. Soon their scent faded, and, with a collective sigh of relief, the regiment continued towards their destination.

Two hours later, deep into the forest and long after they thought they had evaded their pursuers, Yasmina heard a whisper of fabric in the distance, a scuff of boots on the ground. It was an odd series of sounds, as if someone or something was touching down every few seconds. Whatever it was, it was only one creature, but it was moving quickly their way and bound to intercept them.

She told the others.

"There's no time to move everyone off the path," Chooshe said. "We'll have to confront it."

They summoned Elaina to the front. Though she was the most powerful mage in their regiment, she did not practice offensive magic. The Battle Mages had all joined Caleb's group.

Still, Elaina should be powerful enough to combat a single common-born enemy. The fear was more of detection than of mortal peril.

The forest was thick with live oaks, palms, and pine hammocks. Most of the undergrowth was too dense for her to see through. They were forced to wait in apprehension with their weapons drawn until the maker of the strange noises rounded a corner and came into view on the narrow path, bounding towards them with graceful floating leaps that carried him twenty yards at a time. Yasmina shrank in fear, understanding why she had failed to recognize the unusual gait.

The majitsu alighted on the path fifty feet away and took a moment to assess the situation. Yasmina's harpy eagle was ranging far ahead, searching the sky for mages and airships. The great bird would have missed a low-lying threat like the majitsu. Yasmina had no idea how the warrior mage had found them; the Protectorate must have sent out scouts in a wide swath.

He started to reach into his black robe, then stopped as he focused his gaze on Elaina, who had raised her hands and was obviously a mage. Without a word, he started bounding towards her, perhaps deciding he needed to deal with her before he called for help.

The majitsu closed the gap shockingly fast. On the way, he batted away two Chickasaw arrows with magically-hardened hands, twisted to the side to avoid a blow dart sent by Naxan, and ducked to avoid Chooshe's spinning ax. White-faced, Elaina managed to uproot two small trees and send them flying at the warrior-mage. He leaped over one and, with a mighty, *kiai*, split the second in half with a flying kick. Yasmina clutched her staff in fear, gasping at his power.

With his next leap, the majitsu landed ten feet in front of Elaina. Yasmina looked into her eyes and realized she had no idea what to do. The majitsu saw it too—and gave a wry, cruel, self-effacing smile, as if chiding himself for having worried.

Swallowing her fear, Yasmina stepped forward and raised her staff, wondering if it could withstand a direct blow from a majitsu. Either way, she knew that neither she, nor anyone else with her, had little chance against the warrior-mage.

The Brewer bravely moved forward to join her, along with Chooshe and another indigenous warrior at the head of the contingent. As the majitsu blurred into action, a man in a purple, moth-eaten, velvet jacket appeared out of nowhere right in front of the warrior-mage, startling everyone. The majitsu jerked back with his fists up, confused, as a huge insectoid loomed over him that had not been there a moment ago. It was an eight-foot-tall praying mantis with a strangely human face and intelligent eyes. With a start, Yasmina realized she knew both of the newcomers, though she had no idea how they had gotten here from the Valley of the Cursed, or why they had come.

A serrated appendage swept through the air like a scythe. The majitsu's head wobbled and then fell to the forest floor. The body of the warrior-mage collapsed in a heap of black robe at the feet of the man in the velvet jacket.

"A tit for a tat, a bit of this and that," the Dealer said, turning towards Yasmina with a face completely swathed in white bandages. "Fancy, my dear, seeing you around here."

* * *

At the front of another regiment, Lance raised a fist to stop the march. They had come to a fork in the path which caused the Chickasaw guides to confer. Both trails looked the same to Lance, ribbons of mud that wound through low-lying terrain ready to flood with the slightest amount of rain. Swampland was all around them, teeming with crocosaurs and other deadly creatures that plopped and slithered through the marsh. Lance shivered as he remembered his last flight through a swamp on Urfe, when they had tracked Will to the home of a family of humanoid spiders who cocooned their victims in giant webs strewn among the trees.

The buzz of insects was incessant. The swamp smelled like rotten eggs. Despite living in New Orleans for much of his life, Lance hated the swamp. It was too hot, too sticky, too hard to see an enemy coming. He knew the Protectorate soldiers and Congregation wizards were out there, searching for them with trackers and hyena wolves and magical scrying. He could only hope the Chickasaw and their shamans knew what they were doing, because he could no longer even tell which direction they were headed.

As the Chickasaw continued to debate the route, Allira walked a short way down each path. Each time, she cocked her head to listen, studied the sky, and bent her ear to the ground. Lance's eyes roamed her supple body, the inch-high dreadlocks framing her oval face, and the exotic blue tattoo writhing across her arms and torso. This new world had held many surprises for him—most of all his love for a woman from a foreign culture who spoke louder with silence than any voice he had ever heard.

When Allira returned, the Chickasaw guides voted to take the path on the right. Both, they said, could be taken to their destination, but that was the fastest route. Allira shook her head, made a series of hand gestures signaling approaching enemies, and then pointed to the left.

The Chickasaw frowned, but Lance had learned to trust Allira's intuition and wilderness skills. He moved to stand beside her, making his position clear.

After a heated argument, the eldest of the indigenous warriors sent a younger fighter dashing down the path on the right. He returned within minutes, speaking rapidly in their language and waving frantically for everyone to hurry down the path Allira had chosen.

She gave no sign of pride or satisfaction as the native guides ushered the regiment forward. That was okay. Lance was a far pettier person, and happy to do it for her.

As the last rays of sunlight slithered out of view, ushering in the inky darkness of the swamp forest at night and all its attendant shrieks, plops, growls, buzzes, and roars from the native fauna, Caleb and Tamás led their regiment into a grassy glade buried so deep in the wilderness it felt as if they had walked right off the map. The glade was an anomaly in the wetlands; a square mile of grass and wildflowers that blessedly rose a few feet above the surrounding swamp. Caleb could tell by the reverent way the Chickasaw beside him entered the glade and craned their necks to the open sky that it was a holy place to them. He wondered if it was a burial ground.

Yasmina rushed to Caleb's side and threw her arms around him. "You're the last to arrive. I was afraid . . . I was afraid you weren't coming."

He eased out of her embrace as he absorbed the throngs of people working hard to set up camp. Lance, Allira, and the Brewer hurried over to greet him as well.

"All three regiments arrived," Lance said. "Not a single casualty after the battle. What about yours?"

"Mostly intact," he said, glancing back at Aahpo, who was walking next to the Prophet, "except for five Battle Mages, ten paladins, and double that many shamans. We would never have escaped without them."

"The loss of so many wizards is a blow," Tamás said grimly. "Was there any sign of being followed?"

"Not yet," Yasmina said. "You?"

Caleb shook his head. "We picked off a few scouts, and the shamans worked hard to cover our tracks. It's impossible to say for sure, but I think we're good."

Many voices had wanted to flee during the previous night, in the hope of avoiding a confrontation. The Chickasaw convinced Caleb it was too dangerous to travel with that many people through the swamp in darkness, even for the native guides. Knowing the wizards would have a hard time tracking them through the canopy, especially with the shamans cloaking their progress, they had decided to give most of the army a head start, and try to cripple the Protectorate cavalry. Though not without casualties, the risky plan had worked.

Still, Caleb knew it was only a matter of time before the wizards found a way to locate them. And he had no idea how Val, even if he managed to recover the Coffer, would ever find them buried so deep in the swamp.

But for this night, at least, they were still alive and free.

Still able to dream of revenge.

-25-

As darkness fell, a charcoal tendril of smoke seeped out of the ground on the periphery of the burial ground. The tendril coiled like a serpent as it lengthened, expanded, incarnated into a shadowy figure.

Before the necromancer named Malpheus became fully corporeal, he remained in shadow form and drifted higher above the army camping beneath him, these wretched interlopers who had intruded on his swamp. Just as spirit mages traversed the wings of spirit and phrenomancers traveled the pathways of the mind, an arch necromancer could follow the currents of the dead, the most tenuous of tethers to the material plane. And in this sacred Chickasaw place of ancient souls, the residue of the once-living was so faint it took an expert eye just to detect them.

But the residues were still there—and they could be summoned.

Malpheus drifted down to the ground and into the recesses of the swamp. Once out of sight, he became fully corporeal, using the same currents on which he had arrived to call out to his brethren. None of them belonged to the Congregation, for the magic they practiced did not sit well with the Conclave. But on occasion, in exchange for their independence, the necromancers performed tasks for which the New Victoria wizards did not have the stomach.

Malpheus was aware of current events. He knew an airship had fallen from the sky, and that the Congregation would appreciate knowing where the rebels had taken refuge. That knowledge, in turn, would ensure the strongholds of the necromancers remained forgotten places, far from prying eyes.

One by one his brethren arrived, until a coven had formed. As he beseeched their assistance, he apologized for the discomfort that would result from casting spells of summoning on the consecrated ground of the glade. Malpheus knew the native peoples of the region would never forgive them, but that relationship was already marked by acrimony and mistrust—and Malpheus would rather have the natives as enemies than the Congregation.

Following his lead, for he was eldest among them, the brothers and sisters of the coven joined hands and began to chant at the edge of the glade, befouling the hallowed soil as they called out with one voice to the residues of those who lingered through the centuries, commanding them to rise.

-26-

Watching Caleb walk away from Oyster Knoll was one of the hardest things Val had ever done. He had wanted so much to sweep up his little brother and fly him to safety, take him away from all this madness.

But he had no choice but to let him go. Caleb had made it clear he wasn't leaving, and there was no way for Val to extricate him with half the Protectorate watching.

An hour later, when the Protectorate forces began to advance, Val retreated to the middle of the pack. He was not expected to participate in the battle unless needed. As word filtered back that the cursed rebels had thwarted the initial attack and killed a large number of soldiers, and even some Congregation mages, Val had never felt so relieved, and did not have to pretend to be shocked.

How had Caleb pulled that off?

Baltyr and the other commanders were furious. Yet when they tried to pursue Caleb's army, the ground trackers couldn't find the trail, and the wizards couldn't break through the illusion. At every turn, the Protectorate soldiers found themselves plunging into a disguised swamp. Not even the hyena wolves, prized for their ability to follow any scent, could decide where to go. A sylvamancer from the First Protectorate theorized that the powerful cloaking spell had been cast by an indigenous shaman, or more likely a group of shamans working in concert.

The Congregation wizards knew the shamans couldn't keep up the illusion forever, but they maintained it long enough for the rebels to disappear into the blighted terrain. They had retreated into an area of swampy wilderness uncharted by Protectorate maps, and could only have succeeded with the help of natives guides. Again, this enraged Baltyr, and he vowed to punish the tribes who lived in the vicinity—all of them—for the slight.

And they *still* didn't know how Caleb's army had crossed the continent unseen.

By midday, the Protectorate had mostly given up hope of finding the rebels through conventional means. The lull in the action gave Val a good excuse to return to New Victoria. He didn't bother explaining his reasons, and as the protégé of Lord Alistair, no one dared ask. Soon Val was soaring high above the silver arch of the Canal Bridge and touching down on Magazine Street. Every minute counted. Caleb and an army that size couldn't hide from the Congregation for long. Val knew this in his bones. He had to try for the Coffer as soon as possible.

He had to try for it that very night.

On his way into Salomon's Pad to shove down some food and change out of his clothes, he found Synne sitting cross-legged on his doorstep, as she so often did. He had long given up trying to convince her to wait in a more comfortable locale until he sent for her. Her response was always that, until he moved into a proper wizard's keep, with proper defenses in place, it was her duty to stand guard.

He mumbled something about being in a hurry as he swept past her and entered his home. On his way through the entry hall, lit by standing iron candelabrum that never went out, Val eyed the tapestry he passed every time he entered the abode. The stunning piece of art depicted two wizards facing each other on a rock bridge spanning a chasm. Two fortresses, one silver-blue and one gold and crimson, loomed on either side of the bridge. The faces of the wizards were obscured by the collars of their cloaks. One clutched an orb of swirling darkness, the other an azantite rod. Swirls of color ignited the sky, as if some type of galactic event accompanied the confrontation. Bizarre creatures—even for Urfe—swooped through the air and populated the rocky ground beneath the fortresses.

What the hell is this, Salomon? A vision of some apocalyptic future? Or is it a rendition from the past, some battle you fought on this world or another?

Is it a message, a sign, a prophecy? Or just a good piece of art?

As he entered the kitchen, he also thought of the hidden room in the cellar that concealed scores of silver-blue keys similar to the one that had brought him and his brothers to Urfe in the first place. He had never gotten one of the keys to work, but he suspected they led to other worlds Salomon had visited, perhaps other universes. Snarling at the thought of the arch-mage playing puppet master with their lives, Val wolfed down a loaf of bread and butter, changed clothes, and grabbed his staff. He hesitated in the foyer on the way out, having the strange feeling he might not return. Maybe Salomon would lock the doors that had never locked for him and his brothers, for some maddening motive known only to the arch mage, and force them to find another home.

If so, good riddance.

Stay out of my family's life, old man.

When Val strode out of the door, Synne surprised him by barring his way with crossed arms. He tried his best to be patient. "Do you need me?"

"You always invite me in."

"That's true. I'm sorry. I'm just in a hurry today. Lord Alistair needs to see me."

"You're lying," she said.

Taken aback, Val opened his mouth to retort and then slowly closed it. Knowing Synne as well as he did, and how much she valued—revered—a majitsu's duty of service to her mage, he knew how much nerve it took for her to confront him in this way.

"I saw your brother and Mala leaving this morning, just before dawn."

As Val reeled, wondering if she had betrayed him to the Congregation and might even have come to apprehend him, she noticed the look on his face and said quickly, "I don't need to know what happened or why they were here. I only care about one thing, and that is fulfilling my vow to ensure the safety of my mage. Everything surrounding their visit, and your body language right now, tells me that you're in trouble. So please, Val, tell me what is happening and let me protect you."

Relieved he would not have to confront her, he gripped his staff and looked away. "I can't involve you in this, Synne. It would put you at odds with the Congregation and your own Academy."

She leveled her gaze at him. "I'm not sworn to protect the Congregation or the Academy. I'm sworn to protect *you*."

"Is that really true? Does your vow to protect me supersede your duty to your Order?" She looked uncomfortable, and he knew he had hit a nerve. "Your loyalty means a lot to me, Synne. No one could ask for a better friend and ally. But I don't know what's going to happen next. I can't let you throw away everything you've worked so hard for your entire life. This conversation never happened. Go home. I'll send for you when I need you."

He started to brush past her, but she put a hand on his elbow. "You believed in me when no one else did," she said quietly. "If it wasn't for you, I wouldn't *have* a place in my Order. You saved my career and my honor, and you've saved my life on many an occasion, just as I've saved yours. Yes, you're correct. Under our law, my vow to protect you is not higher than my duty to uphold the tenets of our Order. But I'm not talking about that vow. I'm talking about the vow I am making right now, as your friend and ally, to protect you from harm no matter where the danger lies." Her stare hardened. "Even if it derives from within the Congregation or my own Order. I know you, Valjean Blackwood. I have witnessed the integrity of your actions for myself. My Order allowed the man who destroyed my sister to go unpunished, and abandoned me under false pretenses. They failed me. You did not. So please, I beg you, let me fulfill my duty and uphold the vow that matters to me above all others."

He took her hand gently off his elbow and clasped it between his own. "Thank you, Synne. You have no idea how much that means."

After slipping out of Salomon's Pad before dawn, Mala avoided the glow orbs lining the streets of the Garden District, leading Will through the grimy back alleys and snickelways that crisscrossed New Victoria. Every now and then a shadowy figure would emerge from a doorway or a darkened corner, until a flash of steel from Will and Mala sent them slinking away.

They walked all the way from the Garden District to the French Quarter, right through the city center on a clandestine route Will imagined Mala had taken during her days in the Thieves Guild. He had spent his teen years playing soccer, video games, and reading fantasy novels. Mala had traveled the dangerous world of Urfe on her own, an orphan who had clawed her way out of the gutter and fought her way through the ranks of the city's most notorious group of rogues and cutpurses.

Will no longer feared running afoul of thieves or mercenaries. He and Mala could handle that. He feared detection by one of the Protectorate patrols that Lord Alistair had scouring the city for oath avoiders. Even if they won the fight, an alarm could be raised, and Dashi had warned them that low-level wizards had joined the patrols. It seemed that a collective madness had overtaken the city, and Lord Alistair's unreasonable fear of a small group of people minding their own business—people who posed very little threat to him—had infected the populace as well.

There's nothing new under the sun. Not where human beings are involved.

Mala got them safely to the Thieves Quarter, where Will absorbed the serpentine lanes, uneven cobblestone streets, and peaked Victorian roofs that marked the district. Although the sun had risen an hour ago, there was plenty of activity in the dive bars and flop houses, still going strong from the night before.

Ever since leaving Mala's house, both of them had worn hooded cloaks while traveling through the city. Mala pulled hers even tighter as they passed through the Thieves Quarter. As they walked, she pointed out various landmarks, including a street market for mercenaries, gated compounds belonging to the city's crime kingpins, a pawn shop that comprised an entire city block, and the most notorious tavern in all the Realm, as famous for its nightly body count as for the criminal schemes fostered inside its walls.

Ever since entering the neighborhood, Will had the sense they were being followed. He pointed this out to Mala as they entered the central plaza, a busy square with attractive gothic architecture hidden behind the grime. The patterned tiles of the plaza were empty except for a few outside tables belonging to the ring of cafes on the periphery, occupied by dangerous looking types sobering up with their morning coffee.

"Of course we're being followed," she said as they passed a spiked iron gate rising high above the crowd, surrounding a crumbling brick mansion with turrets and peaked towers. "Dashi protects his investments."

"Is that his mansion?"

"Aye, along with a few dozen other high-ranking members of the New Victoria Thieves Guild. 'Tis their headquarters."

She ducked into a muddy lane to the left of the mansion, where two people dressed in rags awaited. Telling Will to stay behind, she walked swiftly to them, had a brief conversation, and returned.

"What was that about?" he said.

"A couple of requests, including the one you made last night."

He thought for a moment. "Dalen and my cousin?"

"Aye."

"Can Dashi help them?"

"I'm uncertain, but if so, I just offered him a hundred gold pieces."

Will squeezed her arm in thanks. Soon they were slipping through a curtain of Spanish moss that led to the red brick streets of the Live Oaks District. Several turns later, down a twisted lane overgrown with bougainvillea and then through a locked iron gate, Will breathed a sigh of relief as they entered the secluded grounds of Mala's bungalow.

With nothing much to do until Val returned, they spent the rest of the day cleaning up after the battle with Ferala. Mala was impressed by Will's construction skills, and after he repaired her staircase in a matter of hours, she slipped up behind him and wrapped her arms around him.

"Thank you," she said.

"For what?"

"I've always called you Will the Builder, but I had no idea."

He felt a tingle of satisfaction that he actually had something to teach *her*.

"A man with a hammer is very attractive, you know," she said, running her hands beneath his shirt and over his muscled chest just as a knock sounded at the door.

"Again?" Will muttered. "This has to be a cosmic joke."

The knock did not sound threatening, but both of them grabbed their weapons as they made their way downstairs. Will stood beside her with Zariduke in hand as Mala looked through the peephole and then opened the door, revealing one of the ferret-faced men who had followed them through the Thieves Quarter—and two very familiar faces behind him.

Apparently neither had been told where they were being taken, because Will's cousin and friend looked just as surprised as Will. For once, even Dalen, the garrulous illusionist Will had befriended when they were both captured by tuskers, was speechless.

"Will?" Mateo said. "Mala? Thank Devla!"

In response, Will dropped his sword and rushed to pick up his cousin and then Dalen in a bear hug. Both men were stunned by their change in fortune, and in need of a good meal.

The thief who had delivered them gave Mala a package wrapped in brown paper. "The tincture you requested."

In return, she handed him a sack of gold, which he accepted with a flourish before closing the door on his way out. Will realized Dalen's wrists were still bound, though oddly, no chain connected the silver cuffs. "You came straight from prison?" Will asked them.

Mateo grimaced and scratched at his filthy stubble. "Alistair said he was sending us home, and sent us right through a portal to gaol."

"Alistair sent me to prison, too—in a dungeon beneath his cloud castle." He turned to Dalen. "What's on your wrists?"

"Wizard cuffs," Dalen said. "They stop me from accessing my magic. I wasn't important enough to send to Wizard Prison, so I got these instead. No sword can break them."

"We'll see about that." Will retrieved Zariduke and pointed the tip at Dalen. "Hold up your arms."

The illusionist did as requested, then closed his eyes as Will laid the magical blade against the silver cuffs. There was a snip of blue-white light, and the bonds split apart. Dalen peeked his eyes open, then rubbed at his arms. "*Krikey*. I'm glad those are gone."

Mateo flexed the fingers of his normal hand, as well as those on the chainmail glove he had acquired in the tomb of the sorcerer king. "Where are we? Who was the man who freed us? How did you arrange it?"

After exchanging a glance with Mala, Will took a deep breath and put an arm around the shoulders of his friend and cousin. "We have a lot to discuss."

Dida was easier to convince than Val expected. He had only a single request to make of his friend from the Kingdom of Great Zimbabwe, a request which would not involve too much risk. Or at least Val hoped it wouldn't. He knew very little about bibliomancy, but if anyone could create a dimensional door right under the nose of the Congregation, it was Dida.

Still, he did not want Dida to put himself in danger, and told him so. The young mage's nose twitched at the challenge, and, in a rare show of emotion, Dida clasped Val's forearm and said he would have died on Asmodeus's torture wheel if Val had not risked his life to save him. The show of loyal friendship caused Val to choke up, and he vowed to do his best to keep Dida out of harm's way. His gentle friend was a scholar, not a fighter, though time and again his composure and quick thinking had proved invaluable in the heat of battle.

Two more stops to make. The second Val dreaded with all his heart, but for the meeting that came next, he was unsure what to expect.

When Val walked into the Gryphon's Beak at dinnertime, the tavern was hopping. Flames leaped off the grill inset into the far wall. Frazzled waiters wove through the rough-edged crowd balancing pitchers of ale and platters heaped with sizzling cuts of meat. There was not a seat at the bar, and barely room to stand. Yet everyone made way for the mage with the azantite staff and the hard stare striding through the dining room.

"What do *ye* want?" Rucker said, glaring as Val set his staff against the wall. "Last I heard ye were planning on sticking to yer own kind."

Val rested his hands on the table and locked eyes with the grizzled adventurer. It was not easy to withstand Rucker's battle-hardened stare, but Val lifted his chin and said, "I came to apologize."

Rucker took a swig of red ale. "For acting like a horse's ass?"

"Yes."

"What about believin' that high-born wizards are better than others?"

"I never thought that," Val said calmly. "Humanity has proven over and over again it isn't capable of living without the rule of law or government, so someone has to do it." He lowered his voice. "But that someone doesn't have to be a murderous demagogue who cares for no one but himself."

Rucker smirked. "Ye finally found the thorn beneath the rose, eh?"

"That bastard put our father in a soul jar, and is trying to kill me and my brothers."

"A wiser man would have warned against the dragon in the sky before it burned down his own house."

The rebuke caused Val to purse his lips and give a slow nod. "You're right."

"Boy, ye got the smarts and the power, I'll give ye that, but ye need to look in the mirror every now and again."

Val spread his hands. "We can sit here all night and rail about my faults, and again, you'd probably be right. But one thing I've never been accused of doing is failing to act. I came to apologize, yes. But I also came to inquire if you wanted to help me do something about what's going down around here."

"Buttering me up with all these apologies, are ye?"

"No. This isn't a request from a friend. This is something you should only do if you believe in it. Or, as you said yourself, if you want to fight the dragon before it breathes fire on someone you love."

"Yer a silver-tongued devil, ye are."

"I came to you because I know where you stand, and because under all that bluster and don't-come-near-me reputation—well-deserved, I know—you're a good man who loves his city."

"Bah. Did ye hit yer head on the way in? Out with it, boy, then leave me in peace. I've got ale to drink and past deeds to ponder. What is it ye want an old one-armed adventurer who's long past his prime to do?"

Val put his elbows on the table and leaned forward. "Help me kill a king to save the republic."

When Adaira arrived at their favorite table at the Oasis Cafe, sheltered from view by the pleasure garden's lush tropical landscaping, Val stood to greet her with a long kiss that caused him to shudder with a range of powerful emotions.

"Mmm,' she purred, drawing away and holding him at arm's length. "My father's looking for you, you know." With her flowing sapphire dress covering the bulge in her belly, Val could barely tell she was pregnant except for the way she eased into her seat, and the healthy glow of her skin. "Why all the subterfuge?" she asked. "Dida wouldn't say a word, and when I pressed him, he looked like a child who's just opened the jam jar without permission."

"Lying isn't his forte," Val said wryly. "Can I ask you a favor?"

"Of course."

"Can we enjoy this meal together without discussing anything serious? Just enjoy the night air, the show, each other's company?" He smiled as he reached out to stroke her hand. A golden circlet swept back her hair, there was a warm crinkle to her eyes, and he thought she had never looked so beautiful.

A sly smile crept onto her lips. "You've found a name for the baby, haven't you? And you're going to make me wait. Is it something to do with Dida? Is that why you sent him? That could be fun, since he's such a dear . . . Val? You're looking at me strangely. And why haven't you checked in with my father?" As she continued to study his face, he couldn't hide his distress. "Is there something . . . is there something wrong?" she said. "Something about us?"

"Us? No, never. Please, Adaira—can you forget about that for a while? Can we dine in peace as I asked?"

She started to fold a napkin in her lap but let it fall onto the table instead. "I don't think I can enjoy myself until you tell me what's going on."

Val wanted so much to spend this time with her before he said what he had to say. But he knew that was selfish.

When the waitress came by, Adaira sent her away with barely a glance. "Val?" Adaira said.

He stopped stroking her hand and gripped it. "I'm sorry," he whispered.

"Sorry? Whatever for, my dearest?"

"For what I have to do, and how it will affect our family."

A peal of soft, carefree laughter floated over from another table hidden among the courtyard, cutting him like a knife, Adaira's face fell, and he regretted his decision to bring her here tonight. Now they would have a bitter memory of this place.

In a quiet voice, he told her what had happened to Will, and what her father had done to their father. As she listened, her hands were rigid atop the table, and her face grew paler and paler.

"I'm sorry," she said, staring straight ahead. "I'm so very sorry."

He expected her to ask why her father would do these things. When he asked her that very question, she bit her lip and looked away. "A few nights ago, when I went to his room to say goodnight, I overheard him talking with someone. I think he might have been using a spirit helm, because no one else was in the house. They were talking about some kind of prophecy—"

"From the Canticles of Urfe?"

"No, not that. Though I'm sure that's on his mind. This seemed specific to a phrenomancer viewing. Probabilities and pathways and such. I heard the sword of spirit mentioned, and . . . your family's surname. More than once."

Val sat back. "I don't understand. He thinks our family is a threat to his power in some way? Because of a phrenomancer? When were you going to tell me?"

"I didn't hear that spelled out. Nothing of the sort. Thinking back on it, though . . ." She steepled her fingers against her forehead. "The predictions of a phrenomancer are never one hundred percent certain. Maybe if you talk to him, you can convince him how foolish this all is."

"Talk to him? He imprisoned Will, Caleb isn't backing down, and our father . . . it's too late for that, Adaira. I'm convinced he was using me to get to Caleb, and if I had returned with my brother in a soul jar, he would have killed all three of us."

A shudder rolled through Adaira that seemed to suck the life right out of her. "There has to be another way," she said in a small voice.

"When I leave here tonight, you're free to talk to him. I'll ask you not to say a word until the morning, but then . . . do what you must."

Her eyes filled with alarm. "What are you doing tonight?"

"Better if you don't know."

"You don't trust me?"

"I don't want to put you in that position. If he asks, you can tell the truth about what you know."

She gripped his hand. "Whatever you're planning, don't do it. He'll kill you, Val. He's so powerful. You have no idea . . . I know he's far from perfect. Believe me, I know. But he's also a leader, and he has to make hard choices."

"He's a tyrant, not a leader."

"He's my *father*. Can't you just . . . let it go?" Her hands moved to her belly. "For our family? For your *child*?"

Val pushed to his feet. "No Adaira. I cannot just *let it go*."

Her mouth opened and then closed, and she buried her face in her hands to cover the tears that started to flow. "Then run away with me. Leave all this behind. I'll do that for you, Val. I'll leave my father, my home, my inheritance, everything I know. We'll go someplace no one will ever find us, and raise our child together."

He squeezed his eyes shut for a long moment, wanting very much to do as she asked, then walked around to kneel beside her, cupping her chin in his hand. "If it was just me, I would without question. But I can't leave my brothers to fight him by themselves. I have to try to save Caleb."

"*How*, Val? Even with the Coffer and the sword, what can you possibly do to my father? To the Congregation?"

"I'm not sure. But I have to try."

Her silent sobs shook her body, and she buried herself in his arms. "Go," she whispered. "Whatever it is you're doing, I'm sure you need to prepare. You shouldn't waste any more time with me."

He clutched her fiercely to his chest. "I love you, Adaira. If I can't be there for our child . . . if I'm in prison or banished or . . ."

She put a finger to his lips. "Then I'll come and find you, wherever you are."

"I'll be waiting."

Her lips trembled, and she brought his face to hers. "Kiss me," she said, and this time his tears mingled with hers.

Later that night, just after three a.m., Will stayed on his brother's heels as Val and Dida stepped out of Gus's carriage and onto the tiled pathways of the Wizard District. The witching hour had always given Will the creeps, even when he was alone on his Papasan in New Orleans, reading late at night with nothing to fear except a stray branch scraping against his window.

Now the fear was real. Now he was approaching a bridgeless moat surrounding a hulking, midnight blue pyramid that served as the headquarters for the Congregation. Dalen was right beside him, working hard to keep the two of them cloaked in illusion behind the mages, an extension of the shadows that lived outside the glow orbs lighting the district. Val was a Congregation wizard, and Dida was an official envoy from the Kingdom of Great Zimbabwe. Both had permission to enter the Sanctum. According to Val, who now bore the imprimatur of the Congregation magically tattooed under his left arm, a polychromatic octopus head that also gave Will the creeps, this sigil provided Val entry through the powerful wards protecting the Sanctum. The aura extended around him to a radius of five feet, and along with the interior portals, this was how the Congregation wizards brought visitors inside.

Will could only hope his brother was right, and that Dalen's illusion held. Otherwise their plan would be doomed before it started. Dida, whom Will had liked the instant they had met, said it was impossible to enter the Sanctum through a Rune Passage without tripping the pluri-dimensional wards. Will didn't understand exactly what a Rune Passage was, but he got the gist of it. However, Dida had said the Sanctum's wards were designed to protect against ingress, rather than egress—and claimed the portal he had set up earlier in the day could get them out.

Will did not get the same warm and fuzzy feeling with the other two people his brother had brought, and who were waiting with Mala and Mateo inside the enclosed portion of Gus's carriage. The surly, one-armed adventurer named Rucker had glared at anyone who tried to engage him, and having Val's majitsu along was simply unnerving. That said, Will had to admit he wouldn't want to meet either of the two in a dark alley.

As the two wizards and their unseen guests approached the monolithic structure, Will's eyes roamed to the pair of thirty-foot tall stone beings flanking the columned entranceway. The two colossi—living guardians straight out of legend—had gigantic swords inscribed with hieroglyphs crossed against their chests. He had never seen them twitch a finger and wondered what, if anything, could make them come alive.

When they reached the moat, Will grabbed onto his brother's waist. He assumed Dalen—still invisible to Will, as Will was to him—was holding onto Dida's unusual attire that was a cross between a silk suit and a tailored robe. As they soared over the moat, Will worried about his brother. Ever since they had met at Salomon's Pad earlier in the night, Val had barely said a word to anyone, including Will. He had looked distraught when he came through the door, and went immediately to his room to study their father's spellbook. Will had never seen him so frighteningly intense.

The entrance to the Sanctum had no door, but the impenetrable darkness filling the archway felt tangible, as if it were alive. Will was sure it concealed powerful unseen wards. A path of beautiful mosaic tile led from the moat to the archway, but Val and Dida never touched down, instead drifting as wizards do towards the entrance. Will gripped his brother tight, shivery with fear and anticipation, knowing that no matter what lay in store on the other side of the occluded archway, there was no turning back.

-27-

A handful of Roma mages and paladins rubbed the sleep out of their eyes as they rose for the second night watch. One of the paladins, Jonton Aleckian from the Lautari Clan of the Făgras foothills, assumed a position on the north-eastern perimeter of the glade housing Caleb's army. Chewing on a root provided by the Chickasaw helped take his mind off the exhaustion from the day's march.

Jonton was proud to be a paladin and perform his duty in the service of the cause. The previous summer, a group of tuskers hired by the Protectorate had raided his clan. The tuskers had killed many of his family members, destroyed their wagons, and stolen their food for the winter. It seemed to Jonton as if the only things left on the Barrier Coast were abandoned villages and Protectorate death squads.

The decision to join Caleb's army had been an easy one. Jonton had nowhere left to turn.

Even though Caleb Blackwood refused to accept the mantel of the Templar, Jonton still revered him. When Caleb had opened the Coffer of Devla and struck down a Congregation electromancer, his place in history was secure. Leading an army through the dangers of the Ninth, navigating *Temmenily Ayawet* to the doorstep of the Protectorate, and taking down an airship had vaulted him to mythic status. Jonton would follow his leader to the ends of the earth—which, at the moment, it felt like he had done.

He sat cross-legged on the edge of the glade, facing the moss-hung trees, his sword and shield by his side. No one expected trouble before dawn. The army was buried too deep in the swamp for a concerted night attack. Yes, the airships would find them in the days to come, if they stayed in the open glade too long, but that was a worry for the morning, and for more important heads than his.

Truth be told, Jonton had never encountered such an awful place as this swamp. Even in late fall, the temperature was still warm, the humidity higher than any he had experienced. And the insects were simply horrific. He spent his waking hours slapping at the beastly little creatures that buzzed, crawled, slithered, and gnawed on every inch of exposed skin. He had taken to sleeping in all of his clothes with his blankets pulled over his head. The paladin who had woken him that night had given Jonton a smelly paste for his portion of the watch, and it helped. But he still spent too much time scratching and slapping at the air instead of peering into the darkness of the trees and scanning the night sky for airships.

Lulled by the remoteness of their location, the powerful wards set by the Battle Mages, and the small army of Chickasaw camped just outside the wards, Jonton almost jumped out of his boots when the ground erupted right in front of him.

Something burst out of the soil and surged upward—something bony, dirt-encrusted, and pale as death—that at first his mind refused to register. Had some strange burrowing creature come to the surface to hunt? Some exotic species indigenous to the area?

It was not until another hand reached out of the ground and grabbed his foot, using it for leverage as the dead thing climbed out of its ancient grave, did Jonton grasp the truth and begin to scream.

The dream had Caleb firmly in its thrall. He and Marguerite were sitting on the old cloth sofa in his family's home in New Orleans, watching Luca open a birthday present, a bright red fire truck with a ladder on the side. Caleb's parents were there as well, enjoying the time with their grandson, beaming with pride and delight. Val was sitting in an armchair unmoving, staring straight ahead, blood dripping from his hands. In a beanbag in front of the TV, Will was jamming on the Sega Genesis, oblivious to the world. Even Yasmina was there, standing by the fireplace in her wilder cloak, watching them all with a solemn expression, as if aware she was inside the dream.

When the screaming started, Caleb looked around the room to see who was hurt, then realized the room had disappeared, and he was awake and in his tent. The screaming was real and coming from somewhere outside. Not one voice, but many. He leapt to his feet, still in his undershorts, as a pair of grub-white hands burst out of the ground beside his cot. Stumbling backwards, he stood transfixed as a skeleton with bits of gray cloth clinging to its bones pulled itself out of the dirt. The fleshless skull swiveled to fixate on Caleb. With unnatural dexterity, the creature leaped onto him and wrapped its spindly fingers around his throat.

The grip felt like iron. Caught off guard by the suddenness and ferocity of the attack, horrified by this undead thing, Caleb gasped for breath as he thrashed to free himself. Their struggle shoved the cot against the side of the tent, almost causing it to collapse. Caleb stumbled, and the skeleton followed him down, shoving him on his back and straddling him. The exposed bone of its fingers pressed deep into Caleb's windpipe, cutting off his oxygen. Desperate, he tried to buck but couldn't free himself.

The movement had brought him closer to his mace, lying atop his pack at the foot of the cot. With no option left, Caleb kept bucking and shifting his hips, moving inch by tortured inch. As the light dimmed in his eyes and he started to hyperventilate, he managed to grab the handle of his mace with a finger. Harnessing a surge of panicked adrenaline, he bucked again, and closed his hand around the weapon. With a flick of his wrist, he brought the diamond head of the mace crashing against the back of the skeleton.

The blow caused the undead creature's spine to crack and the fingers to release, but that didn't stop it from reaching for Caleb again. Scrambling to create space, Caleb put a foot on the thing's chest and shoved it away. He leapt to his feet and swung the mace with both hands. This time the creature exploded, spraying bone and gravecloth across the tent.

Caleb threw on his cloak and raced into a chaotic scene. Everywhere he looked, human skeletons in various stages of decay were crawling out of the ground and wreaking havoc in the camp. Besides the moon, the only lights were a few glow orbs hanging on poles, and logs that people had ignited with lamp oil to use as firebrands. Without the sun to pull from, he thought the Battle Mages would be hamstrung, but they used the light from the moon in a similar way, drawing in power and shooting silver beams from their palms. The magic seemed much less potent, but it was enough to destroy their skeletal opponents.

Panic had set in at the horror of their enemy. Screams of the injured and dying filled the air. Caleb was scared too, but not as much as when he and his brothers had poled through the swamp to face Zedock in his stronghold, or when he had plunged into the nightmarish bog inside the Tower of Elarion and retrieved a key from the guts of his own rotting corpse. His greater fear was that the necromancer who had summoned these foul creatures was lurking nearby.

With a grimace, he whipped around to see where he could help. The only member of his inner circle in sight was Lance, who was fighting off three skeletons with his battle hammer. The brutal weapon was effective against the creatures, leaving them in a heap of bones whenever he scored a direct hit.

"Caleb! On your flank!"

The voice had come from behind him. *Tamás*. Whirling, Caleb noticed the revolutionary and the Prophet trapped inside a ring of skeletons, about to go down. Caleb rushed to help them. As he neared the first skeleton, his cloak began to glow with a white light. The moment he touched the undead monster with the diamond-headed mace, the light grew even brighter, expanding in a halo around Caleb, and causing the skeleton to disintegrate. He grabbed the neck of the next one with his bare hand to pull it away from the Prophet, and the same thing happened. *Pop*. No more skeleton.

In moments he had destroyed the entire ring, leaving Tamás and the Prophet staring in awe at the white light emanating from Caleb's cloak and the power flowing through his hands. The religious leader turned his head to the sky and began to recite a verse in a loud voice, drawing the attention of everyone nearby.

"The simplest touch from the hand of the Templar will destroy the dead and unclean things, will return them to the graves and soil from which they have arisen." The Prophet lowered his gaze. "Thus sayeth the Canticles of Urfe."

Caleb ignored him and raced to the next person in peril, and then the next. Every skeleton he touched or struck suffered the same fate, crumbling into dust before his eyes. His success in battle, and the radiance of the glowing cape, raised morale throughout the camp. Soon a new shout rose, not of terror but of strength and victory.

The Brewer's tenor rose above the din, along with the melodious strum of his lyre. The tide of battle began to turn. Though the skeletons did not retreat, imbued with a preternatural compulsion by those who had summoned them, the last of the undead things was soon struck down, and the terror of the night dispelled.

Not only was the glade destroyed, but the desecration of the ancient burial ground horrified the Chickasaw. They were deeply offended and convinced the spirits belonging to the unearthed bones of their ancestors would seek vengeance on anyone who remained.

A short meeting with his advisors and Chooshe convinced Caleb the incident was the work of a coven of necromancers in the region. The warlocks of the dead favored the isolation of the forests and wetlands outside New Victoria, as well as the biodiversity of life forms the swamps offered. While polite society shunned the dreaded mages, they often performed unpleasant tasks for the Congregation, and in turn were granted amnesty for their dark deeds.

Deciding they couldn't risk a similar incident, Caleb and his advisors decided to leave the swamp in the middle of the night and march to higher ground near the river. Aahpo flew ahead to warn the Battle Mages patrolling the area.

While they avoided encountering more monsters or slipping into hidden bogs, the forced march left the army even more haggard than before. Nor did it bode well for the dawn attack everyone feared. Without a doubt, the necromancers had followed their progress and knew where they were—which meant the Congregation did too.

The wizards were coming, and nowhere was safe.

Weary to the bone, they sheltered in a section of forest strewn with a bed of pine straw. The canopy would help protect them from the airships.

A few short hours remained until dawn. Camp was set as quickly as possible. Most of those who were not on watch or in charge of setting wards did their best to shut their eyes for a few moments.

Caleb did not plan on sleeping. He laid on his back and stared at the ceiling of his tent. He did not bother unpacking the cot and had only set up the tent to give himself some privacy from the crowd of Devla worshippers who were genuflecting and praying outside the flap, more convinced than ever of his status as the mythical Templar.

Snarling, he reached for his mace and held it by his side. Whether or not his brothers brought him the Coffer, tomorrow he would find a way to challenge Lord Alistair. It was the only way to end this madness. Either Caleb would strike him down in battle, or he would die at the hands of the Chief Thaumaturge—and these people would know the truth.

Yasmina found the Prophet on the edge of camp. As the devout man knelt in prayer beside a cluster of ferns, she approached in moonlit silence, her boots a whisper on the pine straw. She laid a hand on his shoulder. He did not jump as most people would, but instead turned his head at the interruption. "Yes?"

"Do you have a moment?"

He rose to face her. "A moment, yes."

Yasmina's sharp eyes glanced into the darkness to ensure they were alone, her night vision enhanced by the power of her staff. "I want you to convince Caleb that he is not the chosen one of Devla."

"I think he is convinced of that already."

"I think, in the back of his mind, he believes there is something to it. Or he *wants* to believe it, despite what he says. He wants to think he has a chance to avenge his wife and child, which we both know he does not. Your elevation of him to this emissary of your god, this mythical figure, isn't helping."

"I find it curious that you know my thoughts better than myself," the Prophet said. "Because I am fully convinced that Devla has favored Caleb Blackwood, and that he is the Templar of legend foretold."

"But he can't possibly be. He's not even from this world." She slammed her staff against the ground. "He doesn't even believe in God!"

The Prophet faced her with a sad, knowing smile. "Devla does not need people to believe in Him to exist. Most of His people have turned away from Him for hundreds of years. And yet here He is, guiding us through the wilderness, performing miracles before our very eyes. Did you not witness the events in the clearing, the power in the Templar's cloak?"

"*Magic*, you fool. This world is full of magic. Why would you think the Coffer and the cloak are any different?"

"Why would you think they're not? What is magic but another manifestation of the divine? From where do you think magic originated? You come from a world of strange technology. The Templar told me the meaning of this word and some of the machines he has seen. To me these are even greater miracles than magic. The wonder of creation manifests in untold ways throughout the multiverse. Yet everything is divine in origin. Else how do you account for creation at all?"

"Not by attributing it to some old man named Devla."

"Who said Devla was a man, or present in time as we know it, or is anything of which we can conceive? We give names to things we do not understand, myself included. We apply human attributes to our gods because that is the only way we can begin to comprehend them. Devla is Creation itself. His ways are not our ways. Why let his people stray so far and for so long in a godless society, and lead them to the brink of annihilation? Why choose a broken man with no faith from another world to lead us? I do not begin to understand these things. Again I ask you, *why not*? Would it not be even more strange if He acted as you expected, and the mystery of existence unfolded in a way your vastly inferior mind understood?"

Yasmina began to tremble. She did not care about these esoteric arguments. "Please. I'm begging you. Help me save Caleb's life."

"You love him, I can see."

"That is none of your business," she whispered.

"I am sorry he does not feel the same. Truly I am. I sense that you are a good woman, and have his best interests at heart."

Yasmina gathered her cloak and prepared to leave. She had known approaching the Prophet would likely end this way, but she had to try.

The Prophet laid a hand on her arm. "The Templar's victory is far from certain. Human beings have free will, and what we do matters. Devla provides the tools, but we have to use them. It is not just the Templar who must act. You and I have our place as well, as do many others. If the Templar did not have us to support him—you and I especially—I fear he would not have made it this far. He may not love you, but he cares for you deeply. This is easy to see. You came here tonight to dissuade me from my path, but I believe Devla led you here tonight, to me, so that I can encourage you to remain on yours. The Templar needs you, wilder. You are from his world. You are his strength, his pillar. This is *your* destiny: to be at his side as he confronts his."

Yasmina turned away to hide the tears in her eye and strode quickly into the darkness. The Prophet let her go, though she could feel his steady gaze lingering on her back as she left.

She blinked a few times to clear her eyes. No good would come of succumbing to her emotions. Not at a time like this. Knowing she would not be able to sleep that night, determined to help in any way she could, she climbed the highest bluff she could find near the river and watched for a sign of the enemy until the sky began to lighten.

-28-

Will hung onto the back of Val's traveling cloak as they flew into the Sanctum. It was an extraordinary experience, like grasping onto a flying carpet. Weightless, free, powerful. *I can see why Val digs being a wizard.*

Dida flew in right beside them, with Dalen hanging on so he could work his magic that kept him and Will invisible to observers. For some reason, Zariduke did not cancel the illusion, as if the sword could sense Dalen's magic was benign. The protective wards guarding the entrance to the forbidding headquarters of the Congregation, on the other hand, did cancel the illusions—but Dalen was prepared for that. The instant they cleared the wards, he manipulated the light and shadows stemming from the globe orbs in the cavernous main lounge to once again cloak himself and Will.

Val and Dida kept to the perimeter, where the dimmer lights would help conceal them, and Will could only hope that no one cast a spell to pierce the illusion. And why should they? No one could enter the Sanctum except for wizards bearing the Mark of the Congregation and their guests. It was the ultimate exclusive club.

Val had argued that he and Dida should go alone, but Will wouldn't hear of it. Not only did he want to watch his brother's back, but if Zariduke was needed in combat, Val and Dida would be out of their depth.

Despite the urgency of their mission, Will couldn't help gawking at the open room beneath the soaring, black marble ceiling. The lounge was the size of an outdoor amphitheater and filled with art installations that boggled the mind. Exotic beasts preserved so well they looked frozen in place, ready to leap out at him. Bronze planters containing flora from a vast range of climatic zones, arranged so artfully that, like the taxidermy, he knew magic had to be involved. Urns housing fountains of living fire that constantly shifted through a spectrum of colors. Slender waterfalls that began in midair and plunged through the floor. Paintings and sculptures that moved in place and seemed to exist in multiple dimensions.

He spied a pair of mages chatting on a plush divan. A larger group was clustered around a gemstone table. One of the mages even nodded at his brother. Will tensed, having forgotten for a moment that Val was one of them. It was disconcerting, even after all that had happened. What if Val decided his ultimate loyalty lay with the Congregation?

No. He would never betray me and Caleb.

Will tried to shrink into the shadows, aiding the illusion, knowing that if the mages looked too hard they might see through it. Dalen's Shadow Walk spell did not render them invisible, just unnoticed by the vast majority of onlookers. Val had been hoping for an empty room at this late hour.

Thankfully, no one accosted them as they drifted past a series of alcoves recessed into the smooth amber walls. The alcoves sheltered displays of jeweled weapons, wizard stones, and other artifacts that made Will wonder at their provenance and power.

Instead of stairs, doors, and hallways, a maze of wizard chutes bored into the ceiling and the floor of the lounge. Floating signs pointed the way to the various sections of the Sanctum. *Chambers of the Conclave. Administration. Banquet Hall. War Room. Arcadium.*

Val flew to a chute in the floor marked *Diplomacy*. Ruby glow orbs ignited and then faded as they descended through a vertical passage made of obsidian. They passed the entrance to the *Diplomacy* section and kept going. Thirty feet down they encountered a spherical intersection of wizard chutes. Val kept heading down, past an intersection marked *Records and Archives*, with a nest of wizard chutes branching off horizontally. At the next four-way crossroads, *Artifacts*, he veered into the tunnel on their right. Will glanced down the chute and couldn't see the bottom, even though glow orbs illuminated the tunnel as far as he could see.

Still following Dashi's instructions—where did he get his information, and could it be a trap?—Val led them down a marble corridor, past a series of doors spaced at irregular intervals. Beside each door was an emblem, similar to a heraldic symbol, carved or emblazoned into the wall with glowing sigils. Most of the doors were made of wood or various metals, though some of the entrances contained nothing but swirling gas or fog, hinting at portals or other types of magical ingress.

At the end of the long passage, Val alighted in front of an oval archway filled with a substance as black as deepest night, with veins of silver pulsing through it. Beside the archway was a sigil—a mahogany shield with a crenellated tower of azantite in the middle, crisscrossed by ruby scepters—standing out in bas relief from the marble wall.

Will sucked in a breath as his feet touched down on the floor. "I've seen that before. In the castle Mala and I escaped from."

"It's the Alistair coat of arms," Val said. "And this archway is made of congealed spirit, a feat only a powerful spiritmancer could achieve."

"That doesn't sound good."

"If Alistair made this door, no wizard short of an elder spirit mage is getting through."

A bead of sweat dripped off Dida's bald head as he stared intensely at the archway. "I detect the presence of multidimensional wards as well."

"Can you disarm them?" Val asked.

Dida murmured to himself as he passed his hand slowly over the archway, illuminating a spidery nest of three-dimensional lines glowing with a ruby light, hovering just on the surface of the spirit door. "The good news is I do not detect an alarm within the wards. While the layering is quite potent and sophisticated, with enough time, I believe I can manage."

Will withdrew Zariduke from the sheath on his back. "Hopefully you won't need to." As he drew the weapon, he noticed that parts of his arm had started to flicker, coming in and out of shadow like a living chiaroscuro sculpture. He looked over and saw the same phenomenon happening to Dalen.

Val noticed as well. "You can drop the illusion."

"*Lucka*," Dalen said, in a strained voice. "I thought you'd never ask."

Moments later, Will watched his body return to normal. The slender illusionist appeared in full beside him, clad in the beige cloak he favored, and which matched his eyes. His boyish face looked drawn and pale, his nimble fingers trembling as if from great exertion. Holding the illusion for so long must have taken quite a toll.

"You did good," Will said, clapping him on the back. "Are you okay?"

Dalen gave a weary nod. "As long as Dida's return portal works. *Krikey*, I doubt I have the strength to get us back. Perhaps. I'm unsure. Maybe if I rested—"

"Save your breath," Val interrupted, "and well done. Our lives were in your hands, and you came through." As Dalen beamed with praise, having been slightly in awe of Will's oldest brother from the moment they met, Val turned back to the door and said, "There's a very good chance the Coffer is on the other side of this door. The bad news is, if the sword doesn't work, getting inside is beyond my power."

"Let's see what I can do about that," Will said, stepping up to the archway. "You sure we're alone down here?"

Val threw a quick look over his shoulder. Except for a small area lit by glow orbs in the immediate vicinity, the rest of the orbs had extinguished, returning the passage to darkness. "As I've said, most of the security measures are designed to keep people out. I'm sure the entrances to these rooms are warded, but we're here now. Let's get on with it."

Will nodded in agreement. Val, as usual, had cut to the chase: all that mattered was getting through that archway. As he raised the sword, Dida lunged to stop his arm, averting the swing. "Wait!"

Confused, Will lowered the sword as the bibliomancer apologized for grabbing him. He released Will and approached the archway, wagging his finger and muttering to himself like a befuddled professor. He passed his hand over the archway again, illuminating another set of lines and squiggles glowing with a sapphire light on the perimeter. Even to Will's untrained eye, the pattern of lines was much simpler than the runes guarding the face of the spirit door.

"It's a different ward," Dida said. "Simpler to unravel, and imbued with far less power. In fact, the simplicity of the design is purposeful: it would pass unnoticed to most observers, overshadowed by the potency of the stronger runes."

"Good thing you're a genius bibliomancer," Val said grimly, "and not most observers."

Dida didn't seem to hear him. He wagged a finger again and said, "The architecture is foreign to me, but I'd wager my dissertation it's designed as a pluripotent relay for the principal ward. Marzo-lineal in origin, perhaps with a Nichtbad confluence point—"

"*Dida*," Val said. "Speak English. Can you deactivate it?"

"Ah, yes. My apologies. To state it simply, the perimeter ward is a remote warning designed to alert the architect of the wards when someone passes through the archway—or if the more powerful ward is tampered with in any way. The runic signature is so faint as to be almost undetectable. Certainly, as I said, it would have been missed by most."

"So what you're telling me is that, even if someone manages to disable the main wards—such as you with magic, or Will using his sword—this other ward will alert someone anyway, unless you disable it first? And by someone I mean Alistair."

Dida blinked. "Exactly that."

"Devious," Val muttered. "He knows Will escaped and the sword is out there. How long will it take to disable the perimeter ward?"

"Only a few hours."

"A few hours!"

Dida looked wounded. "Did you think unraveling the ward of an elder mage, even a simple one, is an easy task?"

Val ran a hand through his hair. "Is there no other way?"

"Not unless you wish to raise an alarm."

"Do your best then," Val said, flustered but unable to think of a way around it.

Dida gathered the bottom of his silk garment as he knelt beside the archway and began using his hands to manipulate the sapphire runes on the perimeter, slowly pulling them apart as if untangling a thread. Val left Dalen with him, and took Will back down the corridor so they could listen for sounds of anyone approaching. At least they had come late at night. Though by the time Dida finished, it might already be morning.

The wait was the longest of Will's life. Unwilling to risk a sound, he stood with his brother in silence next to the wizard chute, just outside the range of the glow orbs, straining to hear a sound. Twice they cringed as voices in the distance drew closer and closer before falling away.

Will had so much to ask his brother but he dared not speak. Val flew back to check on Dida a number of times, and the wait never seemed to end. *Surely it's dawn by now.*

At last Dalen floated over to tell them Dida was almost finished. When they returned to the archway, Dida had worked his way to the other side. The wards looked different than before and were glowing brightly. Will held his breath as Dida stood, swept his hands across the doorway like a maestro, and made them disappear.

"There," he said in a satisfied tone.

"We're fine to proceed?" Val said.

"I believe so, yes."

"Okay little brother, you're on."

With a firm set to his jaw, Will stepped forward and raised Zariduke again, gripping the silver hilt. He raised his knee and stepped forward, thrusting with perfect form at the center of the spirit door. The tip of the sword bounced off the opaque surface as if striking a piece of rubber.

"*Krikey*, what was that?"

"I don't know," Will said slowly. "That's never happened before." He thrust again with the same result. "It's not getting through," he whispered.

He saw Val and Dida exchange a worried glance. "Perhaps the magic is too strong," Dida said. "In general, congealed magic is much denser than fluid magic. And for a door made of spirit, crafted by a wizard as powerful as Alistair . . . it might be too much for the sword to penetrate."

Will gripped the sword and faced the door. "How does magic work? If two spells collide, what determines which one prevails? Is it just a matter of strength?"

"All else being equal, yes," Val said. "Wards are different, because the principal component is the skill of the warder or runemaster. Bibliomancers are considered the best wardcrafters in the world, for instance, and while power still matters, so does skill. Trained bibliomancers can unravel wards and runes crafted by a mage far stronger than they. But yes, when two spells collide, or one magical object strikes another, typically the stronger prevails."

"So in theory, Zariduke could punch through this door if the magic it contains is strong enough."

"I believe so," Val said, and Dida nodded in affirmation.

Will growled as he set the buckler shield on the floor and raised Zariduke with two hands. "Salomon is a crazy old bastard, but he's also a two-thousand-year-old wizard. If he made this thing, then it's getting through that door." Tensing his arms, Will swung the sword downward, right at the center of the archway. He felt the same resistance, as if it had struck dense rubber, but this time he kept pushing.

At first he made no progress, but he tightened his core and flexed his forearms, his muscles bulging like baseballs. Just as his conviction started to waver, he felt the sword sink an inch into the archway, giving him a burst of hope. He wanted to channel his energy with a roar but knew he had to stay quiet, so he gritted his teeth, planted his feet, and pushed even harder, willing the sword to go through, thinking of his father and Caleb and how much he despised Lord Alistair, pushing until his veins popped and his arms began to ache, pushing pushing pushing—

At last there was a flash of blue-white light. The spirit door disintegrated. Unable to arrest his momentum, Will fell forward and almost cracked his head on the floor.

Val helped him up, then gripped him by the shoulder. "Good job, little brother."

Will took a few deep breaths as the lactic acid retreated from his arms. He picked up his sword and shield and said, "Let's get what we came for."

Everyone crowded together as Val funneled the light from the glow orb in the corridor through the archway, illuminating a chamber the size of a family living room. The walls, ceiling and floor were made of solid azantite, similar to the training room in Alistair Castle. The room was empty except for a jade pedestal set against the far wall, atop of which rested an azantite chest covered in runes and engravings. The engravings depicted a team of robed clerics carrying the chest with bronze poles inserted through azantite rings on the sides of the artifact.

"Is that it?" Dida said curiously as he approached the artifact. "The Coffer of Devla?"

"The one and only," Will said. "Let's try not to lose it this time."

The plan was for Dida to open an interdimensional space he called a Rune Box, used by bibliomancers to safely transport items across long distances. Once the Coffer was inside, they could extract it whenever they wished, far away from the Sanctum.

As Dida's spindly fingers inscribed a blue square in midair, Will heard a hissing sound to his left. He spun to see a five-foot long snake the same color as the spirit door slithering towards him. Silver streaks pulsed and rippled along the serpent's inky skin as its head wove back and forth. The snake rose up like a cobra, bared its fangs, and Will barely got his shield up in time to bat it away.

He turned and saw two more snakes in the room. One dropped down from the ceiling atop the Coffer, hissing as it landed. The other was about to lunge at Dalen. Caught off guard, the illusionist stumbled back in fright, tripped, and fell to the ground. Will was too far away to help. As the snake struck, Val whipped his staff down to intercept the attack. He scooped the snake below the head and managed to flick it away. Then he dropped the staff, staring down in horror as the wooden shaft crumbled to dust in his hands. The crescent azantite tip—the only portion still intact—clanged against the floor as it fell.

"They're made of spirit!" Val called out as everyone bunched together in the center of the room. "Their touch means death."

The snakes hissed as they slithered to and fro around the perimeter, gathering for another attack. Will glanced down at his shield, wondering how it had survived the contact. He stepped in front of Dida to bat down the next strike, though it came dangerously close to reaching him, and he had no chance to counterattack.

Val sent a bolt of Spirit Fire at another of the creatures. The serpent evaded the missile, which sizzled as it contacted the azantite wall and left a burn mark.

"Dida!" Val said. "Can you step away to safety?"

"If I have a moment, yes."

"Can you take Dalen with you?"

"Indeed."

"Do it now. Will and I are going to have to fight these things. Will, you okay with that?"

He gripped Zariduke in one hand and his shield in another. "Stop talking and get on with it."

As he and Val worked furiously to guard the center of the room, Dida wove his hands through the air, inscribing a matrix of glowing green sigils. Dalen stayed right next to him and cast a spell that created a replica of both himself and Dida. While the bibliomancer worked, a snake got through their defenses and struck one of the Dalens. Will sucked in a breath but the illusion disappeared, leaving the real Dalen unharmed. As the serpent turned to strike again, Will smacked it with the flat of his blade. The contact made it writhe and wriggle away, but did not destroy it. He was going to have to hit them with a direct blow—and he wondered if even that would suffice.

Out of the corner of his eye, he saw Dida open a green doorway in the middle of the air, step through it, and disappear. A hand reached out from the empty space to grab Dalen and pull him through. A moment later, the door disappeared along with them.

Will had no idea where they had gone, but was glad they had fled. Dida was no battle mage, and Dalen, though crafty, did not have the power to combat the spirit snakes.

"What's your plan?" Will called out to Val. The trio of snakes circled them, hissing and rearing up, sending shivers down Will's spine. *Their touch means death.*

"Stay alive and use the sword."

"Yeah, I had that part covered," Will said, spinning to use his shield just in time to deflect an attack from behind.

Another lunged at Val's chest. He thrust both hands out, Spirit Fire crackling from his fingertips, but a second struck at the same time. Val had no time to deflect them both. Will caught his breath as Val raised his palms and thrust them outwards, but instead of Spirit Fire arcing out like lightning from his fingers, the magic congealed to create a spherical shield made of spirit and similar in size to Will's buckler. It was large enough to repel the attacks of both serpents, and stunned them both when it made contact.

Val looked as surprised as Will by the maneuver. The snakes recovered as the orb of spirit started to dissipate, but Val reformed it and held it out from his body. Another snake struck, and he bashed it with the orb so fast Will could barely follow the maneuver, as if Val had employed the shield with the speed of thought. Will jumped in to swing at the center of the snake's back while it was stunned. Zariduke cleaved through it like cold butter. With a snip of white light, the snake dissolved.

"One down," he said, spinning to catch another lunge with his buckler. As the snake tried to slither away, Val blocked its path with the orb of spirit he had summoned. Will leaped forward and snapped his wrist, slicing downward just below the head. A cloud of black dust formed as the creature dissolved.

Val crouched and raised the spirit orb in front of him. "Make that two."

Together, they tracked down the final serpent, cornering it with their shields until Will got a clean strike. It hissed in fury right before it perished.

Breathing hard, Val extinguished the spirit orb as Will scanned the room to ensure they were alone. "Nice spell," Will said. "What was it?"

"I have no idea. I think I just invented it."

Will barked a laugh as the adrenaline ebbed. "It's a good thing, because I couldn't have taken all three."

Val bent to pick up the crescent moon of azantite that was all that remained of his staff. With a stricken face, he held it for a moment before placing it carefully in an inside pocket of his cloak.

"I'm sorry," Will said. "Maybe you can fix it one day."

Before Val could reply, the glowing green doorway reappeared in the middle of the room. It cracked open and a bald head popped out.

"All clear," Val said.

The doorway opened wider. Dida stepped out, followed by Dalen. Will gave the open archway a nervous glance. "Let's get this over with before someone figures out we're down here."

Dalen kneaded his hands in front of him. "*Krikey*, I second that."

Val nodded at Dida, and the bibliomancer approached the Coffer. After floating the relic off the pedestal and onto the floor in center of the room, he said, "Val, if you will?"

The Coffer levitated three feet off the ground. As Val kept it suspended, Dida began to circumnavigate it, his fingers nimbly inscribing silver lines and sigils as he went, dancing through the air with the grace of a world-class pianist. Eventually a cube-shaped pattern of sigils surrounded the Coffer. The moment the runic structure was complete, and the final thread tied off, both the Coffer and the nest of sigils disappeared.

"There," Dida said, rubbing his hands. "All done."

From their earlier discussion, Will knew he had sent the Coffer to some sort of interdimensional space that no one but Dida understood. All that mattered to Will was that the Coffer was back in their possession, and Dida could recall it once they were safe again.

Still, there was one thing they hadn't discussed, and which made Will nervous. "What happens if, er, something happens to you?"

Dida blinked. "I suppose it would be best if that contingency did not occur."

"And if it did?" Val said. "Will's right. We should know what to do just in case."

Dida looked uncomfortable. "If I am unavailable, the Coffer might be . . . impossible . . . to recall. Perhaps not impossible, but it would require another bibliomancer of equal or greater power from Great Zimbabwe to unravel the Marzo-lineal construct—"

Val put a hand up. "Enough said. We need to keep you alive."

Dida sniffed. "I would hope that was the plan all along. Shall I open the Rune Gate now?"

"Right this second."

Again Dida's fingers took to the air, this time outlining a sapphire-blue doorway similar to the green one but much more involved. He reminded Will of a spider spinning a web as he worked, the pattern of the lines and sigils so beautiful and precise they seemed otherworldly.

When Dida had almost finished, a handsome dark-haired man in a silk shirt adorned with lace and ruffles stepped through the arched entrance to the room. Will didn't recognize him, but he could tell from his expensive clothes and imperious stare that he was a wizard.

"Valjean," the man said in greeting, absorbing the scene in a glance. His eyes narrowed as they came to rest on the empty pedestal. "I knew my doubts about you were true."

-29-

Another forest glade, another bleary-eyed meeting with his advisors.

Caleb just wanted it to be over, one way or another.

Wanted the nightmare to end.

The pre-dawn light had just begun seeping through the canopy of loblolly pine. Tamás, Lance, and Chooshe were leading a discussion on battle tactics for the impending fight with the Congregation. Branyn, Elaina, Lisha, and the Prophet were all sitting on the bed of pines needle that blanketed the glade, chiming in when they had questions. The Brewer listened as he tuned his lyre. Even Allira was there, sitting cross-legged off to the side, stirring dried herbs from one of her pouches into a cup of tea.

Besides Aahpo, who had left to speak with his kinsmen, only Yasmina was missing, which Caleb noticed at once. No one knew where she had gone, though the Prophet had seen her walk into the forest before dawn. *Hopefully she's come to her senses and gone somewhere far away from here.*

At the beginning of the meeting, Tamás provided a summary of their army. They did not have a firm headcount, but on the ground, spread throughout the forest around the glade, he estimated they had well over four thousand Roma and Devlan fighters left, and an equal or greater number of Chickasaw.

Add to that the faction of darvish warriors, a dozen Roma mages, a hundred Chickasaw shamans, and the remaining Battle Mages which Aahpo had brought.

A formidable gathering under normal circumstances—but a pitifully inadequate number against the might of the Congregation.

"If we can avoid the necromancers, I believe we can last a week or more in the forest," Tamás was saying. "We'll camp someplace new each night, and the Chickasaw can harass the Protectorate troops at every step."

Chooshe crossed his burly arms. "They will pay a high price for approaching through our lands. The swamps and forests are our citadels. We know every leaf and unturned stone. The shamans will block the paths, call the creatures to their sides."

"And when the airships hover in the sky and rain death from above?" Branyn asked.

"Before that happens," Tamás said, "we can disperse into the forest in small groups so as not to present a single target. It will appear we have scattered, but the Chickasaw will lead each faction and help us maintain contact, so we can regroup as needed."

"That does not sound like a winning strategy."

"Of course not," Tamás snapped. "We all know there's no hope without the Coffer. This gives us a chance to stay alive as long as possible."

"We'll give 'em hell," Lance said, "and make them think twice about entering the forest. An airship is far less useful away from open ground."

"Take heart," the Prophet said, rising from a squat to face the group. It was rare for him to speak during a strategy session. "The Congregation will come, and yes, they will overrun us, even in the forest. But Devla is coming too. We do not have to last forever—but we must have the courage to persevere until He appears!"

His words seemed make the group uneasy, even the believers. After another half-hour working out the details of the dispersal, they adjourned the meeting so they could relay the instructions to the paladins and other commanders. Just before they left the glade, Yasmina rushed into their midst, breathless, the bottom of her cloak flapping at her ankles. Her harpy eagle cawed as it swooped overhead and settled onto a branch in the canopy.

Caleb hurried to her side. "Yaz, what is it?"

"The forest," she said, gasping in air. "They're burning the forest."

"What do you mean?" Tamás asked.

"I saw it from a bluff above the river. It will be here any minute. The fire is coming from three sides, all around you, like nothing I've ever seen." Her eyes flashed with fury. "They're destroying a whole ecosystem."

"But how?" Tamás asked. "It's mostly swampland." His face crumbled as he answered his own question. "They must be using mage fire."

"Without a doubt," Yasmina said. "I've never seen a fire come out of nowhere like that, and burn that hard and fast.

Chooshe looked unsteady on his feet. "How dare they! They have broken the covenant. Our ancestral lands . . ."

In the ensuing silence, a distant crackle arose, the sound of a million jacks tossed on the pavement at once. A chill coursed through Caleb as the crackling grew louder, accompanied by the dull boom of trees crashing to the ground in the distance.

"You said three sides," Lance said to Yasmina, his voice hard and steady as everyone else looked uncertain. "Where are they pushing us?"

"To the river," she said. "They're pushing us to the river."

The rush to escape the burning forest became a blur, a lurid fever dream of smoke and ash and falling trees. Visibility was reduced to almost nothing as the sky became a gray blanket smothering them on all sides. Forced to leave the tents and supplies behind, stuffing everything they could into backpacks, Caleb had little time to think of anything beyond survival. They had to reach a place where they could breathe and see, away from the smoke clogging his lungs, stuffing his nose, and making his eyes water. He wondered if an aeromancer was directing the winds to push the smoke ahead of the fire, or if this was normal for such a large blaze.

Didn't matter.

Either they outpaced the fire, or they would die.

Even with Yasmina's advance warning, they would have perished if not for the quick action of the Roma mages. Accustomed to the much drier climate of the Barrier Coast, which was prone to conflagrations that swept like an angry djinn through the golden-brown plains and hills, all the mages banded together behind the fleeing army to create a fire break, made of uprooted trees and long mounds of earth, that stretched between a freshwater lake and a swamp. They directed streams of water—giant, magical fire hoses—from the lake and the swamp to help quell the blaze.

Their efforts contained the bulk of the advancing fire. Whenever the flames leaped a portion of the barrier, the wizards would zoom across the sky to douse it with the endless supply of water in the surrounding wetlands. Had the mage fire started in the Barrier Coast, it would have overcome them.

As Caleb and his army stumbled out of the forest and into an expanse of wide flat grassland along the river, he knew at once why the Congregation had shepherded them to this spot. Because if the forest fire didn't kill them, then the sky full of airships approaching in the distance, high above the trees, surely would.

A hush fell across the army as it absorbed the awesome, terrifying sight. As the crackling and dull whoosh of the blaze subsided, Caleb, still wiping tears from his eyes, strode further away from the forest to get a better view of his surroundings. Up ahead, across the stretch of grassland, the Great River cut a gentle curve beneath a bluff on the opposite bank. To the north and south, the savannah extended beside the river as far as Caleb could see.

Behind him, coming from the direction of New Victoria, the war dirigibles flew in a matrix-shaped formation that struck fear into his heart. The airships were too far away for an exact count. Twenty-five, at least.

So many that it didn't matter.

The army kept spilling out of the forest, swarming across the flat terrain like a panicked colony of ants. Now that the threat from the fire had subsided, the paladins worked to restore order among the troops.

Caleb gathered with his advisors. Branyn and Elaina flew in from the forest to join them, their faces streaked with grime and ash.

"The fire is almost contained," Branyn said. His eyes were bloodshot, his long brown hair soaked with sweat. "A few have remained behind to ensure the breakline holds."

"Well done," Tamás said. "Did we lose anyone?"

"Hedina, an aquamancer from the Four Lakes. She gave her life to quell a portion of the fire that got through."

Tamás put a fist to his heart and lowered his eyes. "Thanks to you both, to all the mages, for your bravery. You've saved us today."

"Maybe, but for how long?" Elaina said quietly, unable to look away from the approaching airships. "We can't stand against *that*. No one can."

"What's coming now?" the Brewer said. He was facing to the north, shielding his eyes from the sun.

They all whipped around to see what had sparked the comment. At first Caleb thought they were being attacked by green dragons, but then he realized the winged serpents flying in a V formation were unlike any dragon he had ever seen. The long and willowy bodies reminded him more of a snake or a wyrm, with silver wings that jutted out like handheld fans at the base of their heads. Each serpent bore a rider wearing a feathered headdress, standing proudly atop a wooden platform strapped to the backs of the great beasts.

Yasmina gasped. "Are those *Battle Mages?* What are they riding?"

"Coatls," the Brewer said, as they drew closer. "I've seen them before, when I traveled through the Mayan Kingdom."

"There's got to be a few hundred of them," Tamás said in awe.

"Are we sure they're friendly?" Lance said, taking a step back as two of the flying serpents broke formation and dove straight towards them.

"Does it matter if they're not?" Caleb replied, gripping his mace as the pair approached. The closer the coatls came, the more frightening they looked: crimson eyes and whiskered maws like a catfish; two short, clawed forelimbs tucked beneath their bodies as they flew; forked tongues so long they could scoop up a grown man; and elongated jaws with sword-like teeth that reminded him of a darrowgar, except ten times their size.

The coatls landed on the grass, their sinuous bodies rippling as they came to rest. Both of the Battle Mages had hooked iron staffs strapped to their backs, and wore embroidered tunics with a strip of cloth that hung below their waists. As usual, every inch of exposed skin was covered in leopard body paint. When the shorter rider levitated to the ground and removed his horned helm, Tamás raised a fist and gave a shout of recognition. "Aahpo!"

While the taller rider was just as lean and muscular as Aahpo, Caleb was surprised to see the battle-scarred face of a woman in her fifties beneath the helm. She had black hair cut almost to the scalp and a commanding gaze that drew instant respect. As she approached, the Battle Mages on the ground tucked their helms under their arms.

"I bring you Izel Halach, Supreme Commander of the Kukulcan Caste of Battle Mages," Aahpo said, bowing to her after he spoke.

"Well met," Izel said, in a voice that matched the hardness of her appearance. She eyed the airships approaching in the distance. "The arch-governors know that war is imminent. They've chosen to engage here first, on Congregation soil, rather than on our own. Behind me are a dozen dozen Battle Mages and coatl. An equal number will arrive in two days' time. We hope to spoil Lord Alistair's appetite for crossing the border."

Her words stunned Caleb, and he didn't know what to say.

"Two days? Can we last that long?" Lance said bluntly. "I know war, but I don't know wizards."

Izel turned to face him. "I'm unsure. But perhaps a victory before the full might of the Congregation is unleashed will convince the Conclave a protracted war in the Mayan Kingdom is unwise."

"What's your plan of action? How can we help?"

"We will launch from the bluff and engage the airships before they can establish position. I'm unsure what defenses they will employ after the success of Aahpo's surprise attack, but they will not find us an easy target." She gave a hard smile. "The Congregation has superior numbers and more powerful mages. Yet unlike us, they have not seen battle for a generation. We are at constant war along our southern border. Our mages do not study artisamancy and floramancy. They are steeped in the art of combat from the moment they come of age. I think the Congregation will find their training sessions are not the same as the heat of battle." She turned to Aahpo. "You will continue to lead the command that stays here, below the bluff. It's possible the Congregation will try to land one or more of the airships to establish ground position. If they send more, we will divert additional forces as we are able."

Aahpo bowed. "Yes, Halach."

"We will coordinate in the usual manner. I'll send further instructions after I confer with my advisors." She turned to Caleb. "I assume our help is welcome?"

"Affirmative."

The Mayan commander eyed the advancing airships again, then gave a curt nod. "Then good fortune to you all. Less than an hour remains before we engage."

The blip of time before the warships arrived, the calm before the storm, was a hive of activity. Caleb was no war strategist. He let those with experience—Lance, Tamás, Aahpo, and Chooshe—take the lead in crafting a hurried battle plan. It was all conjecture, because no one knew what was coming. Would the airships land? Stay in the air? How many mages were on board? How effective would the Mayan wizards be against them? If the airships were allowed to hover above the grasslands and rain death on Caleb's army, the battle would be over before it began.

With the addition of one hundred and forty-four Battle Mages, the total number of his army's wizards had soared to over three hundred, counting the shamans. Would that be enough to slow the war machines blotting the sky, bloated with soldiers and wizards?

No one knew.

As the airships soared closer, and his army grew tense around him, the air seemed to grow still, reminding him of the calm before a hurricane hit. Caleb felt less in control of the situation than ever, as if the world had spiraled off its axis and was spinning away from the sun. He had left the Barrier Coast to seek personal revenge. He did not want a war. He did not want a single one of these people to die. He understood in his head that his personal quest represented a miniscule fraction of the harm they had suffered, and they were left with no real choice. They were fighting for their lives and their families, their very existence. But his heart could only see the violence and bloodshed that awaited, the terrible cost of war no matter who emerged the victor.

As the airships drew near enough for him to see the soldiers massed along the side railing, and the wizards standing at the prow, and feel the force of the winds billowing the great sails, he remembered the first true battle he and his brothers had waged on Urfe, when the ogre-mage and his band of thieves had attacked in the dead of night. Even though he had played almost no part in the battle, reduced to hiding in the trees, he recalled vividly the sinkhole that had opened in his stomach, and the speed at which the battle had begun.

It was the same now. Adrenaline and fear still threatened to overwhelm him. Nothing had changed except for the mace in his hand and the white-hot rage coursing through him, allowing him to channel his emotions into something useful.

He had become a warrior, or a Templar, or something else altogether. He didn't know what he was anymore.

He just knew he had power—and that his goal had never wavered.

Before the Congregation's warships reached them, the coatls launched shrieking off the top of the granite bluff, their Battle Mages poised atop wooden platforms, hooked staffs in hand.

Most of the airships, still in tight formation, sailed directly at the approaching enemy. But two of the ships peeled off and began to descend. Caleb's mouth went dry in anticipation. *Two airships.* He realized that, while the action on the ground would be swift and furious, the battle would be won in the sky. If the bulk of the airships overwhelmed the Battle Mages and their mounts, Caleb's army would have no support and nowhere to run. If they returned to the forest, the Congregation mages would smoke them out again.

This is a war of wizards.

"Oo-rah!" Lance yelled from the head of the paladins, thrusting his war hammer to the sky. The hundred paladins were the spearhead of the ground troops, flanked by the Chickasaw on one side, and the bulk of Caleb's army on the other.

Caleb and the rest of the inner circle were positioned just behind the paladins. The Prophet had tried to keep Caleb out of the fighting, arguing they needed him alive for morale, like any king or figurehead. But he would have none of it. He had led them here and wasn't about to watch others die while he shouted encouragement from the sidelines.

The two descending airships touched down. Ladders were tossed over the railing so the Protectorate soldiers could scramble down the tilectium hulls. Caleb's army surged forward, now fifty yards away, aiming to engage the Protectorate forces before they could regroup on the ground.

Caleb looked up as he ran. The sky was alight with pyrotechnics. The coatls darted across the sky like reptilian will o' the wisps, enabling their riders to unleash volley after volley of deadly sunbeams at the airships. It looked to Caleb as if they were attacking with laser guns, and he supposed in effect they were.

But this time the Congregation was prepared. Far more mages had been sent than before, crowding the prows of the ship. Half of them used Wizard Shields and other defensive measures to counter the sunbeams, while the others employed offensive spells across the spectrum of their specialties. Fireballs and lightning bolts and ice spears were unleashed. Aquamancers raised water elementals from the river that fountained skyward to attack the Mayan wizards. Geomancers wielded iron orbs that whisked through the sky, seeking out their targets like guided missiles.

As in the first battle, the Mayan wizards tried to destroy the underbellies and sails of the airships, but this time the Congregation had strategically positioned each ship so that it was protected by the wizards of at least one other. It was a deadly dance of destruction, with wizards on both sides using lightning-fast reflexes to erect their shields, and counterattacking as soon as an opening presented. Both sides suffered casualties in the opening salvo, and neither seemed to have the advantage, which gave Caleb hope.

He yanked his eyes away from the spectacle. Whatever happened in the sky was out of his hands. From up close, the enormity of the airships caused his stomach to clench with fear. The hulls stood eighty feet off the ground and stretched as long as a football field. Soldiers poured down the ladders and massed in front of the two ships. The opposing armies exchanged a volley of long-range weapons, arrows and spears and axes, but the wizards intercepted most of the missiles with simple flicks of their wrists.

Aahpo and his faction of Battle Mages had joined up with the shamans and the wizards from Caleb's army. Together, they surrounded the Congregation mages standing on the prows of the grounded airships or hovering on small daises that Branyn called Magediscs. The shamans did not have many offensive spells, but they confused the Congregation wizards with their illusions, and summoned spirit animals to attack in their stead.

As the wizards faced off, the pounding of the ground armies was like two herds of thundering elephants as they rushed to engage on the grasslands. The paladins led the charge with a wall of shields that pressed hard against the enemy's line. A tall reptilus commander, flanked by a pair of wizards, shouted down orders from one of the ships. The Protectorate soldiers raised their shields in unison, using the hull of an airship to defend their flank, and Caleb could tell at once the Protectorate forces, though outnumbered, were better trained.

That was the last observation he made before the armies clashed and the roar of battle engulfed him. Protectorate soldiers surged against the front line, most of them wielding longswords and round shields attached to their forearms. Yasmina was on his left, Tamás on his right. The Brewer's tenor rose above the din, imbuing Caleb with strength as he threw back the hood of his cloak and joined the battle. His first opponent was a reptilus soldier who thrust a trident at Caleb's midsection. Working hard to corral the adrenaline pouring through him, Caleb blocked the trident with his mace and watched with grim satisfaction as the trident broke in half. Caught by surprise, the Protectorate soldier scrambled to get away. Caleb let him go, instead turning to engage a dual-bladed swordsman that took him longer to dispatch. Beside him, Yasmina held her own with her staff, using her quickness and the long reach of the weapon to devastating effect.

The battle ebbed and flowed, pushing closer to the airships and then further back into the grassy field. Lance and Allira fought with the paladins at the forefront of the battle, and Caleb heard Lance shouting orders the entire time. The Roma and Devlan fighters on the river side of the battle had lost ground, but on the forest side, the Chickasaw had pressed the Protectorate forces back. Lance and the reptilus commander both recognized the situation, and shifted their forces to compensate. Lance sent Lisha and her warriors to bolster the river flank, and the howling darvish beat back the Protectorate incursion, despite being outnumbered ten to one. The Protectorate had no answer for the towering red-skinned warriors wielding lava cannons. Had a team of aquamancers not rushed over to help, the darvish would have stormed the airship guarding the reptilus commander.

On the other flank, the Protectorate forces fought hard to beat back the Chickasaw attack, but the warriors fighting for their homeland continued to gain ground. Caleb glanced up. The attacking mages had the Congregation mages pinned on the prows of the ships, but every time they tried to advance, the Congregation mages pushed them back with awesome displays of firepower.

"Caleb!" Yasmina shouted.

He whirled to find her fighting from her back on the ground. Two Protectorate soldiers stood above her, jabbing at her with their swords. It was clear one of them would get through at any moment. Caleb despaired. He would never reach her in time. Desperate, he screamed for help as a giant insectoid came out of nowhere and landed right behind the two soldiers. The praying mantis man stabbed one through the back with its serrated forearms, lifted him off the ground, and threw him fifty feet away. Before it could reach the other, a great screech rent the air, and Yasmina's harpy landed on the head of the other soldier, clawing out his eyes with talons as long as Caleb's fingers. The soldier screamed and stumbled away, blood pouring down his face. Caleb breathed a sigh of relief and helped Yasmina to her feet.

"Thank you," she said to her saviors. Caleb could see in her eyes how tired she was. He was exhausted too. They had fought the skeletons and marched all night without a break. How long could they keep this up?

As if on cue, there was a lull in the fighting. The reptilus commander shouted orders that caused the Protectorate soldiers to draw back and huddle beside one of the airships. Caleb realized in shock the other ship was empty, and its occupants had fled to bolster the defenses of the remaining airship on the ground. His army had defeated one of the ships!

Lance did not order the paladins forward. Instead, realizing the army needed a break, he also pulled back. A swath of grassland separated the two sides as Lance and the other commanders jogged over to confer with Caleb and Tamás. Two of the wizards, Branyn and Aahpo, flew over as well.

"I think we can take the second airship," Lance said to Branyn and Aahpo as flasks of water were passed around, "if you can neutralize the wizards."

"I do not think we can defeat them without help," Aahpo said. "Their defenses are too strong."

"My power is waning," Branyn said. A glaze of exhaustion coated his eyes, and his face dripped with sweat. "I fear the same is true for most of us. The shamans' spirit familiars are losing their potency."

"Perhaps we should await the outcome in the sky," Tamás said, "before we exhaust ourselves."

"I'm not sure that's the best strategy," Lance said grimly. He had turned towards the river, his face upturned to the sky.

What had seemed like an even battle had turned south for the Mayan wizards. Although mages on both sides had plummeted to their deaths, not a single airship had fallen, and they remained in tight formation near the bluff. Many of the Congregation wizards had left the airships, either linked arm-in-arm or riding atop magical discs and other flying devices. They were all over the sky, pursuing the coatl with streaking missiles of magic. Caleb could not tell how many coatl and Battle Mages remained—plenty—but they were disorganized and on the run.

No one spoke as the dire turn of events settled in.

"They're too strong," Yasmina said finally. "And far too many."

"And there's another one coming," Tamás said, pointing at an airship flying low on the horizon from the direction of New Victoria.

"Good Christ," the Brewer muttered. The ship descended lower and lower as it approached, and it became clear it intended to land to reinforce the ground troops.

"No one's on the prow," Tamás said, raising a spyglass to peer at the ship.

"That's something," Lance said. "If there aren't any wizards, we might be able to hold out. How many soldiers are on board? Perhaps we can—"

He cut off as Yasmina gasped beside him. She was peering at the approaching airship with her magically enhanced vision.

Tamás lowered the spyglass, the color draining from his face.

"What is it?" Caleb said, taking a step forward. "What did you see?"

"There are no mages aboard the ship," Tamás said in a defeated voice, "but the hundreds of people on board aren't Protectorate soldiers, either."

"Then what are they?"

Tamás swallowed. "Majitsu."

-30-

Will looked back and forth between his brother and the tall, handsome wizard who had just stepped into the room. The wizard's imperious gaze absorbed what Dida was doing, rested on Dalen for a brief moment, barely glanced at Will, and then returned to Val. From the dangerous glint in his brother's eye, and the way the two were glaring at each other, Will could tell they knew each other, and there was bad blood between them.

The green outline of Dida's portal was almost complete, but the sudden arrival of the newcomer had caused the bibliomancer's fingers to pause tracing his spidery runes in the air.

Black lightning crackled at Val's fingertips. "You shouldn't have followed us, Braden."

"No? I believe that is *exactly* what I should have done. Lord Alistair will be most unhappy to learn that his beloved protégé, his own daughter's beloved, is in fact the traitor some of us believed him to be." Braden sneered. "You're just like your father. A vile, treacherous gypsy through and through. It will be my pleasure to personally deliver you to the Conclave and see you transported to wizard prison."

"You've been consumed with jealousy ever since I replaced you," Val said. "Do you think everyone hasn't noticed how petty you are? Alistair wouldn't take you back even if I was gone. I've seen the way you look at Adaira, too."

Braden took a step closer. "Shut your filthy mouth! You never deserved her!"

"And you do? A schemer and a torturer? I don't want to kill you," Val said. "Let us go, and you can run up to the Conclave and tell them whatever you want about me. I won't stop you."

A smile played at Braden's lips. "*Stop* me? Have you forgotten, whelp, that I'm the highest ranking cuerpomancer in the Congregation? Spirit mage or not, you have many years before you can challenge the likes of me."

"Last chance," Val said, as the Spirit Fire on his fingertips burned brighter, emitting an impressive shower of sparks. Will hung back for the moment, ready to step in but not wanting to break his brother's concentration. He did not know what powers a cuerpomancer wielded, but how could it compare to Spirit Fire?

"Indeed it is," Braden replied, raising a hand as he began to walk towards Val. "For *you*."

Val straightened his arms to unleash the spell. Just before black fire shot out from his fingers, Braden closed his raised fist, causing both of Val's hands to wrench backwards. He cried out in pain, and the twin arcs of deadly energy went awry, flying over Braden's head and striking the ceiling instead. Before Val could recover, a pair of silver handcuffs flew out of Braden's cloak and whisked through the air. One of the cuffs fastened onto Val's left wrist, and his right hand jerked across his body against his will, like an automaton, to attach to the dangling end of the silver cuffs. With both his hands caught, Val snarled and jerked in vain against the bonds.

Val gritted his teeth, unable to produce a spark of magic. Braden lazily waved a hand and sent Val flying across the room and into the wall.

Wishing he had acted sooner, Will rushed the cuerpomancer as Dida's fingers frantically whisked through the air, trying to finish the portal. Will heard a series of loud snapping sounds that turned his stomach and caused the bibliomancer to scream and back away from the portal. Will saw in horror that the bones of Dida's fingers on both hands were broken and jutting out from the skin at unnatural angles.

Before engaging Will, Braden whipped to his left to face Dalen, sweeping the back of his hand through the air. The terrified illusionist raised his hands, but his head was thrown against the wall behind him, causing his eyes to roll back and his body to slump to the ground.

It had all happened shockingly fast. The cuerpomancer clapped his hands and rubbed them together as he turned, causing Will to slow his approach and circle his opponent, wary of his powers.

"Will Blackwood, I presume?" Braden said. "Now that the wizards are disposed of, I suggest you surrender before I run you through with your own sword."

He doesn't know about Zariduke, Will realized. *Alistair hasn't told anyone that he lost it.*

The cuerpomancer had stepped between the two brothers. If Will wanted to use Zariduke to free Val from the wizard cuffs, he would have to go through Braden.

"I've got a suggestion for you too," Will said, taking a step closer and raising his sword.

"Pray tell," Braden said, "before I rip out your tongue and eyes and sew your mouth closed, what a swordsman thinks he can do against an elder mage of the Congregation."

Will pointed the sword at his chest. "That you know what you're up against before you start running your mouth.

Braden made a circle in the air with his hands. Will felt a gentle vibration run through the sword and down to his forearms, as if he had absorbed an invisible burst of magic. He relished the sudden confusion in Braden's eyes. "How can this be?" he said, and then his eyes locked onto the sword in understanding. He took a step back. "Spiritscourge?"

Will lunged. Braden flew backwards to avoid the blow, all the way to the archway. In the few moments that his action bought him, his arms began to lengthen at his sides, and there was another crackling of bones being broken. Braden screamed as the skin on his hands split apart and blood spattered the wall. Will paused, uncertain what was happening until he saw Braden's arms reform into flesh-colored swords with dagger-sharp points instead of hands. A shudder rolled through the mage, and the agony in his eyes disappeared as if he had healed himself. A gleam of fury replaced the pain, and he came at Will with both blades whisking through the air, in a surprising show of fencing skill.

Will blocked one of the armswords with his shield, beating it back, and parried the other with Zariduke. The armsword did not disappear as he hoped—it must be a part of Braden's body, not a thing of magic—but Zariduke bit deep, causing more blood to spurt and Braden to shriek in pain.

After another furious exchange, Will got in close, managed to smack Braden in the face with his shield, and sliced downward against his thigh. It was a glancing blow, but enough for Braden to realize he was no match for Will in a duel. He swung wildly with both arms to create distance, then tried to escape by flying through the arched entrance. Knowing they were doomed if Braden raised an alarm, Will lunged to strike him down from behind, catching him just before he disappeared through the archway.

Braden screamed in pain as Will shoved the sword deeper into his back. The cuerpomancer grasped the blade jutting out of his stomach, blood erupting from the terrible wound.

"Can't . . . heal myself. Magic . . . of the sword . . ."

His last words gurgled away. After ensuring he was dead, Will jerked the sword out and let the body fall. "Not a friend of yours?" he said to Val, as his brother walked over and held up his wrists.

"He's not a friend of anyone's anymore."

Will pressed the blade against the wizard cuffs, causing them to disappear with a snip of blue-white light. He hurried over to check on Dalen as Val tried to comfort Dida, who was shivering with pain and holding his broken fingers.

Will opened a flask of water and dabbed Dalen in the face until his eyes finally opened. "*Krikeyluckatrokaikekrikey*," he said, blinking and rubbing the top of his head. "That hurt."

Will helped him to his feet, suspecting his friend had a concussion. "Can you walk?"

"Lucka, I'll make do. If Braden knew we were down here, someone else might too."

"Thanks to his pride and ambition, I believe he confronted us alone," Val called out. "But yes, someone could realize Braden's gone missing."

Poor Dida was moaning and cradling his hands beneath his body. "I can't open the portal without my hands," he said in a pain-filled whisper. Will couldn't even look at the fragments of white bone jutting out from his fingers.

"It's fine," Val soothed, gently putting an arm around his friend. "Mala has a healing potion in the carriage. We'll get you fixed up soon."

"*Krikey*, but how do we get out of here?"

"You can't hold the illusion again?" Val said. "Not even to the entrance?"

Dalen swallowed, held up a hand, and concentrated on it. After a few moments, his hand began to weakly flicker, then returned to normal. Dalen hung his head in shame. "I'm too drained."

Will patted him on the back. "It's okay. The plan was never for you to get us back."

"I have an idea," Val said after a moment. "You'll all have to wait here."

"With a dead body?" Will said. "What if someone comes in?"

"Then stab them. I'll be back as soon as I can. I'm aiming for the low-tech escape plan."

"Low-tech?" Dalen said, as Val flew out of the archway and disappeared. "What is this?"

Will chuckled to break the tension. "I'll tell you one day."

After Val left, Will grabbed Braden's frilly white shirt and pulled his corpse into the room. Keeping a tight grip on Zariduke, he walked over to stand near the archway, listening for sounds in the corridor outside. As Dida moaned quietly in the corner, Dalen paced back and forth, muttering to himself and glancing at Braden's corpse from time to time as if it would reanimate.

Long minutes later, Val returned with an armful of hooded brown robes that made Will think of medieval priests.

"Put these on," Val said, handing out robes to everyone except himself. "It's the best I could do on short notice."

"Who do they belong to?"

"No idea. I found them in a closet."

Val gently helped the bibliomancer with his robe, and still he almost swooned from the pain when the cloth brushed his ruined fingers.

The garment swallowed Dalen whole as the illusionist flew in front of the group, barely able to manage the feat. Dida bravely insisted he fly himself. He kept his broken hands inside the folds of his sleeves, though Will worried if anyone looked too closely they would see him shaking with pain.

Val took the rear position, so he could keep an eye on everyone and levitate Will as well. The empty corridor of strange doors and wizard seals was cloaked in silence as they drifted through, but the wizard chute was more active. *It must be well into the morning.* Before they reached ground level, plenty of wizards had drifted past them, either in pairs or alone. Most greeted Val with a friendly nod and gave his robed entourage sidelong glances, but no one accosted them. All it would take, Will knew, was for one person to go looking after Braden, or notice the spirit door guarding the archway to Lord Alistair's artifact room was missing.

They reached the grand foyer without incident. Just as Will grew hopeful they would escape, a wizard in a steel-gray cloak with black runes on the sleeves called out to Val and flew directly at them. Will's breath caught in his throat as Val hovered in midair to greet him.

"Cyrus," Val said, exchanging a friendly arm clasp. "Good morning."

The wizard had a stern, dour face that radiated power and authority. That, along with a set of vertical gold runes on the breast of his cloak, gave Will the impression he was a commander of some sort.

"Alistair is looking for you," Cyrus said in a thick British accent. "The War Council is about to meet."

"I'm on my way," Val said. "These emissaries got turned around in the wizard chutes, and I was just escorting them outside."

Will tried to disappear into his hood as Cyrus gave them all a long look. "I see," the gray-cloaked mage said finally, opening a palm towards the entrance as if to say *it's right over there*.

"I'm stepping out for some fresh air," Val said to defray his suspicions, "and then I'll join you."

"Very well," Cyrus said. "You've heard a large contingent of Battle Mages have joined the rebels?"

"I . . . have."

"They put up a fight, and we lost another airship, but the battle will soon be over. Kjeld has joined Yasir on the ground, and I'll be leading a second wave of airships to ensure there are no more surprises. Not even the combined might of the Arch Governors can stand against our full fleet."

"That's excellent news," Val said, with an almost imperceptible swallow.

Cyrus again glanced at Val's companions, and Val began drifting away to distract him. "I'll see you shortly, then."

All of a sudden, Dida gasped and convulsed as if overcome by pain. He quickly recovered, but not before his hood slipped back, allowing Cyrus to glimpse his face. "Why Dida," he said, his eyes narrowing, "I didn't realize it was you."

"Yes," Dida said, unable to mask the pain in his voice. "Well met, Cyrus."

Cyrus drifted closer, coming face to face with the bibliomancer. "Is everything all right? You don't look well."

Val patted Dida on the arm. "He woke up with a bit of flu."

"I thought you said he was lost?" Cyrus said. "Dida knows his way around the Sanctum quite well."

In the ensuing silence, as the tension grew as thick as morning fog, Will prepared to rip off his robe and reach for his sword. Yet even if they managed to overcome this gray-cloaked wizard—who looked extremely competent—plenty of others were milling about in the foyer. They would never escape.

Val touched Cyrus's arm and spoke in a very quiet voice. "*Please.* Don't ask any more questions. Just let us go."

"What is the meaning of this?"

Val compressed his lips as he debated his next words. "We haven't talked about it before, not explicitly, but I believe you and I share the same objective."

Cyrus glanced quickly around to see if anyone was watching. He took Val by the arm in what would appear to onlookers as a friendly grip, but Will could see the tension in his face as he spoke through clenched teeth. "And what might that be? You know what I am and who I represent."

"I think you know exactly what I mean."

There was a long moment of silence. "You tread on very dangerous ground, Valjean."

"You know me, Cyrus. Please don't ask any more questions. All I can tell you is that I strongly believe that my interests and yours—the Queen's—are not in opposition."

Cyrus's face darkened even further, and he held onto Val's arm for so long that people were starting to stare. Will knew that at any moment someone else could wander over.

"Because you avenged my brother," Cyrus said finally, "I will let you attend to your fresh air, but you should know that if we meet again, my duty is to my Queen and the Realm. If our interests are not aligned, any friendship of ours will not suffice to stay my hand."

"Understood," Val said, and Cyrus removed his grip. "I won't forget this, and remember what I said."

Cyrus didn't answer, and Will could feel the wizard's eyes on their backs as Val flew them through the columned entrance to the pyramid and out into the open air. To his surprise, the sun had risen above the tops of the trees in the Wizard District. *How long were we inside?*

As they flew past the two colossi guarding the outside of the columned entrance, Will scanned the Wizard District for a sign of their friends. Not far away, he spotted Gus's carriage parked alongside a manicured green space crisscrossed by pathways of mosaic tile. All they had to do was reach the carriage, give Mala's healing tincture to Dida, and let him reconstruct the portal to the Pool of Souls he had started beneath the Sanctum. The previous night, Dida had scoured the library of the Abbey and found an old book that detailed the original construction of the spirit mage portal.

Relief poured through Will as they touched down on the street outside the carriage. Gus made a clicking sound, and Rucker threw open the door. The others—Synne, Mala, and Mateo—watched everyone crowd inside the carriage.

"Dida needs help," Will said in a rush to Mala, as Val helped the bibliomancer struggle out of his robe. "Right now."

Mateo swore softly at the sight of the bibliomancer's ruined hands, and Mala hurried to fish out a tiny blue bottle from one of her pouches. She twisted off the stopper and held it to Dida's lips. He drank deeply and, moments later, shuddered as his broken fingers began to straighten. The tendons and ligaments reformed before their eyes, and new flesh grew atop them.

"That's all we have," Mala said, dropping the bottle in the seat. "I tried to buy more from Dashi but the Guild is hoarding them."

"How is it, lad?" Rucker asked.

With a deep sigh of relief, Dida flexed his fingers without pain. "As if it never happened," he said in awe. "We do not have such potent draughts in our kingdom."

"Glad to hear it," Val said roughly, to disguise the emotion in his voice. "Now get that portal up and running. How long will it take?"

"I completed most of it inside," Dida said, "and need only recall the schematic."

"If we're this close to the entrance to the Pool of Souls," Rucker said with a growl, "why doesn't Gus just take us there?"

"Because if we use the front door," Val said, "we still have to navigate the Planewalk. No one but me has a chance of doing that, and I barely survived it the first time. There's another entrance to the pool which the Conclave uses, but I don't know where it is. So it's the portal or nothing."

"Bah. Get on with it, then."

Dida stood as best he could in the cramped space, waved his hands, and summoned the green doorway he had almost formed beneath the Sanctum. It was complete except for a portion of the bottom right corner.

All of a sudden, the entire carriage rose straight into the air at a dizzying speed, as if it were part of an amusement park ride back home. "What's happening?" Synne cried, crouching in alarm.

"Val, is this you?" Will shouted. He and Mateo had gripped onto each other for support.

His brother clutched an armrest with both hands. "No!"

The sudden movement caused Dida to fall across Mala and Rucker in one of the seats. The carriage finally stopped moving, coming to a sudden halt. Wondering if Lord Alistair had found them, Will leaped to a window and saw that Gus and the horses were far beneath them, but still beside the park. Something had ripped the carriage clean away and raised it straight into the air. He leaned out and craned his neck up to see what had happened. When he realized what had lifted the carriage as easily as a marble, his blood curdled, and he struggled to form words.

Before he found his voice, the roof was ripped off, and the others saw for themselves the face of one of the enormous stone beings guarding the entrance to the Sanctum.

"The colossus," Mala breathed in terrified wonder. "It moves!"

They were at least thirty feet above the ground, eye level with the creature of legend whose size exceeded even the storm titan. Its chiseled face resembled a handsome warrior locked in stone. The jaw was solid as a mountain, and one massive hand had unfurled to raise the being's obsidian sword into the air. The carriage rested in the palm of its other hand, its feet were planted in the moat, and Will realized it had reached down to pluck the carriage right off the street. The other colossus stood unmoving beside the entrance to the Sanctum, in the same position as always.

Someone sounded the alarm and brought this thing to life.

"Fly us out of here, mage!" Rucker roared.

Val shook his head. "It's too late. They'll surround us in a second. Dida, open the portal. That's our only chance!"

Good advice, Will thought as he saw the commotion on the street. Every tourist in the district was pointing at the colossus in awe, and wizards in flight were streaming out of the Sanctum.

As Dida worked frantically to finish the green doorway, Will felt a great weight press on his back and slam him to the musty floor of the carriage, his sword trapped beneath him. The force of the blow knocked the wind from him. Gasping for breath, he saw the stunned look on the faces of his friends, twisted his neck to the side, and realized the colossus had pinned him down with a finger.

Why didn't it just kill me? He thought, then answered his own question.

It wants the sword. Alistair sent it after Zariduke.

Dida finished the green doorway and caused it to hinge open. Nothing except for a faint shimmer in the air was visible on the other side.

"Go!" Will said, struggling to free himself. "Save yourselves."

"Shut up," Val said, and sent a blast of Spirit Fire into the hand of the colossus, above where it was holding Will.

No effect.

"Don't bother," Rucker said. "Only an arch mage, and precious few of them, could harm a colossus."

Mala took out Magelasher and whipped the hand of the colossus over and over, in the same spot Val had tried. "It's not working!" she cried. "Think of something, wizard!"

Val snarled and tried Spirit Fire again, with the same result. He cut it off, not wanting to waste his power. "Hold on, Will," he said, unable to hide his despair.

Out of the corner of his eye, Will saw a group of wizards flying above the entrance to the Sanctum, aiming straight for them. "They're coming," he said. "*Take the portal!*"

Rucker pushed Mala and Val aside and swung Demonbane with all his strength. The mighty ax bounced off the colossus as if striking a steel barrier. Synne leaped onto the arm of the legendary being and beat it with a series of rapid, magic-driven blows. It didn't even twitch.

With a roar, Mateo made a fist with his chainmail glove, raised it high above his head, and slammed it down on the back of the finger pinning Will. There was a sound like a thunderclap, and a hairline crack appeared in the stone.

After a moment of stunned silence, Val shouted at his cousin. "Again!" he commanded. "Harder, Mateo!"

The Roma warrior obliged, crashing his gloved fist against the finger of the colossus with all his might. The crack grew larger, and the finger twitched enough to allow Will to wriggle free and grab his sword. Mala and Rucker were also ready, and helped dragged Will away. The colossus did not have fast reactions, and before it could respond, they had all poured through the green doorway.

The transport was instantaneous. Not sure what to expect, disoriented by the sudden change in location, Will stumbled as he emerged into a high-ceilinged cavern lit by an orange phosphorescent glow. In the center of the cavern was a sunken basin filled with a viscous, shimmery, metallic-blue substance.

The Pool of Souls.

Dida whisked his hand across the green doorway as if trying to make it disappear, but it failed to respond. After a moment of confusion, his eyes widened. "They're holding the portal open!"

"Can you keep them out?" Val said.

"Not for long. There must be a team of wizards on the other side!"

Val stepped waist-deep into the pool, causing a rush of images to form in the depths of the semitransparent substance. Everyone except Dida gathered around to see scenes from Val's past rushing by: friends down the street from their old family home in New Orleans, holidays with their mother's relatives, Val at work in his law firm, and a beautiful woman with turquoise eyes and a braid of blond hair, dressed in fashionable Urfe attire. *That must be Adaira,* Will thought. Soon images of Caleb began to appear, and once they did, Val began shouting into the basin. "Caleb! Can you hear me!"

There was no response.

"Hurry!" Dida said. "I can't hold it much longer."

Feeling helpless, Will balled his fists as the images of their middle brother moved faster and faster, skipping forward in time.

Caleb at the Minotaur's Den on their first day in Urfe. Laughing in the forest as Marguerite taught him sleight of hand tricks. Racing through the deadly maze beneath Leonidus's keep. Fighting Zedock in the cemetery. Working as a slave in the Darklands. Watching the Congregation airships rain death and destruction on Freetown. Surrounded by ugly little faeries in a ring of mushrooms. Saving Luca from a waterfall. Slipping a ring on to Marguerite's finger in a crisp mountain stream, his brother's face happier and more alive than Will had ever seen it.

Standing in front of the Coffer of Devla with a befuddled look when it opened.

Watching as a bolt of pure electricity slammed into Marguerite and then Luca, killing them at once.

"Caleb!" Val screamed, leaning as far over the basin as he dared. Feeling ill from that last image, Will joined in as well. "Caleb! Can you hear us?"

Grasping a diamond-headed mace atop an ivory tower as waves crashed against the rocky shore beneath him.

Fighting off a horde of mountain trolls with Tamás and the Brewer by his side.

"Caleb! It's your brothers! We need to come through!

In some strange place made of moonlight, trying to free a little girl tied to a burning pole.

Sobbing in Yasmina's arms.

Watching an airship full of black-robed majitsu land a hundred yards away.

"They've opened the doorway!" Dida said. "I can't stop them—they're coming through!"

"Caleb!!!"

-31-

The airship filled with majitsu touched down on the grassy field by the river. It landed just in front of the other two Congregation airships on the ground, one of which had been abandoned. Caleb had drawn his army back to create some distance. The sight of the black-robed warrior-mages lining the sides of the airship made him want to order everyone to run as far and as fast as they could, but there was nowhere left to go. If they turned and fled, the majitsu would chase them down and slaughter them.

The commander at the prow was a red-bearded goliath gripping the railing with both hands, shouting orders as the majitsu leaped off the airship and floated down to the ground. Even from that distance, Caleb could hear the cruel, arrogant bite in the commander's voice, and he struck fear into Caleb's heart.

All around him, his friends and fellow revolutionaries put up brave faces as they waited for the battle to begin. No one broke ranks or surrendered. In the sky above, the Mayan wizards and coatl were doing everything they could to keep the fleet of airships occupied, but the Congregation forces had them on the run.

On the ground, the battle still raged around the second airship. It seemed like an even fight between the Congregation mages and the combined forces of the Roma and Devla mages, the Chickasaw shamans, and Aahpo's contingent of Battle Mages. Caleb knew the wizards in his army were too preoccupied to help with the majitsu.

The Protectorate troops still on the ground—a thousand or so foot soldiers who answered to the stoic reptilus commander—fell back to let the majitsu lead the charge. Why risk more lives when the warrior-mages would cut through Caleb's army like a battle ax through a pile of kindling?

All of the majitsu except the red-bearded commander had left the airship and organized into a single long line facing Caleb's army. A strange formation for normal troops, but not for warrior-mages with skin like steel and fists that could punch through walls. The common born soldiers filed in behind them, and the strategy was clear. The majitsu at the front would drive deep into Caleb's army, creating a swath of destruction that would break the backs of the rebels.

Beneath the cloudy sky, the air was still and heavy, mirroring the tension on the ground, building towards an afternoon storm. Caleb wiped a bead of sweat off his brow and exchanged a grim look with Yasmina and the Brewer. Along with the rest of the inner circle, they were at the vanguard of the regular army, just behind the paladins, who had bravely fanned out to line up opposite the majitsu.

"They need a word from their leader," Tamás said to Caleb. The Roma warrior was gripping his sword as he stared straight ahead, into the heart of the enemy. "Something to lift their morale."

"False hope isn't my style," Caleb said.

"Have faith," the Prophet murmured from behind them. "The day is not over."

No one bothered to respond.

"I should return to the front," Lance said.

Caleb stepped forward to join him, as did Yasmina, Tamás, Allira, and the Brewer. Together, they walked to the front of the paladins, and as they passed, the paladins raised their shields in respect for the brave gesture.

The majitsu commander on the prow of the airship raised a fist as he roared. In response, the line of majitsu surged forward, moving in their peculiar leaping fashion aided by magic. Unlike a normal army, they did not yell or cry out, and made but a whisper of sound as they advanced, their feet barely touching down on the grass before lifting off again. The supreme confidence on their faces, despite carrying no weapons and being vastly outnumbered, caused a chill to sweep down Caleb's back.

"*Caleb . . .*"

The voice calling his name sounded watery, faraway—and very familiar.

After whipping around in a circle, he looked up and saw, just as he had the night of the funeral pyre during the march across the Ninth Protectorate, a spectral image of Val standing in a pool of shimmery, silver-blue water.

Val held out his hands with his palms upturned and beseeching. "You have to bring us through, Caleb. Right now!"

There was movement beside Val as more people stepped into the shimmery image. Caleb saw a few unfamiliar faces, including a grizzled one-armed adventurer and a female majitsu that made Caleb suspicious, but then he recognized Dalen, Mateo, Mala—and his younger brother.

"We have it!" Will cried. "We have the Coffer!"

Reeling at the sight of his brothers, and at Will's proclamation, Caleb glanced down and noticed the advancing majitsu had covered half the distance to his army. His heart sank as he realized he couldn't bring his brothers through to certain death. Nor did he see the Coffer anywhere near them. "I can't," he said. "There's no time."

Val's face appeared larger and much closer, right in front of Caleb's, as if he had shoved his head into the shimmering pool. Using his authoritative, older-brother voice, he said, "I can see the majitsu coming, and I don't care. There's a dozen Congregation wizards about to come through a portal right behind us. We have to get out. Now shut up and bring us through *right this damn second*."

Caleb couldn't see what was happening behind Val, but he saw the fear and alarm on the faces of everyone in the pool. With a curse, Caleb concentrated with his mind as he had the last time, wishing for their presence beside him, and made it a reality. At the last second, Val reached out with a hand and jerked a final person through—a bald mage with very dark skin and a befuddled, slightly panicked look in his eyes.

As soon as Val arrived, he took one look at the advancing majitsu and began to bark orders. "Dida, get the Coffer. Synne, watch my back. Everyone else get behind me!" In a lower voice, he said to Caleb, "I don't have much power left, but I'll try to stall them."

The line of majitsu was ten yards away. Could Val really do something against that, Caleb wondered?

Yasmina, Tamás, and everyone else near Caleb was shocked by the appearance of the newcomers, but no one had time to process it. Lance and Tamás began shouting orders that Val ignored as he stepped in front of everyone with his wiry female majitsu standing guard beside him. Val raised his hands and unleashed twin arcs of Spirit Fire at the feet of the advancing majitsu. The entire line leaped back or stopped advancing, startled by the sudden appearance of a spirit mage—as well as Lord Alistair's protégé.

"This is your only warning!" Val shouted, letting the Spirit Fire disperse. "I don't want to hurt you. Leave the field of battle! Go back to New Victoria!"

Behind Val, Caleb saw the bald mage who had just arrived work frantically to outline a glowing sapphire door in the middle of the air.

In the ensuing pause, the red-bearded majitsu drifted closer to the battle, flying high like a regular mage instead of leap-walking, glaring at Val as he roared instructions. Grim-faced, the majitsu fell back into a different formation, forming a rough square with twenty majitsu on each side and the rest filling in the middle. The majitsu outlining the square drew closer together and linked arms. After another shouted order, they advanced more slowly, walking instead of leaping, holding their hands out with ridged fingers that made their intentions clear.

Black sparks leapt off Val's hands as his own majitsu adopted a battle stance beside him. Will pushed to the front to stand on the other side of Val, and Caleb joined them.

"Lance?" Will said in a shocked voice as his childhood friend gave the order for the paladins to raise their shields.

"Good to see you, old buddy. How ya been?"

Will gripped Zariduke as he lowered into a crouch. "Never better. How'd you get here?"

"That old wizard sent me. You look different."

"So do you."

The red-bearded majitsu had almost reached his troops and was still shouting orders. The paladins waited steps behind Val to see what he would do. Forced into action by the advancing majitsu, Val grimaced and unleashed the Spirit Fire again, right into the front line.

Instead of ripping through the majitsu and incinerating them, the majitsu in the center put his palms up to absorb the black energy. All along the line, the faces of the warrior-mages were locked in concentration, and Caleb saw a shimmer in the air around them, as if they were all channeling their power or bodily energy into the palms of the single majitsu facing Val.

The defensive formation held off Val's magic for a long moment, but not even their collective might was enough to stave it off altogether. The majitsu in front screamed as the spirit magic broke through his palms and burned his hands to stumps. Screaming, the majitsu fell back and another took his place. Their advance continued in the same manner, forcing Val to renew his assault. Caleb could see the sweat on his brother's brow and how his hands shook with the effort. Some of the paladins launched spears and other missiles that bounced off the majitsu as if striking a stone wall.

They're draining him of power, Caleb thought. *They're going to break through at any moment.*

"I have it!" came a voice from behind him. "It's here!"

Caleb whipped around to find the robed mage that had come through the portal standing next to a large azantite chest covered in runes and engravings. *The Coffer*. Caleb's heart skipped a beat. The last time Caleb had seen the Coffer was the night Luca and Marguerite had died. It fueled his rage anew, and he strode towards it with a fire in his chest as Val struggled to hold back the wave of majitsu.

"Do something!" Yasmina called out. "He's getting weaker!"

Caleb glanced back and saw Val's Spirit Fire sputter and then die. He collapsed in Synne's arms, and she hustled him off the front lines as the red-bearded commander urged his majitsu forward. Without further thought, Caleb reached for the lid of the Coffer and threw it open. At first nothing happened, causing him to wonder with a sinking heart if the Coffer only responded to a direct attack, or if it still worked at all. He realized he knew nothing about it, except that it had saved him once, and that it just felt *right* when it had opened. As if the Coffer had belonged to him all along, a long-lost possession that had returned.

A swirl of golden light gathered inside, so bright Caleb had to look away. Moments later, a beam shot out of the artifact, over Caleb's left shoulder. The beam did not dissipate, and he whipped around to see where it was pointing, shocked to find that it had locked onto Will. No, not on his brother, Caleb realized.

On the shield that had once belonged to Fieran Blackwood, captain of the paladins.

The stream of light from the Coffer made the runes on Will's buckler blaze to life so brightly it hurt Caleb' eyes to look at them. Before anyone had a chance to react, the light spread like a great tentacled web to the rest of the shields the paladins were holding. The rudimentary runes the Devlan had marked on the shields with natural pigments and dyes from the forest glowed just as keenly as on Will's buckler. Once every shield was aglow, the light returned to the Coffer, leaving Caleb slack-jawed with amazement, and unsure what it portended.

After a moment's hesitation, the majitsu attacked the front line with a fury, throwing kicks and punches with preternatural speed.

"Shields up!" Lance cried. "Engage!"

As one, the paladins and Will raised their glowing shields to meet the attack. Expecting to punch and kick right through the barriers, the majitsu instead found that striking the shields had no effect, and in fact seemed to hurt them. Not only that, but when the warrior-mages tried to block sword thrusts with their hands and arms, the weapons bit deeply into their flesh.

The Coffer is working through the shields to deflect their magic, Caleb realized in awe, *just like with the electromancer. It's turning their blows back against them.*

"Guard the Coffer!" Caleb shouted to a group of soldiers standing near to him, so he could rush into the battle.

Val's young majitsu protector, who had hustled him beside the Coffer and eased him to the ground, balled her fists as she stood beside the relic. "They'll have to come through me."

Dida and Dalen joined her, and their support made Caleb feel better about leaving the Coffer's side. The battle raged in earnest as he sprinted over, howling in fury. A dozen or so majitsu had perished in the initial clash, when their powers had failed to protect them. But they had realized that, while they could no longer infuse magic into their blows or harden their skin against the weapons of the paladins, they could still use their martial skill and superhuman speed. They drove their fists into jugulars, executed impossible spin kicks in midair, swept out the legs of the paladins and picked up their own swords to impale them.

When the battle had started, Yasmina, Tamás, and the rest of Caleb's inner circle—everyone except for Will and Lance, who had paladin shields—had dropped back. But Caleb saw Tamás pick up a shield from one of the fallen paladins and enter the fight. A majitsu drove a fist into his gut, but instead of collapsing Tamás's stomach or ripping out his guts, the blow only caused him to grunt. The glowing shield, despite changing hands, had protected him.

Tamás's counter-attack with his sword caught the warrior-mage across his neck, felling him.

Yasmina noticed what Tamás had done, and followed suit. "Stay out of it, Yaz!" Caleb yelled as he engaged a tall majitsu attacking with flying fists. Caleb wondered why the woman majitsu was smiling, then realized *he* didn't have a paladin's shield. Her first strike got through, too fast for him to follow, but her uppercut to his jaw only rocked him back and did not end the fight. He realized that he, too, was under the Coffer's protection from her magic—and then realized he had somehow known all along that he would be, whenever the artifact was near.

Caleb swung and missed with the diamond-headed mace. The woman was incredibly fast. He couldn't seem to touch her, and she landed a series of blows before he finally blocked one with his vambrace.

She somersaulted over him and swept his legs from behind. He crashed to the ground. With an evil grin, she raised a foot to stomp on his face right as Yasmina's staff cracked her in the temple. As the warrior-mage wobbled, the one-armed adventurer who had arrived with Val came up behind the dazed majitsu and swung his gleaming battle ax into her back, severing her spine on impact.

"Maybe *you* should stay out of it," Yasmina said, offering a hand to help Caleb stand.

"Maybe so," he said, climbing to his feet.

Despite not having a shield, Rucker waded into the thick of the battle, weaving his great axe back and forth like a toothpick, seeking out majitsu with their backs turned. When Yasmina spun, another majitsu leaped at her, too fast for her or Caleb to react. A serrated appendage came out of nowhere to deflect the majitsu's ridge-hand strike. The warrior-mage turned and looked up, shocked by the sight of a hulking praying mantis man looming over him. The majitsu quickly recovered, and the two began to circle each other, warily testing defenses.

Caleb whipped around to see where he could help. The fighting was fast and furious, and he could not tell who had the advantage. Despite being hamstrung by the powers of the Coffer, the majitsu were still better warriors. Although the paladin shields burned the majitsu to the touch, not allowing the warrior-mages to remove them from the battlefield, the majitsu fought fiercely to stop new fighters in Caleb's army from picking up the shields of fallen warriors.

Somewhere off to Caleb's left, the Brewer began to sing a ballad of war. The sound of his lyre rose above the din of battle, much louder than it should have been, making Caleb wonder if the Coffer had amplified it. The sweet sound of the lyre, combined with the Brewer's deep tenor, made Caleb feel as invigorated as if he had just woken up from a long night's sleep, instead of fighting and running for his life for days on end. He could see the music was having a similar effect on the rest of his army. Was it the power of the Coffer, or the lyre from *Temmenily Ayawet*?

With his mind and muscles refreshed, Caleb waded into the battle at Yasmina's side, vowing to fight to the bitter end.

The smell of sweat and blood-soaked grass filled Will's nostrils. He kept drying his hands on his breeches and leather jerkin so his sword wouldn't slip. All around him were cries of pain, the clang of steel, and the thump of bodies hitting the ground. Even with the replenishing effects of the Brewer's song, Will's sword arm ached, and his calves and thighs felt on the verge of cramping.

He and Mala tried to stay back to back as much as they could, ready to spring to the other's aid. The combination of Zariduke and Magelasher, in tandem with the power of their paladin shields, proved devastating to the majitsu they faced.

Not far away, Mateo gripped a paladin shield with his chainmail glove and snapped his urumi blade to create distance from his opponents. Tamás fought beside him, facing off with a blindingly fast majitsu who had the upper hand until Mateo broke away from his own fight and lashed the majitsu in the back, giving Tamás room to breathe.

Still unable to believe Lance was on Urfe, Will heard his muscular friend shouting orders and guarding Allira as she sent her boomerangs spinning around the battlefield. Similar to the rest of the paladins, Lance was having trouble dealing with the speed of the majitsu. Allira had also picked up a shield, but even without the power of the Coffer, her missiles often found their mark on the temples of unsuspecting foes.

As usual, Mala fared the best of all, though not even she could match the preternatural dexterity of the warrior mages. Time and again she and Will were knocked down and saved by the other at the last moment, or raised their shields just in time to prevent a killing blow.

Despite the Coffer-enhanced shields, the majitsu would have won the day except for a simple mathematical fact: every time a paladin fell, another fighter in Caleb's army eventually retrieved the shield and replenished the ranks of the paladins.

Every time a majitsu fell, their numbers shrank by one.

Lisha and one of her darvish warriors had managed to retrieve two of the shields. Their ululating cries resounded on the battlefield as they wielded their lava tubes to devastating effect, until a majitsu leaped onto the back of Lisha's companion and broke his neck with a vicious twist. Shrieking in rage, Lisha blasted the majitsu in the back with her lava cannon, then ran to her fallen lover.

When the rest of the Protectorate forces entered the fray on the flanks, Caleb's army and the Chickasaw rushed to meet them. The revolutionaries had greater numbers, but the battle would belong to whoever controlled the center. If the majitsu defeated the paladins and managed to recover all the shields, they would run rampant over Caleb's army. Despite heavy losses to the original paladins, most of the shields had been recovered, and Will felt the tide of battle turning in their direction.

Just as his confidence grew, he heard a series of horrible cries to his left. He turned and saw a swath of destruction in human form stomping through the battlefield, as if a demon from the pits of hell had entered the fray.

This was a demon he knew by name. A red-bearded, marauding, giant of a man who had killed Mala's family and ruined the lives of countless others.

Kjeld barely seemed affected by the Coffer-infused shields and the weapons of the paladins. Will did not know if his magic was that much stronger, or if he was simply relying on brute strength and superior speed, but he plowed through the ranks of Caleb's army like a tank through a street full of bicycles. No one could stand against him. As Will watched in horror, Kjeld broke the neck of a young Devlan woman, then scooped up a paladin, raised him above his head, and snapped his spine on his knee.

Mala saw him as well. Will saw her shrink in fear as the majitsu commander continued to wreak havoc through the ranks of their army. He threatened to single-handedly restore the advantage to the majitsu.

With a shudder, Mala shrugged off her terror, and started towards Kjeld with Magelasher in hand.

Will hurried to keep pace with her, and grabbed her by the arm. "Wait."

"Leave me," Mala said with a snarl, jerking away. "I'm going for him."

"Not alone, you're not."

"He killed my family. This is my fight, not yours."

"You've taught me about my weaknesses, Mala, and made me a better warrior. Your weakness is that you never let anyone in. Don't fight him by yourself. He's too strong. There's no pride in being a hero, as you've told me countless times. Dying for a cause just means you're dead."

Her face contorted at his words, and he expected a stinging rebuke. But he didn't give her the chance to say no. Instead he raised his shield and kept walking straight for Kjeld. "Challenge him, but do it with me by your side."

"I never agreed to this, Will the Builder."

"Good thing we don't have time to argue."

They broke into a run to cut the majitsu commander off before he did any more damage. He saw them approaching, roared in pleasure, and turned to spar with someone who, like Will and Mala, had decided to engage the red-bearded giant.

"Tamás, no!" Will shouted, looking on in horror as the revolutionary leader stepped up to face the commander. "Wait!"

His long hair flying, covered in blood from the battle, the valiant Roma warrior stood to toe with Kjeld. Tamás managed to block the first few punches with his shield, but Kjeld dropped faster than it seemed possible for such a large human to move, and used a leg to sweep out the back of Tamás's knees. The revolutionary crashed to the ground and tried to roll away before Kjeld recovered, but the majitsu sprang to his feet as only a majitsu could do, using magic to lift his body upright, and brought his foot crashing onto Tamás's back. Pinned to the ground, Tamás struggled to free himself as Kjeld bent over, ripped the Roma warrior's sword out of his hand, and plunged it into his back. As Tamás screamed, Will saw Kjeld twist the handle of the sword with a look of pure satisfaction, as if he derived physical pleasure from the other man's pain.

"You bastard!" Will roared as he charged him.

Kjeld stepped off of Tamás almost lazily, eying Will and then Mala. The majitsu circled with his hands raised as they rushed him, dodging Mala's cat o' nine tails and then a sword thrust from Will. He lowered and sprang at Will like a linebacker, and was on him before Will could react. His open hand palm to Will's chin sent him flying off his feet. Will's head thudded against the ground when he landed, and he almost lost consciousness. As the giant rushed to finish him off, Mala caught him on the side with one of Magelasher's azantite barbs. Kjeld grunted and looked down in surprise at the nasty wound and the blood dripping from his side.

"Meet the agent of your demise, Despiser," she said, twirling the cat o' nine tails.

Kjeld cracked his knuckles as they circled. "A gypsy, then? Only one of your filthy race would know me by that name."

"Do you remember a clan outside Londyn you ambushed? I was a little girl trapped beneath a wagon, watching you murder my family."

"I've killed too many gypsy families to count, small one. Why should I remember yours?"

"Because the orphan of Clan Kalev is the one who will guide you to your grave."

He laughed as Mala pressed the attack harder than Will had ever seen her fight. Forced to use a paladin shield in tandem with Magelasher, instead of her sash or one of her blades, she worked the scourge back and forth as she advanced. Despite his far superior speed, Kjeld seemed unable to penetrate her defenses. As Will struggled to his feet, blinking away the cobwebs in his head and fighting off the nausea from the blow to his head, wanting desperately to help her, he could only marvel at Mala's prowess. Of all the fighters he had ever seen, only she could have lasted this long against the majitsu commander. As she had once told Will, when she had trained him to fight with skill and finesses instead of brute strength, there would always be someone bigger and stronger than he. And that someone, that ultimate bully who had no fear, was Kjeld. No normal human could stand against such a fiend, even with the magic of the Coffer-infused shields as protection. His size, strength, and magically enhanced speed were too overwhelming.

Mala used every trick in her book to stay alive. She spun, flipped, dove, twirled, lunged, and parried. She cheated whenever she could: throwing hidden daggers at his eyes, feigning slips to throw him off balance, even spitting in his face before she lowered for a knee attack. It was a legendary performance from a prodigy at the height of her powers, something for the bards to sing about one day—and yet it still wasn't enough. As Mala whipped the cat o' nine tails at the majitsu, over and over, driving him away, he spun to the side at the last moment and caught her by the wrist. With a grin, he forced it backwards, causing a brittle snapping of bone. Her scream of pain was the final jolt Will needed to regain his equilibrium and rush forward.

"Kjeld!" he roared, doing everything in his power to distract the monster before he killed Mala. He got there just in time, forcing Kjeld to turn and face him. The majitsu bladed his arm to ward off the sword thrust, either unaware of the power of the sword or believing he could overcome it. Zariduke bit deeply into his flesh, and Will slid the sword out as Kjeld stumbled back.

Grimacing through the pain, Mala somehow held her shield with her damaged wrist and picked up Magelasher with her good hand. She whipped the scourge back and forth as the two of them pressed Kjeld hard, before he had a chance to recover.

"How does it feel?" Mala taunted. "Tormentors never like it when their prey fights back."

Enraged, Kjeld shrugged off his stab wound and fought like a cornered animal, driving them away and catching Mala with a backhand that knocked her off her feet again. The blow rocked her so badly she dropped the scourge, and this time, Kjeld used a foot to sweep the powerful weapon far away from the fray. Desperate to help her, Will rushed the majitsu before he could pounce on her. Instead of attacking with the sword, he made a split-second decision that, if the tactic failed, would get them both killed. His ploy depended on his lover's almost superhuman combat sense.

"Mala," Will said as he faked a lunge with Zariduke, "catch!"

At the last moment, before stabbing with a blow that Kjeld was sure to evade, Will threw the sword past the majitsu at knee level, too low for him to grab. As he released the weapon, Will threw both hands out to wrap the much larger man in a bear hug. Will was banking on the fact that someone that big never expects to be bum-rushed, not to mention the fact that Will had thrown away his weapon, and hugging Kjeld could only lead to him crushing Will's spine.

Kjeld was caught completely off-guard, and not even his magic-infused agility allowed him to evade the maneuver. Still roaring like a madman, Will wrapped his arms around the barrel-chested commander, barely able to lock his hands on the other side. But Will hadn't managed to trap the bigger man's arms, and Kjeld simply reached around Will's back and grabbed with his own hands, squeezing so hard it felt as if Will was being crushed by a falling building. His breath whooshed out of him at once, and he felt his ribs crack at the pressure. He thought he had made a terrible mistake—right before the tip of a sword exited Kjeld's chest and kept going, missing Will by a millimeter.

"It's a good thing for you, Will the Builder," Mala said as Kjeld's arms fell away and he slumped to the ground, felled instantly by the sword thrust through his heart, "that I have precise aim and an expert command of human anatomy."

Will took a knee, unable to think through the pain in his side. He glanced over and saw that Kjeld was already dead, the center of his heart pierced by Zariduke.

A perfect thrust by Mala.

She put a foot on the majitsu's back and yanked the sword out. "'Tis a pity he died so quickly."

"Let's just be glad he's dead," Will gasped, his breath rattling in his throat. He put a hand on the ground to steady himself and thought he was about to pass out. "Oh, and Mala?"

"Yes?"

"Nice catch."

After the red-bearded commander fell, the remaining majitsu lost their momentum. Surrounded on all sides, their numbers dwindling, Caleb watched as the last two clusters of warrior-mages fled the battlefield and bounded for the safety of the forest. Unable to catch the swiftly moving majitsu, Lance gave the order to stand down and let them go. There was a moment of stunned silence as the realization of victory set in.

Out of nowhere, the Prophet appeared beside Caleb on the grassy field, raising his hands to the sky and shouting praises to Devla. His appearance spurred the army to press the attack on the remaining Protectorate forces, who seemed shocked by the defeat of the majitsu. With Lance and Caleb leading the way, at the spearhead of a hundred fighters with glowing paladin shields, they routed the ground troops and kept on going, surrounding the embattled Congregation mages on the prow of the final occupied airship. Beset on all sides, facing a superior number of shamans and Roma mages, plus a newly-confident army hungry for blood, the New Victoria wizards formed a defensive phalanx and took to the sky, linking arms as they flew away. Caleb raised a fist and opened it, giving the signal to let them go. His army gained nothing by hunting them down and expending more lives.

Dazed by the turn of events, so exhausted he could barely stand now that the adrenaline had ebbed, Caleb turned the army over to Lance and the other commanders and went looking for his brothers. He found Val and Synne by the Coffer where Caleb had left them. Dida and Dalen were with them. Though Val was sitting up by himself, drinking from a flask of water, his face was drawn and pale, his shoulders hunched in exhaustion.

"Healer!" Mala called out from nearby. "I need a healer! Where's Allira?"

Caleb turned to find two paladins holding Will under each arm, carrying him gently as Mala led the way. Caleb hurried over to them. "I saw you fighting that giant—what happened?"

"We kicked his ass," Will said weakly, wincing with every word. "Now get me some water."

"Hush," Mala said, snapping her fingers for a water flask. She was heavily favoring her right hand. Val tossed his flask over, and she pressed it to Will's lips as the two paladins set him down. "I don't believe the wound is grave," she said, "but he won't be able to continue without aid. Are there any healing salves?"

"We gave the last one to Tamás," Caleb said. "It saved his life, but he's lost the use of his legs. So is Will . . . is he going to be all right?"

"I fear he's cracked half his ribs," Mala said. "The Despiser gave him a friendly hug."

"I'm right here," Will said, inducing another gasp of pain and a sharp look from Mala.

Someone had found Allira. The healer ran over with her hands digging into a pouch hanging from the waist of her brown pantaloons. She eased Will to his back and began dabbing his face with a damp cloth that made Caleb wrinkle his nose at the bitter herbal smell. After a few inhalations, the medicine seemed to sedate Will, allowing Allira to remove his shirt without him screaming in pain. She began gently probing his wounds and rubbing a yellow paste over his torso.

The healer shooed Caleb and Val away when they tried to crowd in. They backed off to let her work. Will tried to get Allira to attend to Mala, claiming her wrist was broken, but the adventuress laughed him off.

Yasmina, Mateo, and the Brewer returned from the front lines, joining the rest of the companions as they gathered to discuss their next move. Caleb gave Yasmina a fierce embrace, relieved beyond words to see her alive and unharmed. She cast a worried look in Will's direction as Lance ran over and pointed at the sky, drawing everyone's attention.

"They're coming in," the former Marine said, in a voice hoarse from shouting commands all morning.

Caleb looked up to see the remaining coatl and their riders swooping towards the grassy field in formation. It appeared they had lost well over half their numbers. Higher in the sky, the Congregation airships had gathered above the riverside cliffs, turning to face the grassy field. Caleb counted fifteen of the enormous dirigibles still in the sky.

"Not a good omen," Rucker muttered. "Why do they return?"

The great serpents landed in the field where Caleb and the others had gathered. Aahpo flew over to meet them as one of the riders yanked off her helm, revealing the battle-scarred face of Izel Halach. The stern commander looked almost as exhausted as Val, but she held her head high as she strode across the field to address Caleb.

"There are too many," she said, "and their defenses are too strong. We cannot protect you any more today. Not until we rest and regain our magic. They know this, too. I suspect they will attack now, while you are unprotected."

"Branyn? Aahpo?" Caleb said, addressing the two young mage commanders. "How do we look?"

"I lost a third of my mages," Branyn said, pushing a lock of brown hair off his sweat-soaked forehead. "And the rest are spent. The shamans have already retreated to the forest. They will not return until the morning."

"Less than a score of mine remain," Aahpo said grimly.

Caleb looked down at his feet. They had won a great victory over the majitsu on the ground, a miraculous victory, only to face a sky full of airships filled with wizards.

"I have more bad news," Izel Halach said. "Our scout has spied a massing of ground troops outside the city. No doubt they will march this way soon, arriving with the dawn."

"How many?" Caleb said in a dull voice.

"Ten thousand troops and a thousand majitsu."

Her comment caused a somber silence to descend, right before Caleb heard a loud whoosh from behind. He turned to see a line of fireballs raining down from the closest airship, which had turned its prow around and was sailing towards the three grounded airships, where the bulk of Caleb's army had gathered.

The Fire Spheres slammed into the open field, blasting soldiers on the outskirts, causing the earth to erupt, and setting the grass ablaze. The screams of the dying filled the air as Aahpo and Branyn led a team of weary mages to douse the flames with water from the river.

Another attack came. Caleb threw open the Coffer and stood before it, willing it to do something. The fireballs slammed into another crowd of people, closer this time, filling the air with the stench of burning flesh. A second airship on the heels of the first sent a fleet of mini tornados spinning into the midst of Caleb's army. The Battle Mages worked so hard to disperse the twisters that a few of the mages collapsed from the effort.

They're going to end this right now, as soon as enough airships are in range.

"Do something!" Caleb screamed at the Coffer.

Another volley of Fire Spheres tore through his army, and then another. Branyn's exhausted mages worked furiously to quell the mini blazes that resulted. The lead airship was right above their heads. Sensing victory, the Congregation pyromancers on the prow of the ship coordinated their efforts and unleashed a storm of fire that looked like a meteor shower streaking down. Wishing with all his might for the Coffer to protect them, Caleb watched in shock as a flash of golden light erupted above his head, spreading quickly to illuminate a forcefield-like dome that enclosed an area a few hundred feet around him on all sides. Similar to the first time he had used the Coffer, when the Fire Storm collided with the dome of golden light, it bounced back to its sender faster than anyone could react, causing the airship to explode in midair.

"Take cover!" Lance yelled as bits of wood, tilectium, and scorched bodies rained down on them. The mages nearby helped block the falling debris, and everyone who had a shield ducked under it.

The aeromancers on the second airship in line had already sent a wide swath of mini tornados right on the heels of the fire storm. Either too shocked to react or unable to stop the twisters in time, the Coffer's protective dome redirected the Aeromancy spells as well. The Congregation wizards managed to disperse most of them, but two tornadoes tore through the airship, crushing it in midair and sending its occupants fleeing into the skies.

Caleb was stunned, but as the glow of the golden dome faded, he began shouting orders to bring the entire army within the radius of protection, next to the three airships on the ground.

"Mother of Mary," Yasmina said, stepping out from beneath her shield to stare at the wreckage of the downed airships. "Did you do that?"

"The Templar is but the agent of Devla," the Prophet said, gazing at the sky in rapture. "All power and glory flows through the Coffer and into His hands."

"They're pulling back!" Dalen said. "I think they're leaving!"

"Not quite," Val said, after a few moments. With Synne's help, he rose to his feet to watch as the airships spread out in the sky, gathering into a loose circle above around the grassy clearing, surrounding Caleb's army on all sides.

"Sixteen of them," Rucker said, craning his neck as he turned to count the dirigibles. "Chock full of blasted wizards."

All over the clearing, Caleb's army huddled around the grounded airships, staring nervously at the sky. Next to Caleb, Allira and Lance stood side by side, leaning on one another for support. Mala was bending down to stroke Will's hair as he recovered. Dalen and Dida were talking in low tones as they absorbed the shocking turn of events. Rucker, Mateo, and the Brewer all bore dire expressions, though none more so than Val, whose clenched fists and rigid jaw was evidence that the weight of both worlds was on his shoulders. Together, they all beheld the awesome and terrifying sight of the Congregation airships hovering above them.

Caleb understood the message loud and clear. They might have achieved a stalemate for the time being. The strange powers of the Coffer had afforded his army a brief respite, and protection from a direct magical attack. But they still had nowhere to run, no way to combat the massive ground assault that was coming. Their only safe space on Urfe was a tenuous circle of protection that seemed all too pitifully small.

-32-

Azantite scepter in hand, drawing to his full height with his shoulders thrown back, Lord Alistair knew he cut an imposing figure as he drifted atop the silver-blue dais of hardened spirit near the apex of the Sanctum. The arguments and troubled murmurs from the gathered members of the Conclave faded as the Chief Thaumaturge leveled his most commanding stare at them.

He could tell from the body language of the elder mages that his grip on power had shifted ever-so-slightly after the theft of the Coffer and the disastrous battle by the river that morning. This was as it should be. More airships had fallen. Hundreds of mages were dead or grievously wounded, including Braden Shankstone, a member of the Conclave itself. An entire regiment of majitsu defeated, and the most powerful commander to wear the silver belt in a generation, Kjeld Anarsson, had been slain by the rebels.

If anyone in the room was *not* troubled by the day's events, they had no business representing the most powerful collection of mages in the Realm.

Before he spoke, Lord Alistair waited until an uneasy silence encased the room, demanding the complete attention of his audience. "Not long ago, someone asked me how events on the Barrier Coast could possibly affect the Protectorate at large."

His gaze swept the room before locking onto the cold, imperious face of Kalyn Tern. It was she who had posed the question, at another meeting of the Conclave, soon after the sword born of spirit had returned to Urfe. Although the proud aeromancer was his closest ally, he could see that she, too, harbored doubts that needed to be quashed.

"It seems the impossible has come to pass," Kalyn said quietly. Clad in a topaz gown that fell to her diamond-studded sandals, she floated in place in the center of the semicircle of wizards facing the dais. "We are perhaps not as invincible as we thought."

"As I told you then, it is not the rebels themselves who pose a problem, but the ideology they represent. Yes, we have suffered minor losses. Yes, we underestimated the daring of the rebels and the power of the Coffer." Lord Alistair's expression turned scornful. "And yet the battle is already over. They are surrounded in a glade far from the city, with nowhere to turn."

"So we said when we sent out the first fleet of airships," said Professor Azara, to murmured assent from the crowd. "And yet the rebels survive."

"Prisoners locked in the deepest darkest dungeons survive as well. It does not mean they have a chance to take the throne. We do not even need magic to finish this fight. By the morning, our ground forces will overwhelm them with sheer numbers. Now we understand that the Coffer, when open, provides protection in a small radius. Thus, the rebels pose no real threat unless attacked directly with magic. Not only that, we have struck a decisive blow against the Mayan Kingdom, who treacherously sent its Battle Mages to support the uprising."

Lord Alistair could tell by the darkened brows of some of the elder mages that they knew full well the Arch-Governors were simply responding to the threat of Protectorate troops massed along the border. It didn't matter. Victors rewrote history. Once he conquered the Mayan Kingdom, the scribes and bards would tell of how the Arch-Governors had thrown their weight behind the wrong army, and lost the war in the decisive battle beside the Great River.

He continued, "And yet, as I said, the real threat lies in the *idea* fostered by the rebels. That some . . . some *artifact* . . . should somehow be connected to a mythical deity who intervenes in events on Urfe. No one knows the true origin of the Coffer, but all of us gathered here, and all rational individuals, know the truth: that some long-dead human wizard crafted the relic, perhaps to awe the common-born, or force them into submission. There is no divine power. No wrath of Devla. There is only a chest formed from azantite by an elder mage just like us, in a faraway place and time." He felt the familiar rage bubbling inside him caused by events he could not control. "*We* know this, but the common born of New Victoria are not convinced. Already rumors have started, bestowing godlike powers on Caleb Blackwood and the Prophet. Deifying them. Threatening to upend centuries of progress." He slammed the head of the scepter into his palm. "We will not return to the Age of Sorrow and wizard persecution, to the Culling and the inquisitions and the pyres stacked with corpses of the mage-born! Not while I draw breath!"

He could tell his words had hit home. As powerful as they were, the elder mages knew the common born outnumbered them by vast numbers, and that if they were not careful, history might repeat itself.

"What do you plan to do?" Jalen Rainsword said slowly. "We must not make a martyr out of either of these men."

"Precisely," Lord Alistair said, in a dangerously calm voice. "It is for this reason that our forces on the ground, *common born* soldiers led by Yasir Oofar, will place the Prophet and the Blackwood brothers in chains, and slaughter every last one of the rebels. Under the watchful eye of the airships, they will drag their captives and the Coffer back to New Victoria, to be hung in suspension cages at the foot of the Canal Bridge. The people will watch the flesh melt from the bones of these men, and see the crows pluck out their eyes, and the vultures pick clean their bodies. After the sun has bleached their skulls, in a grand ceremony before thousands of witnesses, I will ground what remains of these *human* men to dust."

His voice had risen to a thunderous crescendo during his speech. As he finished, his body drifted higher off the dais as black fire began to spark not just from his fingers, but all over his body, crackling and rippling in a halo around him. The men and women gathered before him—the most powerful mages in the Realm—were shocked at first, worried his rage had caused his magic to spiral out of control and consume him. Yet as he spread his arms and raised them high, exulting in his power, they realized he was still in full control, and drew back in fear before the awesome display.

When Lord Alistair spoke again, flames of Spirit Fire erupted from his mouth, accompanying his words. "If the people need a god to lead them," he roared in a metallic voice infused with spirit, his body a living torch of pure magic, "*Then I will give them one!*"

-33-

Caleb's entire army had gathered in a cluster on and around the three grounded airships. The Congregation fleet hovering in the sky above, wary of the power of the Coffer, did not attack the rest of the day. It was obvious they were waiting for ground reinforcements to arrive the next morning.

As evening approached, Caleb and his advisors debated their options, and did not like any of them. If they tried to cross the river, the aquamancers on the airships would raise the waters and drown them. If they returned to the forest, the pyromancers would smoke them out. A march of any sort would risk dividing the army and losing the protection of the Coffer.

"I hate to say it," Lance said, as he and the Blackwood brothers gathered around a cooking fire, "but our best bet is staying here and hoping for another miracle."

"The Coffer doesn't protect against swords and arrows," Val said. "There's a thousand more majitsu coming, and ten thousand soldiers. We only have a hundred paladin shields. They'll slaughter us if we sit still."

Lance tipped his head and shook it, unable to disagree.

"We need a way to force his hand," Caleb said, staring into the fire. "Draw him out into the open."

No one needed to ask to whom Caleb was referring.

"As much as I want revenge," Val said, "I'm not sure that's the best idea." He gave a little shiver that unnerved Will. "What if Alistair is stronger than the Coffer and can negate its effects, or even destroy it? It's a big risk."

"I don't care about the risks," Caleb said in a stony voice.

Will shifted his stance to relieve the stabbing pain in his side. Though Allira had given him a bag of analgesic leaves to chew that provided some temporary relief, there was only so much you could do for a set of cracked ribs.

Val was staring straight ahead. "I just don't know what to do against power like that. I saw him reach out with his mind through a portal once—he wasn't even present—and destroy an entire fortress of assassins. He can manipulate reality and walk through dimensions. How do you fight that? If we could figure out how to reach some of the less militant wizards in the Conclave, we might be able to negotiate with them. But I doubt that happens with Alistair in the picture."

Lance yawned. "I've got to catch a few zzzs. I don't think I've slept for three days, and it's a bad idea to go into battle with a head full of fuzz." He patted Will gently on the back. "Goodnight, Blackwood. I still can't believe we're all here. If we ever make it home again, we'll be telling this story at the House of Spirits for the rest of our lives."

"That's the Lance I know," Will said. "Surrounded by airships full of wizards, and all he's thinking about is chicken wings and draft Abita."

"You know it, buddy." He ran an admiring hand over Will's biceps and said, "When did you get so ripped, anyway? You're making me look bad. And that long hair and stubble? No wonder Bad and Beautiful came around," he said, flicking his eyes to where Mala and Allira were sitting off to the side, sharing an herbal concoction. "I always knew you had it in you."

Will winced in pain as he chuckled, knowing his oldest friend was just trying to help them all relax. "Go to sleep, Lance."

As the moon rose high in the sky, Will and Mala placed their bedrolls side by side. She lay on her back, gazing at the stars and the ominous ring of airships surrounding the grassy plain by the river. She had been quiet all evening, and he guessed she was processing the death of Kjeld. How do you act after your lifelong quest is fulfilled? What thoughts go through your head?

He murmured, "'I have spent all these years preparing to find the six-fingered man and kill him in a duel.'"

Mala shifted her violet eyes to meet his. "What?"

He grinned as he eased to his feet. "Nothing. I'll be back in a minute."

"Where are you going?"

"To say goodnight to my brothers. Why don't you get some rest? The perimeter wards are set, and the Protectorate forces won't arrive before the morning."

"I don't think I'll be resting much tonight, Will the Builder. Since it might be the last night sky we ever see."

In response, he reached down to run a hand through her lustrous dark hair. She reached out to pull him closer, and after they kissed, they stared into each other's eyes for a long moment, letting the silence speak for itself.

Will made a detour to say goodnight to Yasmina and Dalen and Mateo, who had all bedded down outside the tent where Tamás was lying. He was still unconscious, and his breathing was shallow. Will worried he wouldn't make it.

After leaving his friends and cousin, Will found Val near the dying embers of a fire, studying a leather-bound journal as Will approached. The Brewer and Dida were snoring lightly on one side of Val, and Synne was sitting cross-legged on her bedroll on the other, looking as if sleep was the furthest thing from her mind.

"Turning in?" Val asked.

"I thought I'd say goodnight first. Want to see if Caleb's awake?"

"Sure."

Val closed the journal, placed it in his bedroll, and stood. Synne rose to join them but Val asked her to stay behind.

Near the center of the quiet camp, Will and Val found their middle brother in his tent, laying shirtless on his back on a cot. Will noticed a silver wedding ring attached to the leather thong necklace hanging from Caleb's neck.

"What is this," Caleb said without bothering to sit up, "an intervention?"

Will folded his arms. "Yes, if I thought it would help."

"It won't."

"Then it's just a brotherly goodnight." Will sat cross-legged on a rug beside the bed. "How long has it been since the three of us were alone together?"

"Far too long," Val said quietly.

Caleb kept staring at the canvas roof in silence. The emptiness in his brother's eyes hurt Will far worse than the pain in his side, or any physical wound, ever could.

An awkward silence descended. The longer it lasted, the more distressed Will grew. These were his brothers, together again at last! For so long he had dreamed of this moment, but so much had happened since they had parted, so many incredible and emotional journeys, that he felt as if he were among strangers.

He couldn't bear it.

"You know what I miss about home?" he said, remembering a conversation he and Caleb had once had on the way to Leonidus's Keep, long before conflicted loyalties and suicidal vows of revenge, before slaughtered family members and broken hearts and impossible choices. He eased to his back and laced his fingers behind his head. "Reese's Piece's and Cool Ranch Doritos."

For a moment neither of his brothers spoke. Val looked down at Will as if he could not believe he had made such a mundane observation at that moment, and Caleb kept staring at the top of the tent.

"Ice-cold AC on a hot summer day," Will continued. "Kicking back at the levee to watch the river, a double matinee with no one else inside the theater, po' boys loaded with fried shrimp. Browsing a bookstore. Getting an Amazon package."

"A night where I pay for my beer with my video poker winnings," Caleb said softly, without shifting his position. "Deuces Wild all the way, baby."

"My two brothers," Val said, shaking his head. "The last two guardians of high culture."

Will cocked his head. "So what do you miss, Sir Val? High tea with the Queen? A long day at the spa covered in Icelandic mud?"

"I miss a Pittsburgh Rare ribeye and a three-hundred-dollar cabernet at New York's finest steakhouse, all on the firm's tab. I miss sushi and a cold IPA after a hard workout at the gym. A night on Broadway. Smoky jazz clubs in Harlem. Gazing at the lights of Manhattan from a nightclub on top of the world."

"Whatever," Will said. "Give me HBO and Premier League on Saturday mornings."

"A show at Tipitina's," Caleb added. "The balcony at Tropical Isle. Tuesday night Rebirth at the Maple Leaf."

"Word," Will said, nodding in agreement. "What I wouldn't give for that."

"Mardi Gras," Val said, and when Will looked over, he saw a big fat grin spreading across his oldest brother's face. "God how I miss the parades, the parties, the food, the feeling the whole city is just alive."

"Mardi Gras," Will said somberly, and with the utmost respect.

"Mardi Gras," Caleb intoned.

"Remember the last time we were—Will, behind you!"

As Val shouted, his finger flew into the air, pointing at Will's chest. Confused, since there was barely any space between where Will was laying and the side of the tent, he reacted to the alarm in Val's voice and rolled to the side as fast as he could. Almost swooning from the pain in his side, he jumped to his feet, drew his sword in one smooth motion, and whirled to see a cloaked form drifting towards him with its arms extended. Streaks of silver light pulsated across a face that resembled a congealed shadow in the faint outline of a human being.

"What in God's name," Val said, "is *that*?"

Will didn't know what it was, but he had seen one before, in Freetown, just before the first attack by the airships. The shadow being he had faced that day had almost killed him, and he knew its touch meant death.

Caleb leaped out of bed, reaching for his mace, as a weak spark of Spirit Fire flickered on Val's fingers. He still had not recovered his magic. Neither brother would reach Will in time, and even if they did, he doubted they could help. He drew Zariduke, remembering how the sword had dispatched the last shadow being, and held it up before him. This caused the thing to stop advancing, hovering in place as it fixated on the sword.

Ready to lunge with Zariduke, Will was shocked when a second familiar figure, this one dressed in ragged pants and a hooded purple cloak, appeared out of nowhere between Will and the shadow being. As before, when Will had met the strange figure in the Valley of the Cursed, the velvet cloak was frayed and moth-eaten, like a prop in a long-abandoned theatre troupe. Every inch of the figure's exposed skin—fingers, hands, and face—was swathed in white bandages. As soon as he appeared, he began calmly shuffling a deck of playing cards, and after a moment, he held one of the cards out to the shadow being.

"What'll it be, I see," the figure in the purple cloak said. "I smell one unknown to me. Or is it whee, me, the same thing I be?"

"Uh, Dealer?" Will said, remembering what the figure had called himself.

"One and the same, same and the one, oh my my we are all undone."

The shadow being had stopped advancing but did not reach for the playing card. Poised to act, Will held his sword in front of him as he risked a glance at his brothers. They both looked as confused as he as.

"Where's the Coffer?" Val said in a low voice to Caleb.

"In the tent right beside me, guarded by the Prophet and a dozen mages."

"Can you use it from in here?"

"No dice."

"Not the one for you?" the Dealer muttered, as he retracted the card. "Maybe we should be in a zoo." He reshuffled the deck and held out another. Will noticed it was the King of Hearts. "Go on, don't run, try this one on for fun."

Tired of the game, the shadow being flowed forward and into the Dealer, causing Will to cringe and grip the sword tighter, expecting the Dealer to dissolve. Instead nothing happened when they made contact, causing the shadow being to rear back as if shocked. Slowly, it reached towards the Dealer's face in a probing manner, and thrust a shadow hand deep into the hood. Will remembered, in the Valley of the Cursed, seeing a bandage on one of the Dealer's fingers start to unravel. Beneath the white cloth, he had glimpsed the flesh of a normal human being—except the finger kept disappearing and reappearing, as if it were blinking in and out of existence.

"I do say," the Dealer said, as the shadow being stuck its other hand inside the hood, as if gripping the Dealer by the face, "this is quite a fine day. What a jolly new thing, such rare tidings you bring! If I were to guess, 'tis a mighty fine mess, no more, no less. Fancy a trip bip while joined at the hip? To find father and mother, or even another, what say you, my brother?"

With that, the Dealer threw the entire deck into the air and stepped forward, right into the center of the shadow being. Will's jaw fell as the two figures flowed into each other, as if forming a new entity. The falling cards vanished whenever they touched the strange pair, and when the last card fell, the conjoined forms of the Dealer and the shadow being vanished with it.

Stunned, the three brothers stood close together, waiting for them to reappear. When it seemed they were truly gone, Val said, "What in the world just happened?"

"I think he saved our lives," Will said slowly, taking it all in. "And found someone else like him. I don't know *what* they are, or where they came from, but I think we know who sent them, or at least the shadow being."

"Alistair," Caleb said grimly.

Val shuddered. "It has to be. It's hard to explain, but I could sense, when I looked at both of them . . . I could sense they were made of spirit. Like they were magic in semi-human form."

"It was looking at the sword the entire time," Will said. "Dollars to donuts Alistair ordered the thing to go after it." As the brothers contemplated the appearance of the two beings, an idea popped into Will's head. "It's right here in front of us," he muttered. "He tried to come to us, so why not go to him?"

"What are you talking about?" Val said.

As Will sheathed his sword, he eyed his brothers in turn. "We need to cut off the head of the snake? But we can't get past the body, which in this case is an overwhelming number of Protectorate ground troops and majitsu headed our way."

"That about sums it up," Val said.

Caleb put a bare foot on the cot and leaned an elbow on his knee. "What are you thinking?"

Will broke into a grim smile. "We've got three airships, right here under our noses. I say we use them."

-34-

At dawn, Lord Alistair woke to the chirping of birds outside the second-floor window of his St. Charles mansion. Beside him, Melina rolled over as he stirred. Her bare arm fell across his chest. Normally the slightest touch of her smooth skin aroused him, but this morning his mind was far too occupied for affairs of the flesh. He rose from the bed, slid on his Bavarian wool trousers, and began to fasten the embroidered cuffs of his dress shirt.

"Is it time already, my love?" Melina said, throwing off the covers and languidly stretching her curvaceous figure.

"It is indeed." He pulled on his boots, donned a jeweled ring on each finger, and floated his azantite scepter off a marble table and into his hands. "I'll be watching events unfold from a scrying portal in the Sanctum linked to one of the airships. Once the Coffer is in our hands, I'll send for you."

Before he left, she rose out of bed to embrace him. "Queen's luck, milord."

As he looked into her mesmerizing lavender eyes, the corners of his mouth curled upwards. "We won't need luck today, my dearest."

His retinue of majitsu awaited outside to accompany him to the Sanctum, but on the way out, he was surprised to find Adaira in the kitchen, holding a steaming cup of coffee. Her eyes looked bleary and puffy, as if she had been crying all night.

"Adaira! Why are you up so early?" His eyes lowered to the tiny swell of her stomach, eliciting a grandfatherly smile. "Did the child keep you awake?"

She stared at him for a long moment. "The child? The *child*? How could you say such a thing?"

He blinked in confusion as his daughter seethed.

"Lest you have somehow forgotten," she said, her voice as cold as a glacier, "today is the day that my fiancé will likely die or be imprisoned. His name is Valjean Blackwood, if you'll remember? The father of my unborn child, and your grandchild? Your former protégé? The man whom I love?"

Lord Alistair stiffened. "He stole the Coffer and betrayed the Realm, Adaira. He's a traitor."

"And I'm your daughter!"

His face softened, and he reached for her. She smacked his hand away.

"Give him amnesty," she said. "I know you have the power. I read the laws last night."

He touched a hand to his temple. "Give him amnesty—do you have any idea of what you speak? He was using me all along, to gain my confidence and help the rebels from the inside." His eyes flicked to her stomach. "He used all of us, Adaira."

"How *dare* you! Stop looking at my child as if it's a bastard already! I loved him, father! I love him still. Whatever he did, whatever his reasons . . . I know that he loves me back."

"That man loves no one but himself. That is who he is."

"No, that's who *you* are! You've always been in love with your reputation and power. The high and mighty Chief Thaumaturge, the greatest spirit mage since the time of Myrddin," she said bitterly, with a mock flourish. "All hail Lord Alistair, ruler of the Realm and beloved of no one but himself. Do you think that harpy upstairs cares about you? Her chicanery can be seen from a mile away!"

"You go too far, child! I loved your mother as I've loved no other—except for you, Adaira. Everything I do is for you."

"If you loved me," she said in a low and venomous voice, "you would spare the father of my child. Banish him. Fasten him with magecuffs and send him off in a boat to the forgotten isles of the Western Ocean. Anywhere. Anything. Because I tell you, father, if you destroy this man today, you destroy your only daughter as well."

"Don't talk to your father like that," Melina snapped, as she floated down the stairs and into view wearing a silk bathrobe. "He deserves better."

"Silence!" Lord Alistair roared. "This doesn't concern you!" He raised a palm and sent Melina flying backwards into a wall so hard that she slumped to the floor.

Adaira was shocked by the brutal display, causing Alistair to feel ashamed. He had never lost control like that in front of his daughter.

"And thus he treats the ones he loves," Adaira said softly.

Despite his guilt, he took a step towards her, eyes flashing with fury, his terrible temper uncoiling like a dragon inside him.

"Go on," she said, placing her hands on her stomach as tears fell down her cheeks. "Strike us both down. We'll join Valjean on the pyre."

Lord Alistair stood in place and quivered, feeling the rage creep up his limbs and into his flushed cheeks. Shuddering to control his emotions, he spun on a heel and strode towards the front door. "I have to leave. We will talk tonight, after the speech I'm scheduled to give at Victoria Square."

"Go on then, father. Do what you must to ensure your legend lives forever."

So hurt and angry he could barely think, Lord Alistair did not even greet his majitsu as he took flight, soaring above the mansions and manicured estates of the Garden District.

That ungrateful child! Can she not see how much I love her, how everything I do is for her and the memory of her mother?

Perhaps not everything, he could admit to himself, even through his self-righteous haze of anger. He knew his ambition knew no bounds, and he was comfortable with that—as long as he had the love of his daughter. To lose that was unbearable. He resolved then and there not to gibbet Val in the suspension cage with his brothers and the Prophet, but to ensure the eldest Blackwood died in an 'accident' during the coming battle. Given enough time, Adaira's broken heart would mend, and she would understand his reasons one day. He vowed to parade the finest suitors in the Realm before her, to work tirelessly to secure her happiness as soon as this unpleasant business was finished. One day she would forget she had ever known a traitor named Valjean Blackwood.

Feeling very alone and sorry he had treated Melina so harshly, he soared into the Wizard District, forcing himself to focus on the task at hand. Soon he would meet Kalyn Tern in the scrying room to watch the Protectorate crush the last of the rebels and seize the Coffer. All of a sudden, he remembered the Spirit Liege. The morning's drama had caused him to forget he had sent his creation after the sword last evening, in a bid to secure the powerful weapon for himself. Why had it not returned? He had known it was a risky move, since the youngest Blackwood had used the sword to slay the previous Spirit Liege.

Had the same thing happened this time? Or had an opportunity to seize the sword not yet presented?

Bah. No matter. Once the Coffer is secure, I will take the sword as a spoil of war.

Just before he crossed the moat to enter the Sanctum, Baltyr burst out of the entranceway, and met him in midair. "Milord—come quick!"

Lord Alistair frowned at the flustered demeanor of the battle-hardened aeromancer. "I'm well on my way. What is it?"

"It's the rebels. They have . . . they've managed to fly the airships."

Lord Alistair waved a hand as he flew, signaling for the aeromancer to follow him into the Sanctum as his retinue of majitsu fell away. "I don't understand. What are you saying?"

"The three ships on the ground they were gathered around—they've boarded them and managed to take flight, with the help of the Mayan wizards. We're unsure how to proceed. Using magic near the Coffer is risky, and the ground troops cannot reach them in the sky."

Lord Alistair sneered. "I assume they're trying to flee across the Great River?"

"No, milord," Baltyr said as they entered the scrying room, where Kalyn Tern was standing in front of a large, oval, mirrorlike object mounted on a wooden stand. Reflected in the three-dimensional surface was a blue sky dotted with airships.

"I assume you've heard?" Kalyn said. Ten other high-ranking members of the Conclave, including Professor Azara, had also come to observe the day's events. Instead of flying into a room full of confident wizards, as Lord Alistair had expected, the gathered mages looked troubled and uneasy.

"I was about to tell him," Baltyr said, turning back to face Lord Alistair. "The rebels aren't trying to flee. They're coming right for the city."

Rage blossomed anew on Lord Alistair's face as he digested the words. He snarled and approached the scrying mirror. "Where is the commander of this ship?"

"He stepped away for a moment," Kalyn said. "To confer with the other wizards on board."

"When he returns, tell him to wait until I arrive to engage. Not a single more life of an Oath-fearing citizen shall be lost to this rabble, be it mage or common born."

"Wait until you arrive? What do you have in mind?"

"It is time to put an end to this foolishness," he said, signaling for Kalyn to join him as he flew towards the entrance. "We will see how this Coffer and the infidels who wield it fare against a mage with true power."

-35-

The wind ruffled Will's hair as he stood with his brothers at the prow of the airship, whisking through the sky above the wetlands outside New Victoria. As the name of the vessel implied, the experience was akin to skimming across the surface of a vast blue lake on a sailboat—except there was nothing beneath them except open sky for a thousand feet.

Up ahead, in the distance, the colored spires of the Wizard District thrust up from the city like a pageant of minarets for the gods. To Will's left stretched the watery expanse he knew as Lake Pontchartrain back home. On the other side, the Great River cut a serpentine course through the forest.

And, trailing less than a quarter mile behind them, flying in battle spread formation behind the three stolen dirigibles, was the mighty fleet of airships manned by Congregation wizards.

It had been dicey when Will and the others took to the sky at dawn light. After the Chickasaw and every member of Caleb's army crowded on board the three airships—no one wanted to be left behind, defenseless, to face the wrath of the Congregation—every single mage worked to lift the behemoth vessels off the ground and pump air into the sails. The entire first hour, Will and his brothers clutched the railing with white-knuckled grips as the airships gradually rose and fell, dipped and tilted, lurched and spun. Finally they gained enough height, and, under the direction of a trio of Roma aeromancers, the army harnessed the combined might of the shamans, Battle Mages, and other wizards to keep the airships afloat and heading in the direction of New Victoria. They also had to keep the ships as close together as possible, within the protective shield of the Coffer. No one knew exactly how far that shield would extend, but so far they had not had occasion to test it. The Congregation mages, wary of a repeat of the day before, had yet to engage the airships, preferring to shadow them as they drew nearer and nearer to the capital city of the Protectorate.

Caleb stared grimly at the approaching skyline. "I really, really want to see the look on Alistair's face when we plow an airship through his precious stronghold."

"They'll never let us get that close," Val murmured. "They'll try something first."

The air that high was chilly, and Caleb placed a gloved hand on the railing. "I sincerely hope so."

Will was not afraid of heights, but the journey through the sky trailed by wizards had left his nerves more jumpy than a bundle of live wires. The airship was stable now, but he knew that if a mage attack pierced the defenses of the Coffer, and managed to destroy or even damage the great ship, all of those not endowed with magical ability would plummet to their deaths.

He glanced over his shoulder. Their closest friends and companions had joined them on the oak-planked prow. The Brewer with his silver-stringed lyre, Yasmina peering into the distance with her harpy eagle perched on the tilectium railing, Allira and Lance shielding their faces from the sun, Mateo and Dalen conversing with Rucker and Dida near the bottom of the billowing headsail. Since the beginning of the flight, Mala had stayed near Will, scourge in one hand, her broken wrist bandaged, balanced perfectly on her feet no matter the motion of the ship. Synne stayed close to Val at all times, her eyes scanning the sky. And near the center of the prow, standing protectively beside the open Coffer of Devla, was the Prophet. Though trying to maintain a serene expression, even the calm and composed mystic could not fail to disguise his wide-eyed awe at the daring nature of their aerial voyage.

Will glanced at the companion airships flying on either side. Chooshe and Lisha stood at the helm of one, and a handful of Tamás's closest lieutenants, commanded the other. All three ships were filled with a mixture of Chickasaw warriors, Roma clansmen, Devlan, and other members of Caleb's army. The mages and paladins, whose rune-covered shields still glowed with the power of the Coffer, were spread out among the vessels.

They had just passed above the main body of Protectorate ground forces sent to annihilate them. Massed for miles along a wide Byway, Will shuddered at how massive a force it was. A spyglass had revealed entire regiments of majit-su, hyena wolves, armored cavalry, and battalion after battalion of foot soldiers.

Will had grimaced in satisfaction as the Protectorate forces were forced to watch, helpless and no doubt enraged, as the rebels soared past overhead.

The gleaming spires drew ever closer. Will estimated they were less than a mile from the outskirts of the city. Just as he wondered how close the Congregation would let them get before responding, the sky a hundred yards ahead of them pulsed as if hit by a shockwave, followed by a sonic boom so loud it made Will's ears ring. For a moment he saw a yawning oval void in the sky, as black as deepest space. When the void disappeared, an airship remained, appearing out of nowhere.

The new airship hovered in place, level with the ship carrying the brothers. It was pointed right at them. Wizards filled the prow of the ship and lined the railings along the sides.

"By the Queen," Mala breathed. "They've brought it through a portal."

"That has to be Alistair's doing," Val said grimly. "No one else has that kind of power."

"Stop!" Caleb said, raising his mace in the air. "Stop the ships!"

The aeromancers on all three vessels responded as fast as they could. At first Will worried they might crash—and wondered if the Congregation would open another portal to escape—but the great dirigibles finally slowed and came to rest in the sky, close enough to the lone Congregation vessel they could see the faces of the wizards gathered at the front of the ship. This included the handsome, broad-shouldered figure of Lord Alistair standing on the prow, holding an azantite scepter in his left hand, clad in a silver cloak that snapped in the wind.

Val scanned the faces of the gathered wizards. "Cyrus is with him. There's Kalyn Tern, Professor Azara, Jalen Rainsword . . ." He swallowed as he turned to his brothers. "Half the Conclave is on board. The power . . ."

"They don't look very interested in negotiating," Will said, noticing the weapons and other talismans bearing wizard stones. A heavy contingent of majitsu was interspersed among the mages.

Mala laid a hand on Will's shoulder. "Will you not reconsider dropping back? You should not risk fighting with a wound like yours."

Will's waist was wrapped in a heavy layer of bandages to protect his damaged ribs. Allira had given him more of the foul-smelling brown paste and an even nastier herbal concoction to help numb the pain, but he knew fighting with his injury was risky. He could die if he received a blow that caused one of his broken ribs to pierce an organ.

Then again, confronting a ship full of angry Congregation wizards was about the riskiest behavior one could engage in, broken ribs or not.

"Thanks for the concern," he said, "but I'm not about to sit this one out."

"Have we not discussed the fate of heroes, Will the Builder?" There was a level of concern in her voice he had never heard before, and it both touched him and brought a chill of fear sweeping down his spine at the realization of who and what they were facing.

"Sometimes, Mala," he said, squeezing her hand and then removing it from his shoulder, "you just have to stand next to your brothers."

She gripped the hilt of her cat o' nine tails. "Then I will stand with you, foolish boy."

Caleb lifted the leather thong necklace from under his shirt. He held it reverently for a moment and, before he dropped it, kissed the wedding ring attached to the bottom. Dressed in his black cloak with silver stitching, holding the diamond-headed mace firmly in hand, Caleb drew to his full height and shouted across the empty air dividing the two airships. "Alistair! You've persecuted these good people for long enough. Tried to control their lives, told them what to believe and how to live. You've sent Death Squads to the Ninth to destroy their clans and settlements. You've lied, stolen, and pillaged. And I have not forgotten, nor will I ever forget as long as I draw breath, that you gave the order to kill my wife and son!"

Will watched in alarm as spittle flew out of Caleb's mouth, his voice so strangled with fury it became almost incoherent. "It ends now, do you hear me? You do not deserve to rule, you do not deserve to live!"

The ferocity of Caleb's speech seemed to take aback the occupants of both ships. For a moment no one spoke. Standing at the tip of their respective prows, the two cloaked figures faced off, the elder spirit mage staring down the fine-boned young man from another world.

Will tensed as Lord Alistair slowly, methodically, raised a fist in the air and held it. In response, the mages gathered behind him and along the sides of the ship summoned attack spells endemic to their disciplines. The pyromancers called forth spheres of golden fire; aeromancers formed tornados shaped like javelins between their palms; geomancers raised spinning metal orbs as large as cannonballs; electromancers extracted crackling electricity from a strange copper box in the center of the ship.

It will be suicide to attack if the Coffer deflects that much magic back at them. Or will they try to overwhelm it?

Despite the open Coffer glowing softly behind him in a spectrum of color that seemed to constantly shift, reminding him of the wildly diverse hues in the Place Between Worlds, the sight of an airship full of Congregation mages with spells ready to unleash caused a line of sweat to trickle down Will's neck.

"Move back," Val said, pulling Will behind him. Caleb resisted until he saw what Val was doing: floating the Coffer to the very front of the ship, the last thing standing between them and the enemy airship. Neither Will nor Caleb had to consult Val to know the Coffer was their only chance of surviving that onslaught of magic.

Will thought he saw Lord Alistair sneer as he watched Val set the Coffer down, though from that distance it was hard to be sure. The brothers gathered behind the artifact, on either side of Caleb. The Coffer did not seem that bright when Will wasn't looking straight at it, but when he tried to glance into the depths of the azantite chest, a flare of intense light seared his vision and caused him to turn away.

Alistair's jeweled rings glittered in the sunlight as he kept his hand raised. On a signal from Kalyn Tern, once every single mage aboard the ship had a spell ready to cast—Will noticed a spark of Spirit Fire from a raven-haired woman—Alistair opened his fist.

The floodgates of magic opened.

As one, the Congregation mages sent their enchanted missiles rushing towards the airship, right where Will and his brothers stood behind the Coffer. A hurricane of Fire Spheres, Lightning Bolts, mini Tornadoes, Iron Orbs, and other assault spells bore down on them as if the primal powers of the multiverse had been released. Will could hear the roar of the twisters and the crackle of electricity, feel the heat from the Fire Spheres, see the deadly whirring of the geomancer orbs, and smell the burning chemical odor of the corralled forces of nature rushing through the atmosphere. It took all the courage he had to stand and face the attack instead of turning to dive onto the wooden deck.

The Blackwood brothers gripped each other by the arms, unflinching, standing together as one. Will had never felt so proud and terrified at the same time. Live or die, he would stand with his brothers to the end.

Just before the heat and wind overwhelmed them, and the Congregation spells annihilated the airship, the sky in front of the Coffer pulsed, similar to when the portal had opened, and returned the onslaught of magic back on the casters. The spells boomeranged even faster than they had arrived, giving the mages aboard the Congregation airship no time to defend themselves.

Or so Will thought, until Lord Alistair roared and thrust his palms forward, creating a vortex of seething black energy that appeared between the two ships, just in time to act as a forcefield against the whiplash of returning magic. The magical barrier reminded Will of the spirit shield Val had created to fight Braden, except Lord Alistair's vortex was on a far greater scale, a spinning maelstrom that instantly devoured all the other spells.

As the brothers watched in stunned disbelief, Lord Alistair rose above the airship, his feet planted on a blue-white circular dais. He left the vortex of black energy in place to protect the Congregation airship, and formed a whirling tower made of Spirit Fire that grew as tall as the storm titan guarding Inverlock Keep. Silver streaks pulsed throughout the tower as it gradually assumed a shape akin to a djinn summoned from a bottle.

"A Spirit Fiend," Val whispered. "I've only seen them in books."

"Can you stop it?" Caleb asked.

"I couldn't even begin."

Two red eyes focused on the brothers as Lord Alistair issued a command. Will raised his sword as the thing surged forth, reasoning he had a chance against anything formed of magic. Before he had a chance to strike, a cone of blue-white light erupted from the Coffer and enveloped the Spirit Fiend. At first, the Coffer's light only slowed the advance of the creature, but the closer it drew, the more Will could see that the blue-white light was slowly tearing it apart, causing the dark magic that comprised the Spirit Fiend to disintegrate until, by the time Lord Alistair's creation reached the airship, it was nothing but an outline of charcoal-colored ash that scattered to the wind.

With a cry of rage, Alistair lowered his hands, causing Will's stomach to surge as their entire airship dropped a foot in the sky. It dropped again, and again, and everyone except Mala lost their footing and tumbled to the deck.

"What's going on?" Caleb shouted, as Will picked himself up on shaky legs.

"He's toying with gravity," Val said.

Will was shocked. "He knows what gravity is? And can manipulate it?"

"Apparently so."

The Coffer flashed every time the ship dropped, which Will took to mean it was countering the spell in some way. The sustained effort seemed to tax Lord Alistair, and he cut off the attempts with a snarl. The rebel airship stabilized and stopped lurching towards the ground.

For a long moment, the scene was eerily quiet as Lord Alistair hovered in place, staring down at the Coffer as if debating his next course of action. Will wished he had a way to attack him directly, and debated asking Val to fly him over, but he knew Alistair would just evade him and, as soon as they left the protection of the Coffer, incinerate them with Spirit Fire. Maybe his sword could stop it, maybe not.

"Your reign is over!" Caleb screamed into the wind. "The Coffer is more powerful than you are. *We* are more powerful!"

His words enraged the elder spirit mage. With another roar, Alistair left his scepter hanging in midair and raised his arms to take control of the vortex of spirit, aiming its gaping maw right at the Coffer. He thrust his hands forward, sending the circle of black energy racing towards the brothers until the Coffer pulsed and emitted a flare of light brighter than any Will had seen yet. As with the other spells, Lord Alistair's maelstrom of swarming spirit hit the invisible wall of protection erected by the Coffer and returned towards the sender.

But it did not go far. With Lord Alistair straining in effort, pressing his palms against the air as if holding back an avalanche, he kept the awesome power of the Coffer at bay, and the vortex halted in midair. It reminded Will of the fight between Alexander and the ogre mage long ago, when the two mages had fought atop a tower of earth, each trying to overcome the raw power of the other.

"By the Queen," Mala said from behind Will. "He's fighting it."

Perhaps thinking all the power of the Coffer was focused on the spirit vortex, one of the pyromancers on the Congregation airship sent a Fire Sphere across the divide, rushing towards the side of Caleb's ship. Will gripped Caleb's arm, worried the spell would pierce their hull, but the Coffer protected them again and sent the Fire Sphere careening back into the Congregation airship.

It landed on deck in a fiery explosion, causing chaos on board and killing a handful of mages.

Lord Alistair did not even notice. All his focus was on combating the power of the Coffer. An enterprising Battle Mage used the diversion to shoot a sunbeam at Lord Alistair, but his cloak absorbed it with no visible effect.

"What happened?" Will said. "Why didn't that spell get through?"

"He's using a Spirit Skin," Val said. "The highest level of protection a mage can have. It's a highly dangerous spell that involves weaving pure spirit into the flesh itself, creating a barrier to all weapons and lesser magic. Not only that, but once formed, it takes no concentration to hold since it's part of the mage himself."

"How long does it last?"

"Long enough. This battle is between Alistair and the Coffer, because nothing else is getting through his defenses." He cut a glance at Will. "Except maybe your sword, if we had a way to reach him."

"Or my mace," Caleb said, causing Will to recall the incredible story his brother had told him about his journey to the Tower of Elarion. *A weapon that can break through any substance.*

Will had his doubts about that, and hoped neither of them had to test their weapons against the godlike power of the spirit mage battling the Coffer. Even as the thought entered his mind, he saw the vortex of spirit advance a foot closer to the Coffer, and then another.

"He's winning," Val said, unable to conceal the awe in his voice. "He's actually winning."

Lord Alistair had seemed on the verge of collapse, but the slow advance of the spirit vortex imbued him with newfound strength. With a triumphant cry, he thrust his palms outward again, causing the maelstrom of black energy to pick up speed. As the brothers watched in stunned disbelief, the vortex passed the halfway point, moving ever closer to their airship. Will did not need Val to tell him that should it reach them, its magic would swallow them in an instant.

Will heard a cry of despair from behind him. He looked back to see the Prophet kneeling beside the Coffer. A crack had formed on the azantite and was spreading along the side. "It's tearing apart! Devla, Oh Devla, help us in this time of need!"

Caleb gripped the rail as his face tightened in concentration, as if trying to bolster the power of the Coffer. When his efforts had no visible effect, Will gripped the sleeve of Val's cloak. "We have to do something."

Val sent twin bolts of Spirit Fire arcing above the vortex, aiming straight for Lord Alistair. As before, his cloak absorbed the powerful spell.

"I can't touch him," Val said. "He's got to be weakening, but it's still not enough."

"The crack is spreading!" Mala said. "I fear the Coffer's about to break!"

Will looked from Lord Alistair to the Coffer, desperate for a solution. He debated trying to have Val float the Coffer closer to Lord Alistair, but if the Coffer left the ship, it would allow the rest of the Congregation mages to destroy them.

"Dida!" Val shouted, whipping around to face the companions gathered behind them. The bibliomancer ran towards the brothers, and Val grabbed his arm. "Can you open a portal quickly? Right behind Lord Alistair?"

Dida's eyes widened in alarm. "Yes, I suppose . . . but with a short time window to work, it would only be one way."

His answer seemed to deflate Val, but then he straightened. "Fine. Do it. How long will it take?"

"A one-way portal that short, and within my line of sight? Only moments."

"Make sure it's big enough for two," Caleb said.

"Make that three," Will said.

"No!" Mala cried. "Your side—"

He took her by the shoulders and looked her in the eye. "I'll be back soon. Tell Allira I might need some more of that awful brown paste."

Val gave a grim shake of his head. "You two can't go with me. I can't fly you and fight him at the same time."

"Or yourself, for that matter," Will said. "What exactly are you planning to do?"

"Give me the sword."

"You're no warrior, Val. You probably can't even lift it."

Caleb snarled. "Shut up, both of you. We go together, Val, or I won't authorize the portal."

Startled by Caleb's harsh order, Val opened his mouth to retort, then looked at Caleb with respect and nodded. "Okay. Synne, where are you?"

"Right behind you," she said, stepping into view.

"Remember those Magediscs we took from the grounded airship?"

"Aye."

"Where are they?"

"On this ship, ready for deployment."

"Get three of them, Synne. As fast as you can!"

Instead of replying, the warrior-mage bolted across the prow so fast it made Will dizzy to watch her. She leaped into the air, clearing a group of people with a single leap, and disappeared down a flight of stairs.

"Magediscs?" Caleb said. "What are those?"

"Flying hoverboards is the best way to describe them. They allow you to fly without expending magic, and don't require magic to use. They react to the motion of your body. Just lean forward if you need to move. You'll get the hang of them quickly."

"I hope so," Will muttered. He glanced off the ship and saw the spirit vortex had drawn perilously close, less than twenty feet away. From up close, he could feel the crackle of energy from the swirling darkness and bolts of silver pulsing in the maw of the great disc, energy that would evaporate anything it touched on impact.

The Prophet was shouting to the heavens with his hands upraised. The rest of the companions on the prow had gathered around the Coffer, faces aghast at how far the crack had spread. *How much longer can it hold?*

There was a cry to Will's left. He turned to see Synne racing towards them with three silver discs the size of trash can lids in her arms. She vaulted over another group of people and dropped the Magediscs at the feet of the brothers.

"Good work," Val said, stepping onto one of the discs.

Will stepped onto the second disc, trying not to gasp as a sharp pain stabbed him in the side. Mala saw his jaw clench and looked away, seething with worry and frustration.

"Hurry!" Rucker said. "It's almost here."

"Dida!" Val cried. "Do it now!"

"What's the plan?" Will said as Caleb joined them on the third Magedisc. His feet felt sticky against the surface, as if there was subtle magic keeping him in place.

Val said, "You go first and stab him as hard as you can."

"That's exactly what I had in mind."

The looming spirit vortex was ten feet from the edge of the ship, blocking their view. As Dida opened the portal, a shimmery displacement of air large enough to step through, the vortex touched the outer railing, causing it to crumble into dust. Will glanced at Lord Alistair. Though locked in concentration, still thrusting with his palms, the elder mage knew he was on the verge of victory, and a smile had crept to his lips.

"It's ready," Dida said. "Go!"

Will did as Val said, bending his knees and willing his feet to move forward. The Magedisc moved with him, leaping a foot into the air with Will on board. As Val had said, it was intuitive and easy to control.

His brothers moved forward on either side of him. Will clutched Zariduke in one hand and the shield of Fieran Blackwood in the other as he soared through Dida's portal.

And then, in the blink of an eye, he was hovering a foot behind the unprotected back of Lord Alistair. Without hesitation, as his brothers popped into view beside him, Will plunged the silver hilt of the weapon straight into the left side of Lord Alistair's back, aiming to slip the sword through his heart.

With a snip of blue-white light, Zariduke penetrated the Spirit Skin of the elder mage—but the powerful spell slowed Will's thrust down enough that it did not go all the way through. It stabbed Alistair in the back more as a knife would, four inches deep, enough to seriously wound but not kill him.

With a gasp, Alistair spun and flew away from them. The vortex about to devour the airship disappeared. Val sent Spirit Fire arcing into the elder mage, but he must have erected more defenses, because the black energy fizzled when it reached his cloak. Still, Alistair's face was drawn and pale, his hands shaking from the prolonged effort of combating the Coffer. He sent two bolts of Spirit Fire racing back at Val, but Will swiped them away with Zariduke.

"You think to defeat me, even weakened as I am?" Alistair said. "*You*? Do you not understand the places I can go, the worlds I have traveled?" He threw back his head and laughed. "Watch now, mortals, as a god walks among you."

With a wave of his hand, a portal opened behind him to a place familiar to Will: a kaleidoscope of color preserved in solid state, a dreamscape of bridges and loops and pathways, honeycombs and grottoes and multidimensional spirals.

The Place Between Worlds.

Alistair's portal did not shimmer, as if the spirit mage had summoned a direct conduit to the otherworldly realm. The portal was so large it concealed the Congregation airship from view, and would allow the elder mage to escape to a place the brothers had no hope of following. The brothers raced towards the Chief Thaumaturge on their Magediscs, but with a sneer, knowing they would never reach him in time and he could simply close the portal, Alistair flew backwards, towards the Place Between Worlds looming a few feet behind him.

Right before he reached it, the entrance to the portal began to glow with a sapphire light. Alistair slammed into the blue light as if hitting a wall. He tried again to pass through but couldn't, stunned and confused by the sudden barrier. Will didn't understand what had happened, but he and his brothers were right on Alistair's heels. Sensing an opening, Will's eyes gleamed with eagerness as he gripped the sword, while out of the corner of his eye, he saw the same sapphire glow emanating from a ring on Val's right hand.

Trapped against the glowing barrier to the Place Between Worlds, a look of sudden desperation whisked across Lord Alistair's visage. As Will surged forward, the elder mage closed his eyes and lifted both his palms—

All of a sudden, Val found himself paralyzed in midair in front of the fabled Place Between Worlds, unable to move or speak. His brothers were in a similar state right beside him. Will was caught lunging towards Lord Alistair, barely a foot away, Zariduke extended for a killing blow. Behind Will, Caleb was clutching his mace, his face twisted in fury.

Try as he might, Val couldn't get the Magedisc to budge, or even move a finger. He could no longer feel the air on his cheek or hear any sounds from the airships behind them. It was as if the entire world had stopped.

Valjean

Unable to move, staring in awe and terror at the otherworldly dimension looming before him, Val recognized the voice in his head. *Alistair*. Val did not know exactly what had happened, except that when the portal opened and he saw the Chief Thaumaturge about to escape, Val remembered the ouroboros ring on his finger, and the words he had read in the old tome on lost artifacts.

The Ring of Planar Orientation . . . bears the true seal of Myrrdin . . . the ability to open and force shut dimensional doorways.

Desperate to stop Lord Alistair from escaping, Val had concentrated as hard as he could on channeling magic through his ring and closing the portal—and it had worked. The wall of sapphire light had appeared at the entrance to the Place Between Worlds, barring the way through.

Since Val couldn't speak, he tried using his mind instead. *Why can't we move?*

Because I have frozen the world around us. Yes, my protégé, over time itself I have dominion.

Since the spell wasn't cast directly at Will, it must have avoided the negating power of the sword, Val reasoned. *Maybe so, but you can't move either, can you? You're weak. I can sense it. You used the last of your magic to do this, and it won't last long. Then we'll avenge our father.*

It doesn't have to be that way. You alone can change your fate. Once I free us, you can use your magic to strike the hand of your brother and divert the sword.

*I could, except I want you dead. *

Do you? I am the father of your fiancé, the grandfather of your unborn child, the ruler of your realm. I can teach you how to walk worlds and travel dimensions. I can give you what no one else can. Power beyond your dreams, the love of your life, a future with your child. Know this as well, Valjean. You are wrong about my power. No matter what happens when this spell wears off, I have enough power left to kill you.

Val felt in his heart that, as weakened as Alistair was, he spoke the truth.

I will spare the life of your brothers. This I swear. I will take the sword and the Coffer, yes, but I will send them to your home world with my last ounce of strength. You will watch as it happens to ensure I speak the truth. You have my word as a father, and on the grave of my beloved.

Did you love her as much as you loved the brother you killed?

There was a moment of silence. *Do not speak of things of which you know nothing!*

Val could feel the spell weakening around him. It was hard to describe, as if the fabric at the edges of his reality was unraveling, coming loose at the seams. Despite how much he hated this man, Val felt conflicted, and tempted by the offer—especially if his brothers could safely go home. Val would never rule the realm at Alistair's side. Not after what he had done to their family.

But Val could marry Adaira and watch his child grow up.

You must decide, Valjean. Our time in stasis is drawing to a close. We are much the same, you and I. We have both committed terrible deeds. It is honorable to make hard choices in life. I told you long ago that you possess this talent as well. The clarity of vision needed to rule. You can stand by my side, Valjean, as we conquer this world and others. Stay with me. Marry Adaira and learn at my side. Prolong your life and live for centuries. Give your child an empire to inherit!

Children don't need empires. That's what you never understood about Adaira.

Then be a better man than I. You've seen for yourself what happens when the common born have power, and ignorance reigns. Help us put an end to this madness once and for all. For your wife and fellow mages, for your unborn child and the good of humanity, stay by my side and embrace your destiny.

My destiny is to leave the world a better place by killing you.

And leave your child without a father?

Better that than a legacy of letting you slaughter all these people.

Fool! the voice in Val's head roared. *I will kill you and your brothers, reopen the portal, and flee anyway.*

If you could do all that, we wouldn't be talking.

Then make this choice and die.

You made it yourself, when you went after our family.

The world restarted as if it had never stopped. Will had control of his muscles again, but as he pressed the attack on Lord Alistair, whose back was trapped against the unmoving face of the portal, he noticed the elder spirit mage had shifted his attention at the last moment. Instead of trying to escape, Alistair raised his hands as Spirit Fire surged at his fingertips—and turned to face Val.

"No!" Will screamed as he thrust with Zariduke. Caleb was right beside him, the diamond-headed mace raised above his head.

Oblivious to the threat, Lord Alistair unleashed the Spirit Fire. Val raised a

Spirit Shield in defense, but the elder mage's magic blasted right through it and consumed Val in an instant.

The sapphire barrier behind Lord Alistair evaporated, leaving him free to escape to the Place Between Worlds. He surged backwards at once—but not in time to avoid the thrust of Zariduke through his heart, or the swing of Caleb's mace that crushed his skull like cracking an egg.

The portal to the Place Between Worlds Disappeared.

Distraught beyond reason, Will flew on the Magedisc to the remains of his brother, a cloud of ash dissipating on the breeze. He saw something bright and crescent-shaped—the azantite tip of their father's staff—begin to fall through the sky. Screaming in rage and despair, Will barely noticed, at the edge of his consciousness, a gray-cloaked mage hovering above the prow of the Congregation airship, lowering his palm to halt the attack.

ONE WEEK LATER

-36-

The funeral took place in the most beautiful plaza in the Wizard District, an azantite tile courtyard surrounded by lush tropical foliage. Will could see the colored spires soaring above the wizard compounds in every direction, and smell the star jasmine, and hear the soothing gurgle of the courtyard fountain, its ruby base shaped by a master artisamancer into a latticework of roses.

He held himself together for the Prophet's short eulogy. Though Val had never professed any religious beliefs, all three brothers had seen enough during their time on Urfe to understand the multiverse was far more complex than they had realized, and that powers were at work beyond human comprehension.

Mala, Lance, Dalen, Yasmina, and Mateo were gathered behind Will. The presence of his closest friends and loved ones gave him comfort. Caleb stood beside his brother, tall and silent, staring fixedly ahead, his emotions locked behind a door Will had not been able to open. After accepting a truce in the sky with Kalyn Tern and Cyrus Ravensill, Caleb had insisted on landing the three stolen airships on a sprawling fairground just across the Canal Bridge, while the two sides worked out the details. The proximity of the Coffer to the city ensured the rebels' demands would be taken seriously.

Tamás, who was still recovering but would be paralyzed from the waist down for life, had appointed Mateo as interim leader of the Revolution and the voice of the Roma clans. The elders had approved the choice, provided that Mateo consulted with the council on his decisions, as was customary. He readily agreed. Together, Mateo and the Prophet had started the process of negotiating with Kalyn Tern, who upon Lord Alistair's death had ascended to Chief Thaumaturge, and Alaina Whitehall, the common-born Governess of the Protectorate. Cyrus had direct access to the Queen and parlayed on her behalf as well.

Although Caleb had no interest in the proceedings, and had barely stepped out of his quarters aboard the airship, Will had attended the diplomatic meetings as an honorary guest—and as the wielder of Zariduke.

It turned out much of the Congregation, as well as the common born populace, did not share Lord Alistair's hatred of non-oath takers. The negotiations were still tense, but in exchange for the rebels' agreement to take the Coffer and return peacefully to the Ninth Protectorate, the ruling powers agreed to end the centuries-old ban on religion, restore a sizeable territory to the Chickasaw and other native peoples, pardon everyone exiled to the Fens for political reasons, and abolish the Oaths. Only the Black Sash remained *persona non grata*, but no member of that organization had been seen in the city for weeks, and it was hoped that none remained.

The concessions were due in part, no doubt, to the rapid expansion of Devla worship that had emerged after the Battle of New Victoria. The word of Alistair's defeat had spread like wildfire, as had the tale of how the power of the Coffer had held the wizards at bay. Though cracked, the Coffer had survived the battle, and none of the Congregation wizards who had spoken out against the truce had the stomach to test the artifact's strength. The runes emblazoned onto the paladin shields had remained in place, still imbued with the power of the Coffer, another sign of the favor of Devla. Remarkably, it also seemed the Prophet and a number of his followers had gained the power to heal minor wounds. It was unclear how this had occurred, the extent of this power, or what it portended for the future. But this miracle, too, had sparked a fervor of belief among the common born, and even some of the wizards. Arcane scholars in the Congregation shouted until their throats were hoarse that the Coffer was simply an artifact of some uber-powerful elder mage lost to the mists of time, as Lord Alistair had claimed. But no one knew for sure, and Will thought no one ever would. He tended to believe that Devla, or God—whatever name one preferred for the mysterious creator of the multiverse—had indeed played a role. But he would save the theological and philosophical questions for another day, when he didn't have to bury his brother.

For now, he was happy that Caleb's army—and every other former oath avoider—could live their lives without fear of persecution for their beliefs or heritage. The Queen had even agreed to give the Roma clans and other freeholders on the Barrier Coast a role in the leadership of the Ninth Protectorate. She announced plans to establish an embassy in Freetown, and ordered the Congregation to help rebuild the city as reparations for Lord Alistair's unjust aggressions.

To ensure promises were kept, Caleb agreed to stay with the Coffer until the rebels' triumphant return to the Barrier Coast. After that, no one, not even Will, knew what he planned to do. Speculation of his next move had inflamed the populace of New Victoria, who were quite smitten with the stoic hero of the revolution. It didn't hurt that said hero was also tall, dark-haired, and incredibly good-looking. A Devla worshipper assigned by the Prophet to watch over Caleb delivered a stack of marriage proposals to his quarters on a daily basis.

Would the middle Blackwood brother return to Freetown and help his people rebuild? Would he marry again and settle down, travel the Realm, reunite with his brother? Would he join the Prophet in reestablishing the temples and stoking the flames of religion that had returned to the Realm?

After the funeral service ended, Will remained standing by the fountain with his eyes closed, unwilling to move on to the final destination of the day, lost in the memory of his brother. He felt as if he had lost one of his legs, and could no longer stand upright without support. As if sensing his imbalance, Mala stayed by his side with an arm looped through his.

When Will opened his eyes, Caleb had retreated to a quiet corner of the courtyard. Arms folded, he was staring into the foliage with his back to the crowd, making it obvious he preferred to be left alone. By the fountain, an impromptu receiving line had formed in front of Will. The Brewer began strumming his silver lyre, a requiem both sad and hopeful. Will took a deep breath, squeezed Mala's hand, and greeted his first visitor.

The sight of his brother's fiancée so resplendent in her turquoise gown, and the swell of her stomach with Val's child, tested every bit of Will's emotional willpower. Adaira did not fare so well, and Will stood awkwardly in place as she broke down.

"Not very becoming of a lady," she said when she composed herself, dabbing her eyes with a silk cloth.

"I think it's the most becoming thing you could do," Will said. "I know you loved him very much."

"Like the sun and the moon," she said softly.

Will reached for the inside pocket of his thin wool coat that Mala had bought him for the service. "I have something for you." When he carefully handed her the crescent moon of azantite that used to top the staff their father had bequeathed Val, tears filled her eyes again. His gaze lowered to her stomach. "I thought it should stay in the family."

Adaira threw decorum aside and threw her arms around Will, causing him to blush. "Thank you," she whispered. "I can think of no greater gift. And I hope the child's uncle is a strong presence in his or her life."

"Oh, he will be. You can count on that."

She kissed him on both cheeks and moved on. Dida took her place, and performed a bow so deep it made him stumble. The bibliomancer from the Kingdom of Great Zimbabwe professed that Val had become not just a fellow mage and friend, but the brother he never had. Will gave him a fierce hug and made him promise to tell him stories about Val's time at the Abbey.

The next person stumped forward with a scowl on his face, and was the only person not garbed in funeral attire. Rucker approached Will wearing the same battle-scarred leather breastplate with a grey sleeve he always wore. "That brother of yers is lucky I didn't take him down a peg or two the first time we met."

"Um, okay," Will said, still uncomfortable in the presence of the grizzled adventurer. Beside him, he thought he caught a hint of a smile from Mala.

"But he had courage to spare, and wasn't lily soft like the rest of his ilk. He was the only one in the pub who had the guts to approach me."

Will allowed a smile to seep through. "That sounds like Val."

Rucker gripped Will's forearm so hard it made him wince. "I'd go into battle with him anytime," he said roughly, then stepped quickly out of line as his voice started to crack.

Next came Gus, who told Will how Val had been so generous to him that Gus would be able to support the Kenefick clan for years to come. "Yer brother might never have showed it in public," Gus said, dabbing at his eyes with a stained white cloth, "but that one had a heart as big as a mule bear."

After Gus, two of Val's professors—Gormloch and Azara—described him as one of the most talented, and certainly the hardest working, students they had ever had. Professor Azara seemed especially saddened by Val's death, and claimed he had saved her life. "*Leh*. He was taken far too young. Who knows what heights he might have achieved?"

The line was long. Aahpo, Lisha, and Chooshe stopped by to pay their respects. Allira gave Will a long hug and laid her head against his chest, as if soothing his wounded heart. A member of the kethropi royal family named Riga, a fish-woman whose strange appearance made Will stutter when he greeted her, had even traveled to New Victoria for the funeral. By the time the last visitor had moved on, Will was overcome with emotion, and happy he had discovered more about his brother's short time on Urfe.

Caleb rejoined Will, and Gus drove them in his carriage at the head of a long procession. They traveled in silence through the wonders of the Wizard District and stopped alongside a building surrounded by columns of red and gold marble. As arranged, the rest of the funeral procession stayed inside their carriages as Will and Caleb entered the Hall of Wizards by themselves. Normally tourists filled the open-air building, but by order of the Congregation, today the brothers walked alone beneath the frescoed ceiling high overhead, past the lifelike statues of important Congregation mages immortalized in stone.

At the rear of the hall, the brothers approached a wall plaque Will had seen once before, soon after they had arrived on Urfe. He remembered how emotional he had once been finding their father's name on the plaque. As he and Caleb knelt beside the new name engraved next to their father's—Valjean Roland Blackwood—Will was overcome with love and grief for his father and his oldest brother, for the memories they had made and all the future ones they had lost. Will reached for Caleb's hand, and when his brother gripped his in return, Will finally let his emotions pour forth.

Late that night, after a feast in Val's honor aboard one of the airships, Will and Caleb returned to the city and climbed to the rooftop of Salomon's Pad. Will stood in silence beside his brother, contemplating the spires in the distance, relieved they were alone at last with their grief. Lance and Mala had both offered to stay the night, but Will rebuffed them both. He needed some time with his brother.

"Lance told me he's staying on Urfe," Will said after a spell. "He's in love with Allira, and they're going to help rebuild Freetown. I think it's good for him. He felt useless back home once his career ended."

Caleb said nothing in reply.

"Yasmina's not going back either," Will continued, "though I think we both knew that. Pretty crazy she's a wilder, huh? She wanted me to tell you she's stopping by tomorrow, before she heads out again."

Though his brother's face tightened at the mention of Yasmina, he still didn't speak.

"Are you ever going to take that cloak off?" Will continued. "It gets pretty hot in the summer around here." He had not seen his brother wear anything else since they had reunited, and even now, the diamond-headed mace was an arm's-length away, resting where Caleb had laid it against the short wall surrounding the roof. "Kinda cool we're going to be uncles. I always wanted to be an uncle. You remember when Uncle Dave let us watch our first real horror movie? Some classic R-rated zombie flick. What was I then, eight? Mom would have *killed* him if she knew."

"Do you think he's found peace?" Caleb said finally, and Will knew he wasn't talking about their Uncle Dave. "Or just . . . gone?"

"I've been thinking about that a lot," Will said quietly. "When I talked to Dad, he mentioned there was something . . . else . . . out there, after we die. He didn't elaborate. So I don't know. I also had the thought, after we found that book in Val's bedroom describing the ring he used to trap Alistair . . . that maybe the ring saved Val's essence somehow. What if he's still alive in some way? You know—" Will waved a hand at the sky "—out there somewhere."

"Our brother had his flaws," Caleb said, "but in the end he gave his life for others. That's what counts, isn't it? Making the right choice, doing the hard thing, even if it's against your nature?"

"Maybe it counts even more. Though I don't know who's keeping score."

"You don't have to be a good person," Caleb said, staring straight ahead. His voice sounded haunted, as if it bore a great weight that could never be lifted. "It just matters what you do."

"An interesting thought," said a new voice, causing Will and Caleb to whip around and reach for their weapons. "Though it brings to mind the philosophical query often voiced in your world concerning auditory repercussions of trees falling in a forest with no one around to hear."

"Salomon," Caleb said with a snarl, taking a step towards the old man with silver eyes who had appeared out of nowhere on the rooftop.

Will let his hands relax but moved next to his brother. "Do you have no shame? Our brother would still be alive if you hadn't intervened!"

"Would he?" Salomon said softly. "Or would you all three have perished at the hand of Zedock long ago?"

Will's retort died on his lips. The old mage had a point.

"It still doesn't give you the right to toy with our lives," Caleb said. "You could have helped us along the way. You could have saved him, you could have saved *them*."

"Perhaps in the moment, perhaps not. And perhaps my intervention would have caused even more suffering, or only delayed the inevitable. You continue to ascribe powers to me which I do not possess. No one understands the true nature of fate and consequence. But I am sorry for your loss," he said gravely. "For all of them."

"Perhaps?" Caleb shouted, taking a step towards Salomon. "*Perhaps?* You could have helped them!"

"Have you not witnessed what has occurred, my boy? It was nothing short of a miracle. A maelstrom of events in which I found even myself, to my surprise, caught up. I admit I thought I had some little control over matters on this plane, but in the end, I, too, was but a puppet. It makes one wonder how much of reality we can actually perceive. To an ant, the anthill is the sum of the universe. What if nature and all she entails—your world and mine, the multiverse, all the strange and wonderful things we all have witnessed—what if *that* is but a small part of the whole, the tip of the iceberg? I'll tell you, my boys, the longer I live, the more I think that is indeed the case."

Will put a hand to his temple. "Are you ever going to tell us *why* you've been following us around?"

Salomon shrugged. "If you wish. Though I have to say, I've learned my own lesson when it comes to that. But there's another reason I came to see you tonight, in addition to offering my condolences."

"We don't need any more of your *help*," Caleb said.

"If that is your desire, I will respect your wishes. But lately I've felt quite guilty about meddling in your lives, as you would call it, and about my role in any grief I've caused. To that end—and again, only if you're keen, and as long as it's within my power to do so—I'd like to fulfill a final request for each of you."

-37-

"Pray tell, Will the Builder, what is this about?" Mala called out as she climbed the ladder to the treetop platform above her bungalow. From there, in case of emergency or a desire for stealth, Will knew they could take to the canopy and emerge on half a dozen streets near her property. "Why did I bring my pouches and weapons?"

A month had passed since Val's funeral. Will had arrived on the wooden platform half an hour ago, and he gave Mala a hand to help her up the final rung. "Like I said, it's a surprise."

She saw the stuffed rucksack at once. "What is that for? Are we going somewhere?"

"We are indeed."

Her dark eyebrows lifted in curiosity.

A dense canopy of live oaks and tropical vegetation surrounded them. It was a beautiful morning, bright and clear and redolent of flowering vines. This high up, the only sounds they could hear were birdsong and the buzz of insects.

"I know you're getting restless in the city," he said, and could tell by a quick shift of her eyes this was true. He shouldered the backpack, and opened his hand to reveal a bluish-white ring in the shape of an ouroboros.

He enjoyed the shock on her face as she stared down at the ring, a look he imagined a wild tigress might produce when asked to step into a cage.

Perhaps one day she'll be ready to wed. I'm in no hurry, and I plan to wait as long as it takes.

"You brother's ring," she said slowly.

"I found it on the ground, near the headpiece to his staff. I don't know exactly what happened when they fought, but I know he used this to keep Alistair from escaping. I know a few other things about it, too."

"Such as?"

He grinned and drew out the surprise. "I know you're not the kind of girl who thinks about settling down, at least not anytime soon. So I thought I'd take you someplace new. Try out a place or two you haven't been before."

"There aren't many places I haven't been."

He winked at her. "We'll see about that."

As always, holding Val's ring induced a sharp pang of longing in Will for his oldest brother. He desperately missed Caleb, too, and hoped he had found some peace on his journey.

"Where did you have in mind?" she asked. "Albion? The Old Country?"

"Someplace a bit further away."

"You win, Will the Builder. My curiosity is peaked."

"Would you say the suspense is unbearable?"

A dangerous glint entered her eye. "I'd say you are close to lying on your back on a treetop platform."

He chuckled and beckoned for her to come closer. When she did, he slipped the ring on his finger, and concentrated in the manner Salomon had taught him. The ring was meant for spirit mages, and Will had no idea how Salomon had managed to grant his wish.

In the center of the platform, a portal opened, and Will caused it to expand until it was large enough to step through. On the other side of the gauzy opening, they could see pathways and grottoes made of melted rainbows, tunnels and bridges and canyons, spirals and honeycombs, a universe of shapes and colors for which Will had no name. And everywhere the semicircular cave mouths that signaled the entrances to new worlds.

More worlds than he could count, and which, as far as he knew, stretched to infinity.

"The Place Between Worlds," Mala breathed. "But how . . ."

"Want to explore a few worlds, milady?"

She threw her arms around his neck and, for the first time since they had met, he could detect no trace of mockery in her laughter as he scooped her up and carried her through the portal.

NEW ORLEANS, EARTH

-38-

The afternoon sun warmed Caleb's face as he walked to work down Magazine Street. He had just returned from Lafayette Cemetery Number One, to lay a bouquet of fresh roses on his parents' graves. Nine months ago, when Salomon had sent him back to Earth, Caleb was devastated to learn his mother had succumbed to a heart attack—until he worked out the time difference between the two worlds, and realized his mother had died on the exact same day Will had opened the Soul Jar, allowing their father's spirit to move on. Maybe it was a coincidence, but Caleb felt sure their father had called to their mother's trapped mind in some way, urging her to let go and join him. How that was possible, he had no idea.

Add it to the list of Impossible Things.

Two blocks later, he approached the bar where he used to work, and which used to be called the House of Spirits. After Caleb had purchased the building with the proceeds from the emerald the size of a robin's egg he had found in his pocket before he transferred worlds, another guilt offering from Salomon, he had changed the name of the bar to *Marguerite's Tavern*.

He had also purchased the oyster shack across the street, named it *Luca's*, and begun the process of turning it into an ice cream parlor.

"Hey boss!" an employee called out as Caleb opened the door and passed through the beaded entryway. Caleb clicked his tongue and threw a salute.

Even though he owned the place, Caleb donned an apron five nights a week to work the evening shift. The routine of slinging drinks to thirsty customers helped him block out the noise and gave purpose to his day.

As usual, the tourists and college girls flirted with him. As usual, he ignored them. A couple of hours into the shift, a customer walked in he thought he recognized from the old days, a retired painter named Red. The nickname stemmed from the reddish-brown goatee streaked with gray, and from the hardline socialist opinions Red flouted to annoy other customers. Caleb hated politics and had always laughed him off.

"Say!" Red said. "I heard you bought the place."

"You heard right. Bud Light and a shot of Jaeger?"

Red blinked. "Color me impressed. By the purchase and your memory."

"If I remember a face, I remember a drink."

"What'd you do, win the lottery? Rob a bank?"

"I found the pot at the end of the rainbow."

Red squinted, wondering if the joke was on him, then grunted and said, "Make it two, why don't you, so we can toast." He gave a conspiratorial wink. "Just like old times."

Caleb poured a single Jaeger and slid it over to join the draft beer in front of Red. "No can do, partner. I gave it up."

"Now why would you want to go and do a terrible thing like that?"

"I made a promise to a girl."

The comment caused a striking blond sitting next to Red to roll her eyes. "I thought you were just playing hard to get," she said to Caleb. "You didn't tell me you gave up the bottle for someone."

Caleb shrugged and reached for a glass to clean.

"Say," Red said, "didn't you used to have a brother, came in here all the time? An electrician or something?"

"A builder."

"He still around? He was good company. Smart kid, too."

"Nah, he moved a while back."

"Oh yeah? Where to?"

"Another world."

Red chuckled. "You mean out of town? I hear you. There's no place like New Orleans."

"No, there's not," Caleb murmured.

A while later, he asked the other bartender, Amy, to watch his customers while he took a break. After purchasing the bar, Caleb had barely touched the place. He had kept the ancient jukebox and the working Atari, the frayed

Mardi Gras posters and the flyers from local concerts plastered on the wall. One of the more recent flyers, a band called *The Brewer and his Magic Flute* that had played last Saturday night and rocked the place, caused him to grin as he thought of his older friend, who Salomon had also agreed to send home.

Caleb stopped by his office to grab a pack of cigarettes. He only allowed himself three a day, one with morning coffee, one on his break, and one after dinner. *A man's got to have a vice or two to keep him sane.*

He took a long moment to stare at the photos of his brothers and Yasmina on the walls of the tiny office. He had installed a large safe, inside of which he kept his diamond-headed mace, his vambraces, and the black cloak he had found in the Coffer. Not once had he opened the safe since installing it, and he didn't plan to.

Not unless someone—or something—came for him.

Caleb grabbed his pack of Camel Blues and a lighter. He pushed through the rear door into the parking lot and stood on the same vine-covered stoop on which he had stood with his brothers when Zedock came to steal the sword. As always, the memories came crashing back as the tip of the cigarette burned down.

The lot was a deserted sliver of blacktop that fed into an alley. When he finished the cigarette, he squeezed the ash out, walked to the Dumpster, and flicked the butt inside. Usually some putrid odor leaked out of the Dumpster, but it must have been recently emptied. The only aroma that night was the sweet smell of decaying vegetation.

Something scrabbled in the banana grove. Probably a rat, though if so, it was a very large one. It could be a stray dog or a cat—or it could be something else.

His instincts still honed from the war, Caleb poised, debating whether to investigate. The scrabbling continued, and it sounded oddly purposeful, almost as if something was trying to communicate with him. After a long moment, he decided to let it go. By the time he returned across the alley to enter the bar, the strange rustling had ceased, and the only sound was the whisper of a breeze ruffling the leaves in the grove.

THE GROVE OF THE ANCIENTS, URFE

EPILOGUE

As day faded to night, Yasmina sat cross-legged on the forest floor, rocking her infant twins to sleep in a hammock made of hemp harvested from the foothills of the Făgras Mountains. She hummed softly the songs her own mother had sung to her as a child, love welling inside her such as she had never dreamed possible.

She had yet to name her children. Having twins had taken her by surprise. She would find the right name for them soon, when the time was right. One of her children, the boy, was dark-haired and fine-boned like his father.

He looks just like Caleb, she had thought the moment she laid eyes on him.

The girl favored Yasmina: the complexion of a light roast coffee bean, wisps of honey-colored hair, and wide searching eyes with the same green hue as the needles of the giant sequoias that formed the sacred grove which surrounded them.

What better place to give birth than a shady bower beneath a canopy so ancient it featured in the creation myths of the tribes who called the forest home? A root system so mammoth and interconnected that Yasmina could feel the geochakric currents thrumming beneath her feet as she walked?

When her duties as a wilder resumed, she would take her children with her on her travels. She smiled at the thought of her children nurtured in the ways of the wilder, at one with the natural world from their very first breaths.

Yasmina heard a whisper of sound behind her, gentle footsteps on the forest floor. She turned to see her doula approaching.

"*Samana*," the young woman said, folding her hands in a prayerlike position as she addressed Yasmina with her tribe's time-honored name for a wilder. "Two people have come to see you. They claim they have traveled very far."

"Who are they?"

"I do not know. They speak your name but their dress is unfamiliar."

Yasmina hesitated, glancing down at her children. "Do you sense any danger?"

"I detect only wisdom, benevolence, and a great urgency. But if I am wrong, your honor guard is alert and ready."

"Thank you," Yasmina said. In addition to the tribal warriors protecting the ring of sequoias, Yasmina's staff was beneath the hammock, within easy reach. She lifted her eyes and saw her harpy eagle in her usual perch, preening her wings as she kept watch over the grove. Now full grown and well-fed, the proud avian stood almost four feet tall and possessed a wingspan over eight feet wide.

I would not want to be the one who threatens my children in her presence.

The doula ushered in two visitors, a man and a woman old enough to be Yasmina's parents. Both had long silver hair swept back with circlets. Yasmina watched curiously as they approached. They wore mud-spattered boots and fine-spun traveling cloaks clasped at the throat, and their exposed skin was a few shades darker than hers. They bore strange runic markings, tattooed with midnight blue dyes, on the backs of their hands and faces.

The visitors craned their necks to peer at the canopy, their eyes roaming the grove with awe and reverence, though Yasmina detected a shadow behind their gazes.

Before the doula retreated, she hung a pair of lanterns on either side of the hammock. When Yasmina stood to greet the visitors, they bowed low before her, causing her great embarrassment. "Please don't," she said. "I'm merely a humble wilder."

The woman smiled as she straightened. "All wilders are due great respect, but it is not before you that we bow. It is before your children."

"What?" Yasmina said, taken aback by their words.

Both of the visitors unfurled their left hands, revealing bluish-white marbles resting in their palms. The man took a knee. "Guided by the stars in the heavens, whose light our people have followed since time immemorial, we have come to present these gifts to those who would stand against the darkness."

"I don't understand. What darkness? Are my children in danger?"

"Soon all of us will be," the woman said. "Perhaps not today, or for the rise of many moons, but in your children's lifetimes the great evil shall come, and the world will not be ready."

"But what does this have to do with *my* children?"

"We only know the stars have foretold their importance," the man said, thrusting his palms forward. "Please, accept our gifts. They will protect your children in a time of need."

Yasmina reached down to put her arms protectively around her babies. "Who are you? Why should I believe you?

"We are travelers from the East who read the stars. A shadow has returned to the heavens, heralding the danger, but another will come first, a ruler from a kingdom who worships the darkness and would see your children destroyed." The man's eyes lowered. "And thus we have come to beseech you: with great haste, you must take your children far away from this place, and hide them as best you can."

Yasmina's throat grew dry, and a chill swept through her. "Hide my children? Who is this ruler?"

"The cloud in the stars has obscured these details. We know only that a powerful leader will appear soon, in advance of the great evil. And they, too, will surely have seen the portent that led us here."

"What do you mean, *soon*? How soon?"

"We do not know. But you should leave this place with all haste."

"Even if I believed you, where would I go? I don't even know who I'm running from!"

The woman's eyes lowered. "Nowhere on Urfe will be safe. It is surely the reason a wilder was chosen as the mother of the star children. You can flee to the remote places, where the land and the animals will shelter you. Perhaps, by then, greater allies will present themselves."

The man pressed the silver bauble into Yasmina's right hand. The woman followed suit. Feeling numb, Yasmina debated jerking her hands away. Except what if these visitors spoke the truth? What if someone was coming to kill her children, and these baubles could help protect them?

Together, gently, the man and the woman closed Yasmina's fingers against her palm.

"We are sorry to bring such ill tidings," the woman said. "One day the future of Urfe will depend on your actions."

Reeling, unsure what to believe or what to think, Yasmina pleaded with the visitors to stay the night. They agreed to talk again in the morning, before they returned to their people. Yasmina could tell they were exhausted and asked the doula to take them to the village for nourishment and rest.

After they left, Yasmina stayed awake deep into the night, holding the strange silver baubles, rocking her children as she debated what to do. *My poor babies. My innocent little babies!*

In the morning she would send messengers to the cities to try to verify these claims. Surely someone, somewhere, knew something about these strange travelers and their hideous predictions.

As she wrung her hands, unable to sleep, a phrase the woman had uttered kept repeating in Yasmina's mind.

Nowhere on Urfe will be safe.

If that was true, Yasmina thought, then it left her with only one choice.

A sincere thank you, Dear Reader, for accompanying me on this journey across the multiverse. I hope we travel to many more worlds together.

To stay up to date on future stories in the world of Urfe, as well as other new releases, it's best to visit www.laytongreen.com and join my VIP Reader's Group.

Until the next adventure,
Layton

About the Author

LAYTON GREEN is a bestselling author who writes across multiple genres, including fantasy, mystery, thriller, horror, and suspense. He is the author of The Blackwood Saga, the Dominic Grey series, the Genesis Trilogy, and other works of fiction. His novels have been nominated for multiple awards (including a two-time finalist for an International Thriller Writers award), optioned for film, and have reached #1 on genre lists in the United States, the United Kingdom, and Germany.

Word of mouth is crucial to the success of any author. If you enjoyed the book, please consider leaving an honest review on Amazon, Goodreads, or another book site, even if it's only a line or two.

Finally, if you are new to the world of Layton Green, for additional information on the author, his works, and more, please visit him on Author Central, Goodreads, Facebook, or at www.laytongreen.com.

CPSIA information can be obtained
at www.ICGtesting.com
Printed in the USA
BVHW040254020321
601389BV00004B/710

9 781733 818865